'Paton Walsh _____
her own _____ ___ __ it. It ___ ___'
_. could have been done better.'
Andrew Taylor, *Spectator*

'Jill Paton Walsh's continuation is superbly (sometimes almost spookily) accurate. Paton Walsh has captured those imperial Sayers cadences perfectly.'
The Times

'With a generous quota of twists and double twists, Wimsey succeeds in restoring the cloisters to their customary tranquillity, leaving the reader to finish the novel with a warm glow of contentment.'
Daily Mail

'This is a charming romp through Oxford, featuring some unforgettable characters - a novel to get lost in on a winter's evening.'
Oxford Times

'A light, agreeable story with ghostly reminders of Sayers.'
Literary Review

'Paton Walsh has Sayers' voice down to a tee and the novel is full of vintage charm – but an underlying sharpness and modernity keep the contemporary reader hooked.'
The Lady

Jill Paton Walsh, born in 1937, is the author of seven novels for adults: the fourth of these, *Knowledge of Angels*, was shortlisted for the Booker Prize. Before writing for adults she won many literary prizes as a writer of children's books. She has also written four novels about the Cambridge detective Imogen Quy: *A Piece of Justice* was shortlisted for the Crime Writers' Association Gold Dagger award.

Visit her website: www.greenbay.co.uk.

Dorothy L. Sayers, the greatest golden age detective novelist, was born in 1893, and was one of the first women awarded a degree by Oxford University. Her aristocratic detective Lord Peter Wimsey was one of the most popular fictional heroes of the twentieth century. She was also known for her religious plays, notably the BBC broadcast of *The Man Born to Be King*, and her translation of Dante's *Divine Comedy*. She died in 1957. Find out more from the Dorothy L. Sayers Society: www.sayers.org.uk.

JILL PATON WALSH

The Late Scholar

Based on the characters of
Dorothy L. Sayers

HODDER

First published in 2013 by Hodder & Stoughton
An Hachette UK company

First published in paperback in 2014 by Hodder & Stoughton

1

A CIP catalogue record for this title is available from the British Library

ISBN 978 1 444 76087 3

Typeset in in Plantin Light by Hewer Text UK Ltd, Edinburgh

Printed and bound by CPI Group (UK) Ltd, Croydon, CR0 4YY

Hodder & Stoughton policy is to use papers that are natural, renewable
and recyclable products and made from wood grown in sustainable forests.
The logging and manufacturing processes are expected to conform to the
environmental regulations of the country of origin.

Hodder & Stoughton Ltd
338 Euston Road
London NW1 3BH

www.hodder.co.uk

In memory of
CHRISTOPHER DEAN
1932–2012
Tireless and imaginative promoter
of the work of Dorothy L. Sayers
in all its varieties

ACKNOWLEDGEMENTS

Tony and Nancy Kenny generously gave time to reading this book in manuscript and removing errors about Oxford ways and nomenclature, as well as assisting in more general ways. I am indebted also to conversations with John De'Ath, and to the forbearance of Carolyn Caughey, my editor at Hodder & Stoughton. My husband, John Rowe Townsend, has given indispensable support and encouragement, and I thank him and all the above-mentioned friends. Elaine Griffiths was a real person, who taught me to read and admire Alfred the Great; I salute her memory.

I have been working with the consent of the Trustees of Dorothy L. Sayers.

I

'Great snakes alive!' said the Duke of Denver, sometime Lord Peter Wimsey, famous amateur sleuth.

'What is it, Peter?' asked his Duchess, sitting across from him at the breakfast table.

The Duchess was sometime Lady Peter Wimsey, and before that had been Harriet Vane, detective-story writer, a person that she still was as often as life allowed her.

Peter was holding a sheet of deckle-edged writing paper, which had emerged from a crested envelope brought to him by Bunter, manservant and friend, who was standing back, but within earshot, evidently having appreciated the possibly explosive nature of the letter.

'I seem,' said Peter, 'to be the Visitor for St Severin's College, and in that capacity to be urgently required in Oxford.'

'How can one *seem* to be a Visitor?' asked Harriet calmly. 'If you are such, don't you know about it?'

'Well, no, as it happens, I know nothing about it,' said Peter. 'I have heard of college Visitors, but I thought they were usually the King – well, it would be the Queen now – or a bishop or a judge or least the Chancellor. I really don't see how a college can have the Duke of Denver as a Visitor, unless there is such a person as a hereditary Visitor.'

Bunter discreetly cleared his throat.

'Yes, Bunter?' said Peter.

'Perhaps the Dowager Duchess might remember if the late Duke had ever had such a role, Your Grace,' said Bunter.

'She might indeed,' said Peter.

'She will not yet be up,' said Harriet. 'Bunter, would you be so kind as to ask Franklin to let us know when it would be convenient for Peter to call on her? Your mother sleeps in late these days,' she added to Peter, 'and at her age, who could blame her?'

The Dowager Duchess was now approaching eighty-five, and both Peter and Harriet were concerned about her, day by day.

That morning, however, she was propped up on her bed-pillows, bright-eyed and as eagerly talkative as in the old days.

'Oh, Peter, how nice!' she said. 'Come in, dears, sit down. Now Harriet, when I first saw what you had put in my bedroom, I thought – I didn't say anything, of course, you had taken all that trouble while I was in New York with poor Cornelia; thank heavens I stayed all that time with her, since it was the last chance for us, if only we had known, though we did know in a way of course, but we thought it would be me that death came for before her, she was nearly ten years younger than I am . . . now what was I saying? Oh yes, when you did up this place for me while I was away I thought why would I want two armchairs in a bedroom? And now here you are both of you quite comfortable, and so you were perfectly right all the time, and honestly, Peter, if I didn't love Harriet so much I would think she is quite right too often for her own good . . . what is it you want to talk to me about, dears?'

'Do you recall, Mama,' said Peter, 'Gerald holding some sort of position in Oxford? St Severin's College, to be exact.'

'Yes, he did,' said the Dowager Duchess, 'and your father before him. It was explained to me once. Something about the college statues having put in the name of Duke of Denver, instead of the role that Duke happened to have at the time, so they were stuck with Dukes of Denver for ever and a day.'

'What did Gerald have to do for them?' Peter asked. 'I don't recall him mentioning it to me.'

'He had to go to Oxford when they elected a new Warden,' said the Dowager. 'He thought it was an awful bore. Luckily it didn't happen very often. Only once for Gerald, I think. He had to be there to help them *install* the new Warden – such an odd idea I always thought, installing someone, as though they were a new boiler, or an electric light system. Has it happened again? That would be nice for you, wouldn't it? Aren't you two rather fond of Oxford?'

'Something has happened,' said Peter darkly, 'but we don't know exactly what.'

Franklin coughed discreetly from the bedroom door.

'We must leave you to get up and dressed,' said Harriet, taking the hint. 'We'll see you at lunch.'

As they went together down the stairs Harriet said, 'Do you think Cousin Matthew might be able to dig up something about all this?'

'Ancient though he is?' asked Peter. 'Yes, he might. I'll ask him. He's always pathetically anxious to be useful.'

At the foot of the stairs they parted, he to go to find Cousin Matthew, lodged in a flat converted from the nearest of the old Home Farm barns; she to her study.

Less than an hour later Peter was standing in the library, contemplating a copy of the statutes – or statues, as his mother had called them – of St Severin's College that Cousin Matthew had found for him in a trice. Cousin Matthew, the only son of a poor collateral line on the family tree, had been wholly dependent on the ducal family at Denver for most of his life, and had occupied himself on cataloguing books and pictures and antiques, and working on the genealogy of the family.

His pleasure at finding at once what was wanted was visible in satisfied smiles.

The statutes thus discovered did indeed declare that the Visitor of St Severin's was the Duke of Denver. Cousin Matthew supplied the information that a seventeenth-century Duke had been a generous benefactor of the college – had indeed effectively re-founded it. Perhaps that was the true explanation for the hereditary oddity, rather than a simple mistake. Matthew didn't think a Duke of Denver had ever been the Chancellor, or held any other office that would have made him an appropriate person to be the Visitor.

'In the fell grip of circumstance,' murmured Peter, 'My head is bloody but unbowed. What are my unwelcome obligations, Matthew?'

'There are ceremonial ones,' said Cousin Matthew, 'to do with appointing a new Warden, and appointing fellows. You are allowed to delegate those.'

'The devil I am!' said Peter. 'To whom have we been in the habit of delegating these delights?'

'Mr Murbles, I believe,' said Cousin Matthew.

Murbles was the family solicitor, an excellent and reliable fellow, now very elderly, who had retired to Oxford to live with his daughter.

'Well, he is on the spot,' said Peter.

'However,' said Cousin Matthew, 'this is much more likely to be about your function as a referee of last resort if there is irreconcilable conflict among the fellows. See here . . .' He turned a page or two, and pointed.

If any question arise on which the Warden and Fellows are unable to agree, the Warden and Fellows, or the Warden, or any two of the Fellows, may submit the same to the Visitor, and the Visitor may thereupon declare the true construction of the Statutes with reference to the case submitted to him.

'Ho hum', said Peter. 'And in all these years they have managed without needing a referee. I am wondering what might have happened now . . .'

'There is also this . . .' Cousin Matthew pointed again.

It shall be lawful for the Visitor, whenever he shall think fit, to visit the College in person, and to exercise, at any such visitation, all powers lawfully belonging to his Office.

'That might be very jolly,' said Peter. 'I'll show it to Harriet . . . hullo!'

He had looked up and seen a car arriving.

Bredon Hall had a long driveway, between an avenue of fine old plane trees, now just coming into full leaf, their branches sprinkled with the bright fresh green of late May, offering a dappled screening to the drive itself. The drive approached what would have been the centre of the great façade before the dramatic fire, which three years earlier had gutted two-thirds of the house. The drive now curved round to approach the remaining wing of the house, giving Peter and Cousin Matthew, standing at the library window, a sideways-on view of a Sunbeam Talbot, crunching its way along the gravel towards the front door.

'Who goes there?' said Peter. The two men watched as the unexpected driver got out of the car, and, taking a briefcase from the front passenger seat, approached the door with unmistakably urgent steps. 'Be thou a spirit of health, or goblin damned, bring with thee airs from heaven, or blasts from hell—'

At which point Bunter appeared at the library door, saying, 'There is a Mr Troutbeck to see you, Your Grace.

He says his business is urgent.' He offered Peter Mr Troutbeck's card.

Michael Troutbeck, MA Oxon, D.Phil, Fellow of St Severin's ...

'What would you say, Bunter, such a visitor portends?' asked Peter.

'He wishes, I surmise, Your Grace, to have your ear before anyone else gets a word in,' said Bunter. 'You could possibly decline to hear him on his own.'

'He comes in such a questionable shape, that I will speak to him,' said Peter, leaving the library with a light step, and skipping down the stairs like an elderly Fred Astaire.

Troutbeck was a handsome man in early middle age, smartly dressed in a conventional three-piece suit, with a gold watch-chain, and a college tie. Peter led him into the morning room, and offered coffee or perhaps a little light breakfast. Troutbeck was visibly tempted. The fellow really had got up in the middle of the night and driven himself from Oxford ... But the breakfast, once served to him, was clearly hard for him to deal with, so eager was he to have his say. He gulped his coffee, and took only a few mouthfuls of the excellent bacon and eggs Mrs Farley had provided before pushing his plate aside with a determined expression on his face.

Peter, sitting opposite him, said pleasantly, 'Now, how may I help you?'

'Ah ... it's rather, Your Grace, that *I* might be able to help *you*,' was the reply. 'I thought it might be useful if some impartial person gave you a coherent account of the college's troubles, before you found yourself deafened by the clamour that will meet you when you come to the college.'

'And you are that impartial person?' said Peter.

'I certainly am,' said Troutbeck.

'I am willing to listen to you,' said Peter.

'I suppose you cannot have any idea what this is about?' said Troutbeck. 'And to put you in the picture I must begin some months ago – last year in fact. At that time the college was offered a spectacular opportunity: a chance to acquire a large tract of land near Oxford. There was immediately conflict among us.'

'What was the trouble?' asked Peter.

'Money. The college's finances have been in a very precarious state for some years; we are deeply in the red. Something would have to be sold to raise the money to buy the land. But the eventual value of a large tract of land on the eastern margins of the city could transform the situation for us. And we were in a position to raise the money – we could sell a manuscript book supposed to be invaluable, but in practice a burden, since it needs to be kept very secure and we have it expensively insured. A white elephant, as the saying goes. And there was very deeply felt disagreement; the book had been a gift from a former scholar of the college and some of the fellows thought it could not decently be sold.'

'And you, I take it,' said Peter, 'were not of that persuasion.'

Troutbeck looked wary. 'Well, no, I was not. I am not – for matters are not settled. Our statutes provide that any two fellows may raise any matter to be put to a vote at college meetings, and unfortunately they do not prohibit the raising again and again of a matter that has already been voted upon; they merely specify that a vote cannot be taken on a matter already voted on sooner than during the term next following the previous vote. The division was so close that the Warden had to use his casting vote, which makes it all too likely that the decision could be overthrown if voted upon again.'

'But the Warden could use his casting vote again. Which way did he vote?'

'He voted against selling the codex. He said that he thought the casting vote should always be used in favour of the status quo.'

'So the matter is effectively settled however often it is put to the vote,' said Peter. 'Where does the Visitor come in?'

'The Warden has taken leave of absence. The fellowship is divided exactly fifty-fifty. And the necessary two fellows to have the matter discussed again have already tabled the question on the agenda for the next meeting.'

'Who, currently, is the Warden?' asked Peter.

'One Dr Thomas Ludgvan,' said Troutbeck. 'He has been the Warden for years; for an absolute age.'

Peter got up and wandered across to the window, as if to contemplate Troutbeck's car, standing in the drive.

'I think I would expect a body of reasonable people to be able to talk such a matter to an agreement, even if there were some left unhappy by the decision arrived at,' said Peter.

'Non-intellectual people overestimate the power of reason among intellectuals, I find,' said Troutbeck. 'Feelings have become so inflamed over this matter that I fear rational discussion is no longer on the cards. That is why we have taken the unusual step of invoking the powers of the Visitor.'

'You have taken a great deal of trouble, Troutbeck, to come this far to talk to me. I think you must hope to persuade me to take your view of which is the right decision.'

'I think any reasonable person would take the view I take,' said Troutbeck. 'The land we are offered is off the Watlington Road; it is mediocre farmland, and obviously open to development as the city expands. Acquiring it would put the college finances on the right path for a generation.'

'Whereas the manuscript?' Peter prompted him.

'Is a small codex of tenth-century pages in an eighteenth-century binding, rendered largely illegible by fire and water . . .'

'Was it in the Cotton fire?' asked Peter, unable to dissemble his interest.

'Or some other fire,' said Troutbeck impatiently, 'rather too enthusiastically put out with gallons of water. The thing is ugly; it has no display value at all. We incur the costs and responsibility and in exchange attract the curiosity of a few, a very few, medievalists.'

'Your benefactor, meanwhile, is not aware of what is going on, I take it?' Peter asked. 'Who is he or she?'

'The benefactor is no longer on the scene. It was a bequest by which we acquired his book. Nevertheless he requested secrecy,' Troutbeck said. 'I do not really feel that I should break his confidence on my own. When you come to Oxford, of course you will be talking with us officially; but I should warn you that by no means all of the fellowship have the interests of the college at heart. There are factions among us – people bitterly at odds with each other. I am sure you will hear the question explained to you in very misleading ways.'

'I don't think you mentioned what the codex is a manuscript of?' said Peter.

'Some Dark Ages martyr called Boethius,' said Troutbeck.

Peter positively smiled at him. 'Then you have no need to tell me who your benefactor was,' he said. 'There is only one person possible. And it seems clear why the book was given to St Severin's. You should stay to lunch. I have much more to learn from you.'

But at that moment Bunter knocked and entered. 'There is a person on the telephone, Your Grace, urgently desiring to talk to Mr Troutbeck,' he said.

'Please show Mr Troutbeck to the telephone,' said Peter.

The morning room door was left open behind them. Peter heard their footsteps across the hall, but although he could hear the sound of Troutbeck's voice, he could not catch the words, and hoped that Bunter was eavesdropping with his usual skill.

Peter easily overheard for himself the words exchanged by Bunter and the guest as they returned across the hall.

'Not bad news, I hope, sir?' said Bunter.

'No, excellent news, in fact,' Troutbeck said. 'Very tragic, of course . . . I thought I was in a spot, though. I had relied on a duke to be more interested in land than old manuscripts.'

'It would depend on the duke, sir,' said Bunter impassively, showing Troutbeck back into the room.

Troutbeck was having some trouble looking sombre. 'I am afraid I have been wasting your time, Your Grace,' he said. 'A senior member of the college having unexpectedly died last night, the voting will no longer be deadlocked. I think we shall be able to manage without troubling you any further. And I must get back immediately; there will be things to sort out in poor Enistead's affairs.'

'Oh, jolly D,' said Peter duplicitously, 'unless, of course, this deceased fellow was a friend of yours.'

Troutbeck had the grace to blush slightly. 'Not a personal friend,' he said, 'but a colleague of many years . . . one is naturally distressed . . . so sudden . . .'

Peter walked his guest to the door and down the steps to his car. He opened the driver's-side door for Troutbeck, and stood watching the car crunch away along the drive.

'And I imagine the deceased was of the party that voted against you,' he murmured to himself.

When the Sunbeam was out of sight he returned to the library and looked again at the letter that had summoned him to Oxford. It bore two signatures, one of

Terence Cloudie, Senior Fellow; the other of John Ambleside, Vice-Warden. It had not been signed by Troutbeck. 'Whatever is going on?' Peter asked, rhetorically addressing the rows of noble tomes on his own well-furnished shelves. 'Wait till I tell Harriet!'

Telling Harriet did have to wait, however. She and Peter had long worked out a way of dealing with the everyday complexities of their lives. They could talk briefly at breakfast and at lunch; between those times Harriet retreated to her study to write. Peter never lacked things to do – he had the estate to run. Not till the evening did they sit together, Harriet reading, Peter sometimes playing the piano, and with time to let talk expand. On the day of the visit from Mr Troutbeck there had, by lunchtime, been two letters in the second post, and a further visitor from Oxford. The letters had evidently been written before the writers knew of 'poor Enistead's' death; they were from fellows taking different sides in the dispute, each putting their case. Peter glanced at them, and put them aside for attention later, partly because the appearance of another unfamiliar car approaching along the drive threatened to cut short his time to consider them properly.

Bunter announced, 'A Mr Vearing to see you, Your Grace,' and retreated.

Mr Vearing was a man of middle age, grey-haired, thin and dignified, casually dressed in cavalry tweeds and a wine-coloured waistcoat. He looked rather crumpled – either he had slept in his clothes or he was not accustomed to trouble much about his appearance. An atmosphere of anxiety and discomfort emanated from him. He had a lean and rather lived-in face, and a slightly short-sighted frown, and approached Peter with extended hand.

'Vearing,' he said, 'fellow of St Severin's.'

Asked to sit, he lowered himself into the available armchair. There was not a touch of deference about him – something that Peter noticed with approval.

'You must wonder why I have taken the trouble to come,' he began, 'when I suppose you will shortly be coming to Oxford to take matters in hand.'

'I have not yet decided whether I must visit Oxford,' said Peter untruthfully, 'or if I may read what you fellows have to say, and deliver my opinion from the safety of my own home.'

Vearing looked slightly disconcerted. 'This is a very important matter, Your Grace,' he said. 'I had thought you would need to hear the views of all the fellows . . .'

'If so,' said Peter mildly, 'why not wait till I arrive at the college, and tell me what you think then?'

Vearing straightened up a little in his chair. 'I have spent many years teaching undergraduates, and graduate students, Your Grace,' he said, 'and I have observed a recurring phenomenon. That is that when invited to consider two sides of a controversy people are apt to give most weight to the position they have encountered, or have had put before them, first. It is relatively hard for a second position to dislodge their allegiance to the earlier one.'

'Really?' said Peter. 'I would have thought that scholars would be more rational.'

'I could give you a familiar example,' said Vearing. 'In the nineteenth century, those who were thrown into misery by losing their faith – Arthur Hugh Clough for example, or Matthew Arnold, or George Eliot – retained a nostalgia for religious belief which pursued them all their lives.'

'Hmm,' said Peter. 'That is an interesting question, although not the one that has brought you here this morning. I suppose you mean that you think if you put your side of the case to me before anyone has put the counter-argument, you will sway my judgement decisively in your direction. But I am not an undergraduate, Mr Vearing, nor even a nineteenth-century agnostic.'

'Of course not, Your Grace. I did not mean to imply . . . the truth is I know nothing about your education, having realised only yesterday that the fate of the college lay in your hands – and by right of birth, rather than a right of office. I hope you will not blame me if I say that that is a situation that should not have been allowed to happen.'

'About that at least we may agree with each other,' said Peter.

Bunter had appeared, carrying a coffee tray with a splendid silver coffee pot and Royal Worcester cups.

When the coffee had been poured, Peter invited his guest to make his case.

'I am afraid to say,' he began, 'that some of the fellows of the college – exactly half of them in fact – are determined to commit a crime against the purposes of the college. For the sake of the money they wish to sell a precious manuscript volume from the college library, and spend the proceeds on a speculative venture in land. The volume in question is an early copy of a work by the saint for whom the college is named. It seems to me – and to my party in the dispute – to be an act of vandalism to auction it off to the highest bidder, who would probably be some unheard-of college in America . . .'

Vearing's strong feelings were apparent in his heated expression and heightened colour. The coffee cup he was holding rattled gently in its saucer. He had not so much as sipped it.

'Don't let your coffee get cold, old chap,' said Peter.

'Forgive me, Your Grace,' Vearing responded, hastily gulping his coffee. 'Feelings run high on this matter, including mine.'

'Well, it's a dilemma, I do see that,' said Peter. 'But surely not a matter of life or death. Even the life or death of a college.'

'It would be a slow death, admittedly,' said Vearing. 'The sale of the manuscript would deplete the resources of the college library. And it would announce to the world that St Severin's is no longer a safe place for the preservation of treasures of the past. That it no longer values scholarship above money . . .'

'Wouldn't that depend upon what the money raised was spent on?' asked Peter innocently. 'Couldn't you have some jolly new student lodgings, or a lecture room?'

'Quite a few of the best minds in the senior common room will resign,' said Vearing, 'so the new lecture room will be given over entirely to the teaching of those who favour money over scholarship.'

'Will you yourself resign if the manuscript is sold?' asked Peter. He watched while Vearing just perceptibly hesitated.

'I would have to,' he replied. 'And I have come to implore you, since matters are so evenly balanced . . .'

'They may not be balanced as evenly as you think,' said Peter. 'Now that Enistead is dead . . .'

Vearing looked blank for a moment. Then, 'What?' he cried, jumping up. 'When? How? But when I left Oxford this morning, admittedly very early, nobody had told me about it.'

'The news reached me this morning,' said Peter. 'As to when or how the man died I am in the dark. You look like death yourself, Mr Vearing – can I offer you a stiff drink?'

'Just give me a minute to compose myself,' said Vearing, sinking back into his chair. 'This is a great shock. There have been too many mishaps and incidents among us recently.'

'I take it Enistead would have voted for the retention of the manuscript?' said Peter, when a minute or two had elapsed.

'What?' said Vearing. 'Oh, yes; he was fiercely of the opinion that the manuscript had to be retained in perpetuity. For the honour of the college. He was the old-fashioned kind of fellow; not a published word to his name . . .'

'So as matters stand now, when the vote is taken again, the let's-sell-and-be-damned party will prevail?'

'I think so,' said Vearing, rather melodramatically sinking his face in his hands.

'What about the Warden?' asked Peter. 'Mightn't his vote even things up again? Stalemate, admittedly, but not the sale of the book? When does his leave of absence expire?'

'Well,' said Vearing, 'he hasn't exactly taken formal leave of absence, so that one would know how to answer your question. He's just gone – nobody knows where.'

'Does anybody know why?'

'I don't, certainly.'

'And how long has he been gone?'

'Since just after the last college meeting. That was in Hilary term, so about three months.'

'And when is the next vote to be taken?' Peter asked. 'Where are we in the academic year?'

'Three weeks into Trinity term,' said Vearing. 'The vote must be taken before term ends at the end of June.'

'I think,' said Peter, 'that I can take neither the one side nor the other in the dispute that so divides you until I have investigated more fully. You are right, Vearing, that it is time your Visitor paid you a visit. Expect me very shortly.'

It took Peter quite a time to explain all this to Harriet at lunchtime. 'Are you sure you are not over-egging the pudding?' she asked him. 'It sounds improbably melodramatic. The sort of thing I might make up.'

'Who, me?' asked Peter. 'No, I am trying my best to convey to you what the gentlemen of Oxford have taken such trouble to convey to me this morning. All the way from Oxford, and driving themselves. Though I suppose the train is rather a bore.'

'The connection to Denver from Cambridge is quite good, really,' said Harriet, musing.

'But Oxford to Cambridge by train is notoriously bad,' said Peter.

'It can't be *that* bad,' said Harriet, 'when there is a don who comes across from Oxford to buy his books in Cambridge. Someone in Heffers told me when I was last in the shop.'

'What can you buy in Heffers that you can't buy in Blackwell's?' asked Peter.

'What he does buy is detective stories, I am told. I have no idea what Blackwell's is like as an emporium for detective stories; we aren't in Oxford often enough. And the oddity doesn't end there. If what he wants is out of stock, and they order it for him, he won't have the books sent to him. They wait until he comes and fetches them in person.'

'All the world is mad, save thee and me,' said Peter, 'and even thee's a bit odd.'

'I should think,' said Harriet, not rising to this, 'that you had better talk to those who have not attempted to talk to you first.'

'Yes. I must go to Oxford, and soon. I could get away the day after tomorrow. Will you come too?'

'What a nice idea, Peter. I would love to. But I can't come on Wednesday; – I have a paper to deliver to the Sheridan Le Fanu Society this Thursday in London and

I haven't written it yet. And one of us should be around on Friday when the doctor comes to give your mother a check-up. You must go tomorrow; I shall join you on Saturday.'

'I am no longer used to doing things without you, Harriet. I don't like the idea at all.'

'You can manage for three days,' said Harriet crisply. 'I am not asking you to do without Bunter.'

And then, when Peter looked woebegone, she said, 'Cheer up, Peter! When I join you in Oxford we shall have lots of fun – you shall detect and I shall burrow in the Bodleian, and we have many old friends to see.'

'Yes, of course,' he said. 'I am supposed to adjudicate, not to detect, but it rather sounds as though detection might be required. Meanwhile, do you have any helpful suggestions to make about this situation, which resembles, as you remarked, something you might have made up?'

'I should institute an immediate search for the Warden,' Harriet said.

2

The journey from Duke's Denver to Oxford is a tiresome trawl along minor roads, none of them seeming to wish to expedite travel. One could go through Haddenham and Huntingdon, Bedford or Northampton, Buckingham or Banbury, Woodstock or Bicester.

The Romans, who were the first road-makers whose work survives on the face of England, needed, evidently, to radiate from London or Colchester, and had no need of cross-journeys.

It was honestly just as easy for Peter to nip down to London on the Great Cambridge Road, have lunch with Freddy Arbuthnot at the Bellingham Club, and then zip up to Oxford on the A40. Which is therefore what he did.

'Is it just my pretty face, Peter,' Freddy asked him, 'or are you up to your old tricks again and wanting to pick a chap's brains?'

'Weeell,' said Peter, 'since you ask ... why don't you have the lobster, Freddy, and we'll get a bottle of Sancerre.'

'I see you really do want something expounded,' said Freddy, visibly brightening and ordering the lobster as invited. 'What do you want to know?'

'I don't exactly know what I want to know,' said Peter, 'you'll have to help me.'

'The blind to lead the blind any day of the week,' said Freddy. 'Give me a clue.'

'Well, what do you know about speculation in land?' Peter asked.

'Not a lot,' said Freddy, easing the thread of pink flesh from a lobster tendril, and waving it around on the end of his prong. 'But I know a man . . .'

'Of course you do,' said Peter.

'Where is this debatable land?' asked Freddy.

'Outskirts of Oxford. Someone is giving an Oxford college a chance to buy it.'

'Ah. Possible building land?'

'That's the idea.'

'Might be dicey, seems to me,' said Freddy. 'There's all this council housing going up everywhere, and the powers that be can requisition land at the agricultural value if they like. Owners wouldn't make a penny. You really need to go and talk to the planners in Oxford. But I suppose your brainy pals will have done that.'

'I don't know if they have,' said Peter. 'But I'll find out. Thanks, Freddy.'

'Have you heard of Crichel Down?' asked Freddy.

'Doesn't ring a bell. Should I have?'

Let's just say that you will have by and by,' said Freddy. 'A word to the wise, if you follow me.'

'And when I have heard of Crichel Down,' said Peter, 'will it tend to encourage, or to discourage the purchase of tracts of land on the verges of urban areas?'

'The fact that I cannot tell you, Peter,' said Freddy, 'is an indicator of a level of risk.'

'Wait and see, you mean?'

'Indeed, wait and see.'

'And if the principals in this affair cannot afford to wait?'

Freddy shrugged eloquently.

The old familiar way into Oxford, then. Down Headington Hill, which offers no prospect of the towery city; along a nondescript street to the roundabout always called 'The Plains', with no sight yet of anything remarkable; and then a turn on to the bridge, on the far side of which rises Magdalen College tower – Gothic at its most austere and beautiful, and shedding like falling petals into the memories of anyone who ever heard them, the voices of the choirboys from aloft, singing an annual welcome to the first day of spring. Peter was far from immune to this bitterly intense nostalgia; he too had lain in a punt with his friends on more than one dewy morning, and heard the song, and adjourned to eat breakfast cooked on a campfire in the meadow below the bridge. Thinking of punts he remembered sleeping in one, overcome with weariness, while Harriet watched him, and when he awoke something unspoken and irrevocable had happened between them.

He nearly missed Longwall Street, and an aggrieved motorist hooted at him when he braked suddenly to make the turn. Peter waved his apology. From Longwall

Street to Holywell Street, and at the spectacular corner by the King's Arms, with the glories of Broad Street ahead of him, and the few further yards to Balliol tugging at him, he turned right into Parks Road, past Wadham College, and reached the elaborate frontage of St Severin's.

The moment he stepped under the arch and could see into the front quad, Peter realised he had never before entered St Severin's. As an undergraduate he had not happened to have a friend there, and on all the revisits to Oxford that he made since youthful days he had gravitated back to Balliol. People do, he reminded himself: Oxford people return to base. Only the most diligent tourist walks in and out of all or most of the colleges to inspect the architecture. And the architecture of St Severin's would have to wait, while he inveigled himself within its ancient walls, and discovered where Bunter could park the Daimler.

Meanwhile the college porter was looking at him with an expression redolent of one who has seen it all, and is prepared to see off boarders. 'Can I help you, sir?' the man asked.

'I am the Visitor,' said Peter. 'Would you let the Vice-Warden know that I am here?'

'The college is closed to visitors at the moment,' said the porter, 'sir.'

'I am not *a* visitor, I am *the* Visitor,' said Peter.

'Indeed, sir. I have not been instructed to expect you.'

'Nevertheless I am here,' said Peter.

'May I ask who invited you, sir?'

Peter adjusted his monocle and treated the porter to a steady stare. 'Expected, or unexpected, invited or uninvited, I am here by right,' he said. 'Please inform the most senior person now in the college of my presence.'

The porter held his gaze only for a second or so before picking up the phone. 'Someone will be with you shortly,' he said in a minute or so, 'if you would care to wait.'

Peter did care to wait. He stood in the doorway arch of the college for several minutes, while undergraduates came and went, picking up their post from a rack of pigeon-holes, and chatting to each other. Peter attracted much less attention than his car, parked outside with Bunter standing guard beside it.

'Who's got that spiffing car?' someone asked.

'Must be something to do with Dawlish,' Peter overheard.

Then a middle-aged man wearing a gown appeared. 'I am Ambleside,' he said. 'The Vice-Warden.'

'I am Denver, at your service,' said Peter, extending a hand, 'come to make the requested formal visitation to the college. 'Can you make arrangements that allow me to do that?'

Ambleside did not exactly look pleased – alarmed, rather. 'Of course I am glad to see you,' he said. 'I had expected it would take you some days to be at liberty to come.' But he was a courteous man, and he escorted Peter to his own room to sit in comfort while he made arrangements.

It took him nearly an hour, during which time Peter inspected the bookshelves, bearing nearly the complete

Loeb classics, and a formidable collection of historians, commentators and critics of classical Greek and Roman literature. Peter felt an unfamiliar pang; his own degree was in history. Given another life he might have liked to be a classicist. But his Latin was good enough to dabble. He picked up the volume of Catullus, and settled quietly to read.

In a while Ambleside reappeared, and announced that he thought the best place for Peter was the guest set in the Warden's Lodgings. The housekeeper was making up the bed, and airing the rooms right now. If perhaps the Duke would like to linger for long enough to take a glass of sherry, he could settle in very shortly.

'Is there accommodation for my valet?' Peter asked.

'I believe so. I think Mr Bunter is helping the house-keeper right now,' said Ambleside.

'And there would be room for the Duchess, should she wish to join me?'

'Oh, yes. But ... are you intending to stay with us long?' asked Ambleside.

'I am intending to stay for as long as it takes to resolve the college's difficulties,' said Peter. 'You may be a better judge than I am as to how long that is likely to be.'

Ambleside offered dry or sweet sherry, or white port. Peter chose the port.

'I am afraid I have no idea how long matters will take to resolve,' he said. 'If indeed they can be resolved.'

'I understand I am expected to resolve them by fiat. Do you wish to give me your own opinion on the sale of the manuscript?' asked Peter.

Ambleside was silent. Then he said, 'I think perhaps it would not be proper for me to advance my own opinion privately, and first.'

'Not all your colleagues take that view,' said Peter. 'Several approaches have been made to me already.'

'Troutbeck, I suppose,' said Ambleside, frowning.

'And another. But perhaps you would prefer to assist me with a different matter – I am stuck on a line of Catullus in your edition. Would you help me construe it?'

Ambleside brightened visibly and, drawing up a chair beside Peter, said almost eagerly, 'Which is the passage that is causing difficulty?'

They read together tranquilly until the housekeeper's knock summoned Peter to his rooms.

The Warden's guest suite was suitably grand and austere, with a splendid stucco ceiling in the ample drawing room, a bedroom with a four-poster bed large enough for an orgy, a tiny cupboard with sink and kettle, and a bathroom of a Victorian degree of discomfort through a connecting door into the Warden's Lodgings. Peter liked it at once.

'Where have they put you, Bunter?' was his first question.

'There is a servant's room in the Lodgings themselves,' said Bunter. 'Just through the connecting door. Quite close, Your Grace, and perfectly comfortable.'

'Excellent. And the Warden's housekeeper is friendly?'

'Rather glad of the incursion, I would say, Your Grace. It is lonely to be managing a house with nobody in it. And she is not exactly on all fours with the other college servants; or she does not feel herself so.'

'What does she have to say about the disappearing Warden?'

'She is worried about him. It isn't like him at all. And he did not take his razor or his toothbrush, or a change of clothes.'

'Didn't he indeed? Hmm.'

'I understand when he returns she will offer her resignation immediately. She is his personal servant; he brought her with him to the college, and she is outraged not to have been taken into his confidence.'

'Well done, Bunter,' said Peter. 'We must instantly take Harriet's advice.'

At that moment a burst of laughter came through the open window. Peter walked across to it.

The guest drawing room was on the first floor, over the archway between one quad and another. The archway served as a kind of hall's passage, with the dining room on one side, and the buttery on the other. A group of undergraduates was standing round the buttery door, eating what looked from above like lardy cake. Their voices floated upwards.

'I found out about that car,' one said. 'Not something belonging to a posh undergraduate, you will be pleased to know.'

'So whose . . .?'

'It's a visitation from our ineffable Visitor.'

'The Duke of Whatsit, you mean?'

'Well, it's high time somebody called them to order,' said a rather high-pitched voice. 'It's not fair to us.'

'How do you mean, not fair, Jackson?'

'Well, I don't know how it is with the sex-life of plankton or whatever it is you biologists study,' said Jackson, 'but we could do with some help in revising and some moral support. All they can think about is this eternal bickering about money and a manuscript; they have only half a brain to spare for us. And they can go on and on bickering for an eternity, but this is our finals year. We get just one shot at a first, and if we miss it it's gone for ever. They ought to be thinking about us and the college position in the annual league table . . .'

'My tutor is okay,' someone else put in.

'Oh, the maths people are so far in the air they are above all this, I suppose.'

'Bunter,' said Peter quietly, 'slip down there purporting to buy me some of that disgusting lardy cake, and find out if you can what Jackson is studying, and who his tutor is.'

Somehow Peter did not feel very tempted by the prospect of dinner in Hall at St Severin's that evening. He resorted instead to dinner at Balliol, where he secured an invitation simply by telephoning his old friend, George Mason. He persuaded himself that he was not actually shirking; finding out if the trouble at St Severin's was known to all Oxford, or still had the status of a private grief could conceivably influence the direction his investigation would take.

Those avatars of Jude the Obscure who yearn for the intellectual glories of Oxford and Cambridge colleges can fondly imagine that the conversations at High Tables are pitched at the highest storeys of ivory towers. But in the real world – and it is only a chimera, an aura shed by ancient architecture, that makes them seem unreal – colleges are conducted by a group of men, or in a few cases a group of women, who know each other very well, dine together often, have long ago exhausted their interest in each other's subjects, are as capable of hating as of liking each other, and who keep the peace by talking of domestic trivia, the day's headlines, the endless stream of gossip, while avoiding incendiary, that is to say interesting, subjects. A comforting and bland conversation accompanied dinner that night; only when the company rose and adjourned to the Senior Common Room for dessert did someone liven things up by asking a medievalist if he had heard a rumour that St Severin's might sell their Boethius.

For the benefit of another guest – a rather bewildered-looking captain of industry – the Master explained that the book was a work of ancient philosophy written by Manlius Severinus Boethius, which had therefore been given to St Severin's.

'Is it worth a lot?' the industrialist asked.

'Perhaps half a million pounds,' said the Master.

'Good God!' said the industrialist. 'For a book?'

The Balliol dons exchanged glances. The medievalist

explained courteously that the book was very ancient. It was written in Latin, of course, but the copy in question had been annotated in Anglo-Saxon, giving rise to the possibility that it was the copy that had belonged to King Alfred.

'Weren't those Dark Ages people illiterate?' asked the industrialist.

'It is a matter of record that King Alfred could read,' said the medievalist. 'And in Latin as well as English.' Then, rising from his chair, he said it was getting late, and he bade the company goodnight.

His departure dislodged the others round the table, leaving Peter with his friend George Mason sitting alone, the fruit and nuts and the port and claret before them. The college silver gleamed gently in the candlelight.

'You are very quiet tonight, Peter,' said George. 'What's got your tongue?'

'I am capable of listening and learning,' said Peter plaintively.

'You were interested in that manuscript, I take it,' said George. 'The person to ask about that is a woman scholar – Mary Fowey at Shrewsbury College. She's your girl for all things late Latin. Where are you staying? At the Mitre? I dare say we could find you a room if you need one.'

'Thank you, George,' said Peter, 'but I am comfortably lodged in St Severin's.'

'The devil you are! Whatever connection do you have there?'

'I am the Visitor,' said Peter, grimacing.

George stared at him. 'I keep forgetting you are a duke,' he said at last. 'It seems ridiculous, somehow, when I think how we used to romp around.'

'It cannot seem more ridiculous to you than it does to me,' said Peter. 'I'm not surprised you forget it. But what I would like forgotten at present is the connection between a duke and Peter Wimsey the detective.'

'Surely everybody knows . . .'

'There isn't anything that everybody knows,' said Peter. 'Which leaves us the fun of finding out.'

'Change your mind,' said George. 'Let me find you a room in Balliol. It's only a step away from St Severin's.'

'A room in St Severin's is right on the spot, though. Why do you want to move me, George?'

'St Severs isn't a healthy place,' said George. 'Must be something in the water. People dream strange dreams, and have improbable accidents there. Fatal accidents, even.'

'Whereas Balliol possesses a fount of immortality?'

'We are both of us immortal so far,' said George.

It was nearly eleven before Peter got back to his rooms in St Severin's. Bunter was waiting up for him.

'Is there a phone any nearer than the porters' lodge?' Peter asked him.

'There is a phone in the Warden's study, Your Grace,' said Bunter.

'None of that, Bunter,' said Peter. 'We are detecting now, and I am my lord, or even Peter when we are in private.'

'As you wish, my lord,' said Bunter.

'Show me the way to the Warden's study,' said Peter. 'Like an impecunious undergraduate I need to phone home.'

Harriet picked up the phone saying, 'Peter?'

'Oh dear life, when shall it be, That my eyes thine eyes shall see . . .' he began.

'Lonely in Oxford?' said Harriet. 'Don't be silly, Peter.'

'It really is like the old days when you rebuke me for expressions of longing,' Peter said.

'I thought you would be having fun,' she said. 'I am a bit lonely here without you.'

'Isn't my mother good company? How is she?'

'As you left her – very lively in spells, and very sleepy in others.'

'How is that speech on Le Fanu coming along?'

'Fine. How is the peace-making going?'

'Starts in earnest tomorrow.'

'Good luck with it then. Goodnight, sweet prince.'

'I have enough titles,' said Peter darkly, 'without that one.'

The Warden's housekeeper was a stout lady of uncertain age, a Miss Manciple, who proved to be in a useful state of anxiety – the kind that provokes logorrhoea. Peter tackled her first thing after breakfast.

'Oh, sir,' was her opening shot, 'thank the Lord you've come, thank the Lord! Perhaps now something will be done about it. I've been worried out of my mind about him, I really have. I lie awake all night wondering what has become of him, and I didn't should have to worry by myself, should I? Wouldn't you think one of his precious college people should be trying to find him? After all he's done for them!'

Peter, who was eating breakfast – warmed-up lardy cake was proving its worth – said, 'Sit down, Miss Manciple, and have a cup of coffee. Or tea if you prefer. Bunter makes an excellent cuppa.'

'Oh, I couldn't sit down, sir . . .' she said.

'Yes, you could,' said Peter. 'Do me the honour of sitting down with me while we try to get to the bottom of this.'

Miss Manciple sat down. She sat opposite Peter, very straight-backed, with her hands in her lap.

'I take it you genuinely don't know where the Warden – Dr Ludgven, isn't he? – may be?'

'No, I don't, sir, and that's God's truth!'

'And I understand you told Bunter yesterday that it isn't at all like him to disappear?'

'No, it isn't,' she said. 'I've worked for him for nearly thirty years, sir, and I've never before not known where he is. He goes abroad a lot, but I've always known his forwarding address. Always. And another thing, sir, he's a very particular gentleman with regard to his person, if you know what I mean and he didn't take his sponge bag, nor his pyjamas nor nothing. Just walked out.'

'What time of day did he just walk out?' asked Peter.

'I don't know that, sir. I am off duty once he goes into Hall for dinner. I turned down his bed for him, like usual, and went to my own little room, and in the morning his bed hadn't been slept in, and he wasn't anywhere to be found.'

'Bunter,' said Peter, 'would you slip across to the lodge for me and ask if any of the porters saw the Warden leave, and if so exactly when?'

'Now, try to remember for me,' said Peter, addressing Miss Manciple, 'if anything out of the ordinary happened that evening before Hall? Anything at all that you can think of?'

'There was a meeting in his lodging, sir, at five o'clock. And voices raised. Not that that was unusual, sir. It's been happening a lot this year.'

'You don't know what it was about?'

Miss Manciple's lip curled. 'No, I don't, sir. I keep away from all that rubbish. Such clever people we are supposed to think, and they carry on like a load of nasty children. And none of it matters to ordinary people, sir.'

'The other servants don't tell you about it?'

'They would if I would let them,' she said. 'What can you do to find him, sir?'

'Drink up while I think about it,' said Peter.

He didn't have long to think. Bunter returned. 'A nil result, I'm afraid, my lord,' said Bunter. 'There are three porters – they take turns. But they are all very sure that none of them saw the Warden leaving college that night.'

'They could have been distracted, I suppose? A mob of undergraduates pouring through the gate, or someone enquiring for a letter by pigeon post?'

'They don't think so, sir. They have naturally been racking their brains over it, and talking to each other about it. And another thing, my lord. It can be a chilly few steps from the Warden's Lodgings here, to Hall, under that open arch. On cold nights the Warden wears an overcoat over his gown, and leaves the coat on a hook at the back of the Hall. It's still there, my lord.'

'Righty-ho,' said Peter. 'Miss Manciple, you have been very helpful. Thank you. I will let you know at once if we find anything. Bunter, ask the Domestic Bursar to step up here urgently, will you?'

St Severin's dining hall was an archetype of such halls. At one end there was a large oriel window, designed to cast light on the dais and the High Table. Its heraldic stained glass dimmed and romanticised the light it offered, throwing gouts of vert, sable, or azure and gules upon the distinguished faces sitting below it. The Hall was lined with ancient linen-fold panelling, adorned with portraits of patrons and past Wardens in golden frames. Above soared a massive hammer-beamed roof. Mr Winterhorn, the Bursar, presented himself quickly enough, and accompanied Peter.

Peter stood on the dais, and contemplated the assembly of college servants gathered in front of him.

'We are about to organise, with your help, a very thorough search of the college,' he told them. 'Every nook, cranny, cupboard, from the roof spaces to the remotest corners of the cellars. Every inch of the gardens, every greenhouse or tool-shed. Everywhere. The Bursar will assign an area for search to each of you. You will search in pairs, and report back to myself or the Bursar when your search is complete.'

A hand was raised among the throng. 'What are we looking for, sir?'

'I shall take you into my confidence,' said Peter. 'You are looking for the Warden.'

A horrified gasp rose to be lost among the roof beams.

'He's not been seen here for three months or more, sir,' said the Senior Common Room butler, Mr Thrupp.

'We are assuring ourselves that the Warden is not on college premises, alive or dead,' said Peter soberly. 'When we can be sure of that we can search the rest of the world for him. I have two other things to ask of you. First, that if you were to find a body, or any suspicious thing, you should not touch or move anything. It would hamper the police investigation that would have to follow. And second, though I think you would all realise this without my asking it of you, the honour of the college – your college – would be badly damaged if news of this morning's activities were to get out. You all know what a hive of busy gossip Oxford is. I hope I may rely on your discretion.'

Peter himself decided to join the party to search the cellars. They were extensive, stretching below ground to the full area of the buildings above them. The old buildings, that is. The search party was led by Mr Thrupp, who seemed anxious, and was keeping a sharp eye out for his fellow searchers.

'People sometimes think, Your Grace,' he said to Peter, 'that all these cellars reveal a riotously bibulous fellowship in the past. But in fact cellars were necessary because of rising damp. The modern buildings, of course, are standing on the ground with good damp courses.'

Peter agreed. 'But nevertheless, Mr Thrupp, there does seem to be plenty of drink down here.'

'The college does keep a good cellar, Your Grace,' Mr Thrupp said. 'Various of the fellows in the past have been very knowledgeable.'

'I'll say they have,' said Peter, gently removing a bottle from the nearest rack, and holding it up, level, to read the label. 'How many of these have you got?'

'Five dozen,' said Mr Thrupp. 'But diminishing, of course.'

'Wine is made to be drunk,' said Peter approvingly, 'and can be kept too long.'

But the search party had moved ahead, into the next of the sequence of undercrofts, and Mr Thrupp hastened after them.

Peter, lingering, reading the rack labels with interest, heard him calling in alarm, 'No, no! On no account disturb the racks! That is port, gentlemen, port!'

Joining them, Peter saw a row of bewildered faces.

'How can we look behind them racks,' one of the party was asking, 'if we can't lay hands on them to shift them forward a bit?'

'I could get under there, I think,' piped up a scrawny youth.

Everyone looked at him. He seemed about fourteen, though he must have been older, and he was indeed short and very thin. He coloured a bit at the blaze of attention. 'I'm Sidney, sir,' he said, addressing the butler. 'I'm new in the gardens, sir.'

'Well, if you can wriggle under there and make sure there's nothing behind it,' said Peter, 'the college will be indebted to you, and you shall have half-a-crown from me. Now, can we have two of the heaviest of you to hang on to each end of this rack, and keep it steady while Sidney here does his stuff.'

Sidney flung himself on to the dusty flagged floor, and wriggled his way forward.

'It's a bit dark down here,' he reported. A torch was rolled under the racks towards him. For a few seconds the rack was lit from below, outlines of bottles and flashes of deep red within them appearing spookily here and there while Sidney wielded the torch.

Then the boy began to reappear, feet first, then waist and shoulders. It looked as if he might have trouble getting his head out, but, turning right ear upwards, he managed it.

'Sorry, sir,' he said, getting on to his knees to stand up, 'there's nothing there but dust.'

Much less dust than before, thought Peter, seeing the amount of it now adhering to Sidney's clothes. A random scatter of applause greeted Sidney as he stood up, and Peter immediately bestowed the promised half-crown.

It must by now have been hitting home to everyone in the party what they might be hoping or fearing to find. There was palpable tension as they moved on through the warren of cellars. The remotest rooms were empty and dusty. Mr Thrupp shone his torch around all four corners of a room, and moved to go on.

'Hang on,' said Peter. He went to the furthest corner, and picked up something. 'Your torch here, Mr Thrupp,' he said.

The torch showed him to be holding an empty bulbous dark-green glass bottle with a long tapering neck, and a small stamped medallion on its side.

'You haven't got any more like this anywhere, have you, Mr Thrupp?' asked Peter.

'Is it worth something, sir?' said Mr Thrupp.

'I'd have to look it up. Consult a friend,' said Peter, turning the bottle in his hands. 'But I can see at once that it is very old, and very valuable.'

An inexplicable tremor went through his audience.

'How old is old, sir?' said Mr Thrupp.

'Seventeenth century somewhere,' said Peter.

'And that'll be worth more than Sidney's half-a-crown, then, sir?'

'I'm not expert enough to value it, Mr Thrupp; my line is incunabula, not glass.'

'Give us a guess, sir.'

'Somewhere upwards of a hundred pounds,' said Peter.

'Just one? Just one bottle?' came a voice from the back of the party.

'Oh, yes,' said Peter.

Whereupon suddenly gales of laughter engulfed the group. Laughter possessed them till they were clinging to each other and weeping with it. The low arch of the vault magnified the sound, and echoed it around them.

'Will somebody let me in on the joke?' asked Peter.

'Well, you see, sir,' said a gardener, 'a bit back there was trouble with the young gentlemen climbing over the wall, and landing in the herbaceous border. Lots of damaged plants, sir, and breaking the head gardener's heart. So the college decided to put broken glass all along the top of the garden wall, like it is now, sir. But the Bursar . . .' – he could hardly speak for laughter – 'when he got an estimate it said ten pounds for the broken glass, and he said, that were rubbish. We got a load of glass ourselves, he said, and he sent two of us in here with lump hammers to smash up dozens and dozens of bottles like that one sir, and take the bits out in barrer-loads to give the men what was putting it atop the wall. So he saved his tenner, sir, didn't he?'

'That was you, George, you musta missed one!' cried someone.

In another storm of laughter Peter managed to establish that the thrifty Bursar was not Mr Winterhorn, but his predecessor, a man who had been not much loved by the staff.

The laughter stopped abruptly when they continued the search. But they found nothing other than the oddly shaped bottle.

Peter returned to his room to await the reports of the other search parties. Not every senior member had readily consented to have his rooms searched; Bunter had threatened a personal search conducted by the Visitor if necessary. The unwilling had conceded. The head gardener's grief at a search of his herbaceous borders, and the chef's grief at incursions into the buttery pantries, had been overcome. Every inch of St Severin's from roof-tiles to underground depths had been inspected.

But not a single trace of the Warden had been found. Wherever he was, he wasn't in college, living or dead.

3

It is hard to sleep peacefully in an unfamiliar bed. Peter woke at five the next morning; tried to go to sleep again, and failed. He got up and dressed, resolving to go for a walk. Would the main gate be locked? No matter; there was a street gate in the wall that enclosed the Warden's garden, and he could let himself out that way. The light was swathed in mist, like clouds of tissue paper, the air was still and cold. Peter walked briskly, going south. He stopped briefly on the corner of the Broad, to admire the just faintly visible volumes of the counterpointed glories – Gothic Old Bodleian, Classical Radcliffe Camera, Gothic St Mary's Church, all seeming to float like faded aquatints on the hazy air.

As he passed All Souls he noticed that some literate vandal had scrawled on the college walls 'Are not two sparrows sold for a farthing?' on one side of the ornate gates, and 'Take heart, ye are worth many such,' on the other side. With regrettable complicity Peter laughed. The Warden of All Souls was John Sparrow. As he passed the Radcliffe Camera he saw that that, too, bore a message – a brief one. 'I am a camera,' it said.

Peter left the buildings to talk to each other, and crossed the High, going down Magpie Lane to Merton Street, and out on to Christ Church Meadow. The great avenue across the top of the meadow was appearing against the backdrop of mist like a Rembrandt engraving, inked in detail on white paper. Peter walked straight across it and made for the bank of the Thames. He thought he would like to revisit the College Barges, moored along the meadow below Folly Bridge. One by one the old ceremonial barges used on the Thames in London by the ancient City Guilds had been bought by Oxford colleges, and towed upstream to serve as boat clubs and viewing platforms when the races were held. Peter had not been a rowing man, but he had shouted and waved his hat and cheered the Balliol eight heartily often enough. By the time he reached the row of glamorous elaborate old vessels, all different, lining the river, the rising sun was infusing the mist with a red-gold glow. In shabby splendour the barges looked like a sideshow for the *Fighting Temeraire*. The dawn gilded them with ephemeral glory.

Peter clambered down the sloping bank, and hauled himself up by the rails to scramble on board his barge. He wouldn't have done this to any but Balliol's, not even St Severin's. Once on the deck he could lean over the rail on the far side of the barge, and enjoy a fine view of the river, gently steaming with curls of the evaporating mist. The river was not quite empty of life; there were one or two gulls circling. Legend suggested that the gulls came inland when there were storms at sea, but if that were so there was very little calm weather to be had on English shores, for there were nearly always gulls on the river. A pair of swans glided past, their wings lifted in graceful curves to serve as spread sails in the light breeze.

A solitary oarsman appeared, rowing smoothly upstream in a scull. The pleasant soft plashing of his oars fell into the wide silence. Peter watched appreciatively as the man came by him, rowing smoothly but strongly against the race caused by the breakwaters in the bridge. The water broke into golden rings at each dip of his oars, and haloed his head, and it was only as he reached the shadow of the bridge that Peter realised he was watching not a blond youngster, but a white-headed older man. An impressively fit older man, Peter noted. Perhaps he himself should add rowing to his activities; he would bet you got good biceps from pulling those oars.

Quite suddenly the sun soared above him, leaving him in the common light of day. The mist softened and retreated. Every crack in old timber, every blister in old paintwork was revealed. Peter climbed back from barge to bank, and began the walk home to breakfast.

The oarsman had looked vaguely familiar to him, but he couldn't place quite who he was. Perhaps he was a chimera from his own remembered youth.

'I need some information from you, and some assistance,' said Peter to Ambleside. 'I would like you to list for me all the deaths or mishaps that have occurred in the fellowship during the last eleven months or so

– effectively since the issue of the sale of the MS became hot – and the cause of death if you know it, and the side on which the deceased would have voted in the dispute, as far as you know.'

Ambleside looked glum. 'If I may say so,' he said, 'the train of thought evinced in that request is a touch melodramatic.'

'It is devoutly to be hoped so,' said Peter. 'But it is my job to eliminate possibilities until only one remains.'

Ambleside looked unhappy. 'Allow me to say, Your Grace, that in my understanding your duties are confined to the settlement of disputes within the fellowship.'

'And if something rather worse than a dispute has been going on?'

Ambleside looked unhappier still. 'There have been two deaths among the fellows in the time you indicate,' he said. 'I will find you the information you asked for.'

'Could you also put a notice in the Senior Common Room, inviting any fellow who would like to put a case to me, on either side of the dispute, to call on me at any time they find convenient, between breakfast and Hall? Shall we say from tomorrow morning for the next three days?'

Ambleside looked happier at that request, and hastened away to set about it.

It was a lovely, sunny, late morning. Of course there would be lunch in Hall, but Peter decided against that. There would be some awkwardness, whoever he chatted with. Instead he trotted down Parks Road into Holywell

Street, and dived into the Turf Tavern. There he found a
seat in a sunny out-of-doors corner, and ordered a pint
and a Stilton ploughman's. The place filled up rapidly
with loudly conversational young people. Peter buried
himself in his copy of *The Times*, dealing with waves of
nostalgia. Had he and Harriet ever eaten here? He
thought not. Harriet in Oxford belonged to his more
adult days. He sighed as he remembered that in those
adult days, try though he had – he really had tried – he
had been enveloped in the aura of grandeur that had for
so long denied him Harriet's consent to marry him. He
would have taken her to lunch or dinner somewhere
quiet and expensive ... more fool he. And now the
grandeur syndrome was much worse, and much harder
to escape. Snap out of it! he told himself, it was dukedom that has brought you here. You will have to Duke it
all the way.

He became aware that someone was hovering at his
table. He lowered *The Times* enough to look over it at
this person: a young man with red hair, wearing a Harris
tweed jacket.

'I say,' this young man said, betraying himself immediately as Jackson from the timbre of his voice, 'are you
that Duke person who is supposed to be calling the dons
to order at Sever's?'

'I am a duke,' said Peter, 'and therefore a fortiori I am
a person. Sit down, Mr Jackson, and let me have the
benefit of your opinions.'

The young man sat down. 'How do you know my
name?' he said, but then like Pilate did not stay for an

47

answer. 'It's no good talking to me, you know. I don't have a vote on the matter.'

'But you have strong feelings about it?'

'If they sell the Boethius this summer, I'm sunk,' Jackson replied. The pitch of his voice made him sound merely plaintive, but his face was sombre.

'Let me buy you a beer,' said Peter, 'and you can tell me all about it.'

'The thing is,' Jackson said, once they were settled with full glasses, 'I am hoping to do a D.Phil when I graduate. I want to work on the college copy of the Boethius. If they sell it I can't. My whole career is derailed.'

'Let's begin at the beginning,' said Peter. 'What are you reading now? History? Greats?'

'English. Course Two.'

'I ought to know what Course Two is . . .' said Peter.

'Lots of Old English. Then Middle English. One third history of the language, the rest literature up to and including Milton.'

'Whatever made you do that?' asked Peter. 'English with not a single Romantic poet? English with not a single Victorian novelist?'

'It was King Alfred,' said Jackson. 'We had to learn Anglo-Saxon in our first term, and one of the texts was his Preface to another thing he translated – besides the Boethius, I mean – *Cura Pastoralis*. I was slogging through it word by word, and I began to realise it was funny – no, that's not what I mean – it was ironical. It was so civilised. And it was the voice of a Dark Ages king. And the Boethius is even more interesting. Alfred put it on his list of the books everyone ought to know, but it was difficult. Abstract. He made it concrete to help his people get it. When it comes to an idea like contingency, he is writing that it's like the way the spokes depend on the hub, and the rim on the spokes of a wheel . . . and he keeps letting you see what he feels about being a king . . . Oh, God, am I boring you? Carrying on too much? My friends say I do . . .'

'Not at all, Mr Jackson. Far from boring me you are educating me. Will you have another drink?'

'Better not, thank you. I have a tutorial this afternoon.'

'A daunting one?'

'You bet! It's with Mary Fowey at Shrewsbury. She's bloody terrifying.'

'Don't you have a tutor in St Severin's?' asked Peter.

'Oh, yes. I have Mr Cloudie. But he's a Shakespeare scholar. When you do an unusual course you get farmed out to someone who specialises in it. It's good in a way, but those women tutors are ferocious.'

'The female of the species is more deadly than the male?'

'That's about it.'

'So if St Severin's sells its Boethius, your plan of studies can't take place, you say. Surely whoever buys it will make it available to scholars?'

'When they've finished "accessioning" it. When their own people have had first go at it. And anyway it will go abroad. Somewhere in the United States, probably. And I can't possibly afford to study abroad.'

'Couldn't you study something else?'

'Possibly. But this is what I really want to do. Being blocked would be like losing a girl one loved.'

At this point a newcomer entered the courtyard – an old acquaintance of Peter's, Helen de Vine. 'Lord Peter, by all that's marvellous!' she said, coming across to him at once.

'I'd better go,' said Jackson, jumping up and offering his chair to the newcomer.

'What are you doing in Oxford?' Miss de Vine asked Peter.

'Travelling incognito as the Duke of Denver,' Peter said. 'I do hope young Jackson didn't hear what you just called me.'

'Well, you can't keep THAT secret,' said Miss de Vine. 'Wait till I tell the others! When will you come to tea with us? Or will you be my guest at High Table?'

'Either would be lovely,' said Peter. 'And soon. Very soon. I would like an introduction to Mary Fowey.'

'You shall have that as soon as I can arrange it,' said Miss de Vine. 'And is dear Harriet here too?'

'She's on her way,' said Peter. 'I expect her soon.'

On returning to his rooms Peter found Ambleside waiting for him, with the list he had asked for of recent deaths and mishaps.

'Come and sit down with me, and let's look at this together,' Peter said.

Ambleside had noted at the top of the list that the question of selling the Boethius had first been discussed eleven months ago. 'It's all taking too long,' he told Peter. 'The offer to us to buy the land will expire shortly, and we will have to buy it on the open market, or do without it.'

'Who is offering us this chance to buy?' asked Peter.

'The vendor wants anonymity. I must admit I can't see why – donors usually want something named after them. But not this time.'

'Hmm,' said Peter. 'For the moment let's stick to death among the fellowship.'

'Well,' said Ambleside, 'the first of those was Robert Smithy. He died suddenly of a heart attack, two days after the first tied vote on the dispute. Not unexpectedly, Your Grace; Mr Smithy had had heart trouble for some months.'

'And Mr Smithy had voted to retain the MS?' asked Peter.

'Yes, he did. So his death left the balance of advantage with the selling party.'

His death had also left a vacancy among the fellow-ships. A Mr Trevair had been appointed. He had been a non-controversial choice: the college had had until then no fellow in economics, and it would save money to be able to teach the PPE students in house.

'However,' Ambleside said, 'I think many people assumed that an economist would vote against keeping the MS. That was part of the support for his appoint-ment. It would clinch the matter. But it turned out otherwise. Mr Trevair very greatly angered some people by voting on the next occasion to keep the MS, thus again leaving it to the Warden's casting vote.'

'So it was stalemate again?'

'Yes, it was. By this time, Your Grace, the college was becoming a very unhappy place to live and work in.'

'And then someone called Enistead?'

'Fell down a flight of stairs and broke his neck.'

'Two deaths, so far,' said Peter. He saw a little involuntary tremor pass over Ambleside's face at the words 'so far'. 'One natural; one a nasty accident. Not a massacre, Ambleside.'

'Well, there were also a couple of incidents,' said Ambleside, not meeting Peter's eyes.

'What were those?' Peter asked. 'I need *uberrima fides* in your account, Ambleside. Tell all.'

'Dr Dancy got accidentally locked into the bell-chamber – you know, Your Grace, that we have a ring of six bells – when a group of bell-ringers were about to start a trial run of Grandsire Doubles. There had been complaints from Wadham College next door about the disturbance of the ringing when students were studying, so the flanges were closed to mute the noise. Dancy had the presence of mind to turn the clock hands continuously, using the adjustment mechanism, and someone passing on Parks Road noticed and stepped in to tell the porter. The ring was stopped, and Dancy was rescued, in a distressed condition. But he has been left with ruptured eardrums.'

'Hmm,' said Peter. 'Any idea how it happened?'

'The bell-chamber is usually locked during a ring,' said Ambleside. 'I suppose it was not realised that he was up there.'

'Was Dancy in favour of keeping, or of selling the MS?' Peter asked.

'He wanted to sell it. He was afraid for the future of music in the college if no money could be found to deal with the financial crisis.'

'You said there were a couple of incidents,' said Peter. 'What was the other one?'

'I'm not sure about this at all,' said Ambleside. 'It might be just moonshine. But we have an unfortunate fellow who needs sleeping pills, our Senior Fellow, Cloudie. He's been on them for years; I think they must be addictive. They give him nightmares, but he can't get himself off them. He's a bachelor; he lived in college. And he woke up one night, he told everybody, thinking there was someone in his room; someone leaning over him, holding his wrist. Of course he was dopey from his pills, and the room was dark – just a faint glow from the lamps in the court outside his window. He thought the intruder was wielding a syringe – a very large one. When he woke he supposed he had had a nightmare; but there was a puncture in the vein in his inner elbow. Everyone was talking about it at the time.'

'And what was everyone saying?' asked Peter.

'That it was a case of self-administered drugs of some sort.'

'And this chap – did you say it was Cloudie? – was not seriously harmed? And had been voting to sell the MS?'

'Cloudie. Not seriously harmed, but seriously frightened. He moved out of college. And yes, he was and is of the sell the MS party.'

'He teaches English?' asked Peter. 'That's odd, then.'

'Cloudie thinks that there is too much Old English in the syllabus,' said Ambleside. 'He thinks if there were less medieval material we might be able to get beyond Matthew Arnold. I believe he is writing a book about Joyce Cary.'

'So a decision was made to invoke the Visitor.'

'I wouldn't call it a decision,' said Dr Ambleside. 'To call in the Visitor doesn't require a general decision. Any two fellows can do it on their own.'

'And Cloudie and you yourself decided to exercise that right. How had you been voting?' asked Peter.

'Rather ironically,' Ambleside told him, 'Cloudie was in favour of selling, and I in favour of keeping. But things had reached a state when most of us on both sides merely wanted the matter resolved.'

'Tell me about Mr Enistead,' said Peter.

'He fell down the stairs, I'm afraid, here in college,' said Ambleside. 'A horrible thing. One of his own undergraduates found him. That boy is still in a state of shock.'

'I have a distinct impression,' said Peter, 'that Mr Enistead's death was not a matter arousing deep distress. Certainly Mr Troutbeck, who heard of it while in my house, seemed, shall we say, less than heartbroken?'

Ambleside found it necessary to lower his gaze, and study his own shoes for some moments. 'Enistead was a long-standing and conscientious fellow of the college,' he said at last. 'Not a man to set the world on fire, I admit. He was an unmarried man who lived in college, and took a good deal of care of the undergraduates. He used to say his students were his children, and his students were his books. I'm afraid Troutbeck, who is another kind of man altogether, must have allowed his partisanship over the MS to affect his judgement.'

Privately, Peter rather agreed, but he held his tongue. 'Troutbeck seemed to think that the next vote would be to sell the MS and buy the land; he thought that my services would not be required.'

'I would very gladly invite you to depart and leave us to our own devices, Your Grace,' said Ambleside, 'were it not for the dark suspicions that you have aroused in my mind. For the moment I would rather that you stayed.'

'Never fear, old chap,' said Peter. 'I'm staying for a while yet. And since I'm here, would you like to show me the staircase down which Mr Enistead so unfortunately fell?'

That staircase was in a new building, rather tightly squeezed along one wall of the gardens, with a covered walkway to connect it to the east quadrangle. The stair-well where the accident had happened had a bare appearance – concrete steps, and a simple handrail decorated at intervals by round brass knobs topping off the uprights. Ambleside explained with visible queasiness that the nature of Enistead's injuries suggested that he had banged his head, in falling, against one of these brass knobs.

'Which knob?' asked Peter.

'I'm afraid I don't know,' said Ambleside. 'It's all been cleaned up now. I'll see if one of the scouts is around. I expect they know.'

The scout he brought to the foot of the stairs was a young man with a brisk and practical manner. He pointed out to Peter a knob on one of the turns in the stair, about two-thirds up from the ground level.

'Are you sure?' Peter asked him.

'Pretty sure, sir,' he said. 'It had been knocked off, sir, and we found it lying right down there, rolled into the corner opposite the exit door. When the alarm was raised about poor Mr Enistead, sir.'

'An undergraduate found him, I understand?' said Peter.

'Yes, sir. And it being rather early in the morning there were scouts around to come running to help.'

'Early in the morning?' Peter asked.

'When he was found,' said Ambleside. 'It seemed he must have been lying there all night, the accident having happened the previous evening.'

'So you concluded that Mr Enistead had dislodged it when he struck his head against it?' Peter asked the scout.

'It looked like that, sir. The knob had blood on it. And there was only one post missing its knob – that one what I showed you.'

'Are these knobs loose?' asked Peter.

'Not to speak of, sir,' the scout told him, 'not usually. We can polish them where they are without they come off in our hands.'

Peter began to grip and turn the knob nearest to the step where he was standing. When he took both hands to it, it turned, and with several turns it came off. About the size and weight of a cricket ball, he thought.

'It must of been loose to come off when the poor gentleman hit against it,' said the scout.

Peter seemed lost in thought. He was looking up, at the large skylight that lit the stairwell. 'That glass must need cleaning from time to time,' he said. 'Where is the access to the roof?'

'Top of the other staircase, sir,' the scout told him. 'I could show you.'

He led the way to the far end of the building, where a second staircase led up to a similar skylight. A small flight of steps to one side led to a door out to the roof. The three of them emerged through this door on to a flat roof the length and width of the building, surrounded by a low parapet, and featureless apart from the two skylights.

'Are those skylights fixed shut?' asked Peter.

'Oh, no, sir,' said the scout. 'When it gets very hot we have to open them up for a bit to let the heat escape. This building does get very warm in hot weather.' As he spoke he stepped forward and opened the nearest light, simply by lifting the entire pyramid of glazed sections, and propping it up on a rod, just like opening the bonnet of a car. 'Easy!' he said.

'And is the door to this roof usually open as we found it just now?' asked Peter.

''Tisn't supposed to be,' the scout said. 'But there's too many people has a key. The undergraduates like to hold parties up here – pyjama parties mostly – and now and then somebody worrits about it in case they throw themselves over the parapet, and the door gets locked for a week or two. But then it gets left open again.'

'Does anyone know what Mr Enistead might have been doing on this staircase so late at night that he could lie here undiscovered until morning?' Peter asked.

'We thought he must have come to inspect the new paintwork,' said the scout. 'And we had moved the young men out of their rooms on this staircase while the paint dried on the stairs. There was nobody around, sir, till the following morning, when one young man came back to fetch his lecture notes.'

'Do you ever find stuff up here?' Peter asked. 'Leaves and twigs and the like – perhaps a stout twig with a fork in it?'

'There's leaves blow up here in the autumn, sir. And one of the scouts, sir, found a pair of women's knickers up here once. Stout twigs I haven't seen.'

'All the scouts have a key?'

'And all the senior members, sir.'

'I thought senior members cavorting about on the rooftops was confined to All Souls,' said Peter.

'This is Oxford, sir,' the scout said. 'You never know who will get up to what.'

All this time, and all the way back to the main building, Ambleside had said not a word.

On reaching Peter's room he said, 'Perhaps, Your Grace, you would like to tell me what all that was about.'

Peter hesitated, and then decided on candour. 'I was wondering if the brass knob that stove in Mr Enistead's head had been used as a projectile from above, rather than simply being passively hit as he fell upon it,' he said. 'I don't quite see how a falling man could have unscrewed a knob so that it fell free.'

'The one he hit must have been loose already,' said Ambleside. 'I don't see how anyone could have dropped it through the skylight with enough force.'

'I was thinking about catapults,' said Peter.

'Oh, I don't think so,' said Ambleside. 'Catapults are none too easy, especially aimed at a small target.'

'Were you a boy-expert in them?' asked Peter.

'Not at all. But we have a medieval tournament in college in the summer term, and catapults are among the ancient artillery that gets used. I am hopeless at it, but some people are better . . . but it's very far-fetched, Your Grace. Where did you get such an idea? Where would anyone get the idea?'

'It is the murder method in one of my wife's detective novels,' said Peter, 'which has, I believe, sold several thousand copies.'

'Oh, detective stories . . .' said Ambleside. 'Anything goes in popular fiction.'

'But in this case the murder method was based on a case of mine,' said Peter. 'That was real enough. When my wife arrives tomorrow you must put your proposition to her that anything goes in detective stories. I shall enjoy hearing her discuss it with you.'

★　　★　　★

The following morning Mr Cloudie was run to earth reading the *Telegraph* in the Senior Common Room. Peter asked him for an account of his nasty experience the previous term.

'I'm amazed to find anyone taking me seriously,' said Cloudie. 'All my colleagues have written me off as a lunatic. Who told you about it?'

'John Ambleside,' said Peter.

'Ambleside's the best of us,' said Cloudie. 'One can trust him.'

'Would you mind telling me what happened to you?' Peter asked him.

'I'm glad to discover that you think something actually happened,' said Cloudie. 'I take sleeping pills, you know. They are necessary to me; that doesn't mean I am crazy.'

'I have taken sleeping pills myself,' said Peter sympathetically, 'to carry me over a bad patch. Best to get off them when you can.'

'I was in the unit that liberated Belsen,' said Cloudie. 'There are things I need not to remember at night. Just the same, I can tell the difference between nightmares and events. Someone assaulted me in my sleep.'

'Would you mind describing the assault to me?' Peter asked.

'It's just what I told Ambleside,' said Cloudie. 'I half woke, because someone was holding my wrist, and turning my arm so the inner elbow faced upwards. The room was very dark, and the person was masked, I think; certainly there was only a black blur for a face. Then a car passed outside, and the headlights briefly lit the room, bouncing off the ceiling – you know the effect. I was looking down at my arm, trying to work out what was happening, and I saw a syringe being pointed at my elbow. A big syringe, large enough to dose a horse I should think. I felt the needle go in quite deep, and I let out a sort of squawk; as a cry for help it was pathetic, but I was still only half awake. He fled at once; I heard the door bang behind him. I couldn't get up; I could only fight off sleep for a few moments, and then I was gone again. But when I woke in the morning there was a nasty puncture in my arm; it had bled a bit on to my pyjama sleeve.'

'That puncture was the evidence that you weren't dreaming,' said Peter. 'Did anyone else see it?'

'My doctor saw it. I was in a flat panic; I didn't know what I had been injected with.'

'What did your doctor say?'

'I think he didn't believe me. He offered to get me help with drug addiction . . . he did clean up the puncture and put a plaster on it. And he told me to watch in case it became infected. I'm afraid I was so angry at the suggestion that I had been injecting myself with heroin or something that I stormed out of his surgery. And I found myself lodgings on the Cowley Road, so I need never spend the night in college again.'

'I'm not surprised,' said Peter. 'For the record, Mr Cloudie, I believe you.'

'Well, that's something I suppose,' said Mr Cloudie. 'Nobody else does.'

'I have a rather special reason to believe you,' said Peter.

*　　*　　*

Dancy next. He had rooms on the top floor of a front quad staircase. The porter thought he was in his room. Peter heard a piano being played as he ascended the stair. He assumed he would interrupt a music lesson, but when he tapped and entered he found Dancy alone, playing in solitude. The poor man had not heard Peter's knock, and was startled at his appearance.

Attempts at explaining his reason for calling were difficult; Dancy really was deaf, at least temporarily. Peter whipped out a notebook and pen and the conversation was conducted in writing on his part. Dancy could speak with ease; and he had not been deaf long enough to have acquired the loud voice that sometimes accompanies deafness. His account of the accident was just the same as Ambleside's. Peter asked him what he had been doing in the bell-tower in the first place, and Dancy said he was comparing one of his tuning forks with the note of the treble bell when it was lightly struck.

'My own fault, don't you know,' he said, 'my own fault. I had forgotten the ringing practice. I am very absent-minded. Though of course, I didn't expect the bell-chamber to be locked. I don't think they usually lock it. But perhaps they do, and I had forgotten that.' He offered Peter a seraphic smile. 'I am often rather absent-minded,' he said. 'On that occasion I was rehearing in my mind a passage from *The Art of the Fugue*, by Bach. Do you happen to know it, Your Grace?'

Peter said, or rather wrote, that he did. Indeed that he tried to play it sometimes. He had wept tears over the last note . . .

'Yes,' said Dancy, 'so have I. The death of Bach is silence . . . for now I can hear nothing except humming and whining sounds. But they tell me I shall recover by and by, at least partly.'

'For now you can't hear, but you can play?' asked Peter.

Once again Dancy's face lit up. 'I can hear it very clearly when I am playing,' he said. 'I can hear any error in the mind's eye, so to speak. It comforts me to play; sometimes I can forget the deafness altogether. And what light it casts on Beethoven!'

'I salute you,' Peter wrote. 'And thank you for your help.'

The invitation to the fellowship to drop in and discuss their views with Peter was not long in bearing fruit. First to appear were a Mr Oundle and a Mr Martin, carrying rolled-up documents, and hoping that they might explain to His Grace the merits of the proposal to buy land.

'Is Troutbeck joining us?' asked Peter.

'No; we gather he has had his say.'

'But we are here as an informal deputation,' Mr Oundle said. 'We thought perhaps that it would be better if just the two of us spoke for all of us who wish to acquire the land. May we show you? Is there somewhere we could unroll these maps and plans?'

Unasked, Bunter appeared and removed candlesticks and a salt-cellar from the dining table at one end of the room, and then removed an embroidered runner, leaving the table bare.

'Sherry, I think, Bunter,' said Peter.

'Yes, Your Grace,' said Bunter, adopting his stiffest pose.

The map was unrolled first. The contentious land was outlined in blue. It was quite extensive, and there was a road on each side, roads running out of Oxford like the spokes on a wheel, so that the land between them was wedge-shaped. A little brook crossed it. Two stands of trees were marked.

'As you see, Duke,' said Mr Oundle, 'this is a sitting duck for development. Excellent road access; a level site. No particular difficulties for construction . . .'

'Is it grade one agricultural land?' asked Peter.

'We understand it is grade three,' said Mr Martin.

'Why?' asked Peter. 'I mean, why isn't it grade one?'

'Too damp for arable,' said Mr Oundle. 'It's grazing land, basically.'

'It isn't so hugely valuable, then,' Peter said, 'unless it gets reclassified as development land.'

'We expect that to happen,' said Martin. 'Oxford is bursting at the seams, and there is a desperate need for more housing.'

'Housing like this,' said Mr Oundle, unrolling a sheet of architects' drawings on top of the map.

The drawings showed blocks of flats arranged round a small park with a pond. A parade of shops and a school occupied one of the two road frontages. Bright blue skies with fluffy clouds had been provided above this panorama, and little sketchy people with shopping bags and children in prams walked the streets. Toddlers were feeding ducks on the pond. Idyllic.

Bunter having appeared with the sherry, Peter invited his guests to sit down and talk it over.

'The gist of your proposition, correct me if I'm wrong, is that you should acquire this land at agricultural prices, get planning permission, and sell it on at a substantial profit. Is that the idea?'

'Not necessarily,' Mr Oundle told him. 'It might do better if we leased it for development and held on to the ground rents for the future.'

Bunter, having poured the sherry, retreated to the far end of the room.

'I do see a snake in the woodpile,' Peter said. 'If the council want the land they can take it from you at its price for agriculture. And when you ask them for planning permission that thought is likely to occur to them, isn't it?'

'Hence the need for haste,' Mr Martin said. 'We need to buy the land and get it reclassified quickly. We need to write contracts with several developers so that it will be difficult for the council to take over the whole area . . . we need to do this before any coherent plan to redevelop emerges. We need to be ahead of the game.'

'Have you heard of Crichel Down?' asked Peter.

Both men shook their heads. 'We need to get this decided, and act with dispatch,' Mr Martin replied.

'But with the best will in the world this is a gamble,' Peter said. 'It might not pay off.'

'But on the other hand,' Mr Oundle said, 'there is very little downside. Honestly, Your Grace, the loss of the manuscript would not seriously damage the college, whatever you may have been told about it. And may I suggest that you should ask the Bursar to put you in the picture as to the college finances before coming to a conclusion?'

'I am always open to suggestions,' said Peter. 'And now may I ask you something. Whose land is this? Who is the self-damaging person who wishes to sell the land cheaply to the college, instead of gambling on its future value for himself?'

The two men exchanged glances. Neither of them, Peter noticed, had more than sipped their excellent oloroso sherry. He noticed Mr Martin's fingers tighten on the stem of his glass. But his voice did not alter. 'A friend of the college. Wishes to remain anonymous. For personal reasons.'

'I see,' said Peter. He hoped the note of anger in his voice escaped them. Did they take him for a fool? He thought of asking if the gentleman in question was a friend of either of the men in front of him; but he thought better of it.

'Well, I can see the force of your argument,' he said, 'but it is a matter of cool calculation, isn't it? Not a thing to get het up about.'

'What we are getting het up about, Your Grace, as you put it,' said Mr Martin, 'is nothing less than the survival of the college in any state to pursue its stated purposes. To continue as a house of learning, rather than as a mausoleum for antiquities.'

'I see that you feel very strongly about it, old chap,' said Peter.

'Nothing like as strongly as some others,' said Mr Oundle. 'You should hear Troutbeck on the subject.'

'Should I?' said Peter. 'Well, why aren't I hearing him? Why does he send you to speak in his place?'

'He has already made himself clear to you, we understand,' said Oundle. 'We thought perhaps you should see that many of us agree with him.'

The moment the deputation had rolled up their documents and left him, Peter dispatched Bunter to a London train, and a trip to Lincoln's Inn to see if it was possible to discover from the Land Registry the name of the shy friend of the college. And then, ignoring the possibility of more visitors responding to his invitation, he went out for fresh air, and punted himself in solitary glory from Magdalen Bridge to Bardwell Road and back.

When Peter returned to his room he found he did have a visitor waiting for him, though not an expected one: a smart, rather beautiful woman in early middle age, wearing slacks and a tweed jacket over a green silk shirt.

'Mary Fowey,' she said, offering him her hand. 'I understand you want to talk to me about the St Severin's Boethius.'

'How kind of you to come,' said Peter, taking the proffered handshake. 'I was hoping to call on you later today.'

'The MS is here,' she said. 'Shall we go and look at it together?'

The two of them descended to the ground floor, and crossed the quad to the library.

The library had been built by someone who thought of it as sacred space; it resembled a chapel, having a fine hammer-beam timber roof, beautifully carved seventeenth-century bookcases, and Gothic windows glazed in plain greenish bubble-filled panes of glass.

The room was dark, and needed the reading lights with which every desk was provided. Along the back wall of the room a row of glass-fronted bookcases displayed the treasures of the house; those, that is, that were not in one of the locked display cases that occupied the centre aisle. 'I took the liberty of asking your librarian to meet us here,' said Mary Fowey. 'Ah, here he is . . .'

A pallid young man rose from a desk where he had obviously been engaged in pasting acquisition slips into a leather-bound folio catalogue volume. He introduced himself and brought a bunch of keys from his pocket, with which he unlocked one of the display cases. He slipped a pair of white cotton gloves on to his hands, and carefully lifted a book to place it on a book-rest on a nearby table. The three of them sat down at this table.

The contentious volume was small and chunky. It was written on vellum, and bound in vellum, once white and now rather dirty. It had been tightly bound, so that it closed if not held open. Two more pairs of white gloves were found for Peter and Miss Fowey. Very gingerly, cradling the volume in one hand, Peter held pages open with the other. He was looking at an even hand, written without word breaks, in ink now faded to brown, in an elegant rounded uncial script. The scorch marks of which Troutbeck had complained disfigured the outer margins of the pages, and had caused the eroded edges to nibble at the end of the lines of text. There were no decorated initials, and no illustrations. In a very small medieval hand and in bluer ink a line of interposed glosses ran along above the Latin lines.

'You are wondering what all the fuss is about,' said Mary Fowey.

'I don't know a lot about manuscript,' said Peter. 'Incunabula are my field. Educate me, Miss Fowey.'

'Well, *The Consolations of Philosophy* is in no way a rare volume,' she said. 'It was immensely popular in its time; a world bestseller in late antiquity. Dozens, probably hundreds of copies of it survive in libraries all over Europe. And it comes up for sale now and then. If you wanted a copy you could ask Quaritch to look out for it for you, or someone in Rome, and it could be had by and by. And this copy, as you see, lacks charm. But it is undoubtedly very old. I believe it has been dated to AD 600 or thereabouts.'

'So what is the fuss about?'

'The fuss is about the gloss. I'm not on firm ground here – we should ask Elaine Griffiths. But the copy is old enough . . .'

'Old enough for what?'

'To have belonged to King Alfred. So this could indeed, as some have been saying, have been the copy he used when he made his famous translation into Anglo-Saxon.'

'So this might be a holy relic indeed,' said Peter, gently laying the book down on the book-rest in front of him.

'Boethius is a saint and martyr, and Alfred is the only king we call Great.'

'Well, I don't get reverent about relics,' said Mary Fowey. 'I'm an atheist and a scholar.'

'You don't get a shiver down the spine at the thought of who might have held this book?' asked Peter.

'No,' she said. 'Each to his own. Do you?'

But Peter did not feel confessional confronted with this brisk, authoritative woman.

He opened the book again, and using his monocle as a reading glass, and choosing a page at random, he inspected the gloss.

Da com thear gan to me heofencund Yisdom . . .

'I wish you luck making any sense of that,' said Miss Fowey. 'As I said, you need Elaine Griffiths.'

She took her leave. Whereupon Peter's new friend, young Jackson, emerged from behind a bookshelf.

'I could help you a bit,' he said.

'Please do,' said Peter.

'This line says: *when I had sung this mournful song, there came in to me Heavenly Wisdom and greeted my sorrowful mind* . . . Well, it doesn't say exactly that because it doesn't bother with the obvious little words like "in" and "to". You are reading the Latin line, and the gloss just helps you with words you might not know.'

'It's a sort of crib, you mean?'

'Just so. This gloss is in West Saxon, which is the sort of English Alfred spoke. And it would have helped him – we know how he worked.'

Peter raised a sceptical eyebrow at Jackson, and waited. The librarian, who had been standing quietly by, went and fetched a heavily calf-bound volume from the shelves, embossed with the imprint of the Early English Text Society. Jackson eagerly opened it. 'Look,' he said.

Peter looked. Anglo-Saxon on the verso of each page, modern English on the recto. The text of the first page said:

King Alfred was the translator of this book, and turned it from book Latin into English as is now done. Sometimes he set word by word, sometimes meaning by meaning as he plainly and most clearly could explain it, for the various and manifold worldly occupations which often busied him both in mind and body. The occupations are very difficult to be numbered which in his days came upon the kingdom which he had undertaken ...

'Poor chap,' said Peter. He felt both awe-struck and ashamed of himself. What was a dukedom to manage compared to a kingdom invaded by the Danes?

And now he prays everyone who lists to read this book that he would pray for him and not blame him if he more rightly understands it than he could ...

'It's good, isn't it?' said Jackson.

'It's very good,' said Peter. 'I shall go and pray for him right away.'

★　　★　　★

St Severin's had, of course, a chapel handy. It was Victorian Gothic, with stained glass designed by William Morris. A holy water stoop at the door. Just the sort of thing that made Peter uncomfortable. He was pleased to find the east window depicting Boethius instructing students, and willing to admire a Jacobean pulpit presumably surviving from an earlier chapel. There was an organ loft or a minstrels' gallery across the back, above the door, with several carved angels, wings spread, purporting to be bearing the weight of it on their backs. Peter inspected them with interest. Much older than the chapel, he thought. Looking properly medieval, though recently repainted and with gaudily gilded wings. Peter liked inspecting church architecture, of any period. But praying? He was perfectly at home with church services, ready to read the lessons in the parish church at Denver, ready to be present at baptisms, marriages and funerals, but solitary prayer was something rather too High Church for him. Nevertheless . . .

'I assume,' he said to the space above the altar, about amidships to the Boethius window, 'that your servant Alfred met with your eschatological approval. I certainly hope so. As for me, I must leave that with you.

'And whether that is a prayer or not,' he added to himself, 'is also a question for whatever God may be.'

He left the chapel and returned to his rooms, deep in thought. He had not felt like confessing to the snappy Mary Fowey what he felt about relics, as she called them. But he remembered, for example, when on a Foreign Office errand to Prague he had stood in the Villa

Bertramka. Someone had lifted the lid of Mozart's piano, and invited him to play ... to touch the very keys that Mozart touched ... had that meant nothing? Or – another thing – Harriet's wedding present to him, an autograph letter from John Donne on divine and human love: were that to be proved a fake would it make no difference? The question answered itself as soon as it was put, with a lurch in the guts ...

There was no doubt about it: Peter had placed himself as a worshipper of relics. But the day's work had put a different light on matters in St Severin's. He had realised – of course he had – that the tensions and cross-currents in the college were inflamed by some very strong feelings. He had assumed that when he got to the bottom of it he would find some bitter rivalry, some old grudge, most probably having nothing to do with the dispute itself; most probably driven by personal hatred. But perhaps the problem with the manuscript was not hatred, but love? A much more dangerous thing.

4

The suggestion that had been made to Peter that he should seek out Mr Winterhorn, the Bursar, had obvious merits, and the day after his encounter with the contentious manuscript, he set about it; he invited Mr Winterhorn for a drink before lunch.

When Winterhorn appeared he had the nervous look of an undergraduate arriving for an admission interview, and Peter took a minute or two to settle his guest with a glass in his hand, and to chat idly about the story of the glass bottles. Winterhorn opened up.

'My predecessor,' he said, 'rather lost his way. He was very thrifty with small sums of money, Your Grace, but out of his depth with large ones. He could see trouble brewing, but he didn't know what to do about it. He resigned his college fellowship six months ago, and I was elected to take over. Now I in turn am out of my depth, I'm afraid.'

'Why did you accept the post?' asked Peter.

'Well, somebody has to do it,' said Winterhorn. 'I'm the maths tutor, you see, and the fellows seemed to think that would make me competent with money. I can add up a rising deficit, all right; but as to what to do about it . . . I can think of economies, but every one I suggest is rejected with indignation. I will gladly show you the books; they will enable you to see why the land offer is so tempting.'

'You are telling me you have responsibility without power,' said Peter.

'In the constitution of this college, yes, that's about it.'

'You could do with some professional advice, I think.'

'Alas; too expensive,' said Winterhorn.

'Ah,' said Peter. 'Are you too, perhaps, very sensitive to small sums and at sea with great ones?'

'I will be grateful for your advice, Your Grace,' said Winterhorn. 'When would you like to inspect the books?'

Peter spent a dismal afternoon with Winterhorn, trying to unravel the story which the accounts revealed. There was nothing wrong with the book-keeping; and the revelation in chief contained in the account books, which should have come as no surprise to Peter, was the huge expense entailed in running a college. It was the investments that appalled him; on that front something useful could be done less controversial than selling the port, sacking half the fellowship, or allowing the beautiful gardens to return to scrubland.

When he left Winterhorn, Peter returned to base, and settled into an armchair, his gown ready draped over the back of the chair, all set to brave the dragons by going in to Hall dinner, when he heard voices outside the door. Bunter's was one of them, uttering the magical words 'Your Grace,'. Although Peter still detested hearing himself so called by Bunter, after long years during which 'my lord' had been his *appellation contrôlée*, since Bunter was not now addressing him, the words could only mean that Harriet had arrived. He jumped up to greet her.

She entered the room saying, 'And hast thou slain the Jabberwock?'

He opened his arms to her, and said, 'Come and be my beamish girl.'

Harriet came. They did not hasten their embrace. But by and by she said, 'No callooing and callaying is allowed, Peter, if the Jabberwock is still at large.'

'I wasn't expecting you till tomorrow,' he said.

'Well, the doctor came a day early to see your mother, and the Le Fanu speech was a lunchtime one,' she said. 'And when it was done I thought I'd come up to Oxford right away. You seem to need a bit of help.'

'So it wasn't that you were missing me?' he asked wistfully.

'Of course not!' she said, laughing, 'but Oxford is a temptation.'

'Oh, bother Oxford!' he said. 'And look, my dear, I am about to go and dine at High Table. Did you think to bring your gown?'

Bunter coughed discreetly at the door. 'I have found a gown, Your Grace,' he said to Harriet. 'There was one behind the door of the study in the main part of the house.'

'The property of the vanished Warden, no doubt,' said Peter. 'It will do. Can you face the old lions roaring in their den right away and without warning, Harriet?'

'I should think so,' she said calmly. 'Can we sit together?'

'You are likely to be the only woman guest,' he said, 'and therefore yours is the place of honour at the right hand of the most senior fellow present. Don't know if that puts us together. It might. But if we're not together we will between us have a larger sample of the fellows dining tonight. Come – the Senior Common Room first.'

There was a lively buzz of voices in the Senior Common Room, which hushed for a moment as Peter and Harriet entered.

For a moment they stood isolated in the crowded room, as though everyone thought they might have flu. Then the intrinsic good manners of the company towards outsiders, if not towards each other, supervened, and Ambleside approached them and was introduced to Harriet.

Peter was soon talking to Mr Vearing; a not wholly fascinating discussion of the various ways to travel between Oxford and Cambridge, with complaints about the time taken waiting at Bletchley to make the necessary change. 'And what, after all, is Bletchley?' Vearing was asking plaintively, when the butler announced dinner was served.

They began to file down the stairs, through the archway below Peter's quarters, and along one side of the quad towards the door of the Hall. In front of them the Hall windows glowed softly with the muted light of candles. Ambleside led the way, and the Wimseys followed him. As Peter had predicted, Harriet was directed to sit on Ambleside's right, at the head of the table. People filed in and took up their places. The buzz of voices from the undergraduates sitting at the long tables in the body of the hall hushed, and a frozen-faced college butler handed Peter a wooden board with the college grace printed on it.

'You are, of course, the senior person present,' said Ambleside, 'but you may delegate that task to me if you wish.'

Peter looked sternly at Ambleside and began to read the grace steadily and clearly.

No *Benedictus benedicat* for St Severin's – their college grace was long and Ciceronian.

Then, with a clatter of chairs being drawn up to tables, everyone sat down.

The table at which they sat, with a long line of silver candlesticks down the centre, was just too wide to permit conversation across the board, unless the speaker raised his voice, especially with the hubbub of voices from the tables below, where the students were sitting. They sat at narrower tables, but were uninhibited about raising their voices. Mr Vearing, opposite Peter and beside Harriet, was talking to her eagerly, but Peter could not hear what was being said. His attention was commanded by Mr Oundle, on his left side, who was trying to engage him in conversation about the latest films. Peter had not seen *Les Belles de Nuit*, he had to confess, nor yet *Limelight*. Mr Oundle gave him up for lost, and began to talk politics. He was a true blue conservative, and very unsure about Anthony Eden. This dislike arose not from anything the Deputy Prime Minister had actually done, but from the fact that he, Oundle, had been consulted by Eden's speech writers, and had seen drafts of the speeches which deviated from the King's English.

'It's the Queen's English now,' observed Peter mildly.

'Is there a difference?' asked Oundle rhetorically. 'I fervently hope not.'

'There will be in time,' said Peter.

'That will be deplorable,' replied Oundle. 'I shall not myself deviate by a syllable from correct usage.'

'My language is foul, and yours is Fowler?' said Peter, and added with one of his sudden quirky smiles, 'or know your Onions.'

This quip crossed the barrier of the table, because the man sitting nearly opposite Peter laughed.

'Onions?' said Oundle.

'C.T. Onions, I imagine,' said the man opposite. 'Editor of the *Oxford English Dictionary*.'

'Oh, I see,' said Oundle. 'Very droll.'

Peter was looking around the table. He observed that Harriet, though perfectly calm, was trying to talk more to Ambleside and less to Vearing. Vearing was ignoring the man on his right, and bending all his attention on Harriet. The ruby in her engagement ring caught the candlelight as she reached for her wine glass, and flashed briefly at him. She caught his eye, and returned his gaze, looking steadily at him as though she had been a queen and he a courtier. Well, he was her courtier, married to her or not. He became impatient with the company, and only courtesy prevented him from looking at his watch.

The man on his left introduced himself and said, 'So you have visited our manuscript, Denver? What do you think?' Peter thought it best if he didn't answer that.

'It is perhaps more interesting than beautiful,' he replied diplomatically.

'Would you sell it if it was yours?' he was asked.

Alas for the King's English, Peter thought. 'How can I answer that?' he replied. 'My circumstances are not those of this college.'

'You'd have enough money to keep it on a whim, I suppose,' said the other. 'But be honest, if the roof was falling off your ducal palace you'd sell a thing like that to keep the place watertight – you know you would.'

But Peter was spared the need to answer that; at that moment the Vice-Warden rose from his seat. Everyone stood, and a shorter Latin grace was presented to the most junior fellow present, who read it rapidly in a monotone. The company filed out, and the Vice-Warden, with Harriet at his side, led the way to the Senior Common Room. Here port and claret, fruit and cheese awaited them on another candlelit table, and there was no formal order of precedence.

Peter joined Harriet and Ambleside.

'I hope this fellow has not been dismissive about your chosen art form, Harriet,' he said.

'Who, me?' said Ambleside, in a tone of injured innocence.

'You told me within these last twenty-four hours that in detective fiction anything goes,' Peter reminded him.

'Well,' said Ambleside carefully, 'I take it that the Duchess would not claim that the same standards of rigour are required of her as are required of the writer of an academic thesis. Nobody imposes that.'

'Nobody but myself,' said Harriet. 'I impose the highest standards of rigour that I am capable of.'

Now suddenly everyone within earshot was listening. 'But after all it doesn't actually *matter* if you make a mistake in a detective story,' said Trevair. 'There are no consequences.'

'There you are wrong,' said Harriet. 'The smallest slip-up, the smallest mistake, brings armfuls of letters from indignant readers expostulating with you, and every one needing an answer. And of course it is humiliating to be found out having made a mistake. It is after all a profession to be a writer, and one should aim at professionalism.'

'Yours is an avocation; but surely not a profession,' said Trevair.

'It is the means by which I earn a living,' said Harriet.

'But duchesses don't need to earn a living,' said Troutbeck.

'But I have not always been a duchess,' said Harriet smoothly.

'Oh, indeed not!' said Vearing. 'You certainly did not need high rank to bring you to public attention.'

Peter fixed his monocle in his eye and bent on Vearing such an icy and disapproving stare that that gentleman fell silent, and uttered not another word while the port was in circulation. When the company rose from the table, Peter said, 'I'm going to mill about, Harriet. But signal if you need further protection.'

'I shall mill myself,' she said. 'Who teaches law here?'

But Harriet, as soon as Peter left her side, was approached by two fellows, one young and one older, eager to discuss her books with her. She sat down at the table with one of them on each side, and allowed herself to bask in their attention.

'At least you can get your work published,' said the man on her left. 'I'm Gervase, by the way. I have spent ten years on a work of literary history, and OUP won't have it.'

'I'm sorry to hear that,' said Harriet. 'What does the rejection letter say?'

'It is too technical. Minority interest. That sort of thing.'

'What is the subject?' asked Harriet.

'The relations of the Vespasian Psalter Gloss and the *Ancrene Riwle*,' he said.

'I must admit that does sound a bit technical,' said Harriet. 'Have you tried other publishers? What about Cambridge University Press?'

'They said it was too popular,' said Gervase gloomily. 'I thought of taking to crime; you know – knock off a detective story when I have the time.'

Harriet asked him to pass the cheese, and turned to her other companion. He too wanted to talk about unpublished work. The problem, he thought, was that work was sent to others who worked in the field in question. They all had a motive to put down aspiring rivals.

'At least I don't suppose you get the kind of review that drives you to suicide,' Gervase said.

'No,' said Harriet. 'Suicidal impulses usually last only five minutes, and are dispersed by crumpling the offending newspaper page and binning it.'

'Ask around a bit,' Gervase said. 'Ask about The Review.'

But around them the company was beginning to disperse. Peter came to the back of her chair, and asked if she was ready to leave, and she gladly got up and went with him.

'Let's get some air,' he said when they stepped out into the quadrangle. It was a clear, moonlit night. Arm-in-arm, they walked out into Parks Road, and turned right. Up past Keble College, towards the University Parks.

'So what did you make of all that?' Peter asked.

'I suppose they are no odder than any other senior common room,' said Harriet. 'But did you notice the oil and water effect?'

'One lot not mixing with the other lot? It was sharp of you to notice that on your first encounter with any of them. What's the magic trick?'

'Only that I saw people suddenly turning away from someone; suddenly taking an interest in the port . . . suddenly changing the subject as the milling around brought different people close to each other. But Peter, that's natural, isn't it? If people are seriously at odds with one another but must still socialise all the time, how else can they keep the peace? Doesn't any cocktail party contain people trying to avoid each other?'

'And people trying to make sure their catty remarks hit home,' said Peter. 'Yes. You are right.'

'I did think that Vearing man was a bit odd,' said Harriet. 'Really rather creepy. He kept telling me he thought he and I must have a lot in common, with a kind of meaningful emphasis. Looked forward to knowing me better . . . That nice John Ambleside kept trying to rescue me, but the table seating made it hard. Eventually I told Vearing that I had nothing in common with him that I knew of.'

Once in the Parks they made for the river and the little footbridge over it. As they passed along the riverside path they heard from under a willow tree the sound of soft laughter, and languorous murmurings coming from a moored-up punt. They laughed softly themselves.

'Come here, Harriet,' said Peter. 'Why should the young have all the fun?'

In a while she released herself and said, 'Still continue as thou art, Ancient person of my heart . . .'

'Hell, Harriet,' said Peter indignantly, 'I need no such assistance as the ancient person in that ditty required! As I shall demonstrate this very moonlit night.'

They walked on as far as the footbridge, and leaned over the rail watching the multiplied moon dancing in the rocking surface of the river.

'I like you in a gown,' said Peter, 'as well as I like you in anything you wear.'

'I have a slight unease about wearing one, just the same,' said Harriet, as their return path offered them a prospect of Keble, its Fair Isle jersey of patterned brickwork softened to near invisibility, and its fine proportions clearer than in daylight.

'Why so, Domina?' he asked.

'It's an MA gown, and I only took one degree,' she said.

'Oh, that,' he said. 'I was afraid you might be spooked, even after all this time, by poisonous messages stuffed into the sleeve.'

'I wasn't thinking of that,' said Harriet, almost unconsciously reaching into the long tapering pocket in which the sleeve of an MA gown ends.

Even by moonlight Peter saw her expression change. She brought out into the air a slip of paper. He saw with relief that it wasn't covered with cut-out and pasted letters.

'What does it say?' he asked.

'It's very small spidery writing,' she said. 'I can't read it in this light.'

'Let's guess,' he said, taking her arm again as they walked on. 'I know – it's a laundry list!'

'It's a reference to a review,' said Harriet. 'Someone was making dark remarks about a review at dinner.'

'That's too tame,' said Peter. 'I think it's the Black Spot.'

'Peter, the Black Spot administered to the vanished Warden might not be funny at all.'

'You are quite right, Harriet. I apologise. It's the piffle habit again.'

They walked on, fairly rapidly now, to the Parks gates, and the streetlamps on Parks Road. By the light of the first streetlamp they read the note easily. It said: *Consider your position.*

5

The following morning found Peter and Harriet sitting at breakfast, with Bunter in attendance.

'Bunter, please sit down with us,' said Harriet. 'This is a professional discussion, and you are part of the team.'

Bunter pulled up a chair and sat down.

'Officially, I suppose, Peter,' said Harriet, 'you could just rule on the matter of the manuscript, and go home. The duties of the Visitor do not include murder investigation.'

Peter looked at her like a little boy denied an expected treat.

She laughed. 'All right,' she said. 'Of course . . . Can't have murderers at large. So what have we got?'

Peter outlined to her the death of Enistead, and the two odd incidents. 'It won't have escaped you, Harriet, that if Enistead's fall was not accidental, and if the two strange incidents were attempted murders, then the murder methods . . .'

'Are from cases of yours . . .' she said.

'Which you have used in detective stories,' he finished.

'Well, after all, Peter,' she said defensively, 'the very first time you proposed to me you offered as an inducement your ability to provide plots for me.'

'So I did,' he said. 'Let's draw a veil over that occasion, however.'

'And all the targets except Enistead have been among those who have voted to sell the MS,' she said. 'And there is also the missing Warden.'

'Well, he might not be dead,' said Peter. 'He might just have considered his position, as we know he was invited to do, and fled.'

'What do you make of this, Bunter?' asked Harriet. She was hoping Bunter's imperturbability would put a cool and rational interpretation on things. But for once Bunter was not cool.

'It looks like serial murder to me, my lady,' said Bunter. 'Or rather, attempted serial murder.'

'In that case,' said Peter, 'we need Charles.'

'Ask him for help, then, Peter,' said Harriet. 'But while he is on his way I shall pay some calls at Shrewsbury College.'

'Good idea, Harriet,' said Peter. 'They know you are expected in Oxford, so the sooner the better. Bunter, would you care to suggest gently to the college servants that there might be a murderer on the loose – well, it will already have occurred to them, won't it? – and see if anyone offers helpful suggestions as to suspects.'

Bunter nodded, and took his leave, taking the breakfast tray with him.

'What will you do?'

'I think I might look out someone called Elaine Griffiths.'

'What will she do for you?'
'She might know if King Alfred could write,' he said.

Harriet spent the first part of her morning browsing happily in Blackwell's, which did, she discovered, stock detective fiction, though only by Oxford-based authors. Edmund Crispin was there, and Harriet bought a copy of *The Moving Toyshop*. Her own had been lent to somebody, and never returned. It's amazing, Harriet thought, how perfectly honest people who would starve rather than steal sixpence, will steal books without compunction.

There was a Michael Innes – *A Private View* – so Harriet also bought a copy of that. Looking for something more literary she found a novel by L.P. Hartley – *The Go-Between*.

Then she wandered out into the morning sunshine, which was doing its best to lighten the soot-engraved buildings along the Broad.

She had timed her arrival at Shrewsbury College for the morning break, during which she expected to find a reasonable number of her old friends drinking coffee in the Senior Common Room, and lo! it was just as expected. Harriet blinked as she entered; for a few seconds she was back before the war, before marrying Peter, before titles and riches, back as the raw, sensitive, uncertain person, fending off her own best chance at happiness, on whom the college had pinned its hopes of clearing up a scandal without a scandal becoming public knowledge. Just a blink, and then Harriet landed in the present day and noticed the changes in the scene before her. New curtains . . . faint traces of anti-blast sticky tape still adhering, irremovable, on the common room windows . . . new faces . . . But here was a familiar face, Dr Baring, the Warden of Shrewsbury, coming towards her, with outstretched arms, and saying, 'Harriet! My dear Harriet, how good to see you! Come and sit among your old friends.'

Soon Harriet was sitting in the centre of a circle of armchairs, with Miss de Vine, and Miss Hilliard, and Miss Martin all beaming at her, as though she were Queen of the May. For a moment she didn't recognise another figure, walking with a stick, coming towards her – Miss Lydgate, by all that's wonderful! But Miss Lydgate with short cropped grey hair, and not a hairpin in sight. The cropped hair framed her wrinkled, slightly harassed face as the swept-up but ever falling long hair had never done. Harriet jumped up and embraced her.

'How long are you to be in Oxford?' asked Miss Lydgate.

'I don't quite know,' Harriet said.

'I suppose,' said Miss de Vine, 'it depends how long it takes your lord and master to sort out the quarrel at St Severin's.'

'Just so,' said Harriet.

'Only – I've retired now, of course,' said Miss Lydgate, 'but I'm doing just a little thing for *Notes and Queries* about prosody in Spenser . . . and I am in such a muddle . . .'

'Yes, of course I'll help,' said Harriet.

This made everyone, including Miss Lydgate, laugh.

Miss Martin was bringing a tray of coffee cups from the sideboard. 'I think yours is black with no sugar,' she said to Harriet.

'How kind you all are,' said Harriet. 'I feel so at home here, I wish I could abandon everything and come and do a B.Litt. here.'

'What would it be about?' asked Miss de Vine.

'Sheridan Le Fanu,' said Harriet.

'You've been working on that a long time,' said Miss Lydgate. 'Write the book, and present it as a dissertation for the B.Litt.'

'Wouldn't I have to keep residence as well?' said Harriet.

'But you wouldn't mind that,' said Miss Lydgate.

'I wouldn't mind it, but I couldn't do it,' said Harriet ruefully. 'I have serious responsibilities at home. But,' she added hastily, 'I am enjoying being in Oxford again, now.'

'I don't suppose your presence here might bring that gorgeous young man – Lord Peter's nephew – what was he called?' said Dr Baring.

Harriet felt the change in her expression in her facial muscles. 'I'm afraid not. He did not survive the Battle of Britain.'

'Oh, my dear, I'm so sorry,' said Dr Baring. 'We seem to have missed that. How dreadful for you.'

'Yes,' said Harriet. 'Infuriating though he was, he was the sunshine in our lives. But I don't blame you for not knowing; he was one among so many.'

Obviously deciding to change the subject, Miss de Vine said, 'So what do you think Lord Peter will decide about the situation in St Severin's? Or mustn't you tell us?'

'Well, it won't be secret when he has decided,' said Harriet. 'But I think he's still weighing it in the balance.' Then on impulse she said, 'How would it fall out if such a dilemma occurred in this college?'

'We'd keep such a manuscript if we had it,' said Dr Baring decisively. 'But then it's different for a women's college.'

'How so?' asked Harriet.

'Money would be different for us,' she said. 'All the women's colleges are as poor as church mice compared to the great medieval foundations like Christ Church and Merton. We are used to getting by. We have to be.'

'Wouldn't years of getting by make money more attractive rather than less?' asked Harriet.

'It depends to whom one compares oneself,' said Dr Baring. 'We don't, like a hard-up men's college, compare ourselves to a rich men's college. We compare ourselves to women's colleges in other universities. And then we live very simply. We don't have many grand dinners, we don't drink port, we don't have immensely expensive buildings to maintain, we don't pay our senior members as much . . .'

'I see,' said Harriet. She wondered whether she should point out that in that case the conservation and insurance of something like the Boethius would be an even worse strain, but decided against it.

'We shall all be very shocked, you know, if St Severin's sells that manuscript,' said Miss de Vine emphatically. 'It will be a betrayal of what Oxford stands for. But forgive me, I must go – I have a tutorial, and I am so sardonic with them if *they* are late.' And she hurried away. The Senior Common Room was emptying rapidly as the clock reached eleven; having promised Dr Baring to bring Peter to Hall dinner before they left Oxford for their unimaginably distant home – even further away than Cambridge! – Harriet left.

An unfamiliar porter nodded to her as she went through the lodge – of course Padgett would have retired.

She walked back down Parks Road, filled with a sudden sadness. *Eheu, fugaces …*

Latin not being her strong point, she reverted to English.

> *Even such is Time, that takes in trust*
> *Our youth, our joys, our all we have,*
> *And pays us but with earth and dust –*

But a sunny morning in Oxford is not the place for mourning. Nor did the slight changes in Shrewsbury College justify such a feeling. They were tiny straws in a very light summer breeze. What had got into her? Perhaps the mention of Lord St George. And rounding the corner of the Broad and Holywell Street, seeing the row of eroded pseudo-Roman faces looking down at her from the railings in front of the Sheldonian, she felt

reminded that Oxford stood for permanence – a quali-
fied permanence – rather than transience.

Since there was still some morning left to spend,
Harriet, on her return to Sever's – how that undergraduate slang stuck to one! – went to the college
library to see what they might have with any kind of
bearing on Le Fanu. She took an armful of books
from the shelves, and went to sit at a table in a nook
between two grand bookcases, stopping on her way to
her seat to look briefly at the manuscript cause of all
the trouble. She had found a comfortable position – a
worn, sagging, leather-seated chair, a desk worn
smooth with age, a window looking out on to the
fellows' garden; she had to take a grip on herself to
give her attention to the books she had found, of which
the most interesting was not directly to do with Le
Fanu, but was a collection of reports on cases in the
Marylebone magistrates court from the nineteenth
century. Harriet began to read of old unhappy far-off
things and judgements long ago, and was deeply
immersed when she heard voices in the bay behind
her. She looked round. There were some gaps in the
row of books on the shelf, through which she could
hear, but not see. Someone was saying, urgently, 'I
have to talk to you.'

The reply with chilling hostility, almost hissing, was, 'I
vowed I would never talk to you again. Never in my life.
Get away from me, I have not changed!'

Harriet froze. Any sound she made, turning a page
even, might reveal her to be within earshot of this

exchange. And although anger shifted the register of the voice avowing the speaker had not changed; Harriet recognised it as that of Mr Vearing.

'That is ancient history now, surely,' said the first speaker. 'And in this present crisis we could make common cause . . .'

'It's ancient history, is it?' Mr Vearing did not trouble to keep his voice low. 'You can bring the dead to life? Until he breathes again I will not talk to you.'

'I did not do it!' said the first voice. 'You guessed, and you guessed wrong.'

'But I heard you defend it,' said the second voice. 'I heard you laugh and say it would put him in his place. And *cui bono*? That's a good question to ask. I will not talk to you!'

Harriet had just decided that she should get up and walk rapidly past the next bay between the shelves to get a swift glimpse at who was talking, but she was forestalled. One of the speakers rushed past her desk and was gone. And as she rose from her seat to try to get a glimpse of the other speaker here was Peter, coming towards her.

'I wondered if I would find you here,' he said. 'What do you think?'

As he spoke the swing door at the other end of the library closed behind her back; she had caught sight of neither of those she had overheard. For the first time in her life she could have wished Peter to be later in joining her.

'What do I think about what?' she asked distractedly.

'Why the Boethius, of course,' he said. 'What else should it be?'

'Peter, did you meet anyone as you came into the library?' she asked. 'Someone in a hurry?'

'Troutbeck barged past me,' said Peter. 'In too much of a hurry to say hullo. Tell me about it later, Harriet, Charles is waiting for us in our rooms.'

'This,' said Assistant Chief Constable Charles Parker, greeting Harriet with a hug, 'is quite like old times.'

The hug was undoubtedly not Assistant Chief Constable-like behaviour; but Charles, as well as being an old friend and fellow campaigner of Peter's, was his brother-in-law, and unapologetically fond of Harriet.

Greetings joyfully accomplished, they sat down together in the armchairs by the fire of the guest suite's drawing room. Bunter brought sherry for Charles, and white port for Peter and Harriet.

'Now then, now then,' said Charles in stentorian tones, 'what's all this there here?'

Eagerly Peter expounded the problem to him, finishing with: 'It looks uncommonly like serial murder to me, Charles. Or serial attempts.'

'Serial murder is very uncommon, Peter,' said Charles. 'But the major flaw in your theory is this: we always catch the serial murderers in the end, because we can identify their methods. They repeat themselves until they are caught. Few though the cases are I have known, both those and any others I have heard about are marked out by the repetitive use of the same methods and oddities – like always leaving a red handkerchief on the scene of the crime, or always taking a lock of hair or a bit of underwear from the victim. Your list – one possible murder and two possible attempts, is it? – simply doesn't meet the criteria.'

'Hell, Charles, it's not like you to be obtuse,' said Peter. 'What is repeated in this case isn't a particular method of murder, but the fact that the murder methods are all in Harriet's books. Naturally she doesn't repeat herself; she wouldn't anyway, from sheer craftsmanship, but she has an ample source of ideas from cases that I have worked on, often with your help.'

'I often ask myself,' said Charles benignly, 'when putting together a case in my mind, how it would play out in court, and what judge and jury would make of it. Once or twice I have been quite sure who has perpetrated a crime, but equally sure that it would seem so preposterous to the man or woman on the jury that the police could not secure a conviction. We have had to let the matter go. Or at least go into the cold cases file.'

'Do you mean, Charles, that if a murderer devises a devilishly colourful and unlikely way to kill, he or she is likely to get away with it?' asked Harriet, appalled.

'Alas, Harriet,' said Charles, 'devilish ways to kill are your province rather than mine. In the world I live and work in murder is usually squalid, the suspects are obvious and the motives are both obvious and squalid. There are only three, as a rule. Take your choice between avarice, lust and vengeance. I have never encountered a motive that has anything to do with a medieval manuscript. Land speculation might amount to the motive of greed, but in this case the greed is not for the benefit of any possible assassin, but for that of a college. The truth is, my dears, I don't believe a word of it. And the most obvious motive of the lot is Peter's.'

'Mine?' said Peter. 'I am only doing my duty as the college Visitor.'

'And you are not in the least in quest of that amusing life of old, when you could detect all over England, and murders came to meet you on every road you took? Why don't you just rule on the sale or retention of that manuscript and take the road home to Denver? Come via London and have dinner with us. Mary will love to see you.'

'I think you might be forgetting the little matter of the missing Warden,' said Peter.

'Hmm,' said Charles. 'Well, it isn't an offence under the law to abandon one's post and go wandering. It may be breach of contract, and damnably inconsiderate, but it isn't against the law. Not a matter for the police.'

'For the missing persons department?' asked Peter.

'I suppose it might be that. Do you want me to add Thomas Ludgvan to the missing persons register? Do we have a picture?'

'The college has a portrait of him in oils when he was elected as Warden,' said Peter.

'Leave it with me,' said Charles. 'We'll run him through the missing persons regime.'

'Right,' said Peter. 'How about lunch, Charles? We could spin out to the Rose Revived.'

Charles looked bashful. 'I have heard,' he said carefully, 'that there is a pub in Oxford at which C.S. Lewis often takes lunch.'

'There is indeed,' said Peter. 'But he lunches with a group of cronies. If just setting eyes on him is inducement enough . . .'

'Do you read children's books, Charles?' asked Harriet, considerably surprised.

'I read *The Screwtape Letters* first,' said Charles, 'and that led me to read more. He's a sound theologian, you know.'

'I didn't,' said Harriet, 'but I'm glad to hear it.'

'Right,' said Peter, 'on with our overcoats and it's off to the Bird and Babe.'

'I think the pub is called the Eagle and Child,' said Charles, and then, 'Oh, I see.'

It was not till the late afternoon that Charles departed for London, having caught the desired glimpse of the sound theologian quaffing beer. Harriet then lost no time in telling Peter what she had overheard in the library.

'Real, seething hatred,' Harriet said. 'And you know, Peter, it seems to me from the moment I heard all this, that it wasn't really a material for hatred. Annoyance, maybe. Grounds for a feud if the fellows wanted to go tribal and play team games with each other – but murder? If I were writing this into a novel I couldn't get away with the honour of the college versus the wealth of the college as a motive for anything worse than throwing a book across a room.'

'Novels have to be plausible,' Peter said. 'Life doesn't. Life often isn't.'

They sat silently for a few moments, contemplating this. Then Peter said, 'Right. What have we got? A disappearance. A fishy accidental death. Two assaults that might have been attempted murder, apparently based on your books . . . and a little hate talk overheard in the library. Anything else?'

'Someone mentioned a review to me at dinner last night,' said Harriet.

'An adverse review, I imagine,' said Peter. 'Who mentioned it?'

'I think he was called Gervase,' Harriet said.

'We could go and ask him what he meant, I suppose,' said Peter.

'From what you told me,' said Harriet, 'you hoped to receive deputations; planned visits deliberately laying out a case to you. What if you could speak to these people one at a time? In confidence?'

'That's a good idea, Harriet,' said Peter, 'but it would take some time. There are about twenty of them all told.'

'I'm here to help,' said Harriet. 'We could split them between us.'

'Well, you take Gervase,' said Peter, 'with his hints about some review or other; and Vearing . . .'

'Do I have to take Vearing?' asked Harriet.

'All right, my dear. We'll take them in alphabetical order; you get the first half and I'll take the second. You will start with Ambleside; he won't frighten you.'

*   *   *

As it happened, when Harriet called on Mr Ambleside in his rooms the next morning he was in conference with the Bursar, Mr Winterhorn. She had obviously disturbed a professional discussion – large account books were lying open on a mahogany table, with rather more red than black ink visible to her skimming glance.

Winterhorn closed the ledgers, and offered Harriet a chair.

'I have come to ask you, Mr Ambleside,' said Harriet, accepting the usual offer of a glass of sherry, 'and I am happy to ask Mr Winterhorn at the same time, what you think is the root cause of the schism in the college.'

They looked at each other, and were silent.

'It's just that I thought there might be more to it than meets the eye,' she ploughed on.

'The college really is in financial trouble,' said Winterhorn.

All the time Harriet was looking as tactfully as she could round Ambleside's room. He had a large and handsome room with a heavily stuccoed ceiling, and wide mullioned windows looking both ways, one into the street and one into the front quad. That was a reward for his status, she supposed. His bookcases overflowed on to the floor in the corners. Hand-tinted engravings of scenes in the Lake District . . . a lavish vase of fresh flowers . . . not much to distinguish him from any other college fellow.

'Can you make economies?' she asked, feeling foolishly obvious.

'We have, of course, tried to retrench,' said Ambleside. 'But although we are all agreed on the need to do so, every proposal to save money is objected to.'

Winterhorn interjected, 'I don't think Her Grace needs to bother herself with our finances, Ambleside. I have offered to open the books to the Duke.'

Of course, Harriet thought, I am not the Visitor. I have no standing here. 'You could probably make a lot of money by selling the contents of your cellar,' she said.

Ambleside uttered a barking laugh. 'Can you imagine getting that past the Ways and Means Committee, Winterhorn?' he asked.

'I was just thinking,' said Harriet, 'that women's colleges get by with a simpler lifestyle. And that there is a kind of dignity in that.'

'They are not more harmonious, though,' said Winterhorn. 'Rather, they are notorious for cattiness and in-fighting.'

'That is what men think about women's groups, I know,' said Harriet. 'But it is not my experience of them.'

'The truth is, Your Grace,' said Winterhorn, 'it is kind of you to concern yourself with our problems, but only a very large subvention of money can get us out of the difficulties. We are deeply in debt, and even the interest on the loans is a heavy burden on us. We shall have to offer no scholarships or bursaries next year, just for an example.'

'That would be very upsetting,' said Harriet. 'But may I ask you: was the college a happy and harmonious one before this question of the land at Watlington arose?'

'We had our ups and downs,' said Ambleside.

Seeing that she was being stonewalled, Harriet finished her sherry, and left. But then, why should they confide in her? A stranger, a woman, and with no authority. Authority belonged to Peter.

Feeling stubborn, she thought just the same she would try Gervase. This latter gentleman greeted her with smiles and warmth. 'The Duchess! Herself in person!' he cried. 'What an effect I must have had on you last night . . . charmed, Your Grace, charmed. What can I offer you?'

'Please just call me Harriet,' she asked. And spotting a kettle and some cups in an open cupboard across the room, she said, 'If it isn't too much trouble, I would love a cup of coffee.'

'Nothing is too much trouble, er . . . Harriet,' he said, but he in fact made a great to-do about making coffee, producing a grinder and grinding fresh beans. Harriet looked around his room while he brewed it. A very different room. Silk cushions in bright colours, a white orchid in an elaborate pot. A strange picture made of layers of white card with cut-outs in them. 'That's a Nicholson,' he said, bringing the coffee. It was good coffee. Perhaps worth the time taken.

'And now,' he said, slightly tipping his head, and looking steadily at her, 'to what do I owe this visit?'

'You told me last night to investigate a review,' said Harriet. 'I have come to ask you what you meant.'

'On behalf of our esteemed Visitor?' he parried.

'Of course,' said Harriet. 'Regard me as the Duke's sidekick.'

'I rather wish in that case that I had not mentioned the review to you,' said Gervase.

'But since you did,' said Harriet, 'will you now enlighten me?'

Gervase sat down opposite her, and stared at his fire-place, apparently thinking. 'If I don't tell you someone else will,' he said in a while. 'But I would be grateful if it were not known all around the college that it was I who told you.'

The Queen's English is the King's English round here, at least, thought Harriet. 'There are no secrets between me and my husband,' she said, 'but I see no reason why it should get any further.'

'Very well, then,' said Gervase. 'There was a review in the *Times Literary Supplement*, about five years back. It was of a first book by a junior fellow of this college.'

'Who was that?' asked Harriet.

'David Outlander.'

'And the review was unfavourable, I take it?' asked Harriet.

Gervase seemed to be pondering how to answer.

'After all, though people do take issue with favourable reviews now and then, they don't cause much heat as a rule,' Harriet prompted him.

'It was unfavourable,' said Gervase, 'but unfavourable hardly covers it. It was savage; gleefully exposing errors – alleged errors I should say – and holding the author up to ridicule – ridicule hardly covers it either – accusing him of stupidity and ignorance, and saying it was shameful that such a person should hold an Oxford fellowship or make himself out to be any kind of scholar; it went on in that vein over the page. You get the impression.'

'Whoops,' said Harriet. 'How unpleasant. How did the fellows react?'

'They formed two camps. There was a lot of bad feeling. Some people wanted to terminate Outlander's fellowship, and that infuriated those who thought he had been attacked unfairly. A lot of hard words were spoken.'

'Which camp were you in?' asked Harriet.

'I was undecided at first. At that time I was a research fellow myself. I would rather have kept my head below the parapet. But I was convinced by Vearing that the review was unfair, so for what it was worth I lined up with the defence.'

'How unfair?' asked Harriet. 'Hostile and unfair are not the same.'

'No. But it seems that there were – are, probably – two schools of thought about one of David's topics. Both have very reputable scholars propounding them. A genuine disagreement. Thank God for a subject like mine where there are right and wrong answers investigated by objective research.'

'Your subject is?' asked Harriet.

'Engineering,' said Gervase. 'If you build a bridge and it falls over you can't attribute personal malice to the universe. But as I say, there was a scholarly difference of opinion going on; and the reviewer, who must have known that, chose to describe David's acceptance of one interpretation as wilful ignorance of a grossly culpable kind, without mentioning the fact that there were scholars all over the world who would have agreed with him. A dirty trick really. And there wasn't anything David could do about it. Various people in the field wrote letters to the editor, but that doesn't put the clock back. The fellowship here split right down the middle about it. He thought people were pointing at him and laughing at him in the street, and there was no safety in college.'

'Where is he now?' asked Harriet.

Gervase turned his head away, visibly upset. 'He resigned his fellowship,' he said.

Harriet let a silence fill the room. Then after a decent interval she said, 'Would I be right in guessing that the split in the college about the attack on David Outlander would be pretty much the same as the split over selling your Boethius?'

'The fellowship has changed a bit,' said Gervase. 'Some gone, some come. But those fellows who were here at the time of the uproar over Outlander's review form the same groups now as they did then.'

Harriet finished her coffee, and got up to look more closely, and somewhat baffled, at the white picture made of cut-outs.

'Do you like that?' Gervase asked her.

'I can't really say,' said Harriet. 'I don't understand it.'

'Its time will come,' said Gervase. 'By the way . . .' He hesitated, and then went on: 'If anyone here knows what the Warden is up to it would be Vearing. They were thick as thieves, to coin a phrase.'

'Thank you,' said Harriet, leaving open whether it was for coffee or for information that she offered thanks.

'My pleasure, Harriet,' said Gervase, holding the door open for her.

Peter, meanwhile, called on Mr Trevair. He was very new in the college, and had been given rather a small set, which still had a provisional air; he had brought few things of his own, and the furniture looked as if it had been provided by the college: bamboo book-cases and side-tables, and a large mahogany desk of lumpish antiquity. Some rather good Piranesi prints might have been his own, as might the chamber organ that occupied a recess beside the fireplace; a thing unlikely to have belonged to the college, and if it were theirs unlikely to have been imposed on a fellow.

'I haven't seen one of those in ages,' Peter remarked, pointing to the organ, once he was settled facing Mr Trevair. He could remember exactly where he last saw one: Miss Twitterton had one in her capacity as church organist. Hers made a rough and raucous job of it, but perhaps euphonious ones were available.

'It belonged to my mother,' said Trevair. 'She used to play hymns; I use it more for Buxtehude. But it's taboo at the moment with everyone revising for finals. And I'm afraid I shan't be able to help you. I had no idea what I was letting myself in for when I accepted an appoint-ment here. And I don't understand the uproar. It's an open and shut case as far as I can see.'

'Well, tell me what you can see,' suggested Peter. 'I have been given to understand that everyone thought an economist would be all for selling a book and buying land.'

'They don't seem to have known much about economists,' said Trevair. 'Or about risk. I am not a monetarist, I am interested in asset values, by which I mean non-money assets.'

'But both a manuscript and a stretch of land are non-money assets,' said Peter.

'Of rather different kinds. The manuscript is, if not unique, diminishingly rare. I took the liberty of consulting a friend at the British Museum. He told me that the museum would be desperate to acquire the Boethius if it came up for sale, but would be unlikely to be able to afford the huge sum that would be necessary. Further, the MS is already in the college's possession.'

'And the land?'

'Have you heard of Crichel Down?'

'Yes, I have,' said Peter.

'Well, consider an entirely possible scenario. The college sells its Boethius, and then the land is bought by some other person before the college has a chance to buy it. They could do something else with the money; but not the something that they are tempted by. Or, worse, suppose they buy the land and then the city council takes it from them by compulsory purchase, paying only its value as agricultural land. They might all too easily finish up with neither the book nor the land. I voted for the status quo as a matter of prudence. I have also been putting out feelers about the long-term planning intentions of the city council.'

'May I ask with what result?' said Peter.

'I have contacts in the city council,' said Trevair. 'One of my old friends – I would rather not say who – tipped me the wink that the council had their eye on that land, and were planning developments of their own.'

'Did you share that knowledge with any of the other fellows?' asked Peter.

'I told Troutbeck, naturally.'

'What did he say?'

'He asked me not to put it around. He said his own contacts had told him exactly the opposite, and he asked me to give him a few days to sort out the conflict of information. I agreed with that; I can't share his view that the matter is urgent.'

'You have made some members of the college very angry with you,' said Peter.

'One of my colleagues in Birmingham University, where I come from,' said Trevair, 'is a moral philosopher. He taught me that one of the ways to judge a course of action is to consider what company it puts one in. I doubt if that's very good philosophy, but I find it a good rule of thumb.'

'I'll bear that in mind, Trevair,' said Peter. 'Thank you.'

That evening Harriet, Peter and Bunter conferred together pleasantly over a light supper, which Bunter had laid out in their rooms. Another dinner in Hall with its cross-currents and bizarre formality did not appeal to them so soon after the last one, and nor could Bunter have been present.

'Just think,' Harriet said, happily eating excellent smoked salmon which Bunter had procured in the covered market, 'of having to eat together nearly every night, as the fellows do. How do they stand it? However do they manage to get along together?'

'I have the impression that some of them rather like it,' said Peter. 'Factions being one of their favourite games. And then the food is quite good and the wine excellent, and finally they don't in practice manage to get along together . . . we wouldn't be here else.'

'How did you fare talking to Mr Vearing?' asked Harriet.

'Well, he's old and doddery and impassioned and loquacious,' said Peter, 'and I learned nothing from him. But I can't quite see what you have against him, Harriet.'

'Who else did you see?' she asked.

'I saw Winterhorn the other day. I now have the college finances at my fingertips. And they are, it is quite true, a disaster area. When all this is over I must drop a tactful word to someone about consulting Freddy now and then.'

'Why are they in such trouble, Peter?' asked Harriet.

'Too many fellows for one thing. More than they can afford to pay. Bad management in the past. When they have been short of money, they have sold their best farms and ground rents, and left themselves with the weaker ones. Short term, that solves things, but colleges are for the long term – the very long term. To do them justice there has also been bad luck. They own properties in London that were blitzed, and have not yet been redeveloped.'

'So they really should sell the Boethius?'

'I didn't say that. There might be other ways.'

Turning to Bunter, who was bringing a rack of lamb, he said, 'Did you cook this dinner for us, Bunter? What is the Warden's kitchen like?'

'Rather traditional, my lord, but sufficient. Its main shortcoming is the presence of Miss Manciple, endeavouring to assist.'

'I can well imagine,' said Peter. 'So what about the Land Registry, Bunter? What light can you shed?'

'Title to the land was registered in 1938, my lord,' said Bunter. 'The land belongs to a Mrs Cutwater. Mint sauce, my lady? I think she is a widow, since the owner till recently was a Mr Cutwater. I imagine she acquired the land by inheritance.'

'Hmm,' said Peter. 'I wonder if that is all she acquired. If he was a farmer, and if she didn't inherit much other than the land she might be very anxious to sell. I wonder if *she* has heard of Crichel Down.'

'I'm afraid, my lord,' said Bunter, having served up the vegetables, and sitting at a discreet distance from his master and mistress, 'that the Land Registry contains no information about motives.'

How comfortable we are together, Harriet thought. She was grateful to Bunter for sitting down with them *en famille*, a habit he had very unwillingly adopted during the hardships of the war, and occasionally still did when they were strictly in private. He himself, she knew, thought it improper and it made him slightly uncomfortable; he did it only because he knew that she preferred it. This was a form of selfishness in her, she thought, a lack of true courtesy; but whereas it was easy to say *Make yourself at home, Bunter, sit with us like the equal we think you are,* it was really strange to say *Make yourself at ease, Bunter, stand on ceremony and serve us like the servant you feel yourself to be.* She hadn't tried it yet.

'I think we might call on Mrs Cutwater,' said Peter happily. 'Tomorrow will not be idle. But for the moment, Harriet, there is a letter from Bredon's housemaster that we should discuss.'

'What has our quirky son been up to this time?' Harriet asked.

'Oh, he's not in trouble of any sort. The housemaster wants to know to which Oxford or Cambridge college he should be directing him to apply.'

'Goodness!' said Harriet. 'Is he old enough?'

'Last time I counted he was seventeen,' said Peter. 'So I suppose he is at least that, and perhaps a little more.'

'Well, the answer is Balliol, isn't it?' said Harriet. 'Although a Cambridge college would be more convenient for Denver.'

'If it were to be Cambridge, there's St John's, I suppose,' said Peter, sounding distinctly dismayed.

'I thought you would say Trinity,' said Harriet. 'Isn't that the apogee?'

'But it isn't twinned with Balliol,' said Peter sadly.

'In any case, he's surely far too young to go up,' said Harriet.

'I think the school's policy is to secure the college place, and then the young man does National Service before taking it up. So he would be twenty before arriving at Oxford, and somewhat toughened up.'

'I see,' said Harriet. 'Shall you tell them to train him up to apply to Balliol, then?'

'He might as well try,' said Peter. 'He might not make it, of course. He isn't the very brightest bunny. But somewhere will have him. One can try for several colleges.'

The mention of the brightest bunny turned Harriet's thoughts to Bunter.

'What will your son Peter do, do you think, Bunter?' she asked him.

'He's a year behind Master Bredon,' said Bunter. 'But he's hoping for the London School of Economics.'

The Wimseys looked at each other across the table. They could read each other's thoughts. How practical Bunter was, how much more in touch with the changing world . . . How many things that passed them unnoticed were clearly visible to him.

'Did you suggest that to him, Bunter?' Harriet asked.

'No, my lady. But economics interests him greatly. More than any of his school subjects. I did not discourage it.'

'How did he discover such an interest?' asked Harriet, who could not, herself, imagine being attracted to it.

'He has had the good fortune of having the run of His Grace's library for many years,' Bunter replied.

'He has found something there that I didn't know we had?' said Peter.

'He found works by Ricardo and Adam Smith,' said Bunter, 'and the *Treatise on Money* by Maynard Keynes. He told me he disagreed with all of them.'

'Economists do rather tend to disagree,' said Peter, 'but it sounds as if my namesake has found his métier. Good for him.'

6

'I thought we might pay a visit to Mrs Cutwater today,' said Peter the next morning. 'Unannounced.'

'Do we have a pretext?' asked Harriet.

'No. But I have a fiction writer at my right hand who might be able to dream one up for us.'

'Perhaps we might allege that we have heard a rumour that the land is for sale . . .' suggested Harriet.

'That,' said Peter, munching his toast, 'has the demerit of being true. The truth is always implausible.'

'You could take a breakdown at her front door,' said Harriet, 'but that would be less likely to lead the conversation towards the sale of the land.'

'We'll see what comes into my head,' said Peter. 'We don't want to upset the poor old thing.'

It was a sunny morning, and Peter was happy to take the Daimler for a run. First they trundled along the Cowley Road through thick traffic, and then found themselves out in the country, going south-east towards the declining Chilterns. Mrs Cutwater lived in an obscure enough house, not in any village, and they had to consult the map several times to find it. At last they turned into a narrow leafy lane, passable by only one car at a time, up which they proceeded with care – a considerable feat for Peter – till at last it emerged on the top of a modest hill, where nothing but farmland could be seen for miles.

'We've overshot,' said Peter, turning the car, and going down the lane again. In a few yards they met a tractor coming up, and were forced to back some distance to the hilltop again, where the road widened, and they could let the tractor pass them. Peter wound down the window and asked the way. ''Alfway down,' he was told, 'and mind the dog.'

'Good grief,' said Peter to Harriet, waving his thanks to the tractor driver, 'this is Oxfordshire, not Wuthering Heights.'

'Perhaps one can wuther outside Yorkshire,' said Harriet. 'If the lady lives alone in this somewhat recherché spot perhaps she needs a dog.'

Soon the presence of a telephone wire across the road alerted them to a possible dwelling, and they turned through an unmarked opening in the hedges and on to a gravel drive even narrower than the road, which brought them shortly to an old and handsome farmhouse standing in a rather attractive garden.

'Farmers usually make bad gardeners,' said Harriet.

They marched up to the front door. 'It's a hall house, I think,' Harriet said. 'Look at the central chimneys.'

But the door was being opened, and Peter had no eyes for chimneys. The apparition who opened the door to them was a strikingly beautiful woman, not out of her twenties, whose oval face featured wide, pallid grey eyes, and was framed in glossy chestnut-red curls falling to her shoulders. She was wearing a very open-necked green blouse. She looked at them and said coldly, 'What do you want?'

Of course, Harriet thought, a daughter can inherit . . . this is, after all, no poor old thing.

'We were hoping to have a word with Mrs Cutwater,' said Peter.

'Well?' she said, and then after a baffled pause added, 'I am Mrs Cutwater. What is your business with me?'

'We understand you have some land to sell,' said Peter smoothly. 'We would like to discuss it with you. May we come in?'

'You have been misinformed,' she said, beginning to close the door.

'Let me put it another way, Mrs Cutwater,' said Peter. 'You are the registered owner of land about which certain stories are circulating.'

'What stories?' she said.

Peter produced his visiting card. Not, Harriet noticed, the ducal one, but one of the old ones: 'Lord Peter Wimsey, private detective'.

Mrs Cutwater took it, glanced at it, and laughed. 'You look whimsical enough,' she said. 'Oh all right, come in.'

She led the way into a plainly furnished farmhouse kitchen. An Aga radiated heat. A big golden retriever lay comfortably spread out in front of it half asleep. It did not look like a dangerous dog. A dark oak dresser of some antiquity bore a row of blue and white plates over which Harriet saw Peter pass an appreciative eye.

'Sit down,' Mrs Cutwater said, indicating the kitchen chairs ranged round the big table. Then, as if collecting herself, she said, 'This is the warmest room in the house.'

Peter sat down with alacrity and Harriet followed suit.

Mrs Cutwater did likewise, taking a chair opposite them. A woman in an apron holding a duster appeared in the doorway, stared hard, and slowly withdrew. A person no doubt responsible for the sparkling plates, the swept and shining floor, the scrubbed deal table – Mrs Cutwater did not look like a woman for housekeeping in person.

'These rumours are what precisely?' she now asked Peter.

Harriet wondered what Peter would say.

'I have been told that you have land to sell, but that it is not, and is not likely to be, on the open market,' he said.

'That is my business, surely, Mr Wimsey,' she replied. 'And not entirely correct. What has it to do with you?'

'Always interested in land, don't you know,' Peter said. 'I have a few acres of my own over in Norfolk. And some wit once said the thing about land is that they aren't making any more of it. Just wondered why it isn't on the open market, that's all. That's usually the way to get the best price.'

'What is it to you if I don't get the best price?' she asked.

'To me personally, nothing, of course,' he said, 'but I don't like to think of someone recently widowed, and a bit in the dark about things, being taken advantage of.'

'Chivalry, is it?' she said with a barking laugh. 'Oh, don't lose any sleep about me. My husband wasn't God's gift to a young woman, believe me. And his death wasn't unexpected – he'd had his three-score years and ten, and he rather liked the bottle. I'm not cut to the quick over losing him. Far from it. And I'm not without advice. Will that answer you?'

'I'm glad to hear you have advice,' said Peter. 'I am interested in why your adviser has suggested a private sale.'

'My adviser has told me not to discuss it with anyone,' she said. 'You never know who people are. I mean how do I know you are who you say you are? And who is this, with you?'

'I am Peter's wife,' said Harriet quickly. Peter was all too likely to introduce her as also Harriet Vane, detective novelist, and she didn't want to prolong the interview with a woman she had taken a strong dislike to.

Mrs Cutwater cast a long considering stare at Harriet, in which 'how did you pull that off?' could rather too easily be read.

'I'm still not supposed to talk to anyone,' she repeated.

'Do you know why you have been instructed not to talk to anyone?' Peter asked. 'Would that be something to do with St Severin's College?'

'Oh, so that's who you're from,' said Mrs Cutwater. 'Well, I'm certainly not supposed to be talking to *you*, then. But to put your mind at rest I'll tell you just this: it's a sentimental matter. My late husband wanted it. And it was his land, after all.'

'If St Severin's were unable to buy it, would the land be sold to someone else?' Peter asked.

But Mrs Cutwater made no reply to that. She sat silently looking down at her hands, clasped on the table in front of her.

Peter got up. He wrote something on a torn-out page of his pocket diary, and put it on the table in front of her. 'If you ever feel you need different advice,' he said, in a surprisingly gentle tone of voice, 'try that number. Mention my name.'

She left the paper untouched on the table. 'Well, perhaps it's a little conspicuous there,' Peter said. He retrieved the paper, and stepping over to the dresser slipped it behind one of the plates. 'Behind the coffee-rimmed pre-willow pattern plate,' he said. 'We'll leave you in peace, Mrs Cutwater.'

She made no move to rise to show them out. Looking back from the kitchen door as they retraced their steps into the hall, Harriet saw that she was shaking where she sat. They closed the front door behind them, and got into the car. Before Peter started the engine, Harriet said, 'You frightened her, Peter. Do you know why?'

'Can't say that I do,' said Peter. 'But it will bear thinking about.'

They entered the narrow lane up which they had found their way to the farmhouse. Even Peter was constrained to drive slowly down it. It seemed a long way. At last the Daimler was nosing out of the blind turning on to, not a main road, but a reasonably wide and navigable country road. Peter peered to his right, and saw a car approaching, indicating a left turn.

'He'll have to wait for me,' muttered Peter, 'there isn't width enough for him to turn in alongside me.'

The other car approached at speed. Harriet closed her eyes, expecting a crash. But at the last minute the other driver drew to a brake-squealing stop, and allowed Peter to get out of the lane in front of him. Peter acknowledged the concession with a wave. And then suddenly the other driver changed his mind, retracted his indicator arrow, and instead of turning up towards the Cutwater farm, continued towards Abingdon. Peter considered this manoeuvre in the rear mirror rather longer than he should have done, though the road they were now on was at that point straight.

'Odd, that,' he said. 'And it was a Sunbeam Talbot.'

'So?' said Harriet, baffled.

'So the thick plottens,' said Peter, putting on speed towards the next steep bend. Harriet saved her breath for the scream she expected to need any minute, but actually they returned safely to Oxford, and restored the car to the appointed parking place. They didn't go into the college, but walked away down the Broad and St Aldates to have lunch at the Elizabeth.

'Was this place here when you were up, Harriet?' asked Peter, sitting across from her with a candlestick or two between them on a pink linen tablecloth.

'I don't know, Peter,' said Harriet. 'I couldn't have afforded it.' She spoke without the simmering anger that would once have accompanied this sort of remark, having forgiven Peter his wealth now that she knew more about how he spent it.

'Well, what do you make of this morning's little trip?' he asked her once they had chosen their food.

'Not much, I'm afraid,' she said. 'I picked up on the fact that there was something a bit odd about that sale – didn't we already know that?'

'To suspect something isn't to know it,' he said. 'Did you notice the contradiction?'

'Between declaring that she had had no love for her husband, and declaring that the land sale was a sentimental gesture to him beyond the grave? Yes, I did. But people are complicated, aren't they? Couldn't she have a conflicted attitude to him? After all, she married him.'

'There's a little detail you don't, I think, know, Harriet,' said Peter. 'Troutbeck drives a Sunbeam Talbot. He arrived at Denver in one. A pre-war dark blue coupé,' he added irrelevantly. 'You were working when he came.'

'Do you think it's Troutbeck who has been advising Mrs Cutwater?'

'Plainly, it might be. Did you see clearly who was driving that Sunbeam this morning?'

'Sorry, no. The hood was up. Anyway the car went on past the turning.'

'But he, or she, I suppose, was indicating an intention to turn up the lane before he spotted us.'

'All right, let's speculate. Troutbeck is having enough influence over the fair Mrs Cutwater to make her frightened of talking to us. Troutbeck is a leading member of the sell the book and buy the land party in the college. Why doesn't he want it talked about? What's in it for him?'

'Well, possibly he is acting out of a sincere desire to see the college safe out of its difficulties,' said Peter. He did not sound convinced.

'There's nothing wrong with that,' said Harriet, 'as long as the college is paying a fair price; and there's nothing much wrong with it if the college is paying a nearly fair price.'

'And there is nothing wrong with it as long as Troutbeck has no personal interest in the matter – beyond, of course, the security of his college salary. They are all interested parties to that extent.'

'Are you saying that the other faction – the keep the MS at all costs people – are relatively disinterested? After all, they are imperilling their salaries rather than securing them,' said Harriet.

'Hmm,' said Peter, 'really they all seem a bit too impassioned for my liking. Something's going on that we haven't got down to yet.'

Peter paid the bill, and they wandered out into a cool Oxford afternoon, taking the route through Radcliffe Square, the scenic route, Peter called it.

When they reached the quiet of their rooms Harriet said, 'One thing that was clearly going on, Peter, was that you fancied that gorgeous woman. But how could she be your type if I am your type?'

'Come here, Harriet,' said Peter, in a suddenly husky voice, 'and I'll show you something.'

She stepped into his embrace. A little time passed. Then releasing her he said, 'A bed for you and me. And don't follow the quote and deny me till we married be, for I distinctly remember marrying you barely a step from where we stand.'

'Oh, I remember that, too,' Harriet said. 'But it's two thirty in the afternoon, Peter.'

'Must, to thy movements, lovers' seasons run?' he asked.

'But it's no good apostrophising the sun on an overcast day,' Harriet objected.

'It will begin to seem, not that I fancy another, but that you no longer fancy me,' he said, pulling a woeful face.

'Not that,' she said. 'Never that.'

'Come, madam, come, then,' he said.

Looking around like guilty children in case Bunter spotted them – though surely Bunter could be surprised by nothing that they did – they went to the bedroom and closed the door.

'What better covering need'st thou than a man?' he said, his fingers clumsy with haste helping her unbutton her blouse.

Later, quite a while later, they were lying entwined in a nest of warm and tangled sheets.

'Shouldn't we be too old for this?' Harriet asked. 'Can you imagine our parents acting like this, at our age?'

'There are limits to the imagination,' he said, his voice muffled by her hair. 'And one's parents' very private lives are off limits.'

Their dozing satisfaction was suddenly disturbed by raised voices off. Bunter, asserting himself. Someone shouting at Bunter. Peter rolled over and looked at his watch.

Five o'clock. A perfectly appropriate time of day for a caller to be shouting at Bunter; a somewhat revealing time of day should the master of the house appear in a dressing gown, even one of Chinese silk. 'I'd better put some togs on and go and see if Bunter needs some support,' he said. 'Linger as long as you like.'

'What do you think is going on?' asked Harriet as another stretch of a raised voice reached them.

'I'll put my money on Mr Troutbeck, hell-bent on calling me out for a duel,' said Peter.

'Don't get involved in a duel, my lord,' said Harriet, propping herself up on her pillow to watch Peter dress. 'I can't afford to lose you.'

'Don't worry,' said Peter. 'If he challenges me, I get to choose the weapons. And I'll choose rapiers. I'm a good swordsman.'

'What if he is a good swordsman too?' asked Harriet, not quite sure if this conversation was in earnest.

'He's rather too heavily built for that,' Peter said, doing up his tie. 'He'll think better of it.' He skipped over to the bed, lifted Harriet's hand to his lips, and then left her to meditate.

It was indeed Troutbeck, pacing around the drawing room seething with fury, whom Peter found waiting for him.

'What in hell do you mean, Denver, by forcing your way in on Mrs Cutwater, and interrogating her? Who do you think you are? You have authority only over the fellowship of this college, you are abusing it by bullying anyone else . . . and who the devil told you Mrs Cutwater's name? What scoundrel exposed her to your intrusion? My God, when I find out who put you on to her I'll teach them a lesson they'll never forget!'

'You must save your wrath for the Land Registry,' said Peter coolly, 'although I don't know exactly what threat from you would make them tremble in their collective shoes. I imagine that they would call the police.'

He watched his words have their effect. 'The Land Registry is, and is intended to be, in the public realm,' Peter added. 'It is not yet compulsory in Oxfordshire, but title can be registered voluntarily.'

Troutbeck took only a few moments to recover himself.

'But what do you mean by thrusting yourself on the owner in person?' he said, cooking up his wrathful tone again. 'You could and should have enquired from me about anything you needed to know. You are acting *ultra vires.*'

'Mrs Cutwater invited us into her house,' said Peter quietly. 'My wife was with me; I did not appear to her as a solitary male stranger – she had looked at my card. Our conversation did not entail the sort of shouting that you are indulging yourself in, first to my manservant and now to me. You tell me I have no authority to investigate the nature of a sale to the college which is the cause of the dispute I am here to resolve. I disagree with you about that. And perhaps you would care to tell me on what authority you take exception to an interview granted to me by Mrs Cutwater who is a legal adult, and has, as far as I know, no need to ask your permission or to consult you about who she may talk to. Exactly what is your position vis-à-vis her?'

'I am her adviser,' said Troutbeck. He sounded sullen but subdued.

'Indeed?' said Peter. 'Do you usually act as an adviser in buying and selling land?'

'I am a family friend,' said Troutbeck. 'That is, I was a friend of her late husband.'

'A drinking friend, perhaps?' said Peter.

'My God!' said Troutbeck. 'I told her not to talk to anyone. But I suppose she took you for a gentleman, as I did.'

'Can you tell me, Troutbeck,' Peter asked, 'why a few questions should have frightened Mrs Cutwater?'

'No, I can't,' he said. 'If she was frightened you must have been bullying her. You will have no further conversations with her without a lawyer present.'

'I suppose such a decision will be up to her,' Peter said. 'Now, if you have nothing further to say to me, perhaps you will leave.'

'With pleasure,' said Troutbeck, turning on his heels, and slamming the door behind him.

'What did you think of all that, Bunter?' asked Peter, confident that Bunter would have been standing quietly out of sight but within earshot. 'I hope he wasn't too terribly rude to you.'

'A somewhat heated gentleman, my lord,' said Bunter. 'He was as rude to me as he knew how to be. My offence was to decline to disturb you and her ladyship at an inopportune moment.'

'Heated or not, then, he is an unmannerly lout. I'm sorry, Bunter. You should not have to put up with that sort of thing. Did you get any clue as to why he was so worked up?'

'I can make sense of it, my lord, only on the basis that he has formed a particularly deep interest in the lady's affairs.'

'Why yes, Bunter. You must be right.'

'Of course he shouldn't have lost his temper with you, Peter,' said Harriet on hearing this sorry tale. 'But she did seem rather fragile, didn't she?'

'You mean she needs a protector?'

'I thought so, yes.'

'But if he is her adviser, he it is who is frightening her,' said Peter.

'The two statements are not incompatible,' said Harriet. 'Perhaps *you* should challenge *him* to a duel, Peter.'

'I won,' said Peter. 'My chosen weapon was words.'

'None so sharp as you, Peter – but should you have made an enemy of him?'

'I didn't!' said Peter indignantly. 'Please, miss, it wasn't me . . . he started it.

The interesting question is why.'

'Perhaps he loves her,' said Harriet.

'It's a funny way to show love though, Harriet – to broker a sale of what is probably her best and perhaps her only asset to his college, in a way unlikely to raise the best price.'

'Perhaps it's a way of getting a better price than the market would put upon it,' said Harriet.

'Hmm,' said Peter, 'I wonder if the college has obtained an independent valuation. I should have thought to ask that when I was talking to the Bursar.'

7

In spite of having slept unseasonably in the afternoon, Peter and Harriet slept deeply and calmly that night. They were getting used to the unfamiliar bed. As they would have done at home they left the curtains wide, to admire before they fell asleep the ascending moon, the dark sky sequined with stars. The effect was not as dramatic as at Denver, since both the quadrangle and the street were lamplit, but they still liked it better than the pattern on the thick damask curtains.

They rose innocently and at peace with themselves, and sat down to breakfast with a very reprehensible sense that all was right with the world. Bells far and near announced that it was Sunday. Harriet felt rather keenly that she should not have been feeling like this when the troubles of the college were without explanation or resolution, but she could not contrive to feel anxious or gloomy, try as she would. Her efforts were not helped by Bunter's breakfast, since he had found good baps in the covered market, besides good kippers, and Women's Institute home-made marmalade.

Peter was masked from view behind *The Times*. Harriet could see on the spread of newsprint across the table from her only the masthead and the small ads. Bunter had brought a copy of the *Times Literary Supplement* for her, and she was reading the fiction reviews. She resolved to read her copy of L.P. Hartley's *The Go-Between* as soon as possible.

'Ho, hum,' said Peter from behind his paper.

'Something afoot?' asked Harriet.

'A long piece about Crichel Down,' said Peter.

'Does it shed light?' asked Harriet.

'I'm not sure what light it sheds,' said Peter, 'but it seems that what happened is that in 1938 the Ministry of Defence requisitioned some land in Dorset, which was part of the grounds of Crichel House. They wanted it for bombing practice. They paid twelve thousand pounds. The Lord only knows what the value of those acres was as a bombing range; bombing is not, thank God, a commercial activity. Then in 1941 Churchill promised in Parliament that the land would be returned when the war was over. But that promise has not been honoured; the Ministry of Defence handed it over to the Ministry of Agriculture, who claim to have improved it, but anyway it's now valued at thirty-two thousand pounds. The family can't afford to buy it back. They are raising a stink, and demanding a public enquiry.'

'I'm not surprised,' said Harriet. 'But didn't you say that Freddy had made dark remarks about all that when you mentioned the college's proposal to buy land? How does that come in?'

'Well, I suppose,' said Peter thoughtfully, 'it is

relevant to any situation in which a public body acquires land from a private person. Can they buy it for one reason, and hold on to it when that reason ceases to apply and they want it for something else? Can a public body make money at the expense of a private person in that way?'

'It isn't hard to conclude that they shouldn't be able to do either of those things,' said Harriet. 'And if the family could afford it and they coughed up, the public purse would have made a tidy profit out of its power to requisition. A bit unprincipled, Peter, isn't it?'

'It's scandalous,' said Peter. 'And I suppose Freddy was inviting us to consider what Oxford City Council might be tempted to do, if the Ministry of Agriculture gets away with it.'

'Or how the college might stand if the city council acquires this contentious piece of land as agricultural land, and then gives itself planning permission and sells it all on for development? Is that what might happen?'

'I suppose I could advise the college to wait and see if the Marten family get their public enquiry,' said Peter. 'But things here have gone rather far for that advice to be welcome. But if there is a public enquiry, it will set the rules for some time to come.'

'You're in a difficult position, Peter, aren't you?' Harriet said. 'You are going to make bitter enemies, whatever line you take; and nobody wants bitter enemies in Oxford.'

'Bitter enemies are not a good idea anywhere,' said

Peter. 'But they are at least as common in Oxford as elsewhere. It's just that we wear rose-coloured spectacles when we return here – we are dazzled by the foolish idealism of our youthful years.'

'I won't have that, Peter,' protested Harriet. 'People really are idealistic here; really do serve learning all their lives, really are admirable.'

'Some of them are as you describe,' said Peter, smiling benignly at Harriet. 'Do you, my dear, know that quotation about Oxford from Matthew Arnold?'

'Home of lost causes? Everybody knows that, Peter.'

'Home of lost causes, and forsaken beliefs, and unpopular names and impossible loyalties,' he said. 'Yours is a somewhat impossible loyalty, my dear.'

'And yours?'

'Oh, mine too,' he said. 'Madly impossible; about to be maintained, like chivalry, in the face of open bawdry and bloody manslaughter.'

'Or even murder, Peter?'

'Murder,' he said gravely, 'is seeming ever more likely, however unlikely Charles thinks the tale may be. Let's have a break; lets go and see the Judgement window at Fairford. An easy drive. What do you say?'

'Yes please,' she said.

A Judgement window puts everything in a different proportion, they found, even, or perhaps especially, intuitions about murder. But as it turned out they met an old friend of Peter's coming out of the Morning Service in the church, and were asked to come home with him and meet his wife. One way and another they didn't get back to Oxford until rather late.

'So what will you do today?' Harriet asked the next morning.

I have an appointment with a certain Elaine Griffiths, to discuss the Boethius,' said Peter. 'Do you want to come too?'

'I'd like to very much,' said Harriet. 'I know of her only by repute.'

'And what does repute have to say of her?' asked Peter.

'Well, do you know that the Merton Professor of English here will not take women pupils for tutorials? With one exception, that is – he will tute girls sent to him by Miss Griffiths.'

'Have I heard of this misogynist professor?'

'Didn't you read *The Hobbit* to the boys during an air-raid?'

'Yes, I remember that.'

'That's him – the Merton Professor is Tolkien.'

'Who makes an exception for Miss Griffiths's pupils? Is that the extent of the information we can derive from repute?'

'Oh, no,' said Harriet. 'There is always gossip, some of it spiteful. She once, it is said, while sitting through a very bad essay being read aloud to her in a tutorial, said, "God! How you bore me!" and reduced the girl to tears.'

'Am I alone,' asked Peter, 'while deploring the rudeness, of course, in feeling a certain sympathy for someone who has to sit through badly written and ill-prepared essays for hours a week?'

'She is supposed,' Harriet continued, 'to send her tutorial pupils, on their arrival at her door, down to the buttery to bring a bottle of gin, to be put on her tab.'

'That story doesn't sound very spiteful,' said Peter.

'This may be at nine in the morning,' said Harriet. 'Or so 'tis said.'

'Does she share the gin with the pupils?' enquired Peter.

'Yes – that's the scandal.'

'It's no less than manners if one is going to drink oneself to offer it to the company,' said Peter. 'I am not very shocked. Come, my dear, off with us to St Anne's.'

As they walked up Parks Road, arm-in-arm, Harriet said, 'I thought Mary Fowey was the expert on the MS.'

'She's a Latin scholar,' Peter said. 'Elaine Griffiths is an Anglo-Saxon expert. She knows about the gloss. Or, I rather hope she does. We shall see.'

Elaine Griffiths had a sunny room in the main building of St Anne's, very recently made a full college and not yet having many buildings to get lost in. Harriet half expected to be dispatched to the buttery on arrival, but the gin was already present and on offer. Miss Griffiths was a compact, rather short woman with nut-brown hair framing a round face. The moment her guests were settled on her capacious sofa she said briskly, 'Now. What can I do for you?'

'You could tell me whether King Alfred could write,' said Peter.

'I take it that you know he could read?' said Miss Griffiths. Her tone was acidic, but not, thought Harriet, hostile, just challenging.

'I have been instructed by a young man called Jackson,' said Peter, 'to believe that he could.'

'Jackson is a pupil of mine,' said Miss Griffiths with unmistakable satisfaction. 'He is sound, if a touch romantic.'

'I am sure you will have heard what we are doing in Oxford,' Peter said. 'I understand that it is only the gloss that makes St Severin's copy of *The Consolations of Philosophy* so valuable. Is it possible that King Alfred wrote the gloss? That is what we have come to ask.'

Miss Griffiths's demeanour suddenly changed. She lost the hard nut-in-a-shell manner she had been displaying, and became unguardedly engaged in the subject.

'Possible; but not likely,' she replied to Peter's question. 'The hand in which the gloss is written is a monastic hand, very similar indeed to the output of scriptoria in the ninth and early tenth centuries. The possibility is not that Alfred wrote that gloss, but that it was the copy he used to make his translations. It is, as far as I am aware, the only surviving copy glossed in West Saxon. It might have been glossed for the King by the scholars at his court. If so it is indeed a relic of him, more personal to him than even his famous jewel. I take it you have seen the jewel?'

'I saw it long ago when I was up,' said Harriet.

'Take your Duke to see it,' said Miss Griffiths. 'It's hardly difficult to get to the Ashmolean.'

'Yes, I will,' said Harriet meekly.

'So, if the copy is merely one used by Alfred,' said Peter, 'it has, in your view, less value?'

'I did not say anything of the sort!' said Miss Griffiths. 'If it is the copy he used, then a careful comparison of the gloss with his translation would allow the identification of any modification or shift in meaning between the two. And any such shift would have been made by Alfred either as an aid to his own understanding, or as a clarification for the benefit of his readers. I believe Mr Jackson is intending to write his B.Litt. thesis on such a comparison.'

'So the great store some people are putting on the retention of that particular copy is not exaggerated?' said Peter.

'If that book were to leave Oxford it would be a calamity!' said Miss Griffiths, with real pain in her voice.

'Surely not that?' said Peter. 'Nobody would buy it who was not interested in it for scholarly reasons . . .'

'At this present time, Your Grace,' said Miss Griffiths, pronouncing Peter's proper title as though it were an insult, 'fully three-quarters of all the people in the world who can read Anglo-Saxon with any fluency, or who know anything much about English culture before the Conquest, are in Oxford. There are even universities, only a train ride away, in which one can obtain a degree in English without learning Anglo-Saxon, or reading a single sentence of King Alfred, or a single line of *Beowulf*. Any physical object that assists the understanding of pre-Conquest England should be here. Does that help you in your unenviable task?'

'It helps me understand why some of the fellows of St Severin's are so determined not to sell their manuscript,' said Peter. 'Thank you.'

'Let me know if you need further help,' said Miss Griffiths. 'I am not a disinterested witness.'

'That is perfectly clear to me,' said Peter, smiling at her.

'Whew!' said Harriet, once they were safely out of earshot halfway down the stairs from the Griffiths lair. 'There's a woman who lives up to her reputation.'

'I rather liked her,' said Peter.

When they reached the Broad, Harriet said she would like an hour or so in the Bodleian Library, and they parted.

Peter strolled into Blackwell's, and browsed happily for a while. He ran into George Mason there, and they went for a drink together in the Turf Tavern.

'Getting anywhere sorting things out?' George asked him.

'Not really. Not yet,' Peter said. 'I'm losing my edge, perhaps.'

'The whole of Oxford is buzzing with talk about you.'

'That's probably not helpful.'

'Can't be helped though. Rumour has it that the balance is going to tip towards selling the book.'

'How does rumour know that?'

'Well, a couple of your fellows are taking straw polls every day. And chaps in Balliol have been laying bets.'

'I didn't know about the straw polls,' said Peter. 'Ear's not close enough to the ground.'

'Ducal ears are somewhat elevated, perhaps?' said George.

Peter shook a friendly fist at him. 'Better go,' he said. 'Harriet will be expecting me to have lunch with her. Like to join us?'

'Would love to, but can't,' said George. 'Got to see a man about his dreadful idleness.'

'We all feigned idleness when we were up,' said Peter.

'This man isn't feigning,' replied George. 'He's totally authentic, and admirably persistent in doing no work. I have to tell him we will send him down at the end of term if he doesn't produce some essays by then.'

'How did this lazy dog get into Balliol?' Peter enquired.

'Don't ask me,' said George, 'I didn't admit him.'

Peter wandered back to St Severin's alone. But as he approached the college gate he saw that a flag was being raised on the flagpole over the main gate. It ascended slowly, and as he watched it stopped at half-mast. 'Oh, lord,' he muttered to himself. 'What now?'

He raced across the front quad, not wanting to be nobbled by anyone before he knew who had died. At the door of his rooms Bunter was waiting for him.

'Assistant Chief Constable Parker is urgently wanting to speak to you, my lord,' said Bunter. 'He has rung three times. I assured him that you would ring back the moment you came in.'

He dialled a number, and handed the receiver to Peter.

'Got you at last!' said Charles.

'What's up?' Peter asked.

'We've got a lovely fresh body on our patch,' said Charles. 'Throat cut.'

'Congratulations,' said Peter. 'If he be not killed for me, what care I how dead he be?'

'He's one of yours,' said Charles. 'He's a fellow of St Severin's. Do you want to see the crime scene before they move the body?'

'Might help,' said Peter.

'Get down here quickly, then,' said Charles.

'Righty-ho. Oh, Charles, who is it?'

'One Mr Oundle.'

'Ah,' said Peter. 'I'm on my way.'

One of those large Edwardian blocks of flats in Barons Court. Heavy red architecture, and too many occupants to form a community. Green paint in the hallways and corridors. A terrified cleaner sitting sobbing in a chair in the bedroom. Crime scene detectives, a photographer, a fingerprint-seeker blowing powder on door handles, and a young doctor looking rather green. Everyone at once deferring to Charles.

The body lay face up on the living room floor, head at an odd angle, which was not in itself surprising, because the neck had been nearly severed with a clean, deep cut. The carpet was soaked with an extensive bloodstain, and a pool of blood beside the dead man's neck looked like port jelly; not yet dry.

On the floor beside the body lay the murder weapon

– a samurai sword, long, sharp and bloody. As it happened, though his career as a private detective had been long and varied, Peter had not seen very many fresh bodies, and this was a man he knew, even though recently and slightly. He felt distinctly sick.

'Glass of water?' asked Charles sardonically.

Peter accepted.

Charles was asking, 'Signs of forced entry?'

'None, sir. And the front door has one of those spy holes that allow you to see who you are letting in.'

'I take it that the cleaner found the body?'

'Yes, sir,' said one of the policemen. 'She arrived as usual at nine thirty this morning, and let herself into the flat. She's a bit hysterical now, sir, but she did just the right thing. She picked up the phone with a hand towel over it so as not to leave her own prints, and she dialled 999 without touching anything. Smart girl. Seems she reads detective stories.'

'Can she cast any light?' Charles asked.

'She says the body is that of Mr Oundle. The flat is his. He uses it very little in term-time, but is here more in the vacations. Quiet gentleman. What she does insist on is that the sword belongs to him. It has stood in the hallstand along with a walking stick and an umbrella as long as she has worked for him.'

'How long is that?' Peter asked.

'Three and a bit years,' the officer said.

'I take it there are no fingerprints on the hilt of the sword?' said Peter.

The officer blowing powder on the door handles and

the drawer handles of the desk in the window bay said, 'Nothing, sir. Wiped clean, or the assailant wore gloves. The girl says she asked the deceased about it, and he said it was a souvenir.'

'Where's the sheath?' Peter asked. 'These things usually have sheaths.'

'It's in the umbrella stand, as usual. Perhaps the assailant pulled it out of the sheath as he came through the hall. Nasty thing to keep in an umbrella stand if you ask me.'

'Can we ask her again?' said Peter. He approached the girl in the bedroom and silently offered her his handkerchief.

'I'm not usually like this,' she said, wiping her eyes. 'It was such a shock.'

'Of course it was,' said Peter gently.

'You read about horrible murders,' she said, her words broken by a sob, 'but you never expect just to come into a room with the vacuum, and see *that*!'

'You are a brave and sensible young woman,' said Peter. 'You did all the right things in spite of the shock.'

'Did I really?' she said. She was quite pretty in spite of her tear-stained face, and she was recovering in the light of Peter's attention. 'I did the best I knew,' she added.

'It would be very helpful now if you could tell us all you know about that sword,' Peter said. 'Do you know where it came from, and why Mr Oundle kept it?'

'He said it was give him in the war,' she said, mastering her tears and speaking calmly. 'He said I was never to touch it, because it was that sharp. Not that I wanted to touch it, but I might have thought to clean it if he hadn't said.'

'Did he say who gave it to him?' Peter asked.

'Not by name, sir, but he said it was give him by a Japanese officer who surrendered to him. He said it was a terrible thing for them Japs to give up their sword. And he said the swords were handed down from father to son. He thought if the man who give it to him was still alive he might come and ask for it back some time, or else his son might come. Oh, sir, do you think that Jap might of come to get his sword and killed poor Mr Oundle with it? Was it revenge?'

'But whoever used it to kill Mr Oundle didn't take it, did he?' said Peter. 'I don't think you need worry about avenging Japanese warriors returning here.'

'Oh, I won't worry,' she said. 'When they lets me go home it's the last time I ever come here. There's plenty of flats wants cleaning, where there's only umbrellas in the hallstand.'

'I don't blame you,' said Peter.

'Oh, sir,' she said, 'I've thought of something else Mr Oundle said. He would of given the sword back to the man. He said he would give it back to him if he ever came for it. He said the war was over, and it didn't do to have grievances more than what one could help.'

Peter realised that Charles had been standing at the bedroom door listening to all this.

He now said, 'I'll just check with the duty officer and if he has nothing more to ask you we will send you home in a police car.'

'I can't go home yet, sir,' the girl said. 'I've got four more flats to clean.'

'You need to go home,' said Charles. 'I'll send somebody to explain to your employers.'

'Thank you, sir,' the girl said. To Peter she said, 'It's exciting in a horrible sort of way, isn't it? Like a detective story. Like one of them Agatha Christies or Harriet Vanes.'

Peter pulled an eloquent face at Charles. But that gentleman stuck to the point.

'Nothing to be learned from the murder weapon,' he said regretfully. 'And no obvious motive that I can see. All the valuables in the flat untouched. No ransacking through papers in the desk. The fact is, Peter, that the motive must be in Oxford.'

8

It wasn't motive, however, that was on Peter's mind as he drove back to Oxford.

It was the murder weapon. An oriental sword had figured in one of Harriet's Robert Templeton mysteries. That was a wild coincidence, surely? But there was a question nevertheless about murdering a man with a sword from his own front hall. If the assailant had planned ahead deliberately, then he must have known that the sword was there; that implied that he had visited the flat before, a fact that was perhaps confirmed by Mr Oundle having let him in. Obviously the murderer could have been one of Oundle's colleagues.

Peter found the college under siege. A row of police cars were parked outside the front gate. The outer doors were closed, and the porter standing guard. 'What's going on?' Peter asked, although he could guess.

'Poor Mr Oundle has been murdered, Your Grace,' said the porter, with less relish than might have been expected of him. 'And the police are here talking to everybody in the college as to where they were this morning. Not just the Oxford police,' he added, 'but some of them's from Scotland Yard!'

Peter felt suddenly inexplicably tired. It was barely six o'clock, and he could have rolled into bed and slept for a week. He doubted he could help the diligent officers with their interviewing, so he sat in one of the deep armchairs in his room, and drowsed there.

By and by Harriet came in, and said brightly, 'Sorry I took so long. Have a good day, Peter?' Then she said, 'What's the matter? What's happened? You look like death.'

'I've looked *at* death today,' Peter said. 'And a nasty one, at that.' He launched into an account of Mr Oundle's violent and messy end.

Harriet was shocked. She was also sympathetic.

'. . . and I'm sure you see, Harriet,' Peter said, finishing his account, 'the significance of a bright sword.'

'Yes, I'm afraid I do,' said Harriet. 'You are referring to the death by sword thrust in my detective story *Blades of Hatred*. But Peter, I hope, hope we are wrong. It's a terrible thing to have been writing jolly puzzle books, and find one has been writing a handbook of murder methods.'

'You could console yourself, Harriet, with the thought that many literary murder methods wouldn't work.'

'I do quite conscientiously try to make them plausible,' said Harriet.

'Well, for example,' said Peter, 'you used the bell-ringing episode at Fenchurch St Paul. But the victim in that case wasn't really killed by bells. He had a weak heart; the ordeal killed him, but had he been a robust fellow in good health he wouldn't have died – he would just have been left deaf.'

'Like poor Mr Dancy,' said Harriet. 'That's not much comfort, Peter.'

There was a light knock on the door. Bunter admitted a police officer, with a clutch of papers in his hand. 'I'm Inspector Gimps, sir,' he said. 'Mr Parker asked me to let you have this, sir, when we had finished the interviews. And for your information, sir, I am assigned to be your point of connection to the Oxford police.'

'The interviews are all done now?' said Peter.

'Yes, thank you, sir. Everyone's in the clear in the college, sir, as you can see from our notes,' he added.

'Thank you, officer. I shall look forward to working with you. Have a pleasant evening,' Peter said.

Inspector Gimps pulled a face. 'That's not very likely, I'm afraid, sir,' he said. 'I'm on duty at the police station till midnight tonight, and there's always something barmy going on here.'

'Like what, officer?' asked Harriet. She never missed an opportunity to collect background detail.

'Well, last night, m'am,' he said, 'we was called out to a nasty accident. Young man had fallen off a wall into Brasenose Lane. Trying to climb into Exeter College after midnight. Fell fifteen feet, and banged his head and broke his ankles.'

'Very foolish, just to avoid a fine,' said Peter.

'Oh, but that's not the half of it, sir. You see a great long bit of the wall of Exeter has fallen into the lane. There's a gap maybe twenty feet wide. He could just have walked in. But there was a notice the Rector of

Exeter put in the gap what said, "Will gentlemen please
not avail themselves of this facility," so that young moron
was climbing up the drainpipe alongside the gap, just as
they was all doing before the wall fell over. What do you
make of that, then?'

'Ah, my vanished youth!' said Peter. 'I would have
done just the same myself.'

'You surprise me, sir,' said Gimps.

'What happened to the young man?' asked Harriet.

'We stretchered him straight into the Radcliffe
Infirmary, and then yours truly has the nice job of
ringing up his parents in the middle of the night to
tell them that their beloved boy might have killed
himself.'

'Has he killed himself?' asked Peter.

'Don't know that, sir. I've been on this all day; haven't
had time to check.'

'What are we thinking of?' said Peter. 'We must let you
go. Many thanks.'

When Inspector Gimps withdrew, Peter spread the
paperwork he had been given out on the table. Every
senior member of the college had been asked to state his
whereabouts between the hours of nine and noon that
morning. And they all had alibis.

And what alibis they were! None of the 'walking the
dog in the park' kind of story, where other passers-by, if
they could be found, might confirm . . .

Vearing and Ambleside and Gervase had all been
lecturing in the Examination Schools. Their presence

there could be confirmed by dozens of easily findable people.

Trevair had been giving tutorials in his college rooms from nine till noon; any of his third-year undergraduates would confirm. Winterhorn, the Bursar, had been in conference with a distinguished architect on the subject of a necessary repair to one of the chapel vaults, and the question of whether there might be a cheaper way to do it. Troutbeck had been in a consultation session with dons from the Chemistry Faculty about the next finals paper to be set. So on, down and down the list.

'Let's get Ambleside to discuss this,' said Peter. 'Will you see if he can step across here, Bunter?'

When Ambleside appeared, Peter asked him, 'It seems that every senior member of the college has a watertight alibi for the time of poor Oundle's death, Ambleside. Does that strike you as odd?'

'Thank God for it, I would say,' said Ambleside. He looked exhausted and haggard.

Peter offered him a whisky, which he accepted at once.

'What seems odd to me,' said Peter quietly, 'is that usually in a murder case a few people can't really remember where they were at an exact time of the day in question. Or they remember, but it is something that can't be confirmed – they were wandering alone in a wood, or they went to bed early with a headache . . . Or they say their wife can confirm their story – perhaps you know that wives have a special status as witnesses. I have learned to be suspicious of very solid alibis remembered in detail. Few ordinary people can come up with those, whereas a criminal might have provided himself with one. So as I say, does it strike you as odd?'

'I don't know what my colleagues have said,' Ambleside answered cautiously.

'Have a look,' said Peter, pointing at the police reports laid out on the table.

Ambleside leaned over the table, studying the reports for some time. Then he straightened up and said, 'No, Your Grace, none of this is in any way odd at all. Just an ordinary working morning. People would have been doing this, or variations of this, on any morning in term-time, and indeed any afternoon in term-time. In the vac they would have been working in libraries, or in their college rooms in full view of servants and librarians, unless they were away from Oxford. But after all, this is term-time.'

'Yours is a very hard-working profession,' said Peter, 'in that case.'

'Most Oxford people work hard,' said Ambleside. 'There are one or two who idle – a rich college can afford to indulge them if they have some valued quality or are resting on work of high repute. St Severin's can't afford old lions, or peacocks. We need the fellowship to work hard.'

'You can afford feuding, though,' said Peter.

'Afford it? No, it looks set to ruin us. It will hurt the reputations of every one of us if we become famous for in-fighting, or if the college goes bankrupt. Some people are already discreetly looking for jobs elsewhere. As for the effect on us of a fellow having been murdered, even if it turns out, as it looks from all this that it must, that it had nothing to do with the college . . . we must put an end to the feuding as soon as possible, and you must help us. If you can,' he added.

'I am doing my best,' Peter assured him.

'Will you eat in Hall tonight, Your Grace?' said Ambleside. 'It might boost morale if people saw you were still concerned with our problems.'

'In that case . . .' said Peter, taking his gown from the hook at the door. He gave Harriet a mute signal that she was not required to suffer with him, and he rattled down the stairs behind Ambleside.

It was indeed a grim experience that evening. Rather few of the fellows were present, those of them who had a home to go to having gone there. There was an uncomfortable atmosphere; the fellows had not filed in and sat together, there were spaces left so that the company was divided into three small groups. The undergraduates, on the other hand, had packed in and were talking loudly and excitedly, no doubt enjoying exactly the news that was weighing on the spirits of their seniors. The college food was not good enough to bear the burden, though the chef had contrived to lay his hands on enough chocolate, in spite of rationing, to make a sickly end to the menu.

Halfway through the meal a quarrel broke out between dons sitting down the table from where Peter and Ambleside sat. Voices were briefly raised, and then someone got up from his place, and moved down the table to sit alone. Stony-faced, the butler moved his cutlery along and reset his place in front of him. A long silence fell among the other diners who watched this little drama, but eventually they managed to resume some sort of conversation. The subject chosen was the college prospect of bumps in the forthcoming Eights. Could they recover the places lost in last year's Eights?

Peter listened in silence, and a very young research fellow sitting beside him kindly explained to him how bumps worked. The river being too narrow to permit side by side racing, the college boats lined up in the order in which they had finished the previous year, and rowed like hell to try to catch and bump the boat in front. If you achieved a bump you moved up one in the order of the next day's rowing, and your victim fell back one. Peter thanked him gravely for the explanation.

When the closing grace was said, the company dispersed rapidly, and Peter did not join the few who went towards the Senior Common Room for dessert, but returned to Harriet.

'How did it go?' she asked. She was curled up in an armchair beside the fire, contentedly reading.

'Ghastly,' Peter told her. 'The whole place will fall apart if we can't get this cleared up quickly.'

'Colleges have long lives,' she said.

'Depends what you mean. The buildings are old; the charter dates back to the Tudors, the shell of the institution is indestructible. Even if the place went bankrupt I expect a richer college would come to the rescue. But if by "the college" you mean this society, this particular group of people, then if this goes on much longer it will implode, and need building again from scratch. They'll claw at each other to destruction judging by what it felt like tonight.'

'Poor Peter,' said Harriet. 'And here was I peacefully eating a rather good omelette made by Bunter, and an apple turnover made by Miss Manciple. Those two have made peace, and are sharing the kitchen without warfare declared or undeclared.'

'Bunter should have been a diplomat,' said Peter. 'He's wasted on us.'

'Something occurred to me in all this tranquillity, Peter.'

'What was that?'

'There is somebody who doesn't have an alibi. Or, rather, who hasn't been asked for one.'

'There are all the college servants; but somehow, it doesn't seem likely.'

'Not them – think again.'

Peter thought. 'I give up,' he said.

'The Warden,' said Harriet. 'What about him?'

9

'This is taking much longer than I thought it would,' said Peter over breakfast the next morning. 'I think perhaps I ought to tootle back home for a quick visit, and see how Mama is faring. Will you come too?'

'I am sure we would have heard if anything bad had befallen her,' said Harriet, 'but it's a good idea just the same. You always cheer her up. Can you do without me? I was proposing a day in the Bodleian.'

'I can manage without you as long as you assure me that absence makes the heart grow fonder,' said Peter. 'I'll go almost right away and be back by tomorrow night. And you can keep Bunter to look after you.'

Peter was as good as his word, and drove himself off, leaving the college by ten. Harriet immediately felt unanchored and slightly at a loss. She took a notebook with her, and trotted off to Bodley. She was in search of the back copies of the *Times Literary Supplement* in which she intended to find the review that had ruined the reputation of David Outlander.

Periodicals were kept in the Upper Reading Room, less theatrical than the Radcliffe Camera, less romantic than Duke Humfrey, but practical and comfortable, its tall Gothic windows giving it an airy and light ambience. Harriet chose a desk, filled out an order slip for 1948 (hadn't Gervase said it was five years ago?) and waited, awash with nostalgia.

It was not long before the librarian brought her the four folio volumes containing the *TLS* for 1948. The quality of newsprint had still been the dreadful wartime kind. It was already yellowing, like the sulphurous paper of nineteenth-century novels, like those of Le Fanu with which she was so familiar. No person with any respect for documents could flip through the pages rapidly for fear of pulling a piece of the page edge off in one's hands.

Harriet settled to a slow deliberate turning and scanning of the pages. She found what she was looking for in the third issue for April 1948.

The volume had a tendency to close itself under its own weight, and risked pressing a fold into the flimsy pages as it did so. Harriet carefully propped it open at an angle by supporting its covers on piles of books. Then she opened her notebook on the desk beside it and began to read and copy.

Mr Outlander has prefaced this work (which incidentally has not been published by OUP) with the usual statement of gratitude to various scholars in his field, and the announcement that all the errors are, of course, his own. In that case he has almost nothing to be grateful for, since his work is a tissue of egregious errors from start to finish ... Before indulging in relief that at least the distinguished names who have allegedly helped the author are free from

*the extraordinary degree of ignorance on display here, it
would be well to remember that Mr Outlander himself is an
Oxford graduate, and a research fellow of St Severin's
College . . .*

Golly! thought Harriet. Of course she was familiar
with adverse reviews, having reaped a good few of those
herself, especially in her novice days as a writer. She had
noticed, as any 'trade' writer would do who strayed into
a scholarly field, the particular vitriol with which learned
disputes were pursued on review pages . . .

The room was suddenly swept and brightened by a
passing minute of sunlight. A librarian arrived beside
her, and lowered a white canvas blind to keep the sunlight
off the books on the desk. Restored to low-contrast cool
illumination, Harriet bent to her task of note-taking, and
then read on.

*The very least that one might expect from a supposed
scholar of Alfredian writing would be familiarity with the
handwriting of tenth-century scribes, sufficient to permit
distinctions to be made between genuine productions of the
period and later productions such as the obvious forgery of
the gloss on the St Severin's manuscript. Even the clue
offered by the colour of the ink used for this gloss has been
ignored. Of course, the Boethius continued to be read for
many years after the reign of Alfred – no less a later lumi-
nary than Chaucer translated it. The manuscript gloss
itself has been made by a no doubt honest later scribe who
had no disreputable intent. The scandal arises, and the*

appropriate use of the word forgery, when contemporary pseudo-scholars seized with sentimental and romantic desires unalloyed by more than minimum knowledge of their subjects create attributions that are absurdly without foundation ...

Harriet carefully copied the review into her notebook. She was flinching as if it had been directed at herself. By and by she took a rest, sat back in her chair and thought. She had often enough been stung by a review, especially when it was adverse but with a grain or more of truth in it. But it is in fact easy to tell when a reviewer is motivated by spite or private axe-grinding. When once that had happened to her she had found herself blithely rising above it; only a reasoned and reasonable assessment of her work had power to hurt; a vendetta could be ignored.

And other people's reactions to reviews could be very unexpected. She had once had a severe ticking-off in the *Manchester Guardian*, in a long review of *Murder by Degrees* which had stretched down the page. Several friends had congratulated her on it. When she told her publisher about this, deeply baffled, he had replied, 'My dear, never read the things, just measure the column inches!'

In terms of column inches, David Outlander was doing fine – the demolition of his work covered an entire page, and turned over to a column on the following page before reaching its *coup de grâce*.

There is, I am afraid to say, another possible explanation for the jejune errors and ridiculous fantasies in a book

*written by a fellow of an Oxford college, who surely ought
to know better, and that is that a monetary consideration is
involved. The manuscript whose value would be immensely
enhanced, should the foolish attribution promoted in the
book under review gain ground, is the property of the college
of which the author is a member. Corruption takes many
forms.*

'Whew!' murmured Harriet. And then, 'I wonder who
wrote it?' But reviews in the *TLS* were anonymous, and
the yellowing sheet of newsprint at her elbow was not
going to tell her that.

Carefully she closed the volume, and took her way
home. Passing Shrewsbury College she remembered her
promise to help Miss Lydgate, and dropped in on her to
see what was needed. Miss Lydgate's problems were all
about prosody in Spenser's *Faerie Queene*, the proofs of
which were scattered all over every surface in her room.
Her delight on Harriet's appearance was immense. With
deep relief Harriet put nasty reviews and violent deaths
behind her, and buried herself for the moment in how
exactly to define and describe the song-like, music-
derived rhythms of the poems of Edmund Campion.

No breath of faction fluttered Miss Lydgate's scattered papers. Nor was any of the confusion in her mind
– it was all in the paperwork. Luminous clarity, however
hard won, would emerge before the proofs were sent to
the printer. There was such a thing as learning for its
own sake, as devotion to a scholarly life. Harriet began
sorting and ordering the paper according to the page

numbers, and laboured happily till halfway through the afternoon, when, both of them feeling hungry and realising they had had no lunch, they adjourned to the common room for tea and buns.

Harriet relaxed, surrounded by old friends, by the common-sense mutuality of a group of women who had once sought her help, and then befriended her, who had resisted quarrelling for many days under pressure, and of whom Peter had said that they had saved their college by their solidarity. She could hardly resist the thought that the fact that the fellows of Shrewsbury College were women, women to a man so to speak, whereas the fellows of St Severin's were men might have something to do with the in-fighting that Peter and she had been treated to. With a shudder she reflected that although the crisis in Shrewsbury College had seemed exceptionally nasty at the time, it had not involved all-but severed heads and blood-soaked carpets. She had herself, long ago, witnessed a death involving that sort of thing, and she was not surprised that Peter had been visibly upset yesterday. All that blood . . .

'You are far away, my dear,' said Miss Lydgate, breaking into her thoughts. 'And look, here is Dr Baring, and Miss de Vine coming to join us. They will want fresh tea –would you like another cup?'

'I'm so sorry,' said Harriet. 'I was wool-gathering. How rude of me.'

'Oh, but I do understand!' said Miss Lydgate. 'I have the greatest difficulty myself in remaining on the scene where I actually am at the time; shall we have more tea?'

'Yes, please,' said Harriet, jumping up. 'Let me get it. I shall bring a tray and everyone can put in sugar and milk as they like.'

When she brought back her loaded tray the two newcomers had pulled up chairs, and there was a cosy circle to sit down in.

'Do tell us, Harriet,' said Miss de Vine, 'how the investigation at St Severin's is going along . . .'

'I'm really not sure that I should,' said Harriet cautiously.

'Well, at least tell if it looks as if you will be leaving Oxford shortly,' said Dr Baring.

'I think not,' said Harriet, smiling at the transparent ruse.

'In that case,' said Miss de Vine, 'would you consider giving a talk to one of our undergraduate societies?'

'Hmm,' said Harriet. 'What would you want me to talk about?'

'Perhaps about the relationship between detective stories and real life,' said Miss de Vine, and then blushed deep crimson as she realised that Harriet might take that as a reference to her trial for murder, long ago now, but never forgotten.

'Really, Helen!' expostulated Dr Baring.

'Let me rephrase that,' said Miss de Vine, recovering herself. 'Would you talk to us about the relationship between detective stories and literature?'

Audibly indrawn breath in the circle of people round the tea-tray told Harriet that that, too, was seen as a *bêtise* by her companions.

'Yes – I could manage that,' said Harriet amiably. Everyone relaxed.

'I'll make arrangements as soon as I can,' said Miss de Vine, 'and offer you a choice of dates.'

By and by Harriet headed back to St Severin's, with the tactlessness of excellent people, and bloodshed, competing as the focus of her thoughts.

Peter had driven himself home to Denver in record time. Without even the discreet Bunter riding with him offering an occasional indrawn breath, he had indulged his boyish taste for speed. He had a curious impression that seized him every time he drove through the gates at Denver into the park. He had never got over the sense that it was his brother the Duke's house that he was approaching; but why were the gates standing open? Why wasn't Jenkins in the lodge? For the few moments when his memory resisted the reminders that he was in the present time he recovered the younger son's insouciance, the younger son's carefree tomfoolery . . . then as his car took the turn in the drive that brought the greatly altered house into view gravitas reclaimed him, and his responsibilities enveloped him again.

A few minutes later he was sitting with his mother beside the fire in her drawing room.

She, too, was a shock for the first few seconds when he was here again after an interval. She was now very old; she had always been a little lady, but she had been a bundle of energy for so long that the passive person she had now become would have been unrecognisable but for her animated expression.

'Peter! Darling Peter!' she cried. 'How lovely to see you! Is it all sorted out over in Oxford, then?'

'I'm afraid not, Mama,' said Peter. 'It will be a few days yet. So I just thought I'd motor across to see how you are.'

'You should know better than to ask an old lady that,' she said. 'You might get told.'

'You are perfectly yourself, I see,' he said, smiling at her.

'Will you have to go back at once?' she asked. 'You've left Harriet behind?'

'I have left Harriet,' he said, 'to mind the shop. And I can certainly spend the night, and talk to you over dinner.'

'That will be lovely, dear,' she said. 'There's venison pie tonight, I think. One of the deer from the park. I'm always so surprised at how dark the meat is from those pretty pale creatures – wouldn't you expect only the red deer to be red meat? And Cousin Matthew will be glad. He has something to show you.'

Franklin appeared, and reminded the Dowager Duchess gently that it was time for her nap.

'I'll see you at dinner, Mama,' said Peter.

Cousin Matthew was usually to be found in the library, which was, thank God, part of the house that had been barely scathed in the great fire, and still contained the greater part of the library accumulated by successive

Dukes of Denver, who had evinced an impressive desire to collect books and line the walls with them in fine bindings, if rather less enthusiasm for actually reading them. Peter's mother had been used to tell him often that he must be a throwback to her side of the family – the Delagardies having, by her account, been pillars of the Enlightenment.

'Hullo, Matthew,' said Peter, entering the library. 'I understand there is something you want to show me.'

'Oh, yes, Peter,' said Cousin Matthew, rising to his feet and extending a hand to meet Peter's proffered handshake. 'I just thought I might have a look to see what else we might have on St Severin's, beside the charter that I found for you when all this blew up.'

'Tally ho!' said Peter. 'And did you run a fox or two to ground?'

'Well . . .' said Cousin Matthew doubtfully. He was not a hunting man, or not in the field, anyhow. 'There are copies of the college charters right the way back; not quite to the foundation, but as far back as the intervention of the Duke who first interested himself in their affairs.'

'Anything interesting in them?'

'Well, this is the earliest one we have,' said Cousin Matthew, unrolling a parchment scroll on the library table, 'and it says here that no property of the college worth more than fifty shillings can be sold or given away without the agreement of the Visitor. And it says why: *that any who are disposed of their good will to make gifts to the aforesaid college, may be secure and in safety, trusting*

*that such gifts shall be held in perpetuity, and that the donors'
names shall be inscribed in the memory of the college, and in
the prayers offered by the college for their members and bene-
factors.* That's interesting, isn't it, Peter?'

'Extremely interesting, Matthew. It settles the matter,
doesn't it?'

'Well, it would, Peter, if the charters had remained
unchanged. But the college has a right to modify its
charter from time to time, and that sentence has been
removed from more recent charters.'

'Did earlier Visitors consent?'

'The consent of the Visitor is not required. He must
enforce the proper interpretation of the charter, but he
doesn't get to write it or take a hand in rewriting it.'

'Bother. And I suppose it's not the sort of thing that
my esteemed ancestors would have troubled their noble
heads about.'

'Not really. Most of these charter rolls have obviously
not been looked at for many many years.'

Cousin Matthew, however, was speaking with, for him,
unusual animation. Peter looked at him, and said, 'Come
on, old chap. Spill the beans. What's up your sleeve?'

'I don't keep beans up my sleeve,' Matthew said.

Peter was dumbstruck. When had he last heard his
cousin attempt a witticism? Something was exciting him
enough to enliven his usual gravity and gloom.

'The charter has been updated pretty regularly over
the years,' Cousin Matthew said. 'So I thought I would
just look through and see exactly when the proscription
of sales of college property was first omitted.'

He paused.

'I give up,' said Peter. 'Tell me.'

'That paragraph runs through all the charters until the last but one,' said Matthew triumphantly. 'It disappears from the charter before the present one – drawn up in 1945.'

'How drastically do these successive charters change?' asked Peter.

'Oh, not much at all through the nineteenth century. St Severin's changed its charter to allow non-Anglican fellows in the 1860s sometime – I should have made a note of when ...'

'That doesn't matter at present,' said Peter. 'But I am interested to know what other changes were made in 1945.'

'I thought you would be,' said Matthew. 'So I checked carefully. None.'

'Well done, thou good and faithful servant,' said Peter blasphemously.

Of course, now he was in the house, other matters engulfed Peter, and demanded his attention. His land-agent needed to discuss an exchange of fields between neighbouring tenant farmers, one of whom wanted more arable, the other more pasture. The hunt had ridden roughshod through some hedges and over some fences during a time when Peter had been in London months back, and they were dragging their feet over paying to make good the damage.

'Tell them to pay for the work, or I will withdraw permission to hunt over my land,' said Peter.

'Very well, Your Grace,' said the agent, and then cleared his throat and said, 'They as much as told me, Your Grace, that you would not do that, because you yourself ride to hounds. They said in your brother's day he would have made good the damage or had one of his farmers do it.'

'Times have changed,' said Peter. 'I'm getting too old to hunt.'

'Perhaps Master Bredon?' the agent said.

'I gather he thinks hunting is cruel,' said Peter. 'We won't be held to ransom over this.'

After the land-agent, Peter's sister-in-law, the Dowager Duchess Helen, arrived with a series of complaints about the management of the stretch of the park between the Dower House and the Hall, which she could see from her windows. The grass had not been cut, and wild flowers were appearing. Peter explained that he was making economies – but she would be welcome to have the grass cut herself if she wished. Helen pleaded poverty, and Peter suggested sheep.

All this brought it home to Peter that being the Visitor for St Severin's was by no means the most boring or burdensome of his duties in life, and he resolved to be back in Oxford the next day as promptly as he could.

He dined quietly with his mother, listening to her rattling on about the old days, and complaining about Helen's behaviour. 'The moment you and Harriet aren't here to keep her at bay, she comes over and begins to order the servants about as if they were her own, and asking if the family jewels are safely locked up, and that sort of thing.'

It was a pity, Peter thought, that Helen's tenure of the Dower House was not subject to a charter of some kind.

His mother went early to bed these days, and Peter rang Harriet to bid her goodnight.

She said she was lonely in the college rooms by herself.

'Lonely from Oxford is becoming as familiar as Indignant from Tunbridge Wells,' he said. 'But cheer up, Domina, I'll be with you tomorrow early.'

'Oh, not too early, Peter,' she implored him. 'Don't drive too fast!'

IO

Peter probably did drive much too fast. He arrived mid-morning, just as Bunter was bringing coffee to Harriet, and in self-defence he pleaded that he had left very early; before breakfast, in fact. A life-saving infusion of coffee would be just the ticket. Bunter, who should have known better, produced not only coffee, but a late breakfast of bacon and eggs, and Peter could not well decline it without breaking his cover-story. He saw the exchange of glances between his wife and his man, and defiantly consumed his second breakfast and demanded more. How he was then to manage lunch remained to be seen.

Mid-morning breakfast offered a good opportunity to confer. Gently Harriet persuaded Bunter to sit down and join in. She feared losing the easy-going informality between the three of them that the war had imposed, and returning to a way of life that now seemed not only grandiose, but preposterously dated. Bunter, reluctant but courteous to his backbone, usually complied if the discussion was professional, as it clearly was on this occasion.

Peter explained the result of Cousin Matthew's burrowing through the college charters.

'But 1945 isn't so long ago!' said Harriet. 'Could selling the Boethius already have been under discussion?'

'It might have been,' said Peter. 'Although as far as I know the sell-the-manuscript row is recent, having been triggered by the offer of the land. Perhaps somebody foresaw it? To be honest, Harriet, I think that simply knowing that the college finances were ropey might have made the fellows or the Warden drop that clause – just in case they had to sell something.'

'What else did they, do they, have to sell?' asked Harriet.

'There is a playing field,' said Bunter, 'at Marston.'

'Good grief!' said Peter. 'What would the college cricketers say to that? Or the rugger men?'

'Is this a particularly sporting college?' asked Harriet.

'Quite a few undergraduates read law,' said Peter.

'So?' said Harriet, lost.

'Well, when they wanted to tighten up the law exams,' Peter told her, 'someone said, "What will the rowing men read now?"'

'I think you make some of this up, Peter,' said Harriet. 'Whoever heard of oarsmen needing a playing field?'

'Let's return to our sheep, then,' said Peter.

'I have some sheep of my own,' said Harriet, producing her notes on the *TLS* review. 'The blackest literary sheep I have ever had the displeasure of reading.'

Peter and Bunter read the notes in silence, passing the pages between them.

'I'm amazed that the *TLS* published this,' said Peter. 'It's actionable.'

'Reviewing, however harshly, counts as fair comment,' Harriet said.

'Yes – but this goes beyond commenting on the book and comments on the possible motives of the writer. I'm amazed they let it pass.'

'Even Homer nods,' said Bunter.

'I have heard that this particular Homer is often on his travels,' said Harriet. 'His staff hold the fort for him. And all the reviews are anonymous in the *TLS*.'

'I should think it's much easier to mount attacks on people if the piece is unattributed,' said Peter. 'One would think twice about what one said if the words stood above one's signature.'

'That's the whole point, I think,' said Harriet. 'That it enables comment without fear or favour.'

'Hmm. Well, the fact is that we need to know who wrote this vitriolic attack.'

'Good luck to you,' said Harriet. 'I have known lots of authors desperate to find out who to thank or who to hate, or to whom to give a nasty review in return. The *TLS* is incorruptible.'

'Let's put that to the test, shall we?' said Peter.

'Who tries – you or me?'

'You try first, Harriet,' said Peter. 'Keep me in reserve; I have a card up my sleeve.'

Harriet went to the phone to mount her attack.

In her absence Peter asked Bunter if he had any thoughts on the situation.

'Well, my lord,' said Bunter, 'I have spent some time, as you realise, these last few days in the company of Miss

Manciple. I have had the opportunity of observing her while we are jointly employed on cooking your meals. It is my opinion that she is not entirely consumed with anxiety and grief for the absent Warden.'

'Really? You do surprise me, Bunter. She put on a jolly good show when she talked to us.'

'Show might be the word for it, my lord. She has told me a good deal about her young life on the London stage as an actress, and her continuing interest in amateur dramatics.'

'Does she arouse suspicion in any other ways?' Peter asked.

'She has sent several parcels,' said Bunter.

'My dear chap,' said Peter, 'long association with me has made you unreasonably suspicious. She might have an impoverished aunt, or a needy nephew, or a charitable disposition. There are people still sending food parcels to Poland.'

'Yes, my lord, but Miss Manciple's parcels are never addressed. They are in her shopping basket, ready to be taken to the post, with no address as yet written on the brown paper wrapping.'

'That is certainly odd,' said Peter. 'Has she just mislaid her address book?'

'The parcels are duly taken and posted,' said Bunter, 'and that itself is odd, my lord. There is a cubbyhole in the porters' lodge in which one can put items for the post, and the porters attend to them. A trip to the post office is not strictly necessary at all.'

At that point Harriet returned to the room. 'No luck,' she said. 'I didn't expect it, as you know, but it's a stone wall. They put me through to the editor himself, and he's perfectly charming, but of course he won't budge. It's the paper's set policy, and always has been.'

'Right,' said Peter. 'Now it's my turn.'

'What makes you think he will tell you what he won't tell me?' asked Harriet, somewhat miffed. After all, the *TLS* was in her territory.

'Oh well,' said Peter, blushing slightly, 'the editor's name is familiar. I was at school with him.'

Off he went to the phone. Harriet and Bunter could hear his familiar light and bantering tone, and then various darker tonalities in what he was saying, but could not make out the exact words. Indeed, the knee-jerk embarrassment at overhearing someone made them take cover from eavesdropping and begin to talk quietly to each other, mostly about Peter Bunter's progress at school, and about Mrs Bunter's new photography studio in Putney. Bunter said Hope would like to take photographs some time of various Oxford colleges whose alumni might like them as souvenirs.

'I think many people buy copies of the *Oxford Almanack*s from the OUP shop in the High,' said Harriet.

'I understand some of those are now in short supply,' said Bunter.

'Please tell Hope she is very welcome to join us in this set of rooms while we are in occupation here,' said Harriet. 'It would be good to have her with us if she can spare the time.'

Bunter said he would convey the invitation.

Then Peter returned with a sheet of paper in his hands.

'How did you get on?' asked Harriet.

'Modified rapture,' said Peter, pulling a face. 'He wouldn't tell me what we want to know, even when I threatened him. Nicely, of course.'

'What did you threaten him with, Peter?' asked Harriet, astonished.

'Well, perhaps *warned* would be a better word than *threatened*. I warned him that the police might want to know what he wouldn't tell me, and that it is a criminal offence to obstruct the police. And he said that he would wait till the police asked him, and then consider whether to tell them or go to prison. I do have some trouble imagining him in prison, but we might really have to set Charles upon him.'

'You don't sound entirely frustrated, Peter,' said Harriet.

'Well, although he wouldn't tell who wrote the review, he thought he could tell me something else. He didn't realise that what he would divulge might be even more useful,' said Peter. 'He mentioned that there have been quite a few people asking just what I was asking; and he thought he could let me know who those people were. I made a list.'

Peter pushed his notes across to Harriet.

Mary Fowey had asked; so had Elaine Griffiths. So had Professors Lewis and Tolkien and Wren. Miss de Vine had asked. All these people ought to have known better. Well, anyone who asked the *TLS* to break the anonymity rule, including herself and Peter, ought to know better. There were four names from St Severin's: Mr Enistead, Mr Vearing, Mr Oundle, Mr Gervase.

'Why have you asterisked Vearing?' asked Harriet.

'He, I gather, rather more than just asked. He kicked up an enormous fuss, and threatened the paper with a suit for libel that would force them to disclose the perpetrator.'

'Did the threat work?'

'No. They held their ground and the fuss died down.'

'Peter, does any of this get us anywhere?' asked Harriet. 'Or is it a massive red herring?'

'Well, it's another fuss about the manuscript,' said Peter, 'and it's only five years ago. It might be to the point – we can't tell till we find what the point actually is. And it does tell us that although a lot of people were angry, a group of the Anglo-Saxon warriors rode to arms defending their manuscript and their fellow scholar, yet the one who was particularly wrought up was Vearing. I suppose we might ask why?'

Bunter cleared his throat. 'I might be able to cast light on that question, my lord,' he said.

'Cast away,' said Peter.

'Well, it is a theme of the gossip among the college servants,' said Bunter, 'among whom I have inveigled myself as a colleague, that Mr Vearing is not the man he used to be. He was like a father to David Outlander, who was, I understand, a somewhat nervous and volatile young man. The servants assure me that the most brilliant of the college students are more or less mad, in their eyes at least. Mr Vearing intervened several times to defend young Outlander; for example he paid the university fines when Outlander broke the rules. What happened to Outlander broke his heart.'

'What did happen to him, Bunter?' asked Harriet. 'We know he was damaged by that review, and has left the college . . .'

'He left the world, my lady,' said Bunter. 'He hanged himself.'

'God help us!' said Harriet. 'Oh, how shocking, how sad!'

'Mr Vearing's own son was killed in the war,' said Bunter. 'And his wife, too. Their house was bombed. When he came out of the army he moved back into college and became a sort of uncle-at-need to some of the undergraduates and the research fellows. Mr Thrupp told me that Mr Vearing had even befriended one or two of the servants, when a small loan could avoid a large problem. Thrupp says he always knew where to go when such help was required, if it was more than a whip-around among the servants themselves could settle. He says Outlander's death was too much for Vearing. He has been rather odd since then.'

'And now,' said Peter quietly, 'he is determined at all costs to stop the college selling the manuscript. And the manuscript is the only arbiter that could settle the question whether Outlander's book is justified.'

'Well, at least we can see the origin of some of the passion all this arouses,' said Harriet. 'Gervase said that the split in the fellowship about Outlander and the split about selling the MS is roughly the same.'

'I don't at all like the shape of what begins to emerge,' said Peter.

'Is there a clear shape yet, Peter?' asked Harriet. 'And what about the other side in the dispute? What is motivating them? Have they too got a grievance simmering away against the *TLS*?'

'Well, on the face of it they don't need a hidden motive,' said Peter. 'When short of money it's entirely rational to sell a valuable asset. Dukes are selling off their Van Dykes all over the country to pay death duties. Is this different?'

'And what about Enistead?' asked Harriet. 'Wasn't he in favour of keeping the book? So did someone have an animus against him?'

'Well, however suspicious we may feel about round knobs on banister rails,' said Peter, 'and accidental braining of self thereupon, the only undoubted murder is that of Oundle, and that happened in London and may have nothing whatever to do with matters in college.'

'You don't believe that, Peter.'

'No, I don't,' he said. 'I don't like coincidence any more than you do. But, Harriet, suppose it's the wrong book?'

'What do you mean, Peter? Which book?'

'*Twixt Wind and Water*, perhaps.'

'In which all the alibis,' said Harriet, thinking aloud, 'were rock solid, but turned out to be for the wrong time of death . . .'

'Just thinking,' said Peter. '*Wind and Water* was based on the case at Wilvercombe which we were both concerned in solving. In that case, the alibis had been carefully devised to cover the time of the murder; but the fact that when you found the body it was lying in a pool of fresh blood . . .'

'. . . had us all racking our brains because the time of death had been mistaken, and we placed it at two o'clock, perhaps two hours later than it had really occurred. I don't see how that would fit the present case. Am I missing something?'

'At Wilvercombe,' Peter said, 'that preposterously horrible gang of homicides were wrong-footed by the mistake. They didn't have alibis for the supposed time of death; only for the real time of death. Turn it round, Harriet and you'll see what I mean.'

'I don't get it yet, Peter,' said Harriet.

'Well, the hapless victim in the Wilvercombe case,' said Peter, 'was a haemophiliac, and the murderer didn't know that. But suppose someone was a haemophiliac, and you did know it. You would know that the time of death would appear much later than the actual time of death.'

'But are you suggesting that the entire college was in a plot to murder Oundle? That they all organised an alibi . . .'

'We'll apply Ockham's razor to that suggestion,' said Peter. 'That is to suppose more than is necessary. If Ambleside is right, then alibis for an ordinary morning in term don't need organising; everyone would have one, and everyone would expect everyone else to have one. So suppose the murder took place at around seven thirty or eight in the morning. The murderer can be back in Oxford giving a lecture by ten easily, safe in the knowledge that nobody is going to ask him where he was at around eight.'

'But he would need to know that Oundle was a haemophiliac. And for a start, Peter, do *we* know that?'

'It's a wild speculation, I admit,' said Peter. 'I shall ring Charles at once.'

'Charles?' Peter said down the line. 'Could you get forensics to check if Oundle had haemophilia?'

'And Charles said,' Peter reported to Harriet when he put the phone down, '"How in hell did you come up with that, Wimsey? I was about to tell you that . . ."'

'Which leaves us with an interesting question, doesn't it?' said Harriet. 'Poor Alexis, you remember, had kept his haemophilia secret; it would affect his job prospects, and his marriage prospects too. Did Oundle do the same? Because if everybody knew about it, somebody might tell the police in the course of an interview, and the alibi for the time of death would be finessed. So the question now is, who knew? How do we find that out?'

'I think we will start by asking them,' said Peter. 'I think it's time I gave them a pep talk, don't you?'

In the Old Library then. Meeting in the Hall too public – all the undergraduates would be aware of something afoot. The Senior Common Room too small for everyone at once. The Old Library was now very little used and sometimes hired out for conferences or weddings. Harriet slipped in right at the back, and at the last minute, to listen inconspicuously.

Peter spoke in a grave and level tone. 'I believe that the college is in more trouble than has yet been acknowledged among you,' he said. 'I am here to resolve a dispute; but that dispute is rooted not in simple disagreement, but in rivalries of an impassioned kind that date back to before the question of selling your Boethius was ever raised. Of course you, or some of you, know and understand quite a lot about these rivalries, which you are reluctant to divulge to me. I understand that. But things have gone far beyond a question about buying or selling college assets. We are now looking at an undoubted murder of one of the college fellows. And that murder makes it likely that the accidents and supposed assaults that have recently occurred must be re-examined as possible attempted murders. In this new and darker state of affairs the absence of the Warden – coming up to four months now – also arouses grave concern; graver than ever. I am asking you now for your own collective safety as well as your collective honour to set aside any considerations except the need to find and stop the murderer who is in all probability one of you. If you do not wish to talk to the police, you may talk in the first instance to me. You know where to find me.

'Any information you can give is likely to be helpful. Remember that information is as likely to exculpate someone as to incriminate them. For the moment I have a question to ask. Did anyone here present know that Mr Oundle suffered from haemophilia?'

No hand was raised.

After a pause Peter said, 'Mr Oundle has been a fellow of St Severin's for many years. It is likely that someone knew about his health problems. If, on reflection, there is somebody who you think would probably have known about it, then will you in confidence name that person to me? And in the meantime, please keep your doors locked. Do not walk back to the college alone after dark; take care on staircases. And should any of you who served in the war have kept weapons as souvenirs, please keep them under lock and key.'

As he left, stepping rapidly down the centre of the room and making for the door, an uproar of voices broke out. Mostly, Harriet thought, angry voices. Certainly she heard among the hubbub somebody saying, '. . . has no right to talk to us like that! No right!'

11

Angry they may have been, but Peter's appeal produced a number of visitors to his rooms with whom he had not yet had a one-to-one conversation. The first of these was a junior fellow who suggested that the college nurse had probably known of such a dramatically dangerous condition. She might have had to intervene. Come to that, surely the college servants would have been alerted, and once something was known to the college servants, the whole of Oxford knew.

Peter thanked him for his insights and said he would investigate the college nurse.

The next visitor was Tom Ranger, the fellow in medicine.

'I didn't know about poor Oundle, but I'm not surprised,' he told Peter. 'There were indications; but the man wasn't my patient, so I didn't think hard about it and put two and two together.'

'What are the two and two you didn't connect?' Peter asked him. 'Were they anything very obvious?'

'Reasonably obvious, but capable of less exotic explanation,' said Ranger. 'He used a stick, and moved rather stiffly for his age – he wasn't above fifty. His hands were rather gnarled – thick joints like arthritis; in fact I thought it was arthritis. But when you asked your question of us all just now, I remembered an incident in which Oundle bumped his face against one of those pestilential self-closing doors, and got a nose-bleed. We offered the usual remedies – key down the back of his shirt, head tipped back, holding nose between finger and thumb – but he took himself off to the college nurse very promptly. He seemed rather bothered about it. But you see I didn't think of any of this until you mentioned haemophilia. I'm rather kicking myself for obtuseness.'

'You don't think the signs you now recall were obvious enough to allow somebody else to guess?'

'As I say, I saw some signs. I thought he had severe arthritis. That's very common, and haemophilia is very rare. Medical students like to diagnose rare conditions, but experienced doctors usually don't. I'm afraid this is not much help.'

'On the contrary, Dr Ranger, it is very helpful. Background information is often the source of insight, I find,' said Peter.

When Ranger had left, feeling that he himself had better sit and wait for any further visitors, Peter asked Harriet to find and interview the college nurse.

That lady's services were shared between nearby colleges: between St Severin's and Wadham, and Keble and Shrewsbury. Harriet ran her to earth in Keble. Miss Havershaw was as stiff and formal as a hospital matron, and clearly capable of terrifying the undergraduates out of hypochondria. The mention of Mr Oundle's name, however, upset her.

'I wasn't surprised he had passed on,' she said to Harriet, when Harriet had introduced herself, confessed to being an emissary for Peter, and explained her errand. 'The poor gentleman was always at risk, even from a slight accident. But when I heard what had happened to him, I was horrified. Horrified is the word.'

'We need to find who did it, and quickly,' said Harriet. 'And what I have come to ask you is if you know how many people knew about Mr. Oundle's haemophilia?'

'If you mean, did I go around telling people—' said Miss Havershaw, bristling.

'No, of course not,' said Harriet. 'But since, as you say, he was at risk, he might have let some of his colleagues know, just for safety.'

'That would have been sensible, yes,' she said. 'I told him so more than once. But he wasn't having it. He said he couldn't live a normal life if people knew. He wanted to be left alone to take his own risks. And he was a brave gentleman; he could have been exempt from call-up in the war, but he kept it all dark, and served as a soldier. You have to respect that.'

'I do respect that,' said Harriet. 'But are you saying he took no precautions at all?'

'Precautions wouldn't have helped him having his throat cut,' Miss Havershaw said with asperity. 'That would have killed a healthy person. But there was one precaution he did take; or rather it was what he didn't take. No aspirin. He considered his condition was mild. But I worried about him. He left with me an infusion of certain herbs he had learned about in the Far East which were supposed to assist in blood clotting. I was to keep it handy, which I did. It's in the case I carry from one college to another when I do my shifts.'

'Did you see that work?' asked Harriet.

'Either the herbs, or pressure applied to the cut and maintained for a considerable time,' she said. 'It was always a crisis if he cut or grazed himself.'

'So as far as you know his illness was a well-kept secret,' said Harriet. 'You don't think he would have told anybody in the college?'

'I'm sure he wouldn't,' said Miss Havershaw. 'He wouldn't even let me put his name on the herb extract. I had to have the bottle handy in case he came running for it, but it wasn't to have his name on the label, not by any means. I had to put "Tincture of Comfrey" etc.'

'For that to work,' Harriet said, 'it would have to be a powerful clotting agent – have I got that right?'

'Quite right,' said Miss Havershaw. 'And as I say I have no idea if it was a potent concoction or a folk legend. You seem knowledgeable, Duchess. Unusually so for a non-medical person. Or were you a nurse in an earlier life?'

'I'm a GP's daughter,' Harriet told her, 'and I write detective stories.'

'Do you write under your own name?' Miss Havershaw asked.

'Yes. Or my former name, rather. Harriet Vane.'

'I'll look you out next time I am in a library,' said Miss Havershaw.

'Thank you,' said Harriet meekly.

On her return she found Peter in conference with a very young man; he looked hardly out of school, but he was, it turned out, Timothy Smith, one of the junior research fellows.

'This chap has been telling me that the junior research fellows have been making bets on the voting,' said Peter, 'as though the MS and the land were a pair of horses in a race.'

Peter sounded extravagantly shocked, but young Smith looked perfectly at ease. 'We junior research fellows don't have a vote,' he told Harriet apologetically. 'So where's the fun in it all for us? We just laid bets on how it would go each time.'

'Are there enough of you disfranchised folk to make a worthwhile kitty?' asked Peter, 'or are you telling me that fellows both voted and bet on their own votes?'

'Oh, no, not that,' said Smith. 'They were all pretty stiff about it. But there's a bookmaker in Jericho who would take the bets. And some of the undergraduates like a flutter now and then . . . and there are people in other colleges who were interested. And we began to try to research the form, you see – we took to asking every-one how they were going to vote each time the thing was due to come up. And when you asked for help I just thought you might like to see how our polls turned out.'

He put a file down on the side-table, and pulled out of it some scrappy sheets of paper. 'I'm afraid they're not in any sort of order,' he said.

'Can you leave those with us?' asked Peter. 'I think they might be very helpful indeed.'

'Oh, you can have them,' said Smith. 'Nobody has the heart to bet on this now.'

'Look here, old chap,' said Peter, 'I think it would be much better if you didn't tell anyone, not even your fellow junior fellows, or any of your fellow punters, that you have left these papers with me. I think for your own safety you had better have lost them. Do you understand?'

Smith went pale. 'Oh, surely not . . .' he said.

'Probably not; but not surely not,' said Peter.

Smith said, 'I think perhaps I'd better go now.'

'Bunter will show you out the back way,' said Peter, 'by the Warden's back door on to the street. Then you can just walk round and get back into college through the front gate.'

'Thank you, Your Grace,' said Smith, and then added with a lopsided smile, 'I'm a socialist. I do feel silly calling anybody that.'

'I'm right out of sight from your position,' said Peter, 'but I feel silly being called it. Thank you for your help. And take care.'

When he had gone, Peter spread his notes out on the table. The fellowship had been polled four times. Nearly all of them had taken a position and stuck to it, but not quite all. The Warden, who might have been above it all, or might have decided to play his hand close to his chest, had intended each time to vote for the keeping party.

'Our mysterious Warden seems to have two votes,' said Peter. 'One in his own right, I suppose, and one ex-officio, the casting vote. Well, at least he wasn't voting for both sides each time. Oh, ho, Harriet look at this . . .'

It was the name of Mr Enistead that Peter was pointing out to her. In each of the first three polls he had declared he would vote to keep the MS. But on the fourth occasion he had said he would vote to sell it.

'So where did that leave things?' Harriet asked.

'It would have left a decision to sell the book, and acquire the land,' said Peter.

'And the Warden's votes?'

'He would have had only one vote,' said Peter. 'His casting vote would not have come into play; it is only available to break a deadlock, and Enistead's shift across the divide moves two votes – one less for the keeping party, one more for the selling party. No deadlock – no casting vote. But all that is subjunctive, not factual. There would have been a majority enough to settle things if Enistead had not unfortunately fallen downstairs and brained himself after he told Smith and co. how he meant to vote, and before the vote was taken.'

Harriet sat down abruptly. 'Peter, I'm hating this,' she said. 'Poison pen letters at Shrewsbury were bad enough, but murder . . . In *Oxford!* It's horrible.'

'Sick roses, you mean? The invisible worm that flies in the night? It will take more than this to destroy Oxford, my dear,' he said. 'But for once in my life I shall be glad to get out of it when this is over. Where shall we go?'

'Could we go to Venice?' she asked him. 'I've never been there . . .'

'A thousand years their cloudy wings expand About me, and a dying glory smiles,' he said. 'Sounds rather like Oxford, but with gondolas. Very well, Domina, Venice the most serene it shall be. Soon, let's hope.'

But for the present they were sitting in the Warden's guest suite, available to be visited with information. For an hour they sat and read. Then Peter said, 'Harriet, will you hold the fort for me? I'm having keyboard fidgets. I'd like to slip across to the chapel, and play the organ for an hour.'

'Off you go then, Peter,' said Harriet cheerfully. 'I can always send a visitor across there to find you.'

Shortly after Peter had gone, there was another knock on the door, and Troutbeck appeared. 'I was looking for the Duke,' he said, on seeing Harriet sitting alone.

'You'll find him in the chapel playing the organ,' said Harriet.

Troutbeck pulled a face, and sat down uninvited. 'Perhaps conveying my meaning through you would be more effective,' he said.

'I doubt it,' said Harriet coolly, 'but convey away if you so wish.'

'It seems to several of us,' Troutbeck said, 'that your lord and master is exceeding his rightful role. He has appraised the situation; but instead of giving us the decision he is entitled to give, he is entrenching himself in the college, apparently pursuing a private hobby and investigating a murder – one that happened in London and has in all probability no connection with college business. Perhaps you can induce him to go home and leave us to settle matters by simple vote—'

'Before you go on, Mr Troutbeck,' said Harriet, 'I must correct you. There has probably been more than one murder; and one of those was on college premises.'

'Whatever do you mean?' he said. 'Are you referring to poor Enistead? That was an accident. The coroner found accidental death. This is exactly the sort of melodramatising that some of us object to . . .'

'I don't suppose you are a reader of detective stories, Mr Troutbeck?' said Harriet.

'That rubbish? Certainly not!' he said. He was redfaced now, and clenching his fists. He seemed to be someone living very near the limit of his power to contain his temper. Had Harriet not felt pretty certain that Bunter was within call, and probably within earshot, she might have quailed; Troutbeck was a big and powerful man, and plainly used to dominating.

'There are special reasons for fearing that Enistead's death was not an accident,' she told him.

'Kindly inform me what those reasons are,' he said.

'No,' said Harriet. 'You must take my word for it.'

'I wouldn't hang a dog on your word,' he said, 'with your past.'

'Thank you,' said Harriet. Her quiet tones seemed to infuriate her visitor further.

'Are you going to get the Duke to leave us alone?' he demanded.

'No,' said Harriet, 'I am going to suggest that you reconsider that request. Perhaps you do not realise that the Duke has a formidable reputation as an investigator, and has powerful friends in the police. They are content at the moment to leave matters in his hands; if he were to leave Oxford, as you seem eager to have him do, a full-scale murder investigation would at once be launched by the police. You have had a mild taste of what that would entail when the Met sent officers into the college to record a number of alibis. Believe me, that is as nothing compared to a full police investigation. I do not believe for a moment that my husband would accede to your request; but I think also that if he did you would have good cause to regret having made it.'

'I see that I had better wait until I can talk to him man to man,' said Troutbeck.

'Good day, Mr Troutbeck,' said Harriet, standing up.

Bunter appeared instantly, holding the door open for Troutbeck's departure. He went in a dash.

'Are you all right, Your Grace?' said Bunter.

'I'm not quite sure that I am,' said Harriet, who found herself to be shaking. She felt ashamed of herself. Troutbeck had not actually threatened her, had he? It was all in tone of voice and demeanour.

'Let me bring you a stiff drink, Your Grace,' said Bunter, 'and fetch the Duke from the chapel.'

'No, don't fetch him, Bunter,' said Harriet. 'I'll walk across myself and bring him. I could do with the fresh air.'

She stepped across the quad, and opened the chapel door. At once she was engulfed in the cascading notes of a fugue by Bach. She sat down in the nearest pew. It was like having all the tangles of one's soul combed out straight. Or like being a beach washed smooth by a gentle, lucid wave. It calmed her utterly. She sat quietly waiting for Peter to finish. He was not as good an organist as he was a pianist, but that had an effect she had noticed before: tiny errors or hesitations made the listener hear how difficult the piece was, and that was part of the truth about it. By the time the fugue had ravelled and unravelled its complex patterns to the end she was completely calm, and ready to tell Peter what Troutbeck had said.

But they did not talk of that as they walked back across the quad; they did not talk of anything, but enjoyed the dreamlike trance the music had left them in. And when they reached their rooms Troutbeck had to wait; Mr Vearing was waiting for them.

Of course both Peter and Harriet expected Mr Vearing to make an impassioned case for the retention of the manuscript. But what he actually said startled them.

'I was hoping not to have to tell you this, Your Grace,' he said, addressing Peter with a steady gaze. 'But I see that I must. To sell the Boethius will disgrace the college utterly. It is a fake.'

'You will have to justify that statement, Vearing,' said Peter. 'It is a controversial one. Why do you think so? Don't you teach Modern Literature? How is the Boethius MS within your expertise?'

'David told me,' said Vearing, looking wan. 'His expertise was sufficient.'

'David Outlander?' Peter asked.

'Ah. Someone has been talking. There is no privacy in our lives here. No merciful forgetting and moving on. Who told you?'

'Outlander's death is public knowledge, Vearing,' said Peter, speaking gently. 'Reported in the *Oxford Mail*. Not a secret – it could never have been that.'

Vearing was silent.

'Didn't Outlander's book claim the opposite of what you now say?' asked Peter. 'Didn't he say the MS was genuine, had been used by King Alfred, perhaps had been glossed for him by his scholars?'

'His thesis was wrong,' said Vearing. He opened his briefcase, and brought out an old and slightly yellowing copy of the *TLS*. 'Read this,' he said, putting it down on the table.

'We have read it,' said Harriet. 'That is an evidently personal attack; not the usual magisterial calm and accuracy of the *TLS*.'

'David was convinced by it,' said Vearing stubbornly. 'He thought it was right.'

'And so all this time you have been opposed to the sale of the MS because you feared it would lead to the thing being discovered to be a fake? Not because you thought that it was an incomparable antiquity that the college ought to hug to its bosom for ever?' Peter asked.

'Yes, that is so,' said Vearing.

'And not because you despised and hated somebody in the faction who wishes to sell it?'

Vearing looked startled at that, and coloured up. 'Who, me?' he asked. 'I am not a man for hatreds. Whereas they—' He broke off, and then said, 'I think I had better go. I have said enough.'

'Please stay,' said Peter, 'long enough to tell us what David Outlander thought was correct in that review.'

'He was mortified by it,' said Vearing. 'Humiliated.'

'But why do you say he thought it was right? Did he tell you that?'

'He must have thought so. He would have defended himself – fought back – if he had had grounds to do so.'

'That is speculation, surely,' said Peter, 'however well you knew him.'

'I am not alone in thinking the MS is a fake,' said Vearing obstinately, pointing at the *TLS*. 'As you can see.'

With a sudden hunch, Harriet asked him, 'Mr Vearing, do you know who wrote that review?'

'No, no, no,' he said. 'How could I? All anonymous. Always.'

With that he took his leave, retrieving his copy of the *TLS* as he went.

'Whew!' said Peter. 'What do you make of that?'

'I don't quite know,' said Harriet. 'But I notice that he offers a new reason in support of the position he has taken all along. Is it possible he is trying to push you into supporting his side in the dispute with a fairy-tale?'

'This much is true,' said Peter, 'that the putting up for sale of the MS would cause many experts to examine it on behalf of possible buyers. I think it quite likely that a consensus would emerge about the gloss which might be that it was uncertain if it ever had any direct connection with King Alfred. *Proving* that it did not is quite another thing.'

'Oh, bother the manuscript!' said Harriet. 'It's a red herring – I'm sure it is. Charming and arcane and Oxonian though a question like that may be, it feels like wool-gathering to me; not something that might generate all this *sturm und drang* extending to homicide. If I were writing this investigation, my lord, I would think it time to uncover some serious grounds for murder.'

'Yes . . .' said Peter. He was only half listening to her as he scribbled a note, folded it, and tucked the folds into one another. He called Bunter and asked him to put the note in Jackson's pigeon-hole.

Then he returned his attention to Harriet. 'Right,' he said, 'what have we got?'

'Who knew about Oundle's illness, and about Oundle's sword?' said Harriet.

'Who, if anyone, found out who was the author of that review?' said Peter.

'Why was Mrs Cutwater apparently frightened?' offered Harriet.

'Is the MS kosher, or is it dicey?' said Peter.

'Was Enistead felled by a bit of banister loaded into a catapult?' said Harriet.

'Is that all?' asked Peter. 'No – I've got another one: who is it who buys his books in Heffers instead of in Blackwell's, and is he a fellow of St Severin's?'

'And finally,' said Harriet, 'where is the Warden, alive or dead, and why is he wherever he is?'

'Well,' said Peter dryly, 'that should keep us busy for a day or two.'

'Where shall we start?' asked Harriet.

But the starter's pistol was about to be fired in a new direction. There were footsteps hammering up the staircase to the door, and the head porter rushed into the room past Bunter, saying as he came, 'You're needed at once, Your Grace, please come, please come . . . poor Mr Trevair has fallen and broken his neck, sir!'

12

Trevair was lying sprawled on his back, on the chapel floor below the organ loft.

He appeared to have hit a spreadeagled angel on his way down, for a gilded wooden wing lay under his body. One of the porters made as if to climb the tiny winding staircase to the organ and the minstrels' gallery. 'No,' said Peter, 'leave that completely untouched for the police.'

'It did ought to be locked, that door to the stair,' remarked one of the porters. ''Oose got the key?'

'God forgive me, I have,' said Peter, reaching into his pocket and producing it. It was an ordinary key for a modern lock fitted to the door quite recently. 'Is this the only one?'

'Mr Dancy has one,' said Thrupp. 'There's only the two. Did you lock up behind you, Your Grace, when you had finished your bit of playing?'

'I'm afraid I forgot,' said Peter miserably.

'And I forgot to come and get it from you, sir,' said Mr Thrupp, sounding fatherly. 'I knew as it was you what had it.'

Seeing the expression on Peter's face, Harriet took Peter firmly by the arm, and led him away. Once she got him into their rooms she said, 'First telephone Charles.'

He did that and returned to the drawing room ashen-faced, and sat down silent.

'So, Peter, you forgot to lock up the organ loft. People do forget things,' said Harriet. 'People forget to lock up their sporting guns; people leave their car keys in the lock while they dash into a shop. Silly women leave their jewels around for the room-maid to see. Does that make them responsible for murder with a shotgun, for a car-chase in which someone gets killed, for a theft of a family heirloom?'

'Implicated,' said Peter. 'They are, I am, implicated.'

'The responsibility for Trevair lying dead on the chapel floor lies entirely with whoever pushed him off the minstrels' gallery,' said Harriet firmly. 'People are implicated if they should have foreseen the consequences of their negligence. The worst you could have foreseen was someone making an ugly din on the organ, or throwing paper darts made with the sheet music. Be reasonable, Peter.'

When he did not reply, she said, 'This is turning into a massacre, Your Grace. Someone needs stopping. Time we found him.'

'Yes, Harriet,' he said. 'You are right. So which of our questions shall we tackle first?'

'Easiest first,' she said. 'Who buys his books in Heffers?'

'All right, m'dear. You take that one; I'll take the one about who knew about Oundle and his sword.'

'I think I would have to go to Cambridge for my clue,' she said.

'That's survivable,' he said.

'I'll run up to Denver while I'm that way,' said Harriet, 'and just see how your mother is.'

'You are a woman in a million,' said Peter. 'And I am the luckiest dog in England.'

'Piffler!' said Harriet, smiling at him.

'I would help if I could,' said Dick Fox, the bookseller in Heffers. 'But I'm not at all sure that I can.'

'Doesn't he pay you? Isn't there a name on his cheques?'

'Well, no. He pays before leaving the shop, and he pays in cash. And before you ask, no, he doesn't have them sent, even when he has taken quite a few. He carts them off in bags.'

'How do you know he's from Oxford then?' Harriet asked.

'We wouldn't know if he hadn't bumped into a friend in the front shop once. The friend was surprised to see him, and made a small to-do about it. "Whatever are you doing here?" sort of thing. Our man didn't seem pleased to see his chum at all. "Visiting friends," he said. "Anyone I know?" chum asked. "Extremely unlikely," said our man. By this time we were all listening. Chum then noticed the bags full of books. "Those are for your friend, I suppose," he said. "You wouldn't need to lug them home, would you? There are book-shops in Oxford."

'Our man first said, "Mind your own business," and then said, "My friend is a voracious reader. Shot up in the war. Can't walk into the shop himself."'

Harriet saw her trail going cold before her. An Oxford man *could* have a disabled friend in Cambridge for whom he bought books . . . a man in Cambridge who didn't have any obliging local friends? That wouldn't be very Aristotelian; didn't Aristotle prefer the probable to the possible improbable? But that was about fiction, of course, and this was real life.

'So you are telling me that you don't know anything about him?' she asked. 'Just that he's from Oxford; not that he is an Oxford don, not his name, nothing?'

'He's probably a don,' she was told. 'Donnish sort of speech; and then once or twice he has bought a book that isn't detection.'

'Aha!' Harriet said. 'In what subject were his non-fictional books?'

'Pass,' said Dick Fox. 'I'm a fiction buyer. But I could ask some of my colleagues and let you know if any of them remember. If it would help, of course.'

'Anything might help; we would be very grateful,' said Harriet, and then a thought struck her. 'You wouldn't fancy a trip to Oxford, would you?' she asked. 'At my expense, of course. Because you might recognise him, mightn't you?'

'Oh, I'd recognise him all right,' said Dick Fox. 'But I don't get a lot of time off.'

'Have you been to Oxford?' Harriet asked him.

'I haven't, as a matter of fact,' he said. 'Not on my trade routes, somehow.'

'It's beautiful,' Harriet said.

'So is Cambridge,' he told her.

'Indeed,' she conceded. 'Look, I won't press you to come on the off-chance; but if matters come to the point where we really need an identification, and if I asked you then, would you come?'

'Yes, if you twist my arm, I'll come,' he said. 'But, Miss Vane, he can't really be a murderer you know; he's too, well, dithery for that.'

And, looking round her, Harriet realised at once that the splendid selection of books on the shelves could not have been achieved by a man who had time to wander over to Oxford on an off-chance.

Harriet took the train to Denver, and was gratified to find that in her absence and that of Peter – and more to the point that of Bunter – everything was ticking along nicely. The Dowager Duchess's maid, Franklin, who was getting old and cranky, was well able to keep things in order, and had even acquired the knack of fending off Helen, the younger Dowager Duchess. There were of course things to see to, but the best bit of being home again for a few hours was seeing how Peter's mother was doing.

'Are you having a lovely time, dear?' her mother-in-law asked her. 'Do you have to wear those horrid black gowns all the time?'

'We wear them if we dine in Hall, Mother, and we would wear them if we went to lectures; but we can cavort in punts, or go shopping without them. I don't mind wearing mine at all.'

'Well, of course, dear, I never went to university. Finishing school in Switzerland was what I got. I don't think I knew any woman friend who got a degree. Did I miss much, do you think? I wouldn't have wanted to be draped in black bombazine. So unflattering.'

Harriet wondered what best to say to that. Her delectable mother-in-law would not have got into Oxford, except possibly reading French, which she spoke with complete fluency, and would have looked gorgeous in a gown, however little she fancied one. Subfusc would have set off her blue-eyed blonde colouring to perfection.

'I didn't mind it,' she said at last. 'It took so much hard work to win the right to wear it. I don't remember even wondering if it suited me.'

'Of course you were proud of it, Harriet dear,' said the Duchess. 'Silly of me. But then in my day we were rather encouraged to be silly, in case being clever put off the men. I suppose it would always have depended on the man, really, though; a silly wife wouldn't have suited Peter.'

'Peter,' said Harriet thoughtfully 'is unusual in that.'

'Is there anything at all in which my second son is ordinary?' the Duchess wondered aloud.

'If I detect him being ordinary I will let you know at once,' said Harriet. 'I shall go back to join him tomorrow, unless you need me urgently for something.'

'I always like it best when you are here,' the Duchess said, 'but I don't need you at the moment. The time will come, I dare say, but for now don't indulge me; it makes me feel old.'

*   *   *

Next morning in Oxford Peter was bending his thoughts to the question of who could have known the necessary about Oundle. Just the knowledge, of course, fell a long way short of proving that he-who-knew was the murderer; and now he came to think about it, not having known would not entirely prove a person not to be the murderer; the murder could have been committed with no intent to rely on alibis in the *Oxford Gazette* and elsewhere about teaching duties in St Severin's. Peter stood at the window of his room, looking over the back quad, eating toast, and musing.

Why had he and Harriet assumed that poor Oundle's haemophilia was an important part of the scenario? Because they had assumed that the murderer was one murderer, a serial killer of great malignity, who was using the methods of murder described in Harriet's novels.

If that were the case, then of course Oundle's haemophilia was relevant; the murderer was using the fictional account of the murder at Wilvercombe where conspirators had been wrong-footed by the time it took for blood to clot.

We must, in that case, Peter thought, be looking for a lunatic. If I wanted to murder somebody, and I needed to know how it might be done, I would be looking at a manual of forensic medicine, not one of Harriet's novels, brilliant though they are. Then he asked himself in exactly what way were Harriet's novels brilliant? Certainly not in the gritty realism of the modes of death. Peter's own cases were not run-of-the-mill affairs, but the odd ones. The ones where the police had been baffled. And Harriet had, naturally, chosen the most peculiar and exotic murders from that already recherché selection. In real life, he thought, sadly, for the most part murders were a matter of blunt instruments, drunken fists, ligatures round the neck . . . done using things that were handy in nearly every place, done on impulse from obvious nasty motives. No fun at all. Then he pulled himself up abruptly. Was he telling himself that Oundle's death had been *fun*?

Stick to the point, Peter, he told himself. I think we can believe the college nurse that Oundle's colleagues would probably not have known of his illness; he was at pains to keep it from them. But what about friends outside Oxford? What about school friends, for a start? He prowled into the Warden's part of the house – he was using only the guest suite in that house – and looked for the shelf of reference books. He found *Who's Who?* easily, but Oundle, in spite of his doctorate, was not eminent enough on the wider stage to figure in it.

Peter got dressed and went in search of the Warden's secretary, who had a little ground-floor room on the front quad, shared, at St Severin's, with the fellows' secretary.

'I suppose when you appoint someone to a fellowship, you get a CV from them?' he asked. 'Do you have them on file somewhere?'

'Yes, Your Grace, we do,' said the Warden's secretary. 'You'll find them all over on that bookshelf. It's the file called the Domesday Book.'

Peter took down the thick folder, and laid it on the table.

'You want to know where poor Mr Oundle was at school, I suppose?' the secretary asked.

'How do you know that?' asked Peter, surprised.

'Mr Bunter asked me that yesterday, Your Grace,' she said, smirking.

'And what answer did you give him?' Peter asked.

'The Salter's Grammar School in Woodford,' she said.

Peter would have asked her the next question, but preferring to play his cards closer to his chest, he thanked her and went in quest of Bunter.

He found that gentleman industriously polishing shoes.

'The Salter's School,' Peter said to him. 'And who else was there?'

'I could find no other senior member of this college who was at Salter's in Mr Oundle's time,' said Bunter.

'Blast!' said Peter. 'Another red herring bites the dust.'

'That, my lord,' said Bunter affectionately, changing from shoe brush to polishing cloth – it was a pair of Harriet's shoes he was cleaning, Peter noticed – 'if you will allow me to say so, is a mixed metaphor.'

'I will allow you to say so, Bunter,' said Peter, 'but only since you already have.'

'Thank you, my lord,' said Bunter. 'So, as you would expect, I looked at the files about undergraduates. Of course there are very many more of those, and I would have been all day at the task had I not been afforded some help. It seems that for the most part Salter's sends its boys to Cambridge; but David Outlander was at Salter's, though of course long after Mr Oundle. They did not overlap there as schoolboys.'

'Alas, my dear Bunter,' said Peter, 'thank you for your efforts, although to no avail. As someone said: There is always an easy solution to every human problem – neat, plausible, and wrong.'

When Harriet reached Oxford again that evening and they compared notes it was evident that they had not made much progress. 'The police have been here all day,' said Peter gloomily. 'The Oxford police, that is.'

'Did they ask you about that key?' said Harriet.

'Oh, yes. With a form of extreme icy politeness that is actually an insult,' Peter said. 'The key doesn't get them far. A college servant went into the chapel to clean the brass and put flowers on the altar while I was playing, it seems. I didn't hear her. But she was still there when I left and nobody was lying dead on the floor then. And of course once I was back here there were witnesses, including you – I'm afraid you will have to give them a statement tomorrow, Harriet, but in the meantime they have one from Bunter and one from Miss Manciple.'

'What do we know about Trevair?' Harriet asked.

'We know he was an economist. With laughable naivety the fellows supposed that an economist would be interested in money, and therefore the solvency of the college. The selling party were delighted to have him. And then he voted for keeping the book.'

'Did anyone ask him why?'

'He told me he thought long-term assets outweighed present gains.'

'It would be hard if he has been murdered for such an arguable opinion as that,' said Harriet.

'It's hard to be murdered for any reason,' said Peter mildly. 'But the problem we seem to be having here is unreason; the murderer is a madman. It is hard to unravel or predict the actions of such a person.'

'Or persons?' asked Harriet. 'Do we actually know that the murders are the work of only one person?'

'Well, more than one murderer in a fellowship of about twenty-four people is not very probable,' Peter said. 'Do you think there might be a contaminant in the drinking water that produces urges to homicide?'

'That would be a lovely scenario for a murder mystery, Peter,' said Harriet, 'if such a potential contaminant exists.'

Peter suddenly struck himself on the forehead. 'Harriet!' he exclaimed. 'I've been missing something so blatantly obvious – I'm losing my grip. Harriet, in which of your books is someone killed by being pushed off a balcony? By defenestration? By being tossed out of an organ loft? By being thrown off a roof?'

'In none of them,' said Harriet.

'But in the other incidents, murder or attempted murder, there has been a precedent of sorts in your books . . .'

'And in your cases, Peter.'

'And have you ever written a book in which someone disappears without trace?'

'No. You know I haven't. You need a trace to make a story. But perhaps Miss Manciple's parcels are a trace.'

'We could try the third degree on Miss Manciple,' said Peter, 'although I gather from Bunter it might have to go as far as thumbscrews to persuade her.'

'Disgusting idea, Peter,' said Harriet.

'Very well then, best beloved, we will continue to try intelligence before violence. Let's make a careful analysis of what we do know. The college first voted on whether to sell the manuscript in Michaelmas term last year. Deadlock. The Warden used his casting vote in favour of keeping the book, and told everyone that he would always cast it in favour of the status quo.

'The next vote was tabled to take place in Hilary term, this year. No doubt there was lobbying going on, but what also happened in the run-up to that vote was a pair of strange assaults on fellows; first Mr Cloudie either was threatened in his bedroom at night with an intruder wielding a large syringe, or dreamed that he was so threatened. The second oddity was Mr Dancy getting locked in the bell-tower during a ring of bells. Both of these men had voted for selling the MS, so had either of them died in the course of these odd events the deadlock would have been broken, and the book would have been safe. However, both of them survived, though severely frightened. The voting in Hilary term was deadlocked again.

'The third vote is tabled for Trinity term, this year. As we know from the egregious Mr Smith, Enistead had threatened to change sides. Who knew about that, I wonder, apart from Smith's pollsters, and the bookies? Certainly when the news of Enistead's death reached Troutbeck at Denver he thought the vote to sell would be carried, and my services would not be required.'

'And since you became involved there have been two deaths – Oundle and Trevair. Both horribly successful; the murderer is getting his hand in,' said Harriet. 'So where does the voting stand now?'

'Its where it was before,' said Peter. 'Oundle was for selling; Trevair was for keeping. There is still stalemate.'

'Unless, of course,' said Harriet, 'the Warden returns to his post and votes in favour of keeping the book.'

'Yes,' said Peter. 'Unless that.'

'Let's pick up another trail,' said Harriet. 'What about the "who wrote the terrible review?" trail. How do we pursue that?'

'With difficulty. Might some of your bohemian friends have a lead on that?' asked Peter. 'Eiluned Price, perhaps? The *TLS* does review books about music, after all.'

'I could give it a try,' said Harriet. 'I could ask Eiluned to round up the old gang, and I'll take them all to tea at the Ritz.'

'I always knew you had a secret life as a temptress,' said Peter.

'Artists are always hungry,' she replied.

13

There is of course also tea at the Dorchester, and tea at the Savoy; but Harriet had no knowledge of either of those. Very lucky authors are occasionally entertained at the Ritz, perhaps by their visiting New York editors, who presumably find the décor familiar after the glories of transatlantic liners. As a result Harriet thought of the Ritz as an appropriate place for a treat. It has a light and airy dining room with a terrace overlooking the park, and numerous gilded nooks where tea can be had in comfortable seclusion. Harriet opted for one such side-table, for the purpose of confidential conversation.

Her guests arrived together: Eiluned Price – looking shorter and stouter than ever, composing being a sedentary occupation – leading Sylvia Marriot and Marjorie Phelps behind her.

Harriet had already ordered the tea, which was being borne towards her by several waiters following behind the guests. It was the full High Tea: mounds of small delicately cut sandwiches, scones and cream topped off with fresh strawberries, three kinds of cake, and a choice of exotic teas, from Assam and Earl Grey to Lapsang Souchong.

'Oh, jolly D!' exclaimed Marjorie. 'You're the girl to know, Harriet!'

'Nothing for nothing,' said Harriet. 'I need some help. But tuck in first, and tell me how you are all doing.'

Eiluned was eager to tell Harriet all about a commission she had just won in open competition to write music for a film about lovers who had met in an internment camp on the Isle of Man. 'Lots of smoosh,' she said happily.

Marjorie had 'sold out to Mammon' as she put it, and was making figurines for a pottery firm in Stoke-on-Trent. 'Pays the rent,' she said, 'and I eat well, and sleep at night. And I have to admit they do a lovely job of making my designs. They have a perfectionist attitude to mass production. It's all very nostalgic, of course. I offered to make them a wartime sequence as souvenirs – Home Guard figures, and night watchmen, and Winston and Monty – but they didn't think they would sell. So it's back to shepherdesses. I managed to sneak in the Scholar Gipsy, I'm glad to say. They got the pastoral, and missed the literary reference.'

'How about you, Sylvia, dear?' asked Harriet. She knew perfectly well how Sylvia was: writing amazingly and living on bread and jam. Harriet had quietly and secretly been subsidising Sylvia – even Peter didn't know this, but since he had insisted on providing her with an income of her own, or at her own disposal rather, she didn't feel the need to tell him. Sylvia came to Denver from time to time for fresh air and a bit of coddling, and Harriet thought she would stop if she thought it was known that she couldn't break even on her own efforts. Naturally Harriet had wondered about her own motives. Gratitude? Sylvia had spoken up for her at her trial. If it was gratitude it was very inconsistent of Harriet who had for years refused to marry Peter, mostly because she was grateful to him. Or perhaps it was that sneaky sense of guilt that very successful authors feel towards others who they know write better than themselves, and go unrewarded – unpaid and unread. Or perhaps she just liked Sylvia; that was the larger part of it.

Sylvia embarked on an account of her latest novel, a strange affair about a sister shipwrecked in life by the misfortunes of her brother. 'Not incest, I promise you,' she said, 'the girl doesn't much like the brother, and finds out that she loves him only when it's too late to save him.'

'I'd like to write the music for that,' said Eiluned. 'When they make it into a film.'

'I should be so lucky,' said Sylvia dryly, 'but thank you, Eiluned.'

Most of the sandwiches and all the cream scones had disappeared. Harriet ordered another plate of scones, and fresh tea.

'Now, how can we help you?' Marjorie asked.

'I need to know how one would find out – discreetly – who wrote a certain review in the *TLS*,' said Harriet.

'Can't be done,' said Eiluned briskly. 'I have a friend who only wanted to say thank you to a reviewer for a lovely notice of her book about Purcell. They wouldn't tell her. They said they would forward a letter to the reviewer.'

'What do you suppose happens, though, in the depths of Printing House Square?' asked Harriet. 'Someone must know, or they wouldn't be able to pay the reviewers. Are they like other papers do you think, who pay by the column inch of material used? Who keeps track?'

I don't know,' said Marjorie, 'but I know a man who might.'

'Can I talk to him?' Harriet asked.

'He's a printer,' said Marjorie. 'Printers are odd fish, and they drink like them, or some of them do. They can work very late; when they finish putting the paper to bed the buses and the tube have stopped running, except the night buses at very infrequent intervals. So they go off to a dive and drink till the transport system starts up again. Manly men, you might say. I do know where to find him, but not till halfway through the morning tomorrow.'

'I'll stay in London overnight, then,' said Harriet.

'What fun, Harriet!' said Marjorie. 'Shall we all go to the flicks together, like old times?'

'We could go to *From Here to Eternity*,' said Eiluned.

'That's where we are all going in the long run,' said Harriet, 'after all.'

John Taylor worked late and rose late. He was having breakfast when Marjorie and Harriet arrived at his digs. His landlady showed them into the dining room in which their man was eating in solitude, and offered to make more coffee. Harriet feared Camp Coffee, but accepted;

Marjorie, a step more canny, declined. Taylor was wearing an open-necked shirt, and no tie. His jacket was hanging over the back of his chair, and he had not yet shaved. He looked like the morning after the night before; but then, Harriet supposed, with working hours like his every morning was the one after the night before.

They introduced themselves, and waited for him to finish his eggs on toast. Harriet, sipping her coffee, regretted it bitterly – bitterly was the appropriate word.

'Well, ladies,' said John Taylor at last, 'what can I do for you?'

'It's a long shot, Mr Taylor,' Harriet said, 'but we were wondering if you might be able to help us identify the author of a certain review in the *TLS*.'

'Risk my job?' he said. 'Why should I?'

'You might be saving lives,' said Harriet. She briefly outlined to him the story that there had been bad feeling about the review, which might lie behind events in the present. He heard her out.

'I can't help you anyway,' he said. 'I'm just a poor lowly compositor; it's the people in the dolls' house you want to talk to.'

'The dolls' house?' said Marjorie.

'The folk upstairs on the subbing floor,' Taylor said. 'Those who send the copy down for us to set up in print. Any of us could teach any of them the rules of grammar and punctuation, leave alone the rules of valid deduction. And not a man of us has a college education. Just an apprenticeship that goes back to Wynkyn de Worde.'

'Yours is a learned trade,' Harriet said. 'I salute you. Unfortunately we can't get to talk to anyone in the dolls' house.'

'So round you come to the back door. I blame you for this, Miss Phelps.' He glared at Marjorie, but he looked grumpy rather than angry. 'See here,' he said, 'the copy comes down from the editorial department. We put it down on the bench beside the linotype machine, and we type it out. Then the lines of type get set in formes; we stroke the surface of the type like it was a girl's cheek to make sure it's smooth and level; then the formes are locked and sent to be inked and proofed. We don't see the proofs; we're working on the next copy on the linotype machines. Get the picture?'

'And if it's the *TLS* the names of the reviewers have been removed before the linotype operator sees the copy?' asked Harriet.

'If it's the *TLS*, yes.'

'So if it were a particularly hostile review, of, shall we say, a book about a medieval manuscript, that wouldn't attract notice on the printing floor?'

John Taylor was suddenly looking directly at Harriet, with sharp attention.

'I do remember noticing one like that, some time back,' he said.

Harriet asked, 'Did you type it out?'

'No; I read it in the forme,' he said.

'But that would be back to front, wouldn't it?' asked Harriet. 'Mirror writing?'

'We can all read stuff in the forme,' he said contemptuously.

'You noticed it because it was so hostile?' Harriet asked.

'I noticed it because I knew the man who wrote the book it was about,' said John Taylor.

'David Outlander? Do you mind telling me how you knew him?'

'I had him under me just after the war,' Taylor said. 'I was his sergeant. Brave young fellow – foolhardy almost. We were defusing some of the hundreds of bombs lying around in London. I was chuffed when I heard he had got a degree. Would have liked one of those myself. So the review got me narked. Anything else you want to know?'

'You were narked; so did you do anything about it?'

'What could I do?'

'You could have found out who wrote it.'

'And how do you imagine I could do that?' he asked.

This is a game of chess, thought Harriet; I need a strong move. 'The *TLS* pays its contributors,' she said. 'And the newspapers that I review for pay by column inch of the copy they print. So someone keeps track; someone measures the column inches and relates that to the person who will get paid.'

'Not me,' he said. 'That's the Father of the Chapel.'

Marjorie interjected, astonished, 'Whoever is the Father of the Chapel?'

'He's the King and Emperor of everything that happens on the printing floor,' said Taylor. 'Even the editor of *The Times* pays him respect. He sticks up for us, and we do what he says. He would never let out information that was supposed to be confidential.'

'But there must be a clerk to whom he gives those column inches,' said Harriet. 'You could have asked him.'

'Strewth, lady, there's no shaking you off, is there?' he said. 'All right; I did go and ask someone in accounts. He owed me a favour, he won a packet on a race tip I gave him. But I'll have you remember my job is on the line if you go blabbing about how you found this out.'

'I don't want to do you harm, John Taylor,' said Harriet. 'I want to put a spoke in the wheel of someone who is malevolently harming others.'

'So you say,' he said.

'Mr Taylor,' Harriet said, 'do you know what happened to David Outlander?'

'He's dead,' said Taylor. 'I heard that.'

'Did you know he hanged himself?'

She saw him flinch. He hadn't known. She followed through. 'We think it might have been because of the review.'

He took his time thinking about that. Then he reached behind himself, and pulled a notebook from his jacket pocket. From the notebook he tore a blank page. Then he groped for a pen, and scribbled something on his piece of paper. He folded it over and handed it to Harriet. 'Here,' he said. 'Now let me be a while. I've to be at work in an hour or so.'

'Thank you, Mr Taylor,' said Harriet. She put the piece of paper in her pocket, and left with Marjorie.

'God, that news upset him,' said Marjorie as they walked towards the underground.

'It naturally would,' said Harriet.

'Is that why you're muted and glum instead of skipping along, saying "mission accomplished"?' asked Marjorie.

Harriet deflected the question. 'How did you get to know him, anyway?' she asked.

'Known him for ever,' said Marjorie. 'He lived on my street in Finchley when we were children. We used to play in his house or mine. He played with my John Bull printing set and I played with his plasticine. We both made a mess of the kitchen table, whichever kitchen table we played on.'

Harriet thanked Marjorie, promised to see her again soon, and took a bus to Paddington to get the next Oxford train. She was indeed feeling morose. She had not played fair with John Taylor. She had not told him that it might be to protect the reviewer that Peter wanted to know who he was. Had he known that, John Taylor would not have divulged what he knew.

The train was past Reading before Harriet got out the piece of paper, and looked to see what she had extracted from John Taylor. It said:

Thomas Ludgvan

Not having trained as a compositor, Harriet took a second or two to decipher it.

And when Peter saw it he said, 'Well, well. So the King over the Water re-enters the scene . . .'

'But why?' Harriet wondered aloud. She was sitting with Peter over a pre-dinner drink, and had just completed a long and detailed account of her London trip, describing to him as carefully as she could the conversation with John Taylor. She had also confessed her unease at not having played entirely fair with that gentleman.

Peter said, 'My dear Harriet, if we played all our cards face up on the table with every person we talked to in the course of an investigation, how could we get along, do you think?'

'Of course you are right, Peter,' Harriet said. 'I suppose I'm just out of practice.'

'Weigh your scruples in the balance against a further possible death,' he said.

'I did,' she declared, 'and I cajoled the information out of him. But I don't have to feel good about it.'

'No, you don't have to do that,' he said. 'In fact getting a blunt conscience is one of the risks we run. Of course, what we do is always in a good cause; but thinking oneself necessarily in the right is a serious moral hazard. But you have, Harriet, advanced matters triumphantly by finding the author of the dreaded review. So don't be too hard on yourself.'

And Harriet repeated, 'But why?'

'Why what, exactly?'

'Why should the Warden launch a savage attack on one of his own fellows?'

'Let's try to think why. I concede at once that it is a very odd thing for someone to have done.'

'Did he want to get rid of Outlander?' said Harriet. 'I mean, by forcing his resignation, rather than by killing him.'

'That supposition just re-poses the question why?' said Peter. 'We haven't heard that Outlander was loathsome. We haven't heard that he spilled the port or ate peas on the wrong side of his fork. And he had quite a phalanx of people who supported him, either for his work or his person.'

'So he did. Well, suppose the Warden wanted to spike the guns of someone who was Outlander's friend and supporter? How would that seem?'

'Rather extreme,' said Peter.

'No, not necessarily. Because the review writer would not have expected to trigger suicide; just resignation. Or perhaps merely the non-renewal of Outlander's junior fellowship.'

'People aren't usually thought responsible for the unforeseeable consequences of their actions,' said Peter.

'Why did the *TLS* let the Warden review a book about an Alfredian manuscript?' said Harriet. 'Did he have the expertise?'

'I believe he is a historian. Or was a historian. And he was clearly a sort of titular owner of the manuscript,' said Peter.

'I think that's what's nagging at the back of my mind as odd; too odd to be true. How could it be that the Warden of this college wants to cast doubts on the authenticity of a college treasure?' said Harriet.

'You read my mind,' said Peter. 'I was just wondering that. Speculate, Harriet.'

'I'm going to take into account the use of that casting vote, always to keep the MS,' said Harriet. 'And I wonder ... Peter, if people here were already casting lustful eyes on the MS, or the value of it rather, to solve college problems, before these controversial votes began to be cast, is it just conceivable that someone could think that casting doubt on its authenticity would make it not worth selling? Would make the college keep it?'

'Well, that's an interesting idea,' said Peter. 'And we both of us concluded that that is what Vearing was doing when he came and told us that the MS was a fake. But in the event quite a lot of people in Oxford sprang to Outlander's defence, and asserted the signal importance of the MS. So the result of the review was effectively to enhance, rather than diminish the importance of the thing. So was that what the Warden hoped to achieve?'

'Either one thing, or its opposite, you mean?' asked Harriet. 'Does either possibility get us anywhere?'

'Didn't someone tell us that Vearing was close to the Warden?' asked Peter. 'Perhaps that gentleman could tell us which way round that reason should run. Worth a try, anyway.'

'We need your help, Vearing,' said Peter. They had decided to visit him in his room rather than summon him. Most people are more at ease on their own ground. Vearing, as befitted his position as a fellow of long standing in the college, had fine rooms with glorious mullioned windows overlooking the gardens. Over one of the windows an oar was hanging horizontal, with a painted inscription on the blade. His study was book-lined – that was natural – but the books were leather-bound sets of antiquarian appearance. If he read anything new, he kept those books in his bedroom. A tapestry hunting scene hung on the end wall; the chairs round the fireplace were deep and comfortable, and the table was Victorian with an elaborate inlay of garlands of roses, interrupted in their circuit of the rim by the books and papers laid out upon it. A gentlemanly aura of a country house had been imported into the college rooms. There was, thought Harriet, looking round, nothing in sight that was newer than that oar, dated 1918.

Peter opened the discussion. 'We have come to talk to you, Vearing, quietly, about the Warden.'

'I don't know where he is, if that's what you mean,' said Vearing at once. And then: 'You'd better sit down.'

They sat; Harriet a little further from the fireplace, leaving Peter and Vearing face to face across the hearthrug.

'Are you worried about him?' asked Peter.

'I am, I am,' said Vearing. 'Of course.'

'We were wondering what you could tell us about the Warden's reaction to Outlander's book,' said Peter.

'Not much,' said Vearing. 'He took a friendly interest of course. We all did.'

'And then that review . . .' said Peter.

'An outrage,' said Vearing. He had begun to look warily at Peter, with equally wary glances at Harriet.

'We understand you are close to the Warden; one of his friends,' said Peter.

'I was, yes. I mean to say, I am,' said Vearing.

'But you don't know where he is?' said Peter.

'No; he did not confide in me so far as to explain himself.'

'But since you are his friend you might be able to guess where he would go – to a family member somewhere, or some favourite retreat at home or abroad?'

'He and I went on a walking tour in the Dolomites once,' said Vearing. 'It was before the war.'

'But you cannot guess where he might have gone now?'

'If I knew I would have told the Vice-Warden. His absence is very inconvenient to us all. Very inconsiderate.'

'What sort of a Warden is he when he is here?' asked Peter. 'What sort of a fist does he make of being captain of the college?'

'He was very good when first elected,' said Vearing. 'Very active and shrewd. But that was a while ago; more than twenty-five years. He is an old man now; we ought to have a fixed age for the Warden to retire, but we don't. Most colleges don't. He hasn't liked the dispute about the MS. Rather at sea about it all, I would say.'

'Could he just have fled?' asked Harriet.

Vearing turned his gaze on her. 'That might be right,' he said. 'That might be just what he has done.'

'We can't ask him,' said Peter. 'So we are asking you.

Bear with us, Vearing. Do you know what he felt about the MS? Not in his public stance about it, but in his secret heart?'

'Historians tend to like documents,' said Vearing. 'In that he was true to type, I would say. It's not his period, of course; he was a sixteenth-century man.'

'So you don't think he would have talked down the MS, as you did the last time you spoke to us, transparently to devalue it and make it seem less desirable to sell it? That wouldn't have been like him?'

Vearing got up abruptly and began to stride about the room. 'He didn't want it sold,' he said. 'And he thought he was losing the battle against the Troutbeck faction to sell it. He was as sick of the whole thing as we all are. But I don't think he would put a pretend opinion in circulation to get his way. He isn't a dirty tricks sort of man. Is that any help?'

Peter was silent.

'Ah, I see what I have just said,' said Vearing. 'I myself tried just such a dirty trick on you. I am condemned out of my own mouth. It's a great mistake, isn't it, Your Grace, to love anything or anyone too much. I used to think the bachelor life of an unmarried don was a bleak and narrow one. But I think of it now as safety.'

'I might offer many terms of description about life in St Severin's,' said Peter quietly. 'But at the present time, the word safety would not be one of them.'

'I feel perfectly safe here,' said Vearing coldly.

'I hope that you are, Vearing,' said Peter, rising to go. Harriet rose too, and walked to the window.

'You have a lovely view of that copper beech here, Mr Vearing,' she said. The bay window she had walked to had a window-seat in it, with ornate cushions piled in it at each end. A book had been slid behind one of the cushions, just a corner showing. The book was no calf-bound antiquity; it had a yellow dust-cover. Of course any book could have a yellow cover; but the detective fiction published by Victor Gollanz was so well known for yellow jackets that the Italian for a detective writer like herself was actually 'Giallista'.

14

'Whoever he is, he is getting increasingly efficient, and increasingly violent,' said Peter. 'Whereas we, I'm afraid, are getting increasingly bogged down and ineffectual.'

'Peter, what would stop this happening, if we cannot?' asked Harriet.

'Strings of murders, do you mean? Sooner or later the murderer makes a mistake, or is caught red-handed. But the body count is already pretty dreadful. No mistake so far.'

'I meant, what would resolve the conflict in the college, and make further homicide pointless?'

The two of them were walking round the Parks in the dusk, before going to supper with Peter's old friend George Mason.

'The sale of the Boethius would conclude the matter. And so, perhaps, might the withdrawal of the offer to the college to buy the land,' said Peter. 'And if this goes any further there won't be enough fellows left to constitute a college.'

'Yes; there will be a group of tutors in traditional subjects and an inviolate library.'

'Colleges teach, Harriet.'

'And do research, Peter.'

'Which ought to come first?' he wondered aloud.

'Both,' said Harriet firmly. 'One doesn't work without the other. To learn from someone who is still alive above the neck, and still learning themselves, is like drinking from a fresh spring, someone said, but "he that learneth from one who learneth not drinketh the foul mantle of the green and standing pond."'

'What about All Souls?' he asked her. 'No undergraduates to be taught there. Does that stymie their research?'

'All Souls is the odd one out,' she said.

'Consider how frightfully odd is,' he began to quote to her, 'The fate of the fellow whose goal's . . .'

'To prove that men are all bodies,' she went on happily.

'While inhabiting rooms at All Souls!' they finished in unison.

'We are incurably frivolous,' she said, penitent. 'We ought to be appalled and sombre at what we are discussing.'

'We need the frivolity,' he said. 'Neither the sun, nor death, can be stared in the face.'

They walked on to their evening with George, during the whole course of which they managed not to talk about St Severin's, nor to quote to each other or to him. George was a gentleman who appreciated their need for a break. He was also very amusing talking about politics, meaning those of Westminster, not of Oxford. So many figures in public life had attended Balliol that there was endless gossip to be had at George's table. The Minister for Housing, for example, one Harold Macmillan, had been a Balliol man. But at Eton, George told them, he had been so sickly he had not been thought to be going to amount to anything. Pneumonia nearly killed him, and he had been withdrawn from school to the care of private tutors before coming up to Oxford.

'If we had a degree in building houses he'd be eminent enough,' George said. 'He's the Right Honourable now, but do you know something? If his firm employs you, or publishes you, you have to address him, and refer to him, as "Mr Harold".'

'I rather like that idea,' said Harriet.

'George,' said Peter, 'you weren't at school with Macmillan, were you?'

'Didn't overlap him, no, Peter. Neither of us did. He's much younger than us. But his illness was in the gossip stream; and of course we get a lot of Etonians at Balliol. Why do you ask?'

'A floating thread, that's all,' said Peter, and they began to talk about cricket.

Harriet sat, sipping her port, and listening to this talk about and in Peter's world. This was just what she had once so feared in prospect – the whole deal entailed in 'marrying above herself'. She would have to admit now that it was often fun, and fascinating, and that she could justifiably pride herself on having made a good fist of it, and above all of having made Peter happy. She would not grudge him a short wallow in nostalgia with an old friend like George. And sure enough, by and by George remembered his manners and turned the talk towards her. He had just read *After the Funeral*, and he wanted Harriet's views on Mrs Christie's technique.

Harriet obliged him. Mrs Christie was an admirable technician, in many ways, but not perhaps brilliant at conveying subtleties or depths of character. Her work was not likely to engage one's sympathy, only the kind of keen curiosity that the element of mystery in a detective story evokes.

'That's just it!' said George. 'I simply hate getting engaged as you call it. I don't like my emotions molested when I'm reading something. I like the challenge to brain-power.'

'I think then you are likely to enjoy Agatha Christie more than something by me, George,' said Harriet. 'I rather hope so.'

'Oh, but now I have met you, Harriet, of course I shall read you,' said George.

'That's such an odd reason for wanting to read a book,' said Harriet. 'If you meet a brilliant doctor, George, do you wish to contract the disease they specialise in?'

'Ah,' said George. 'Pax. I admit defeat. That's quite a sparky girl you've got there, Peter.'

'Thank you, George,' said Harriet, smiling. 'It's quite a while since anyone called me a girl.'

'Don't mind old George,' said Peter, as they walked home, arm-in-arm, past the vacant gaze of the Caesars on the rails of the Sheldonian.

'Of course I don't,' said Harriet. 'I'm not a shrinking violet, Peter.'

'Quoting again,' he said. 'It's getting extreme. Perhaps we should have a quoting box, like a swearing box, and owe it sixpence every time we utter someone else's excellently phrased thought.'

'Sounds ruinous to me,' said Harriet. 'What was that floating thread you mentioned to George?'

'School legends,' Peter said. 'The way people know things about other people they weren't at school with, if they were at the same school at some later time. Stories about ogre schoolmasters, tricks played on matron, naughtiness and bullying and illness . . . things that float down from generation to generation. Do you get it now?'

'You are thinking about Oundle's illness,' said Harriet.

'Exactly. And it would have been rather spectacular if he bled dramatically as a boy, in class, or on the playing field.'

'Dramatic enough for Outlander to have heard about it years later. But Peter, Outlander was dead long before poor Oundle.'

'Yes. But what Outlander knew, someone else he talked to might have known. Think how casually we now know about Macmillan's pneumonia.'

'It's a bit of a job to try to pick up now on gossip that Outlander might have indulged in, several years ago.'

'It's my old obsession, Harriet. It's when you know how you know who. And it might help matters along a bit to know how something might have got known.'

'But Outlander might have talked to anyone or everyone.'

'I know. This rabbit won't run forward; it won't allow us to deduce who knew about Oundle. But it might run backward; when we have someone in the cross-wires it might explain how they knew.'

'But Peter, the murderer didn't have to know about Oundle. Perhaps he didn't. Perhaps we are just determined to connect Oundle's death with one of my stories, one of your cases. And what about Trevair?'

'I grant you, Trevair doesn't fit in either my corpus or yours,' said Peter gloomily.

'He voted to keep the MS; all the other victims have been sellers. And he died by a fatal fall. Neither of us ever encountered or used that.'

'It's all coincidence you think?' asked Peter.

'Trevair is very odd,' said Harriet, pursuing her own train of thought. 'It's like an Agatha Christie murder – a crime could conceivably have been done like that, but you couldn't plan to do it. Nobody could foresee your sudden need to play Bach, or your forgetting to lock up and return the key.'

'I suppose murderers are as impulsive as any other sort of people,' said Peter. 'Maybe more so. But it's time to think intensively about Trevair.'

'I suppose he was Cornish, with that surname?' asked Peter. He and Harriet were talking to Ambleside about Trevair, the following morning.

'Yes, I think he was,' said Ambleside. 'He was a friend of A.L. Rowse, the famous historian, that I do know. But he might have met Rowse through the LSE, rather than through Cornish connections.'

'And he angered some of the fellows here by voting to retain the Boethius, we understand.'

'Yes. Since I happened to know that he was a friend of Rowse, I wasn't surprised; but people assumed that an economist would take a rational rather than a sentimental view. I can't think why,' he added wryly.

'Who was particularly angry with him?' asked Peter.

'Well, Troutbeck of course. But Troutbeck was the cheerleader for the selling party. I don't know of any personal animus against Trevair on Troutbeck's part. But then Trevair hadn't been here long enough to acquire a portfolio of enemies.'

'What a thing to say about the college!' said Peter.

Ambleside winced. 'I have loved this college, Your Grace,' he said. 'It admitted me as a scholarship boy, and has been my home ever since. Before all this uproar it was a gentlemanly, and a gentle community, with only the sort of grouches that are bound to arise when people see too much of each other, and which blow away over a glass of port in a day or two. I am grieved at what is becoming – has become of us. I have applied for a post in the University of Western Australia.'

'As far away as it is possible to get?' asked Harriet.

'No need to go that far, old chap,' said Peter. 'We will get this sorted out, I promise you. Now, is it possible to give us access to Trevair's rooms?'

'I have a set of keys,' said Ambleside.

Trevair's rooms were orderly, and bleak. There were books, of course; there was Adam Smith and Ricardo, and Frank Hahn. One or two books about Cornwall; well, after all, his surname indicated where his roots were. The bookshelves did not seem revelatory . . . a row of photographs displayed a mature couple who were probably his parents; grieving parents now. And perhaps the happy family photo with three children sitting beside a sandcastle, and a mother and father standing behind them, were of Trevair's sister and brother-in-law, nephew and nieces, or brother and sister-in-law ... Trevair's bedroom also contained a bookshelf, and this one was full of detective stories: a good dozen by Agatha Christie, a few Edmund Crispins, some Margery Allinghams, three Harriet Vanes ...

Peter returned to the drawing room and opened the desk drawer. A large brown paper envelope, unsealed, lay in full view. Peter slid the contents out on to the desk. A short paragraph had been written several times on college headed paper.

Dear —
  I am writing to alert you to a difficulty I have been informed of on good authority, in the way of the college making a profit on the proposed purchase of land. The City Council has already drawn up in outline plans to develop the land in question ... this plan is still confidential.

It was all ready. Trevair had only to write in the names of fellows at the top of the letters; they would each look like a handwritten individual approach. Showing someone in advance had cost him his life.

A typewriter on a side-table had a sheet of paper in it, typed halfway down; an article about the price of gold, it seemed to Peter's glance. The top copy was a sheet of onion-skin; an expensive paper that allowed for erasure and clean correction. Peter lifted it to read it right down to the last typed line, just above the keys, and saw that Trevair had been making two carbon copies. Something struck him; he looked at other papers lying on the desk, all in very straight piles, either as Trevair had left them or as the police had left them after searching the room. There were typescripts of several more articles, all with carbon copies sorted out, paper clipped, and lying together in a stack with the top copy.

'Harriet?' asked Peter. 'Do you make carbon copies of your work?'

'Yes, always,' she said.

'Of a novel, of course; I know you do. But what about something transient – a review perhaps?'

'Especially of a review,' she said. 'The top copy might get lost in the post.'

Peter struck himself a mock blow on the head. 'Come,' he said, 'never mind poor Trevair; let's go and hunt the Warden.'

To the Warden's Lodgings they had the easiest possible access: they just had to open the door between their suite of guest rooms and the rest of the house. There was a guardian there, of course, Miss Manciple. She appeared in the corridor as soon as she heard their footsteps.

'Mr Bunter is not here, Your Grace,' she said. 'He has gone shopping.'

Peter decided to face down opposition. 'We aren't after Bunter,' he told her, 'we need access to the Warden's study.'

'I don't think Dr Ludgvan would like that at all,' she said.

'I'm afraid it is necessary,' Peter told her. 'It can be myself and my wife, or it could be the police. Which do you think the Warden would prefer?'

She stood in their path, thinking for a moment. Then she said, 'He will have to be told – when he returns, that is.'

'Miss Manciple,' said Peter gently, 'when do you think he will return?'

She was silent. She had coloured slightly; perhaps she was aware that she had betrayed herself.

'My guess would be,' said Peter, 'that the Warden, if he is safe somewhere, as we all hope he is, will not return until the crisis in college is sorted out. What do you think?'

She stood staring at him.

'I take it that you would like him to return; that you enjoyed looking after his household? If that is the case, let us look at the papers in his study. May we?'

She stood aside. 'Third door on the left,' she said.

Peter walked, with Harriet following, into the Warden's study.

Everything was orderly. A large, book-lined room. A desk with no papers on its tooled leather top. Miss Manciple stood in the doorway.

'I thought the Warden had left in a hurry?' said Peter. 'Is this how he left things?'

'No, I tidied up for him,' said Miss Manciple.

'Did you often do that?' Peter asked.

'Nearly every day,' she said. 'He was an untidy man. Always losing his work. I used to put it away for him.'

'You served as his secretary, as well as his house-keeper?' asked Peter.

'I can type; he cannot,' she said. 'I served as his secretary when there were matters he preferred not to send across to the college office.'

'And you filed his papers for him too?' asked Peter.

'I filed things that he had me type for him here,' she said.

'So you could easily put your hands on the file copy of his review of David Outlander's book?'

Miss Manciple began to shake. She stepped into the room and sat down in a chair.

'How do you know that?' she asked. 'Who told you that?'

'Never mind how, or who,' Peter said. 'We do know.'

'I didn't tell you!' she almost wailed. 'It wasn't me! I promised; and it wasn't me!'

Harriet stepped in. 'No,' she said. 'It wasn't you, and we will stand up for you if the need arises. We found out for ourselves. Don't get upset.'

'Could you find us a copy of that review?' Peter asked again.

'No, sir, I can't,' she said, still shaking. 'I'm sorry, but I can't.'

'Why not?' asked Peter. He was speaking softly to her now. 'Wasn't there a carbon copy?'

'Of course there was,' she said, defensively indignant. 'I always make one.'

'So, why?'

'It was stolen,' she said. 'Someone just walked in here from the guest suite and took it.'

'Now, Miss Manciple,' said Peter, softly now. 'I would like you to be very sure of what you are telling us. Are you perfectly sure that it was not a case of your losing a document from the files; that beyond all doubt someone stole it?'

'Yes, I am sure, sir,' she said. 'I came back from a shopping trip to meet my sister in London, and choose a new dress; and I took that particular day off because the Warden was in Manchester doing a lecture. I got back before him, and the moment I walked in here I could see someone had been here. The filing cabinet was open, and lot of papers strewn about. I looked at once to see if the review copy had been found. And it was gone, and nothing else was gone, just thrown about on the floor and the desk.'

'What did you do?' asked Peter.

'I tidied up, sir, and I waited for the Warden to come in, and I told him. He was very put out, sir. Very put out indeed. But he didn't want to call the police, or question the college servants to see if they knew who had been in here. He didn't want any attention called to it at all.'

'By your account,' said Peter, 'you knew exactly what to look for. You knew exactly what might have been taken.'

'Yes, I did, sir,' she said. And then she began to weep, holding her hands in front of her face to hide her tears. 'Poor Mr Outlander,' she said. 'Poor, poor Mr Outlander.

Such a nice young man. And I never heard of him harming so much as a fly, nor ever quarrelling with anyone.'

'So were you upset by the Warden's review of his book?' asked Harriet.

Miss Manciple took a while to recover herself. 'I asked him about it,' she said. 'And he told me it was all in the day's work for scholars. We have to have thick skins, he said. So I asked him was it what he really thought about Mr Outlander's book. And he said it would put things back in proportion. People were saying silly things about the manuscript and talking it up to be worth a lot more than what he thought it was. And he said if that went on the fellows would be selling the manuscript just for the money. So he was putting things right. Sir, he didn't mean to harm Mr Outlander; really he didn't. He was dreadfully upset about him killing himself; it made him ill for months. He took to walking round his rooms at night, like he was haunting himself.'

Her tears had dried up, but she was looking grey and gaunt. 'And as to what happened next,' she said, 'he said he had brought it upon himself, and it served him right. He said that more than once to me; over and over would be more like it.'

'What did happen next?' asked Peter.

'If I told you I knew, I would be telling more than I know,' she said, 'but I think he was being blackmailed. I think that's what it was.'

'For money?' asked Peter.

'Oh, no, sir, I don't think it was that. I looked after his bills for him, and so I saw his bank statements. There wasn't a penny of extra money going out. It was about that voting they kept having. His vote, and his casting vote. And now he isn't here, and they'll have to do without his vote, either one way or the other.'

'What do you think has happened to him?' Peter asked.

'It's got too much for him, sir, and he's run away,' she said.

'So much for the anonymity of *TLS* reviews,' said Harriet ruefully, when they were back in their own part of the house. 'Usually anger and indignation at hostile reviews rage impotently in the void; but once one knew who the reviewer was . . .'

'The question now,' said Peter, 'is who the blackmailer was; or is, rather. Did we keep that note from the sleeve of the Warden's gown? Someone might know the handwriting.'

'I'm sure we kept it,' said Harriet. 'Bunter will have it safe somewhere. But it's very revealing, Peter. Anyone who saw it and recognised the writing would know who had been threatening the Warden. Are we ready for that?'

'Hmm,' said Peter. 'Is there anyone here we think reliable?'

'Mr Gervase seems cool and rational,' said Harriet.

'And there's Ambleside,' said Peter. 'We'll try them.'

15

But what they actually did next was to drive themselves, Bunter included, through the hours of darkness back to Denver, driving home in aching anxiety and unhappiness. The Dowager Duchess had fallen down some stairs; she had broken three ribs and an ankle. Worse, the doctors thought she might have had a stroke, and that had caused the fall.

She was being treated in hospital at King's Lynn. There was a horrible revived memory of the drive to Denver the night the house had partly burned down. The night that Peter's brother Gerald had died, and he had become a reluctant Duke. Going to an emergency, and not knowing what one will find . . . Peter had to be allowed to drive; it was purgatory to him to be driven, even by Bunter, and he was tense enough already. To Harriet's relief and astonishment, however, he pulled to the side of the road on the way out of Cambridge, and handed over to Bunter. 'I'm not fit to drive,' he said apologetically. 'Too worried.'

'Sit in the back with me, Peter,' Harriet said, 'and hold my hand.' Meekly he did so.

'Feeling my age,' he said.

But it was his mother's age that was on all their minds. The Dowager Duchess was eighty-four, still buzzing around her life like a queen bee, although often tired now, needing a nap after lunch, going early to bed. If she had had a stroke there was no knowing what would survive of her, at such an age. King's Lynn was beyond Denver; they drove straight past the gates of their house, and on up the A10. Long before they arrived there was silence in the car. They had given up making cheerful remarks to each other, and were wrapped in their own inner worlds; three thinking islands, entire of themselves.

Harriet wondered what it would mean for Peter to lose his mother. She couldn't imagine. His mother had always been his champion, always the one who understood him, who saw through the surface. Then Harriet wondered how she herself would feel. The answer was – desolate. Peter's love had secured his mother's love for her, before they had even met; no, that was not quite right – the Duchess had attended Harriet's trial, and had read her books. She had not been surprised by Harriet, but Harriet had been astonished by her. So utterly unlike what she had supposed a duchess to be! So amusing, so affectionate, so zany and practical at once . . .

They pulled up at the hospital entrance; Peter stalked in and asked for his mother.

Staircases, painted cream above, green below. Ward numbers. Signs. Swing doors. They asked the matron where to find the Duchess.

'Do we have a duchess?' she said.

'Honoria Wimsey,' Harriet tried.

'Of course. Last bay on the right.' Peter was instantly on his way there. Harriet asked for news.

'We've set her fracture,' the matron said. 'And we're keeping her in because we understand she has never had a fall before, and the doctors want to observe her for a few days to see if there are signs that she has had a stroke.'

'What do you think?' Harriet asked.

'I don't think so, but it's best to be sure,' the matron said.

Harriet walked down the ward to the Duchess's bed. Beside the bed on one side sat Franklin, hollow-cyed, white-faced, clearly utterly exhausted. The woman was nearly as old as her mistress, and this must have been dreadful for her, thought Harriet. On the other side of the bed Peter was now sitting, holding his mother's hand. She appeared to be asleep. A nurse brought a third chair, and Harriet sat down. The Duchess had a dramatic black eye, which gave her a piratical appearance, and the lump in the blankets indicated a cast also on her left leg. Harriet thought she remembered her father saying that old bones took longer to heal.

'Don't go, Mama,' Peter said softly.

An hour passed, and then Helen appeared. 'Oh, if you are here, I needn't have come,' she said to Peter. Her unmoderated voice woke the patient.

'Oh, lordy, Peter,' she said, 'I was just dreaming I was holding your hand, and here you are! And Harriet too.

How lovely. Did you say don't go, dear? Soon, perhaps, but not now. Have they offered you a cup of tea?'

Helen said, 'I'll be off, then, and leave it to you, Peter.'

Harriet said, 'Could you drive Franklin home, Helen? She needs to rest.'

Helen blinked. It was not a welcome request, but she acceded to it. Harriet began to persuade Franklin, who was trying to refuse, when the Duchess said, 'Go home and get some sleep, Franklin. Don't be a silly goose.'

'I'd rather stay, m'am, if you don't mind,' said Franklin.

'I do mind,' said the Duchess. 'I'll be home later today, and I need you on your feet to look after me there. Off you go, there's a good girl.'

'What makes you think you'll be home today, Mama?' said Peter, when Helen had swept Franklin away with her.

'I haven't had a stroke, Peter,' the Duchess said. 'I can remember perfectly why I fell; I didn't black out at all, I just tripped over the loose sole on my old slipper. And I reached out for the top of the banister rail to steady myself, and it was just a bit too far to reach, so I toppled over right at the top of the stairs. And down them a bit. Just a fall. Nothing to worry about.'

Peter laughed. 'You should see yourself, Mama,' he said. 'All right; I'll go and talk to the doctor about you.'

He came back looking more cheerful. 'I can get you sprung from here tomorrow,' he told his mother. 'Shall I get you into a private room for tonight?'

'Oh, don't do that, Peter,' the Duchess said. 'It would be lonely all by myself. And they are so kind here. And there's a lovely woman in the bed opposite who has been telling me all about her hens and her grandchildren. She has little ones, called Bantams, and they lay delicious eggs – the hens, I mean, not the grandchildren. The hens hide the eggs on her farm, and the grandchildren are good at finding them. She might be hurt if she thought I had asked to be moved.'

'Just as you like, Mama,' Peter said. 'We'll go and find some lunch, and come back later.'

Harriet was glad to hear lunch mentioned; the moment anxiety abated, she realised she was very hungry.

The appropriately named Duke's Head supplied lunch, and would provide a bed for the night. Since visiting was allowed only between five and seven in the afternoon – an exception had been made for the first visit after an emergency, and that exception was no longer judged necessary – they had an afternoon to spend.

'Let's go and look at Castle Acre,' Peter suggested.

'What's there?' Harriet asked.

'The remains of a motte and bailey castle, and the remains of a grand and important priory,' Peter said.

'Let's go,' said Harriet.

Castle Acre was like one of those Batsford books, Harriet thought, about the history of England. One end a Norman castle, the other end a ruined priory; from Conquest to Reformation it illustrated the history of England. In between was a street of modest houses, mixed in age and style. Some pretty front gardens, some front doors giving straight on to the street.

The River Nar, only a stream really, made its southern boundary. There was a parish church with a grand

Perpendicular tower. The Wimseys entered. They found features to admire: a fine painted rood screen, an odd tall font cover and some misericords. A brass lectern supported an open copy of the Bible. Peter stepped up to the lectern, and began to read:

Man, that is born of a woman, hath but a short time to live, and is full of misery. He cometh up, and is cut down, like a flower; he fleeth as it were a shadow, and never continueth in one stay. In the midst of life we are in death: of whom may we seek for succour, but of thee, O Lord, who for our sins art justly displeased?

'You read like a believer, Peter,' said Harriet quietly.

Peter left the lectern and came to sit beside Harriet in the pew. 'Most of the time,' he said to her, 'I am not that. I am a lover of the fine words and the fine art and the lovely architecture of the Church by law established. But as to belief: no. It seems to me unchallengeably false, or only metaphorically true. Only sometimes, on some few days, it flips over, and I think instead that it is atheism that is unchallengeably false; a shallow adolescent sort of thing that I should be ashamed of not having grown out of. This is such a day. That's all. Normal service will be resumed as soon as possible.'

'Has it flipped, as you put it, because you thought your mother was dying?'

'That must be it, mustn't it?' he said, smiling foolishly at her. 'But also . . .' the sentence died on his lips.

'Also?' she prompted him.

He escaped into frivolity. 'Doctor, doctor, shall I die? Yes, said the doctor, and so shall I.'

Harriet was not to be distracted. 'You must hope to have to face your mother's death, Peter,' she said, 'sooner or later – let's hope it's later, much later – because the alternative is that she has to face yours.'

'It's the enormity of it; of death, I mean. I'm not thinking only of Mother, but of those deaths in Oxford. To take a life for reasons such as we suspect is appallingly frivolous, it's sacrilegious. To make light of death; to secure it as a move in a game, to treat it with less than fear and reverence as the common fate of all.'

'We will find and stop him,' Harriet said. 'I know we will.'

'As in "I know that my Redeemer liveth?"' he asked her. 'Shouldn't you be content to simply hope that we will find the murderer?'

She mused on that as they left the church, and walked out through the graveyard.

Perhaps to claim to know what was not yet accomplished was too bold; merely to hope, since so many hopes were ill-founded seemed not strong enough. There wasn't a word to express the kind of faith in Peter that she felt.

'We'll be late back for the evening visiting time if we don't get a move on, Peter,' she said.

It took so long to discharge the Duchess from hospital the following morning that by the time they got her safely home to Denver, limping on brand-new crutches, and settled in under Franklin's impeccable but over-anxious care, there was no prospect of getting back to Oxford that day. Peter had solved the problem of the stairs up to his mother's part of the house by swinging her off her feet and her crutches, and carrying her upstairs as if he were carrying a child. Harriet, watching him, felt proud of him. He had never looked like a strong man, but at need . . .

The Denver house had taken on the strange unfamiliarity of the very familiar briefly abandoned. There were mounds of letters waiting on Harriet's desk. And on Peter's, no doubt. They had not been away long – no more than a fortnight in Oxford – but resuming life in Denver was like putting on spring clothes that one has not worn all winter, or a swimsuit not yet completely dry.

Harriet knew they must return to Oxford after breakfast next day, and that time was short to deal with all these chores. But she couldn't settle to them. In the time they had been accumulating they had acquired a different feel altogether; perspectives had shifted, and all this felt trivial. She would get the things done, but not feel the usual satisfaction in doing them. She laid her pen down on her desk, walked to the window and stood looking over the garden, to consider this. Bredon Hall was a beautiful building; older than many Oxford college glories, and just as beautiful as many. The garden she looked out over had all been redesigned after the fire, and she had herself taken satisfaction in doing that job. The strange sundial, a gift to them from an Indian friend, was in its way a masterpiece. But the sense of unease persisted. What exactly, Harriet quizzed herself, was wrong with home?

The question once posed, the answer was unavoidable. Bredon Hall was private. Its lovely rooms and wide grounds were for Peter and his family only. A greatly reduced group of servants and gardeners looked after it all, and, she hoped, enjoyed working there. Peter regarded them all as family and without pause for thought looked after any of them who were in need, and all of them when they retired. He remembered their names, and their children's names to the third and the fourth generation. Some of them felt safe enough even to cheek her, by way of a tease. But how many were they? She counted eleven, including Bunter. A small fraction of the community of an Oxford college, even a small one.

And it wasn't a matter of numbers only; there was also a question of purpose. Colleges pursued learning; whereas the purpose of Bredon Hall was to keep itself going long enough to hand the whole thing over to her elder son, Bredon. A private purpose. Not a selfish one; Peter would rather not, and Bredon would rather not . . . but they would take it to be their duty to preserve what they had. Thinking about that she realised that although her own father had left her nearly nothing in cash – he had not been ruthless enough to charge his poorer patients, of whom therefore he had had many – what he had left her was the ambition to get to Oxford. From him she had inherited the life of the mind. It had never for a moment crossed his mind that a daughter was less worth educating than a son.

'I'm moon-gathering,' Harriet told herself crossly. But before settling back to her letters and bills she picked up the phone to Bredon's housemaster, to find out how his university entrance was going. She hadn't much idea how clever her son would seem if judged in a class of his contemporaries; he certainly wasn't as brainy as Bunter's son. And these days there was competition for those cherished Oxford places from a cohort of clever grammar-school boys.

It was all under control, she was told. Chances? Of Oxford or Cambridge, fifty-fifty. Of Balliol, well, sometimes the boys surprise us . . .

Peter was not nervous about driving back to Oxford. So Bunter sat in the back, and they made extraordinarily good time, leaving after breakfast, and arriving in time for tea.

As they drove up Parks Road, Peter wondered if they would see a flag at half-mast over the gate, but flag was there none. It seemed from the porter's casual greeting that nothing had happened in Oxford during their absence. They both felt a faint sense of surprise, as one might if finding everything just the same after an absence of several years.

As they crossed the quad, they encountered Gervase. 'Nice little break?' he said. 'No new bodies for you, I'm afraid.'

'It's a relief, of course,' said Peter to Harriet. 'A pause for thought in the Dance of Death.'

Perversely their college rooms displayed the same prickly reluctance to be taken for granted as their great house at Dukes Denver had done, and leaving Bunter to smooth things over and resume the daily round, they took themselves off for a walk. Up Walton Street where the cinema offered a film called *The Robe*, over the Aristotle Bridge, past the fish and chip shop called Aristotle's Plaice and out on to Port Meadow. Wide and watery, it stretched out all the way to Godstow, where they ate a pub supper. It would have been a long walk home, but as they crossed back over the canal on their way back they stopped to admire a narrowboat. The boat was carrying coal, but the cabin was beautifully decorated with roses and castles. The name Friendship adorned the cabin side, in the sort of sign-writing you see on fairgrounds. A painted water can stood on the cabin roof, and the upswept tiller was decorated with elaborately knotted cord. It glided beneath them in silence, being pulled by a mule on the towpath.

'Come far?' Peter called to the boatee as his boat glided beneath the bridge.

'Brum,' said the man.

'Nice boat,' Peter offered. 'Is it hard to steer?'

'Want to try?' the boatee said. He steered into the bank to let Peter and Harriet jump on. They joined him on the tiny back deck, and he swung himself up on to the cabin roof, with his legs dangling through the hatch, to make room for them. 'Push her out,' was the only instruction he gave Peter. It took Peter a few minutes to get the hang of it. The weight of the towrope and the tug of the mule tended to pull the boat into the bank, unless the tiller was set to steer against it. The length of the boat pivoted on the attachment point of the rope, on a painted post some way down, standing in the mounds of coal. Soon they were gliding down mid-channel, in almost complete silence, apart from the occasional sound of the ripples down the side of the boat.

'How far can we go?' asked Peter, in a while.

'Not all the way no more,' the boatee said. 'They've filled in the basin at the end to make another college. Him what makes cars done it. Jordan's Yard in Jericho is the end now.'

'Can we ride that far with you?' asked Peter.

'Please yourself,' said the boatee. Then he disappeared into his cabin, and popped up again a moment later with a piece of paper in his hand. He offered it to Harriet. 'What does that say?' he asked her.

She looked at it in surprise. It said in large clear capital letters:

BRITISH WATERWAYS BOARD.
CLOSURE NOTICE.
CROPREDY LOCK
WILL BE CLOSED FOR REPAIRS.
MAY 23RD TO MAY 28TH.

Harriet read it to him, and he nodded. 'Nothing to do with me, then,' he said. 'I'll be back through Cropredy before then.'

Jordan's Yard came slowly into sight ahead of them. Peter stepped lightly on shore with the stern rope in his hand, and helped tie up. Harriet wondered if one offered to pay for the ride, but Peter didn't offer. He put half-a-crown on the cabin hatch and, having thanked the boatee, he said, 'Drink our health tonight, will you?'

The man nodded, and they went on their way.

'A wordless man,' Harriet said, as they walked through Jericho. The streetlights were just coming on, golden glows in a deep violet sky.

'For an awful moment I thought you might laugh,' Peter said.

'Me? Laugh? When?' she said.

'When he gave you a notice in thirty point sans serif to read to him.'

'No, I realised in time. It must be scary, Peter, really not knowing what signs and warnings say.'

'They are nomads, along with their children,' said Peter. 'No fixed abode; no way of going to school.'

'There's a school for their children at Brentford, I think,' said Harriet. 'I seem to remember donating some signed books to one of their fund-raising efforts.'

'Not all the boats ran down to London, I think,' said Peter. 'Our chap was bringing coal for Oxford fireplaces. He may never have been to Brentford in his life.'

They walked on.

Halfway along the Broad Peter said, 'You know, Harriet, I think we too may be failing to read the signs. Signs written in large clear letters plain to see, but we are somehow not getting the message.'

16

Mr Gervase said, 'No, I don't know that handwriting. I can't help you, but I can pour you a drink. What will you have?'

Over his pleasant sherry he asked, 'To whom was this monitory message addressed, may I ask?'

Peter and Harriet exchanged glances. 'To the Warden,' Peter said.

'Was it a threat of some kind?' Gervase asked.

'It reads like one, don't you think?' said Peter.

'Was that why the poor old duffer skedaddled?'

'Perhaps,' said Peter diplomatically. He considered Mr Gervase. A suave person, completely at his ease.

'The troubles of the college do not, perhaps, cut you to the quick, Mr Gervase,' he said.

'Was that a bow drawn at a venture, Your Grace?' Gervase replied. 'Speaking of bows, I have more than one string to mine. My fellowship here is not the only position open to me. Whereas some of the other fellows will be on the dole if they lose their places here. Naturally they are agitated.'

'What are these other resources that you have and others lack?' asked Peter.

'My books,' said Gervase. 'I have written diligently ever since the publication of my B.Litt. thesis. The result is that I now regard teaching as a sideline. Also my books have made me well-known outside Oxford. I can get a fellowship somewhere else by raising a finger. But those of my colleagues who have concentrated on teaching and neglected to publish would be left high and dry if the college could no longer employ them. Nobody has heard of them, except their own students of course, and the name of St Severin's on a CV is not going to be an advantage, given the reputation the college already has for internal warfare.'

'So the state of the college finances doesn't bother you?' asked Peter.

'Not personally, no. Of course I am fond of the place . . .'

'You referred to the Warden as a poor old duffer,' said Harriet. 'We have neither of us ever met him. Why did you call him that?'

Gervase seemed at last a little wary. 'He has presided over the decline of the college's wealth,' he said. 'No doubt a line of bursars and advisers have brought the problem about but then the Warden had appointed, or had a hand in appointing, those bursars and advisers. And latterly he had found it difficult to make up his mind about anything. He kept trying rather transparent cunning tricks to get round problems. He was past it, effectively.' With that he glanced at his watch.

Taking the hint, Peter and Harriet rose to go.

'You are sure you don't recognise that handwriting? It doesn't remind you of anyone's that you know?' Harriet asked him.

'No. We don't spend much time writing notes to each other,' Gervase said. 'Try the college office. The secretaries type things out for people.'

'It's not fair to hold ambition against people,' said Harriet, about Gervase. 'How can people spend their whole lives at something without wanting to succeed in it?'

'You should have said, "without wanting advancement in it",' said Peter, 'and then it's what counts as advancement.'

'He isn't the perfect Clerk of Oxenford, I'll grant you that,' said Harriet.

'And gladly wold he lerne and gladly teche? That one?' said Peter. 'Surely there are some like that around. Even in St Severin's.'

'Like who?' Harriet wondered aloud.

'I was told that Enistead was like that,' said Peter. 'And what do you say to Vearing? And Ambleside? What about him?'

'I never met Enistead, and Vearing gives me the creeps,' said Harriet. 'I'll settle for Ambleside.'

'And he's leaving for Australia,' Peter reminded her. 'There's a rather painful contrast with your college, Harriet, with Shrewsbury. They held together admirably through a crisis. Just a little bitching; a few sharp words, but basically loyalty to the college and each other. But

Severin's is beginning to smell of desertion. *Sauve qui peut*, and the devil take the hindmost.'

'Like proverbial rats, you mean? That isn't fair, Peter. Shrewsbury was facing nastiness writ large, but not murdered bodies right and left, only the fear of murder. Whereas the fellows here have both the fear and the fact of it to face. Moreover,' she continued, 'you've seen a lot of murder. I wonder if you realise how appalling it is for ordinary people to encounter it? How shattering it is?'

'I accept rebuke, Domina,' he said. 'You may chastise me.'

'I shall share your punishment,' she said, 'which will be to dine at High Table tonight, and keep the home flag flying.'

'My wife is a wise woman,' said Peter to nobody in particular. 'Let's ask Ambleside for a drink before dinner, and show him the handwriting in his turn.'

'Looks a bit like Troutbeck, to me,' said Ambleside. 'But not quite. The Y isn't right; and I have never seen him use brown ink. Where does this come from?'

When Peter made no answer he said, 'To whom was it addressed? Do we know that?'

'To the Warden,' said Peter.

'Is it a threat?' asked Ambleside.

'What would you say?' Peter countered.

'Well, it doesn't sound friendly,' said Ambleside. 'Are you telling me that someone was threatening the Warden?'

'We might know if we knew who wrote this,' said Peter.

'If I had to guess, I'd say Troutbeck,' said Ambleside.

'Shall we ask him?' Peter wondered. 'Just shove it in front of him and say, "Is this your writing?"'

'If one wants to know something,' said Ambleside, 'it's an obvious move just to ask.'

'Shall we try that, Harriet, do you think?' asked Peter, when Ambleside had left them.

'Might we trigger trouble, Peter? If Troutbeck is a villain, perhaps even a murderer, what would he do if he thought we suspected him?'

'What could he do?' asked Peter. 'His best defence would be to keep up the pretence of virtue.'

'He could flee; he could cover his tracks,' said Harriet. 'And after all, Peter, that threatening note might have been a prequel to the Warden's death; we don't know the Warden is alive; we do know there is a murderer at work here.'

'Yes, we do,' said Peter. 'A strange and whimsical one, to be sure, but certainly a murderer whatever Charles may think.'

'Charles is a very experienced policeman, Peter. We ought to pay attention to what he thinks.'

'How right you are,' said Peter. 'Let's walk our thoughts in Charles's footsteps and see things his way for a while.'

'We start with two assaults, on Mr Cloudie, and Mr Dancy,' said Harriet. 'Both of them wishing to sell the MS. Both assaults are unsuccessful.'

'And if we are Charles we will find both dubious,' said Peter. 'The bell-tower one could have been an accident, and the midnight attacker with a syringe could have been a nightmare.'

'Indeed. So why are we convinced they were the work of a would-be murderer?'

'Because of the methods of attack,' said Peter, 'both being in books written by you.'

'Then the death of Enistead. I liked the sound of him. I should like to have met him.'

'Charles thinks that serial murderers have a consistent pattern of attack. A favourite method that they don't vary. But we think this murderer has a favourite source of methods. An idea that is backed up by the death of Mr Oundle; haemophilia has also figured in a book of yours.'

'It is presumably the murderer who buys his books in Heffers,' said Harriet. 'Shall we cajole Dick Fox into coming across here and having a look around?'

'That would certainly alert the murderer, Harriet.'

'Would it? Couldn't I have a friend who is a book-seller, and invite him to dinner? I could ask that nice lady from Hatchard's as well, as a sort of cover.'

'Let's stick with Charles for a bit longer,' said Peter. 'To be convinced he needs both an obsessively repeated method of murder, and a down-to-earth squalid motive. We offer him an improbable variety of means of attack, and a motive to do with scholarship . . .'

'Hold it there a minute, Peter,' said Harriet. 'Are we a pair of ivory tower dreamers ourselves? What about the money? We aren't paying enough attention to the money.'

'Well, this particular money would not be in the pockets of any single person,' Peter reminded her. 'Do you think someone might murder for the sake of the college solvency? Charles would find that at least as hard to swallow as the idea of murder for the love of learning.'

'What about you, Peter?' Harriet asked. 'Haven't I heard you say that you think motive is a distraction? You concentrate on how the deed was done. I know I have heard you say "when you know how you know who."'

Peter looked a little sheepish. 'Well, the how is staring us in the face in each of these deaths,' he said. 'No fun to be had there. My thoughts stray to why. When we know why . . . and of course, there's one death right out of line. Trevair is the only casualty of a manner of death not suggested in your work. And he is also the only one to die who had voted to keep the MS.'

'Are we looking for two murderers?' asked Harriet.

'Charles would regard that as right off the scale of probability,' said Peter. 'But yes, I think we are. Come, my dear, we will be late for our penitential dinner.'

Hall dinner was poorly attended, at least at High Table. The undergraduates in the body of the Hall were as numerous and rowdy as ever. The conversation was muted. Troutbeck was there, talking to Mr Cloudie, who had summoned up the courage to reappear at the High Table, about the quality of the new applicants for college places, and the search for new appointments to replace Trevair and Oundle.

When they rose at the end of the meal, and filed out into the quad, Peter stopped Troutbeck.

'A word with you, Troutbeck,' he said. They were standing under one of the ornate Victorian lamps that lit the path between the Hall and the Senior Common Room. 'Do you know anything about this?' Peter asked, and showed Troutbeck the scrap of paper.

Troutbeck looked at it.

'Do you know whose handwriting it is, Troutbeck?' Peter asked.

'Yes. It's mine,' said Troutbeck. 'What is it? I don't remember writing it.'

'Found in the sleeve of the Warden's gown,' said Peter. 'Surely you must remember writing it.'

'Well, it might have been just before one of the votes,' said Troutbeck. 'I was putting pressure on him to vote for the sale, rather than pussyfooting about trying to placate both parties. I expect I wrote it before the last vote we took. Yes; I'm sure that was it.'

'It is unsigned, Troutbeck. You gave it to him by hand?'

'Yes, I would have done.'

'You were not threatening him? The note has a menacing tone.'

'Threatening? What could I threaten him with?' said Troutbeck. 'The worst I could threaten would have been an appeal to you. Now if you will excuse me . . .'

A cool head, and a hot temper, Peter thought. An interesting combination.

In the archway below their window a shadowy figure was waiting for them.

'Who's that?' Peter called.

'It's only me, sir,' was the answer. The slight, willowy figure of Jackson stepped into the light of the quad. 'You wanted to talk to me,' Jackson said. 'Is it too late?'

'Not at all,' Peter said. 'Just the right time for a little nightcap.'

'Oh, I can't drink,' said Jackson. 'It breaks my concentration.'

'A mug of cocoa, then?' suggested Harriet. They both saw the boy's face light up.

Once Jackson was settled in a chair in the drawing room, Harriet studied him. Painfully thin, deep shadows below the eyes, slightly trembling hands . . .

'You've been working too hard,' she said in a tone as accusing as if charging him with a crime. 'And when did you last have a good meal?'

'I can't stop for food,' Jackson said. 'Really I can't. I'm behind with revision already.'

Harriet put her head round the door and called for Bunter. 'What do we have handy to eat?' she asked him.

Bunter offered to warm up the supper that he would have served to them had they not decided to eat in Hall.

'What I wanted to ask you,' said Peter to Jackson, 'is what you thought of Outlander's book about the Boethius. I take it that you read it?'

'Yes, of course. It's my bible,' said Jackson.

'But your B.Litt. thesis was going to cover the same ground as that book,' said Peter. 'Have I got that right?'

Jackson looked uneasy. 'There's a bit more to say,' he parried.

'I suppose you also read the notorious *TLS* review?'

'I heard about it,' said Jackson cautiously.

'But since you say Outlander is your bible, you don't agree with the review?'

Jackson was looking more and more unhappy. 'Well, Outlander's book isn't perfect,' he said. 'He got a bit carried away.'

'You seemed rather carried away yourself last time we spoke,' said Peter.

Jackson stared at Peter, then at Harriet, then back again. He looked cornered. Then he looked at the floor. 'I think he's basically right about the MS,' he said. 'But he didn't look hard enough. He missed some stuff. I was going to improve on him a little.'

'Cheer up,' said Peter. 'You can still do whatever it is you were going to do.'

'You can stop them selling the MS?' said Jackson. 'But I'm going to fail my finals. Not get a first, I mean. I can't do a second degree without a grant.'

'You can't improve your chances by failing to eat, either,' said Harriet.

At this point Bunter entered, holding aloft on one hand, posh waiter-style, a laden tray. With the other hand he flicked open a white tablecloth, and spread it on the sofa table near Jackson's chair. Then he put down the tray, revealing a generous plate of chicken Marengo, a cheeseboard and an apple pie. He set out the cutlery, and withdrew.

'Tuck in,' said Peter.

And Jackson did. He ate as if it were the first and last meal of his life.

Shortly, Bunter reappeared and said, 'More chicken, sir?'

Jackson took more chicken. Then he moved on to the apple pie, and, one large slice at a time, consumed it all.

How the young can eat! thought Harriet. Her own boys could do the same. And if this chap had been skipping lunch and dinner . . .

'You said Outlander had missed some stuff?' said Peter, when Jackson had slowed down a bit. 'What stuff?'

'You see, if I tell people and it gets around,' Jackson said, 'if everybody goes and looks at it, then it loses its value in my thesis. It won't be my discovery, just something people know.'

'I do see that,' said Peter. 'I am inviting you to trust us.'

Jackson gave Peter a long meditative stare. He had lost the famished look, but was looking at the cheeseboard through the corner of his eye.

'Promise?' he asked.

'Cross my heart and hope to die,' said Peter.

'Well, Outlander didn't look closely enough at the colour of the inks,' Jackson said, taking the plunge. 'He seemed to think that Alfred might have made the entire gloss. But there's a brownish ink in which the Latin text is written; then there's a bluish-black ink in which the gloss is written; then there are a few words here and there in a blacker ink. Those words are not so elegantly written, and the lines are not quite straight.'

'What do you make of your observation?' Peter asked.

'I thought perhaps the text was glossed for Alfred by his scribes, but that when he was using it, he made some jottings in his own hand, and the different ink would be the one he used.'

'Apart from you and now us,' Peter said, 'is there anyone else who knows about your theory?'

'Miss Griffiths knows,' said Jackson.

'And what does she think of it?'

'She would like some analysis of the different inks. To back me up. But I can't see how I could do that without scraping the words on the page to get a sample of inks for analysis. And I'm not going to be allowed to do that; it would damage the pages. I'm supposed not to be thinking about this till after my finals.'

Bunter, standing in the door, cleared his throat.

'Yes, Bunter?' said Peter.

'I was wondering, my lord, if the dubious ink was darker or lighter than the main text?'

'Oh, it's darker,' said Jackson. 'But only ever so little.'

'So long as what makes it different is that it is darker, my lord,' said Bunter, 'then photography might help.'

'How would it help?' asked Peter. 'Explain yourself, Bunter.'

'At the print-making stage, my lord,' said Bunter, 'one rocks the print in the tray of developer, and the darkest part of the print becomes visible first. I think it possible that the sensitivity of the printing paper might be greater than that of the human eye.'

'It's worth a try, don't you think, Jackson?' said Peter.

But Jackson did not reply; he had fallen asleep where he sat.

Peter and Bunter between them lifted him out of his chair, and laid him on the sofa. Bunter brought a blanket, and covered him to the chin. Then the three of them tiptoed away to their own more comfortable but less urgently needed beds.

In the morning their bird had flown. The blanket Jackson had slept under was neatly folded, and a note saying, 'Thank you' was laid on it. The Warden's door to the quadrangle was still bolted on the inside; Jackson had let himself out through the garden door.

'I wonder how many people know about that door?' said Peter.

17

'Can we play by ourselves, Bunter?' Peter asked. 'Would you have to run back to Denver, or can we obtain the necessaries in Oxford?'

'There is a college photographic society, my lord, with a simple darkroom in one of the attics. That would have all that we need.'

'How do you know that, Bunter?' Peter asked.

'A member of that society spotted me using the Leica IIIf which your lordship generously gave me for Christmas,' said Bunter, 'and got into conversation with me. I have been invited to speak to the society on the subject of Leica cameras next week, my lord.'

'Have you indeed? Did you accept?'

'I did, my lord. As also an invitation to speak to the college Wine Society, on the subject of port.'

'I perceive, Bunter,' said Peter peevishly, 'that you do not expect me to solve the college mysteries in the next day or two.'

'I did consider that possibility, my lord,' said Bunter. 'But then I recalled that I have not had a holiday as such since 1949, and I supposed that you would not grudge me two days' absence in Oxford to fulfil these commitments.'

'You suppose right,' said Peter, abashed. 'So what next?'

'I must inspect the darkroom,' said Bunter.

'Can I come too?' asked Peter.

'If you wish,' said Bunter.

Leaving Harriet to her own devices, her two menfolk collected a key from the porter, and went in search of the darkroom.

It was up a lot of stairs, in the oldest part of the college, and through a door labelled in large red letters: DO NOT ENTER WITHOUT WARNING. Bunter knocked and waited; then they entered a room crouching under the sloping eaves. There was a sink, a bench, a darkroom light with a deep orange shade, a washing line with tiny pegs on it for hanging prints to dry, a shelf of chemicals, and some stained plastic trays in various colours and sizes.

Unfortunately there were also some chinks of light showing through the window blind, and creating splashes of sunlight on the opposite wall.

'Doesn't that make the room useless?' asked Peter. The chinks of light seemed brighter and brighter as their eyes adjusted to the general gloom.

'I expect these young tyros manage to make prints of their snapshots,' said Bunter disapprovingly, 'but it will have to be fixed for the experiment we wish to try.'

'How can it be fixed?' Peter asked.

'Something pinned over the window. I'll see what I can find,' said Bunter.

'Meet me in the library,' said Peter. 'I'll make sure the book is ready for you to photograph when you've fixed the light problem.'

Bunter clattered down the stairs ahead of him, and Peter followed at leisure, lost in thought.

As he had supposed he would, he found Jackson head down over his revising, in a corner of the library. He had regained the haggard expression that had been briefly lifted last night; could he be hungry again? At Peter's insistence he suspended his work long enough to find a page with one of the supposed jottings in different ink on it. And the librarian arranged the book open on the best lit desk, with its pages held open by weighted ribbons.

Long before Bunter appeared with his Leica Jackson had gone back to his work.

'Fixed?' Peter asked.

'All fixed now,' Bunter told him.

Bunter was a careful photographer. Peter sat on a library chair, and watched him work. He used a tripod and a light-meter, measuring the light at the camera position, and then the incident light on the manuscript page. He took a tape measure from his pocket and measured the distance required to focus the camera.

'You used not to go to such trouble, Bunter,' Peter said.

'I have learned a lot from my wife,' Bunter told him.

'As have I from mine,' said Peter.

At last Bunter was satisfied, and took several exposures. Peter, listening to the silky click of the shutter, counted twenty. Then without a word spoken, Bunter directed the camera at Jackson, sitting in a window bay, leaning over his work, his head aureoled in sunlight. Two more exposures.

Before the MS was put away Peter took a look at the page Jackson had chosen. There was only one short sentence that was out of line with the steady march of the gloss over the Latin words. Peter would not himself have seen any difference in the colour of the ink in which it was written.

'Perhaps, my lord, you would like to give me a couple of hours to develop and wash the film, and allow it to dry,' said Bunter.

Peter returned to sit in his room, and opened the window to let in the sweet warm air.

Once again voices rose to him from people walking through the archway beneath him. Idle chatter in broken phrases ... He began to read, and not listen. Then suddenly he heard a voice speaking urgently.

'Why is Troutbeck so agitated?' a speaker asked. 'You would think it was his own money at stake ...'

'That's a good question,' Peter told himself, looking out of the window in time to see two unidentifiable backs receding across the quad. 'Follow the money. That's what Freddy would say.' And the money led to thoughts of Troutbeck.

Having allowed Bunter due time, and knocked on the darkroom door before entering, Peter stepped into total blackness.

'As black as hell, as dark as night, Bunter,' he said into the void. Bunter threw a switch, and the room was bathed in a very dim orange-red light. There was a strong smell of chemicals, but no chinks of daylight. 'How did you fix the window?' Peter asked.

'I asked around,' Bunter said, 'and it turned out that Miss Manciple had kept all the blackout curtains from the Warden's house. In case they should be needed again, she said.'

'God forfend!' said Peter. 'Although he isn't as a rule to be relied upon to forfend, any more than he is to forbid. Now what, Bunter?'

'I am about to make a print, my lord,' said Bunter.

As Peter's eyes got used to the gloom he saw that the enlarger, which had been covered with a cloth, was now ready. Beside it on the bench was a row of three dishes, containing liquids. Bunter switched on the enlarger, and a negative picture of the photographed page appeared on the base plate. There was some fiddling about, while Bunter centred a paper frame to contain the projected picture, raised the enlarger head a little, and focused the enlarging lens.

Then he switched off the enlarger, placed a sheet of printing paper in the frame, and switched it on again. A metronome, pressed into service as a time-elapsed clock, ticked through ten seconds. Then with the dexterity born of experience, Bunter removed the paper from the frame, and slid it into the first tray of liquid.

'Now we rock the dish,' he said. The dish was designed to rock; pressing gently on one corner achieved it. At first the print lay submerged pure and undefiled; then a just perceptible shadow appeared on it. And then the little phrase Jackson had pointed out showed ghostly, and alone.

'Whew!' said Peter. But very rapidly the rest of the words on the page sprang into view, and darkened, along with that first appearing phrase, until the whole print looked like the manuscript. Bunter whipped the print out of the developer, slid it through the adjacent tray of water, and then slipped it into the final tray of fixer. Then he switched on the light, leaving Peter blinking.

The two friends gazed at the print. They could not now see any difference in the darkness of the various inks on the print; it abolished the colour difference between Latin and Old English text, showing only that the gloss was not quite so dark.

'Can you see any difference now?' Peter asked.

'No,' said Bunter, sounding triumphant. 'When the print is fully developed it is just the same as looking at the original. But on the way there, the difference in tone shows, as I hoped it would.'

'You are a genius, Bunter,' said Peter. 'Can we do it again?'

'Indeed we can,' said Bunter, 'and we should.'

The second print got whipped out of the developer when the solitude of the phrase was just being challenged by the rest of the text. Bunter got it into the fixer at that stage.

'I believe this is a proof, my lord, that the ink of those words is indeed darker,' said Bunter.

'Jackson ought to see this,' said Peter. 'I shall go and get him.'

Jackson of course had not left his desk in the library, and though he demurred, Peter insisted that he come. 'It's worth your while to see this,' he said. 'Trust me.'

Grumbling a little, Jackson followed Peter up the stairs, and into the darkroom.

'I don't get this,' he said.

'Watch,' said Peter.

And so Jackson saw the phrase emerge on its own, pursued by shadows of the other words.

His reaction was not at all what Peter had suspected; he burst into tears.

'Why does it do that?' he asked Bunter.

'Because you are right,' Bunter told him. 'Those words are written in a different and darker ink.'

'Don't get carried away, old chap,' said Peter. 'There might be other reasons; it might be that when they ran out of ink and mixed a new pot it varied a bit.'

'It doesn't otherwise vary on this page,' said Bunter. He switched on the light, and they could see a row of prints he had made while Peter fetched Jackson; the procession of prints had been stopped at different moments in the developer. They showed gradients of depth in the words, starting from the phrase entirely alone and changing till the whole page looked equally dark.

'Can I have those?' Jackson asked, in an incredulous voice, like one asking if he had won the football pools.

'You can when they are dry,' said Bunter.

*   *   *

While Peter and Bunter were playing happily with hypo behind blackout curtains, Harriet received an unexpected visit from her sons, Bredon and Paul. Harriet, who was sitting in the window-seat, had as much warning as the time it took them to cross the quad.

She expressed delight, and received their manly embraces before asking them what accounted for their appearance. She learned that a whole party of sixth-formers were in Oxford, looking round, and talking informally to college tutors, where the school had been able to arrange that. Next term they would decide which college to apply to. Bredon had inspected Balliol and Hertford the day before. Paul had come along just to get a look at Oxford; his turn to apply was not yet. The school charabanc would return them to Eton mid-afternoon, leaving them a free morning in Oxford.

'Thought we'd just drop in on you, Ma,' said Paul, with his crooked grin.

'We're not interrupting something, are we?' asked Bredon.

'Nothing as good as a morning with you two,' said Harriet.

'Where's our father?' asked Bredon.

'I believe he is buried in a darkroom somewhere with Bunter, conducting a photographic experiment,' said Harriet.

'Well, that's good in a way,' said Bredon.

Paul said, 'I think I'll go and find Blackwell's, Ma, and have a look around.'

'Shall we all go?' Harriet asked.

'No, thanks,' Paul said, 'I can manage,' and he left.

Harriet immediately clicked into emergency mode. This suddenly looked serious.

'All right, son,' she said to Bredon, when Paul had left them, 'what is this about?'

'Can't you guess?' he asked her.

'You preferred Hertford to Balliol?' she hazarded.

'Worse,' he said. 'Much worse. I don't want Oxford at all.'

Harriet flinched at the thought of how Peter might react to this. 'Explain yourself,' she said severely to her son.

'I want to go to Reading,' he said.

'*Reading?*' Harriet failed to conceal her surprise. 'Why ever do you want to do that? And what do you know about Reading?' At his age, she thought, I wouldn't even have heard of a university there.

Bredon tackled the easy part of this inquisition first. 'The school has us all apply to Reading, Ma, as a practice for being interviewed. We aren't supposed to want to go there. I'm surprised they go on interviewing us; they must have noticed that we don't take up the places we are offered there. As a rule, that is. Of course if you fail Oxford and Cambridge, then at least you have got somewhere.'

'Is that what it is? You don't think you will make it into Oxford?'

'No, that's not it, Ma,' said Bredon, sounding insulted. 'I think I might make it here if I really tried. I'm trying to tell you that I don't want to try.'

'Don't get agitated, son,' said Harriet. 'Just tell me what's in your mind.'

'I don't want to do Greats, or History, or English,' Bredon told her. 'I'm not bright enough. Everyone thinks I will follow in Father's footsteps. My housemaster thinks Balliol will be kind to me because of Father. If that's true I think it's all wrong. I don't think I should have to follow Father's footsteps, or not to Balliol, anyway. And they shouldn't let chaps in for reasons like that.'

'I completely agree with you,' said Harriet, 'and I don't think they do. Not unless it's choosing between two people so exactly matched that it amounts to tossing a coin. However it is very high-minded of you to object to being looked on favourably for a reason you don't approve of. Perhaps you are following in your father's footsteps more than you know you are.'

'He's so damned *clever*,' complained Bredon. 'And you are no slouch. And Peter Bunter can run rings round me any day of the week, whatever we are talking about.'

'That might all be true, my dear, and not amount to your being stupid,' said Harriet.

Bredon was silent. He was looking as miserable as his mother had ever seen him.

'Enough of what you don't want, Bredon,' she said. 'Tell me what you do want.'

'I want to do Estate Management,' he said. 'Or, failing that, Forestry.'

'Talk to me about that idea,' she said.

'I want to be useful,' he said. 'And estate management is what I am interested in, and what I might be good at, and what I seem likely to be called upon in the long run to do.'

'That sounds sensible to me,' said Harriet. 'But you could do that, or, failing that, Forestry, here.'

'But I like the look of the course at Reading, Ma. It's got something of everything in it: agriculture and forestry, and buildings . . . and I shan't feel overshadowed by people expecting me to be like Father.'

It occurred to Harriet that Bredon was not only Peter's son, but Gerald's nephew. She remembered crusty, preposterous old Gerald talking about planting oaks that would take a hundred years to reach maturity. She remembered him caring for the Denver estates as conscientiously after his own son died as while that wild young man lived. It wasn't for Peter and then Bredon that he lived and laboured as he had; it was some sort of sense of duty to the land itself. Not a bad thing for her son to inherit. And since it would hit him eventually, in all probability it had to be a good idea that he was embracing it gladly, and wanting to be ready for it. It wouldn't be as hard for him as it had been for Peter.

She realised that her long musing silence was tormenting her son.

'You realise, do you,' she asked, 'that things are changing? That a government might arrive that will confiscate landed estates, or grind them down with death duties? That a choice to be the manager of Bredon Hall all your life might not be viable all your life?'

'I've thought of that. There will still be land,' he said. 'Farms and houses and woods and rivers. Somebody will have to look after them, even if it isn't the owners any more.'

'Very well, son, you have my blessing,' said Harriet.

And then the killer question: 'Will you tell Father?'

'No,' said Harriet. 'It will be much better if you tell him. But if necessary, I will speak up for you.'

There was a knock on the door. 'Is it safe to come in?' asked Paul, putting his head round the door.

'One down, and one to go,' said Bredon to Paul.

It wasn't long before Peter and Bunter turned up, bearing damp prints that needed to be squeegeed to mirrors and windows to dry. Peter was delighted to see his sons, and demanded an account of the interviews that Bredon had had.

'Peter, take Bredon punting, why don't you?' said Harriet.

'Of course,' said Peter happily. 'He'll need a bit of instruction. Makes a fellow look an awful fool in his first term if he doesn't know how. Shall we all go?'

'Paul might get seasick,' said Harriet.

A brief, speaking glance between her and Peter was exchanged. 'I'll look after Paul,' Harriet said.

'Off we go, then, Bredon,' said Peter.

Standing at the now familiar viewpoint window, Paul and Harriet watched them go.

Bredon had grown to about the same height and build as his father. He had not inherited Peter's ridiculously blond hair; Harriet's contribution had generated a tawny-bronze shade for him. It was extraordinarily painful, Harriet found, to watch two people she loved more dearly than her life going off together to hurt each other badly.

'I'm glad I'm not in Bredon's shoes,' said Paul feelingly.

That gave Harriet a thought. 'No, indeed, Paul,' she said. 'If Bredon can be his own man, so can you. Let me show you something.'

She picked up the Warden's gown, and they set off together to climb into the cupola on the roof of the Sheldonian Theatre. As they went she explained to Paul that the Sheldonian had been built by Christopher Wren to serve as the assembly hall for the university. Harriet's gown would admit them without fuss.

'Does it still count when you have left long ago?' Paul asked.

'You don't exactly leave Oxford,' Harriet told him. 'You can, of course. But if you take your MA you're a member for life. I can still use the Bodleian Library; in fact it's easier by far to work here than at home.'

'I didn't know you had an MA,' Paul said.

'You just leave your name on the books, and pay the fees for five years, and then your BA becomes an MA,' Harriet admitted.

'Not fair,' said Paul.

They were both preoccupied. But when they reached the little cupola, scrambling up a narrow and rather ramshackle ladder through dusty space between the roof timbers, and came out into the light, Harriet let the view speak for itself for a while.

Then she said, 'Towery city, and branchy between towers, Cuckoo-echoing, bell-swarmed, lark-charmed, rook-racked, river-rounded ... It's lovely, isn't it, Paul?'

Visible from the cupola is a southerly vista of extraordinary beauty. First the little Gothic lancets on the roof of the Bodleian; then the large rounded mass of the dome on the Radcliffe Camera, which convinces the eye at once that every city should have a dome; then the airy Gothic spire of the university church, St Mary the Virgin, the square tower of Merton. And Tom Tower off to one side and beyond it all in every direction soft and gently rising vistas of green hills.

'Worth going on paying those fees, I should think,' said Paul.

'I think so,' said Harriet.

'Would it please you if I had a shot at coming here?' asked Paul.

'It would please your father immeasurably,' Harriet said.

'I asked if it would please *you*,' said Paul.

'It would please me very much if you were happy here,' said Harriet. 'But then I would be pleased for you to be happy anywhere.'

'If I was a dustman in Notting Hill?' he asked her, extending a supporting hand to her as they negotiated the steep steps down again.

'As long as you were a happy dustman, son,' she said firmly.

Then he gave voice to what was on both their minds: 'I wonder how that punting lesson is getting on?' he asked.

When they reached base it was immediately apparent that the punting lesson had not gone perfectly. Pools of water on the floor indicated that somebody had taken a dipping. Hearing them come in, Peter emerged in a dressing gown, and with very damp hair.

'Heavens, Peter,' Harriet exclaimed, 'you haven't fallen in after all these years?'

'I didn't fall,' said Peter, outraged, 'I was pushed!'

'Bredon pushed you?' asked Paul, round-eyed.

'Not Bredon, I'm glad to say,' said Peter, 'but some incompetent person swinging their pole around horizontally without looking who else was on the river. But it did serve me right.'

'How so? You sound like an innocent victim.'

'I was demonstrating to Bredon how to propel a punt from the Cambridge end, in case he ever needed to. It's hard to get a firm foothold on the deck end. So I just slid off. And all in vain, I gather.'

'Where is Bredon now?' asked Harriet.

'Being dried off by Bunter,' said Peter. 'He jumped in after me.'

'To save you?' said Paul incredulously.

'He said he didn't know if I could swim,' said Peter, beginning to laugh. 'He said there had to be something I couldn't do, and he was afraid it might have been that.'

Just then Bredon appeared, wearing Peter's clothes. There was no hope of drying off his own in time for the charabanc.

'Right,' said Harriet firmly, 'hot food before you two have to get on that bus back to school. The Turf Tavern, as fast as wc can get there.'

Over soup and steak and kidney pie Harriet deduced that the crucial conversation had taken place, duckings notwithstanding. Bredon had lost his tense apprehensive manner, and Peter did not seem sunk in gloom. They were entertaining herself and Paul with vivid descriptions of the dismay of Peter's inadvertent assailant. He too had jumped in, and hogged the limelight, since he really couldn't swim, and having been rescued, gasping, he was held upside down by a burly friend to drain out.

Talk and laughter over food – just what family life should be like. Peter would confide in her later.

It was much later before he broached the subject. They were lying in bed by moonlight. He said into the silence, 'I am bitterly disappointed, Harriet, and bitterly ashamed of myself.'

'Why are you ashamed, Peter?' she asked.

'Because I am disappointed,' he said.

'Raising children is not like doing topiary, Peter,' she said. 'One has to wait and see what comes up. I find I am rather proud of him myself.'

'Am I tyrannical, Harriet? As my own father was? Why did he find it so hard to tell me?'

'Not because you are a tyrant, Peter, but because he knew it would hurt you, and he loves you.'

'Meanwhile you were doing a bit of opportunistic

topiary yourself, weren't you, taking Paul to a high point and showing him all the kingdoms of the world, and the glory thereof?'

'I shouldn't have done that, should I?' said Harriet. 'It was the devil who took Christ to a high place, after all.'

'You are a benign and maternal devil, my dear,' he said.

'It's a fine line, though, isn't it, Peter, between loving someone and wanting to control them?'

'We do our best. We haven't made too bad a job so far,' he said.

'So it isn't a disaster if the eldest son doesn't go to Balliol?'

'Not when I've had an hour or two to think about it. Of course not. He's making perfect sense to me.'

'Peter, exactly *when* did you and Bredon have this showdown? Before or after you fell in?'

'I didn't fall; I was pushed.'

'Before or after you were pushed, then?'

'After. We had only just got going upstream past Mesopotamia when it happened.'

'So you were talking about it while both soaking wet?'

'Yes. I suppose that standing together in dripping clothing at the epicentres of a pair of spreading puddles of river water was a great leveller. Perhaps it would improve political life if our masters were given a thorough soaking before entering the House of Commons, and not allowed to dry off before reaching agreement . . .'

'I'm glad you're straight with Bredon,' she said. 'I love you, Peter.'

'Don't change the subject,' he said.

'I wasn't,' she said, and then they were soon asleep.

18

They were woken by the phone ringing insistently through the door to the Warden's quarters. It stopped abruptly as Bunter answered it. Then they heard him knock gently at their door, and when Peter said, 'Come,' he stepped in.

'More bodies, Bunter?' Peter asked.

'Not as far as I am aware, my lord,' said Bunter. 'It is Mr Charles Parker wishing to speak to you when you are able to take the call.'

'I'll be right with him,' said Peter. 'I can take a call in my pyjamas, as long as Miss Manciple isn't about; and if she is about these are, after all, Harrod's pyjamas.'

'Don't be silly, Peter,' offered Harriet, propping herself up on her pillow. 'It might really be a body and you can't go haring down to London in pyjamas, wherever you bought them.'

'Tell Charles I'll ring him back,' said Peter.

In a short while Peter consulted Harriet again. 'Can I go haring around after bodies without shaving first?' he asked her.

'Certainly not, Peter,' she said. 'There is an implication

of inattention in an unshaven man that gives the impression of intellectual weakness.'

Nevertheless it was only a quarter of an hour before Peter rang Charles back.

'Ah, there you are,' said Charles. 'We've found your Warden for you.'

'Excellent, Charles. Is he alive or dead?'

'Alive.'

'Better and better. Where is he?'

'Not far from you at all. He's in the Radcliffe Infirmary' – here Charles paused for dramatic effect – 'suffering from arsenic poisoning.'

'I should have expected that,' Peter said. 'I should have known.'

'Failure of clairvoyance, Peter?' said Charles. 'Clairvoyance usually fails.'

'Of course, we didn't know where he was. No way of warning him. Can I talk to him?'

'I don't see why not. There's an Oxford copper at his bedside, but *nihil obstat*. Unless the hospital objects.'

'I'll hop over there and see,' said Peter.

First, of course, he gave the news to Harriet and Bunter. Bunter told him that Miss Manciple was weeping her eyes out in the kitchen, and Peter went down to talk to her.

'I take it you know what has happened to the Warden?' he asked her.

'It was me that called the ambulance,' she said.

'You were with him? You have known all this time where he was? Sworn to secrecy, I take it?'

'Yes, sir.'

'Well, you kept the secret very loyally, if not very wisely,' Peter told her. 'Where has the Warden been hiding then?'

'Yarnton, sir. He has an old friend with a lovely house there, and lots of space. There's a gardener's cottage tucked away in the garden, behind the house gates. He was hid away safe from prying eyes.'

'So you have been sending him things he needs – all those brown paper parcels?'

'Sending or taking them, sir. There's a good bus up the Woodstock Road.'

'Is that why you were there last night? Taking him something?'

'Not exactly. I was there cooking a dinner for him to have with a friend.'

'Who was that?'

'I don't know, sir, and I didn't see. I got the food all laid out in the kitchen ready to serve, and then he sent me off to the cinema. There's a nice cinema in Kidlington. He gave me money for the tickets.'

'He didn't want you to see his guest?'

'He said they had things to talk about, that's all. All quite natural, sir. But when I got back to clear up he was in a terrible way; he was moaning with pain, and throwing up everywhere, and there was blood in the vomit. So I called an ambulance, though he told me not to.'

'You were right. You probably saved his life. What about the guest?'

'I don't know, sir. He had gone before I got back. What is wrong with the Warden, sir?'

'I'm afraid he has been poisoned,' Peter told her.

'Not with his dinner, sir. I cooked every morsel of that myself, and I ate the leftovers when I was clearing up, and I'm quite all right, sir, as you see. How is the Warden, sir? Will he be all right?'

'I'm off to see him now,' said Peter. 'I'll tell you what I can when I get back. And, Miss Manciple, I should warn you, you will have to deal with many questions from the police. They will want to know all about that dinner that you cooked.'

'They'd do better to find out who the guest was,' said Miss Manciple stoutly. 'It has to be him that poisoned the poor Warden. Like I say, it wasn't my dinner.'

Not surprisingly, perhaps, the Warden was not fit to be seen. By good chance Peter intercepted a doctor leaving his room and, claiming his status in St Severin's, obtained a little information. The doctor said his patient had ingested a heavy dose of arsenic, which had not proved lethal only because of the prompt and disobedient action of his servant. (One up for the devoted Miss Manciple.) He was being treated by chelation, and was expected to live, though not perhaps to recover completely from the impact on his heart and liver. Try visiting tomorrow, Peter was told; the chelation should have had some effect by then. Peter asked for an explanation of what, exactly, chelation was. It was, he was told, the action of a chemical that bound itself to heavy metal and made it soluble in the bloodstream, causing it to be washed out of the human body through the kidneys. Arsenic was a heavy metal. Peter thanked his informant, and returned to the college.

He more than half expected to find the Oxford police interviewing Miss Manciple, but they had not yet arrived. Perhaps they were handing it over to the Scotland Yard Poison Unit; perhaps they had not yet realised the Warden had eaten a meal with a guest, and were assuming an environmental source of arsenic. They would shortly be on the trail, going over the gardener's cottage at Yarnton with due diligence. Peter decided to steal a march on them; he swept up Harriet, Bunter and Miss Manciple – best not have anyone around to be questioned by the police at this juncture – and took them all on a quick drive to Yarnton Manor.

The owner of that beautiful house was abroad; his housekeeper said she had not yet been able to contact him to tell him what had happened. She had never heard of anyone being taken ill at Yarnton in such a manner before, and she had kept well clear of the gardener's cottage other than bringing some food when requested, because it was supposed to be kept secret that anyone was living there. Also the Warden – she called him Mr Ludgvan – had told her that he was working on something very demanding, and needed peace and quiet. The secrecy was now presumably blown away, and she had no objection to a party from the college, including Miss Manciple whom she knew to be a trusted friend, inspecting the cottage. 'You won't find anything wrong there,' she added, 'but have a look by all means.'

The cottage was in fact a small house, standing alone in a quiet corner of the grounds. On one side its windows faced into an orchard, on the other into a small wooded copse. Its seclusion was complete. There was a living room, looking unloved and unlived-in with dark Victorian furniture, and an empty grate cleaned of ashes. There was a dining room with utility furniture, smelling of wax polish, a small kitchen and scullery, cleaned of any trace of any meal.

'I didn't know any better than to clear it up,' said Miss Manciple unhappily.

Upstairs there were two rooms under the eaves, with little dormer windows. One was the bedroom, smelling of sickness, with disordered sheets; the other had a desk under the window, and had obviously been used as a study.

'Can I clear up the bedroom, sir, and wash those sheets?' Miss Manciple asked.

'Best not,' said Peter.

He walked through to the study bedroom. The desk was covered with papers. The Warden's handwriting was sprawling and untidy; no wonder Miss Manciple had typed for him. Just to make sure, he summoned her to stop grieving over the sheets, and come to inspect the handwriting. Yes, it was the Warden's.

Peter whipped a handkerchief from his pocket and, using it to cover his own fingers, opened the top drawer of the desk. The drawer contained the usual desk clutter of paper-clips, rubber bands, pencils and pens, and a single Woolworth's exercise book. Carefully, holding it through the handkerchief, Peter laid it on the desk and opened it. The top line of the top page was a heading: APOLOGIA. '*If I die in suspicious circumstances . . .*' Peter read. He urgently wanted to read on.

'That is probably the whole *fons et origo* of all this,' said Harriet, looking over his shoulder.

'But we can't touch it,' said Peter. 'We mustn't interfere with a crime scene, even if we think the police when they get here will do just that.'

'That's harsh, Peter. They probably know their job.'

'They'll be out of their depth with this case, I think,' said Peter. 'But then we're not exactly in our depth ourselves. I'm glad we know that this book exists. But for access to it I suppose we must apply to Charles.'

The three of them went downstairs, to find that Bunter had been burrowing in the dustbin. He had extracted two wine bottles: one of Châteauneuf-du-Pape, and one of Sauternes. He was handling them with gloves.

'Shall I fingerprint these, my lord? Since we are here?'

'Good idea,' said Peter.

'Miss Manciple, do you recognise these bottles?'

'Oh, yes, sir,' she said. 'I bought the red one from Mr Thrupp in the college, because the Warden asked for it. I told Mr Thrupp it was for you, sir. Sorry about that. And the other bottle I didn't see before I came to clear up. The guest must have brought it.'

'I suppose there isn't the least dribble left in either of those bottles?' said Peter wistfully.

'What could we collect a sample in, my lord?' asked Bunter.

Miss Manciple piped up, 'The Warden smokes cigars that come in metal tubes, each one separate,' she said. 'I'll find a couple of those.'

Very gently Bunter upended each bottle over one of the empty aluminium tubes. Just one drop from each bottle was collected.

'I take it we have taken the last but one, rather than the very last drop from those bottles?' asked Peter.

'There is enough left for the police. What now, my lord?' Bunter asked.

Peter looked at the bottles, each having a powdered area around the neck, where Bunter had dusted the fingerprints prior to photographing them. 'Hmm,' he said. 'Well, we can't clean them off to cover our tracks; that really would be interfering with a crime scene. We'd better just leave them on the kitchen table, and confess if asked. On the other hand . . .'

'On the other hand what, Peter?' asked Harriet.

'Reading the Warden's Apologia would leave no traces. We can't take it; and of course the police may arrive here any minute, but I could read it.'

'They're not likely to arrive here soon,' said Harriet. 'Unless the Warden recovers enough to be interviewed. The only other person who could tell them about this hide-away is Miss Manciple, and she's with us here.'

'So what are you suggesting?'

'I suggest that I take Miss Manciple and Bunter out to lunch at the Turnpike Inn, that we passed on the way here, and you sit and read that exercise book.'

'Don't I get any lunch?' asked Peter.

'Choose between lunch and duty,' Harriet told him.

'Oh well, there's always dinner in prospect,' Peter said.

'If I may say so, Your Grace,' said Bunter to Harriet, 'I might be of most use lurking in the grounds, in order to give the Duke time to leave by the back door if the police are arriving at the front.'

'You, too, put duty before nourishment, dear Bunter,' said Harriet. 'Come along, Miss Manciple. Don't argue; you deserve a treat.'

Harriet, having talked herself into having to drive the Daimler, left very cautiously to cover the short distance to the pub, and resigned herself to learning all about Miss Manciple's early career on the stage.

Peter, feeling disconcertingly like a small boy raiding the larder, went upstairs and settled at the Warden's desk to read.

APOLOGIA

If I die in suspicious circumstances, this memo will offer background to the situation in which I died. This mess is my own fault, my own doing. It was a fool's trick to slate young Outlander's book as I did. I went about it with gusto and I even remember enjoying using immoderate language in the task. Of course, I had no idea that Outlander was fragile; I did not intend to hurt him at all, which even I think was strange of me, looking back on it. Why did I do it? Not to damage a research fellow of my own college, but to damage the claims being made for that accursed manu-script. People were putting a huge monetary value on the thing, and that was triggering greed in a section of the fellowship, and the fellows were forming factions that were tearing the college apart. I did not think our problems could be resolved for long without reducing the number of fellows, a very unpopular idea. The whole idea of buying our way out of making that hard decision by selling a book and buying land was flawed.

As I say, although I thought his book rather speculative, I had no animus against Outlander, and I was appalled at his death. And it was all for nothing, since the dispute in the college did not die down, and there seemed to have been no effect on the insurance value, and presumably the sale value of the MS. The likely buyers of the MS if it were put up for sale were American university libraries, and various American scholars were writing papers in support of Outlander's views. I became a very unhappy old man. It served me right, I think. I was living with a heavy heart – I had had no idea how literal that expression is.

What made matters much worse was that X, one of my few friends in the college, was distraught at Outlander's death, and made a determined attempt to find out who the reviewer was. He wanted me to use my position as Warden to bring pressure to bear to unmask the reviewer. I refused, on the grounds that the interests of scholarship demanded that reviews should be fearless and free, however unreasonable they might be in the eyes of some.

My friendship with X cooled immediately and then quite suddenly became icy and remote. I am very isolated in the college now. I wondered if X had in fact managed to find out that I wrote the review, although I did not see how. Then I went to Manchester to deliver a lecture, and Stella Manciple took a day off in London. On her return she found my papers disturbed, and the carbon of the review missing. There was no sign of damage to the house locks, and a discreet enquiry to the porters' lodge showed that the master key had not been borrowed; indeed Stella was assured that the porters would not have lent the key to my Lodgings to anyone in any circumstances. Then I remembered that when we were close friends I had given the spare key to X. A quick look for it showed us that he had not returned it. A further search through my papers made it certain that the carbon copy of my submission to the TLS *was missing. Of course I should have destroyed it – my God, why didn't I destroy it? I thought, X has stolen the carbon copy. But I couldn't ask him about it without unmasking myself as the reviewer.*

Then as if all that were not enough, Troutbeck revealed that he knew about it. He began to blackmail me. Unless I vote to sell the MS *he will reveal to the whole world that I am the author of the review. That would destroy my authority as Warden. I accused Troutbeck of stealing my papers and he just laughed at me. Finally he threatened me with physical violence, and I fled. I am safe here, I think, but I cannot live here for ever. I have a lot of time to think. X is the only person that I know to have had a chance, albeit a brief one, to look for that carbon. But I cannot imagine X of all people empowering Troutbeck of all people. Nor do I imagine that Stella Manciple is at fault. I would trust her with my life; indeed, in view of what Troutbeck was threatening to do to me I am trusting her with my life since she knows where I am.*

I can see no way out of this situation. But I ought to reappear in college for the next vote. I quail at the thought, and am deeply depressed at my confinement here continuing without limit. I have decided to try to mend bridges with X, and have invited him to dinner with me here tomorrow. Perhaps if I offer true remorse we can resume some sort of friendly relations.

Peter read through this effusion twice, and then sat thinking for a considerable while. It was evidently important to know who X was. And rather odd, now he came to think of it, for a man making effectively a note to post-mortem investigators to refer to a colleague as X. What good was this note if it concealed the name of one of the main players?

Peter read it through again, and then went to find Bunter in the shrubbery. The two of them walked down the road to the pub, to join Harriet and Miss Manciple. Those two had found themselves to be both daughters of country doctors, and were happily comparing notes about their adored and high-minded fathers.

Although it was nearly two o'clock Peter and Bunter were allowed to order ploughman's lunches, so duty had not really come at the price of nutrition. Peter was preoccupied, and Harriet, supposing that he didn't want to discuss what he had read with Miss Manciple present, held her peace, and a desultory conversation took place, partly between Bunter and Miss Manciple, on the question of the exact nature of an authentic ploughman's lunch: was it bread and cheese and onions? Was it denatured by the inclusion of slices of ham? This diverted their thoughts from the hapless Warden and his situation.

Peter asked the publican about the authenticity of his ploughman's, and was told that the lunches were as authentic as the ploughmen who ordered them. For that retort he got a generous tip when they left.

Peter parked the car at the top end of St Giles, within a few yards of the Radcliffe Infirmary, and handed over to Bunter to take the two women back to college, though Harriet elected to walk.

When Peter showed up at the Warden's bedside he found the man ashen white, and semi-conscious. A nurse hovered at the bedside. 'He is much better,' she told Peter. 'Out of danger. But we have given him heavy painkillers to help him through the next few hours. I am told that when he can be interviewed the police must talk to him first.'

'That's only right and proper,' Peter said. 'Just the same, there is something you could do that would be very helpful. Could you take note of anyone who comes visiting? Just their names. I don't think the police would object to that.'

'I will if I can, sir,' the nurse said.

Peter walked, musing. Someone had poisoned the Warden; the arsenic had to be in the bottle the guest had brought, because Miss Manciple had eaten the food without harm. Someone the Warden did not want to name. Peter had no doubt poison would be found in one of those samples. Who taught chemistry in St Severin's? Bunter would need apparatus to perform a Marsh test for arsenic. Probably wisest to confide in Charles, and get official help.

As he crossed the quad, he encountered Ambleside. 'I'm just going to drop in on Vearing,' Ambleside said. 'He didn't turn up to give a lecture this morning. On the Gothic novel, I believe. I'm just going to make sure he's all right.'

'I'll come with you,' said Peter.

19

Vearing was 'sporting his oak': that is, the outer door of his room was closed, the traditional sign that the occupant did not want to be disturbed. Peter knocked on the wooden panel, tapping against it with his signet ring to make a sharp sound. There was no answer.

But the outer door was not locked. They stepped through it and knocked on the inner door. Likewise, no result. Ambleside called through the door; silence; then a faint groaning sound, which they both heard. The inner door was locked.

'Are you all right, Ex?' Ambleside called. 'Come to the door, old chap, and let us in.' After what seemed several long seconds they heard the key in the lock the other side of the door, and it was opened. Vearing faced them unsteadily on his feet, looking greenish-white, and with his clothes stained with vomit. Then he collapsed to the floor at their feet.

Peter and Ambleside between them picked him up and laid him out on his sofa. There was a telephone on Vearing's desk, and Peter lifted the receiver. The porter answered at once. 'Call an ambulance,' Peter said, 'Mr Vearing has been taken ill.'

The ambulance didn't take long to come. But before it arrived Vearing began to rave at Peter. 'You stinking hypocrite!' he cried. 'Don't touch me – don't come near me. I know what kind of man you are, you lying duplicitous devil!'

'In the name of God, Ex, what has possessed you?' said Ambleside.

'*He* knows what I mean,' said Vearing, waving at Peter. 'Ask him why he wanted to marry a murderess; ask him that! He cooked up a wicked, wicked, false story to nail an innocent man, and get himself a woman out of a hangman's noose! I know it wouldn't work, I know what he said was a farrago, but someone hanged on the strength of it, and she didn't.

'It doesn't work, does it, *Your Grace* – Your lying conspiring Grace! Look at the state of me – you can't tell me it works! Putting about rubbish like that amounts to murder . . . but you don't mind that, do you? You sleep every night in the arms of a poisoner, a sloppy unscholarly poisoner who can't be bothered to get her facts right, and pretends to be a virtuous woman. Nothing in common with me that she knows of, that's what she told me, the slut! We'll see about that, we'll . . .' He began coughing, and vomiting. There was telltale blood in the vomit.

Peter stood rooted to the spot, thinking only, Thank God Harriet isn't here to hear this.

His ordeal didn't last long. Soon the ambulance men were clattering up the stairs, issuing orders, getting Vearing on to a stretcher, carrying him away.

Ambleside said, 'He has gone mad.' Ambleside himself was looking white-faced and shaken.

'I think he has been mad for a long time,' Peter said.

'What is wrong with him now?' asked Ambleside. 'I never heard that madness makes a man vomit blood.'

'What is wrong with him now is arsenic poisoning,' said Peter. 'Let's get out of here, Ambleside, and I'll tell you about it.

'I feel as though I smell,' said Peter, as they emerged into the quad. 'Let's stay in the open air.'

Ambleside led the way into the Fellows' Garden, and they found a bench near a flower bed planted lavishly with tobacco plants and bordered with lavender.

'Why did you call him Ex?' Peter asked.

'I've known him a long time,' said Ambleside. 'Of course we use just our surnames usually. Or when anyone else is present.'

'Sorry, I don't follow you,' said Peter.

'Oh, Vearing's first name is Xenophon,' said Ambleside. 'His friends call him Ex.'

'That's pretty conclusive, then,' said Peter. 'Look, Ambleside, I'm glad to fill you in on all that somewhere where my wife can't overhear us. And this is in confidence.'

'Thank you for trusting me,' said Ambleside. 'In the context that's a compliment.'

'What Vearing was accusing me of was manufacturing a false story that implicated a man in murdering his nephew, and thus exonerating my wife and obtaining her acquittal. His deduction was that because the method of murder I had uncovered would not work, it followed that Harriet was in fact guilty, and was, and is, a murderess.'

'Why does he think the method you suggested would not work?' asked Ambleside. 'He has to my knowledge no medical expertise at all.'

'He has tried it himself,' said Peter, 'with the result that you see.'

'I'm afraid I don't understand what I see,' said Ambleside. 'Was he trying to kill himself?'

'No. Not himself; someone he was sharing a meal with. What the abominable Urquhart did was to ingest arsenic over a long period in very small but increasing amounts. Treated like that the human frame acquires tolerance. Eventually it is possible to eat a lethal dose of the stuff without coming to any harm. Then you can share a meal or a bottle of wine with your victim, and he dies while you are unscathed. Plainly the poisoning of the victim cannot have been due to the shared meal – or so it would seem to the police and the courts. The blame can be thrown on someone else. In the case he refers to the person framed and in danger of hanging was Harriet.'

The first words out of Ambleside's mouth were not about Vearing. 'How terrible for her,' he said. 'And, I should think, for you. I didn't know about this.'

'For a long time she was inclined to think that everybody knew about it,' Peter said.

'I won't mention it. You can trust me for that,' said Ambleside. 'But I am still in the dark. Are you saying that Vearing was acclimatising himself to arsenic? But we have just seen him in dire straits because of it.'

'He has botched it,' said Peter. 'Probably by trying to achieve his immunity too quickly.'

'How did he know about it?' asked Ambleside 'Is it in one of your wife's books?'

'Yes. Eventually she achieved the objectivity to write about it. There's no denying it's a good plot. And the case also is in several legal textbooks, and books of forensic medicine.'

'I see.'

'You don't tell me that your dear friend could not have been capable of such a thing?'

'No. I find him a very odd character. And if I had not known and liked him long ago I doubt I would like him on meeting him newly now.'

'You haven't asked about the victim,' said Peter.

'Are you telling me he got round to trying it on a victim?' said Ambleside in obvious horror. 'Was it Troutbeck?'

It was a double botch,' said Peter. 'Vearing did not escape unscathed, and the victim did not die. And it wasn't Troutbeck. It was the Warden.'

'How does one poison a missing man?' asked Ambleside. 'That poor old chap . . .'

'He isn't missing now,' said Peter. 'He is in the Radcliffe, pulling round from a near-death experience, with a copper for company. No doubt he would like a visitor with a friendly face.'

'I'll go at once,' said Ambleside.

Peter remained seated on the bench, thinking. He thought so long that Harriet came looking for him. The porter told her where to find him, and she came and joined him. They sat for a while in companionable silence.

'How did Troutbeck come to know?' he said in a while.

'How did he know what?' Harriet asked.

'Oh, lord,' said Peter. 'Sorry, Harriet. You live so closely in my mind I had for a moment forgotten that you need to be filled in. A lot has happened since lunchtime.'

He began to tell her about what the Warden's notebook had contained, and then about Vearing. He toned down what Vearing had said to him as much as he could.

Harriet became thoughtful and sad. 'The past has long claws,' she said.

'But we have escaped them,' he said. 'We struggled free into happiness. I don't tell you often enough, Harriet, what it means to me that you are happy with me.'

'It isn't my happiness that is my escape from the past,' she said, 'it is yours.'

'There never was a better bargain driven?' he said.

'Just so. Now to our sheep, my lord. Where are the loose ends in this dreadful tangle?'

'The one that presents itself to me most prominently,' said Peter, 'is the question how Troutbeck got to know what Vearing knew. Plainly Vearing wouldn't have told him.'

'It's that carbon copy of the review,' said Harriet. 'That's the dangling thread. Where is it now?'

'Last heard of in Vearing's possession,' said Peter.

'Can we go and look for it?'

'I think we can. The Visitor can do most things around here.'

'Let's start there, then,' said Harriet.

Vearing's room was just as they remembered it; in perfect order. His scout had cleared it up and nobody would gather that the occupant had nearly died in it only a few hours before. Peter began by opening desk drawers, and then drawers in that lovely inlay table.

'Basically we are looking for something stolen,' Harriet reminded him. 'Nobody would keep such a thing in an open and obvious drawer.'

'You're right,' Peter said.

A short passage led from Vearing's drawing room to his bedroom. The passage was lined with deep book-cases full of box-files, but box-files all covered with beautiful art nouveau wallpapers. They made a lovely patchwork effect. Harriet resolved to imitate that in her own study. 'Somewhere among these?' she asked. They were all labelled with subjects and dates. Peter began to check; the subjects and dates were all correct – the contents matched the labels. Vearing had been an assidu-ous note-taker and lecture-giver for many years. But it would plainly take days of work to be sure that the notorious carbon was not in any of these files.

Harriet walked through to the bedroom. It felt intru-sive to enter it; it contained not much other than the bed and a large chest of drawers, on top of which there were half a dozen framed photographs. A man and a woman in a park somewhere with a little boy holding a cricket bat. A sporting picture of a rowing eight. A picture of a woman in ATS uniform. A glamorous-looking portrait of a young man in a silver frame . . . it was this last that caught her attention.

Peter said to her from the passage, 'You said, "Nobody would keep such a thing in an open drawer."'

'Yes, I did. Come and look at this.'

'But what you should have said surely was: nobody would keep such a thing. Vearing had stolen it from the Warden's papers. Wouldn't he have destroyed it?'

'Perhaps he would hang on to it as evidence.'

'Why would he need evidence? It had told him what he wanted to know. You don't need evidence to attempt to murder someone. It was Troutbeck who needed evidence; it's certainly useful to a blackmailer.'

'So it isn't here – somehow Troutbeck got hold of it?'

'Not easily, though. Think how long it would take to search this place thoroughly. And Vearing might have returned to base any minute. Or the scout might have arrived. He's got it somehow, but not like that. I think we are wasting our time here, Harriet.'

'Just look at this a minute,' she said to him, pointing out the photograph of the young man on the chest. 'Who is he? He looks vaguely familiar to me, but I can't place him.'

'Hang about; it's signed.'

'I missed that,' said Harriet.

'Very black ink, right against the frame,' said Peter. 'Warm regards, David. David Outlander, I presume.'

'Why does he look somehow familiar? We haven't either of us met him.'

'He's just a generic handsome young man,' said Peter. 'Firm chin, neat ears, nice eyes . . . matinee idol sort of fellow. They come by the dozen.'

'No, they don't, Peter,' said Harriet. 'Every one is different.'

'Well, he looks vaguely familiar to me too,' said Peter. 'Perhaps we bumped into him at some London party thrown by one of your publishers. Or sat opposite him on a bus or train.'

Harriet, having thought of something else, wandered back into the drawing room to see if the book hidden in the window-seat cushions was in fact one of hers, or only something with a similar yellow dust-jacket. The book had gone, but in disturbing the cushions she noticed that the window-seat was a box with a lid. She thrust the cushions aside, and lifted the lid. The base of the box was covered with modern books, spines upwards, like a bookshelf lying on its back. Among many other authors' works there was a line of Harriet Vanes. She pulled one out, and opened it. On the purple endpapers that her publisher used to give her books a distinctive look and style was the little green and white round sticker of Heffers bookshop in Cambridge.

'But we already know,' said Peter, coming up behind her. 'We know he is a murderer. The game has changed. It is the other murderer we are after. It is fish for the Troutbeck now.'

They closed the door behind them, and left.

'Shall we quit this pit of vipers for a while?' Peter asked. 'Let's have dinner at the Rose Revived.'

'The pub Charles scorned in favour of a glimpse of C.S. Lewis?'

'The very one. Unless you would prefer the Ferryman at Bablock Hythe.'

'You obviously had a car when you were up,' said Harriet. 'You're the expert.'

'If I am to choose,' said Peter, 'let's seek the pure spirit of the Scholar Gipsy, crossing the stripling Thames at Bablock Hythe. A few pure spirits wouldn't come amiss.'

'There's John Ambleside,' said Harriet. 'And the swarm of worker bees at Shrewsbury College, and surely Balliol is full of pure spirits?'

'I stand rebuked,' said Peter. 'Come. Let's be off.'

The stripling Thames is beautiful. It flowed calmly, full of the reflected skies of the summer evening, and it was pleasant to sit outside at rough-cut wooden tables, and listen to a nightingale somewhere in the bosky woods on the further bank. They drank draught beer, and ate roast rabbit, and allowed themselves to reinhabit themselves as if all the world were young.

They let their contentment last into the dusk, but eventually Peter said, 'Come, Shepherd and again begin the quest.'

Harriet said, 'Can we hear out the nightingale?'

Peter held his peace. But soon the nightingale sounded more distant, and then fell silent.

'Fled is that music, do I wake or sleep?' he said.

'Change of poet,' said Harriet crisply.

'That's allowed,' he said.

'How does your interim report go, Peter?' she asked.

'I think we know what Vearing did,' said Peter. 'He started with two assaults, presumably intended to kill. He trapped Dancy in the bell-chamber, and he injected Cloudie with air into a vein. He had literary licence for both of those, but neither of them worked. His third attempt did work; he killed Enistead by using a catapult on him through an open skylight. That did work.'

'It worked in the sense that it killed the unfortunate man,' said Harriet. 'So why didn't it fix the vote?'

'Because they appointed Trevair, and he took the side in favour of the MS,' said Peter. 'So then Oundle had to die.'

'Peter, is Vearing strong enough to have dealt a blow like the one that killed Oundle?'

'He's an oarsman,' said Peter. 'And still rowing, I think. I believe I saw him on the river the other morning. Good for arm muscles as well as legs. And that sword was ultra-sharp.'

'But what about the alibi? Didn't he need to know that Oundle was a haemophiliac? And wasn't that a well-kept secret?'

'I suppose he could have risked it without knowing that,' said Peter. 'But actually I think he did know. I think somebody who was at the same school as him might have known. Remember Macmillan?'

'Gossip down the generations, you mean?'

'Outlander was at the same school as Oundle. And Outlander was a buddy of Vearing's.'

'And haemophilia was a strand in one of my books.'

'That young man seems to be at the end of many a line of thought,' said Peter.

'Including playing a part in the show-stopping finale,' said Harriet, 'in which Vearing diced with death by arsenic, and lost on two counts.'

'It's Trevair who is the odd one out,' Peter said. 'A newcomer to the college, of whom John Ambleside said he had not yet acquired enemies.'

'And killed in a fashion that I have not written about,' said Harriet.

'And declaring that he would vote to retain the MS,' said Peter. 'The odd one out in three ways at once.'

'Four ways,' said Harriet.

'Your most excellent reason?' Peter asked.

'It's the only one that could not have been planned,' she said. 'And spontaneous murder is a different kind of thing, isn't it?'

'Well, I suppose someone might be seething with rage and hatred, and ready to kill, and then suddenly find they had a chance ... Planners might have to be full of rage and hatred too,' said Peter. 'Cold-blooded, though.'

'My colleagues don't pay much attention to this,' said Harriet thoughtfully. 'There's a tale I read somewhere – Agatha Christie, I think, but I can't be sure – in which someone fired a gun from one flat that killed someone through a bathroom window in an adjacent flat, who just happened to be standing in view shaving. Possible, but entirely unpredictable. Nobody could plan it. It would have to be done on a moment's impulse.'

'A moment's impulse might be enough to throw somebody out of an organ loft. Somebody slight and unprepared.'

'And only because they have voted to keep the MS? That sounds cold-blooded to me rather than hot-blooded,' said Harriet.

'It isn't difficult to imagine someone –Troutbeck, say – crossing the quad, and seeing Trevair go into the chapel, and following him in. Following him up to the organ loft, and getting into a confrontation with him there; perfectly possible.'

'Why did Trevair go up into the organ loft?'

'Perhaps he fancied a chance to play,' said Peter. 'And he saw the stair door was open, and not, as usual, locked – mea culpa!'

'Do we know he was a keyboard player?' asked Harriet.

'Yes, we do. Or rather I do. He has a chamber organ in his rooms.'

'That must make revision hard for his entire staircase,' said Harriet.

'It's taboo this term. All the more reason why he might have wanted a chance to play.'

'So Troutbeck, or somebody – Peter, we don't know for sure that it was Troutbeck – wants to buttonhole Trevair about something. And it turns nasty, so they fight, and Trevair falls over the gallery balustrade.'

'Or is just thrown over.'

'Why?'

'Each player removed from the game is worth a vote.'

'Hmm. What are we going to do about Vearing?'

'Get him arrested as soon as he can stand up. Perhaps we ought to talk to Inspector Gimps right away.'

When they reached the police station they found Inspector Gimps writing up reports.

'You have saved me stepping over to the college, Your Grace,' he said. 'I've got something here I think you ought to see.'

He found office chairs for Peter and Harriet, and passed a report across the table to Peter.

Peter was reading an interview with Mrs Dancy. He handed each page to Harriet as he read. Mrs Dancy had been looking for her husband, who was somewhere in college. It seemed he might well have been in the chapel, being a devout man prone to sharing his burdens with the Lord. When she entered the chapel she could hear voices raised from the organ loft. Someone was speaking 'very rudely' to Mr Trevair.

'Could she see the speakers?' the interviewing constable had asked her.

No; she was standing almost immediately under the organ loft, and could not see anyone above her.

How then, had she known that one of the speakers was Mr Trevair?

The man who was talking to him – shouting at him actually – was calling him Trevair.

Had she heard what the quarrel was about?

Mrs Dancy had at first told Inspector Gimps that she never eavesdropped.

He had pressed her. He was only asking her to

remember what she had actually overheard, quite without intending to.

She had overheard Trevair saying that he had legitimate doubts. The project was extremely risky. He had written a brief note to the fellows explaining why he thought so, what he had heard. 'Naturally I gave a copy to you first,' he had said.

The other voice had said, 'I am asking you not to put this around,'

Mrs Dancy was not quite sure how Trevair had replied – 'ask all you like,' or something like that. It amounted to refusal.

'There will be consequences,' the other voice had said. And at that point she had collected herself and left.

'I didn't want to know,' she had told Inspector Gimps. 'Sometimes it's best not to know. In my husband's position . . .'

'What position was that?' Inspector Gimps had asked.

'A fellow of this college who hates controversy,' she had told him.

He had pointed out to her that the conversation in the organ loft had probably been about the sale of the land. Yes, she had realised that. He had pointed out that if she could recognise that second voice, she would help the arrest of a very wicked person.

Mrs Dancy had steadfastly refused to identify anyone by an overheard voice. She had told Gimps that at her age her hearing wasn't what it used to be. You lose the finer points of voices, or of music, she had told him. She simply couldn't be certain who it was, and she was not going to point the finger at somebody on a suspicion. She had told him all she could.

When he had pressed her she had declared that she would say not another word without her lawyer present.

When Peter and Harriet had both read this through, Harriet handed it back to Inspector Gimps.

'I mistook my witness, I'm afraid,' he said ruefully. 'I took her for what she looked like: a pleasant old bird, everybody's granny – you know the type. But once I pressed her and she mentioned a lawyer, I knew there was no point in going on.'

'Oxonian old grannies are a special breed,' said Peter sympathetically.

20

As they walked through the college gate, the head porter came hastening after them.

'I have been telephoned three times this evening, Your Grace,' he said, 'by a woman urgently wanting to speak to you. She was very agitated, sir, and wouldn't tell me what it was about. She wouldn't leave a name or a number. And she twice broke off the call in mid-sentence, and then phoned again later. She kept mentioning a willow pattern plate, sir. Sorry I can't be more helpful.'

'Thank you,' said Peter. 'That's more helpful than you know. If she calls again, put her through to the phone in the Warden's house, will you?'

By the time they had crossed the quad and let themselves into the house they could hear Bunter's voice on the phone.

'I can give him a message as soon as he comes in,' Bunter was saying. 'No, I don't know when that will be – wait a moment, madam, I think I can hear him coming in now.'

Peter galloped up the stairs to take the phone. A frantic voice at the other end said, 'I am so frightened, so angry; and so frightened!'

Peter recognised the voice of Mrs Cutwater, the owner of the land the college wanted to buy. He thought of the remote farm, and of the narrow difficult lane in the dark. 'Meet me at the turning off the lane,' he said.

'I am locked in,' she said. 'He has got them to keep me locked in. They have gone out somewhere, otherwise I wouldn't dare phone you. Oh, what can I do?'

'Try to keep calm,' Peter said. 'Pack a small suitcase of just the least that you need. We will come and get you out of there, and bring you somewhere safe.'

He put the phone down, and came to talk to Harriet. 'She does sound very frightened,' he told her.

'More than she was when we saw her?'

'Quite a bit more, I would say. And she says she is locked in the house. She said "he" had got "them" to keep her locked in. Why she was angry as well as frightened she didn't say.'

'Peter, what will it take to rescue her?'

'We can probably break in,' he said. 'But if the servants, or whoever "they" are, come back before we get her out there might be a nasty scene.'

'Shouldn't we get the police?'

'Yes,' he said. 'On reflection, I think we should.'

It took a bit of talking to the duty officer in Oxford police station to get Inspector Gimps's out-of-hours phone. Once the Inspector was on the line he listened to Peter's account of a woman locked in and asking for help. 'If this is just the usual sort of domestic spat,' he said,' we usually leave well alone.'

'That won't do,' Peter said. 'Habeas corpus applies to civilians as well as to the police.'

'You'd be surprised how often the woman won't press charges,' the Inspector said. 'But what do you want me to do?'

'I was hoping you would go round there and ascertain that she is being held against her will. And if so get her out.'

'Yes,' said the Inspector, 'I think we can do that much.'

'Thank you,' said Peter. 'Can you go in some force, and can I come with you?'

'Yes, to both of those questions,' said Inspector Gimps.

'I'll meet you at the foot of the lane,' said Peter.

'In half an hour,' said the Inspector.

'Someone should go with you, Peter,' said Harriet, 'and Bunter would be more useful than I would.'

'You don't trust contingents of the Oxford constabulary to keep me safe?' he asked.

'Not as I trust Bunter,' said Harriet.

'Thank you, Your Grace,' said Bunter.

The lane was in darkness, of course. There was just about enough moonlight to let Peter see the telephone wire that crossed the road, and drive himself up to the farmhouse. The house too was in darkness, except for one upstairs window. A police van followed Peter up to the house, and six constables got out of it. Three of them moved round to the back of the building. The Inspector hammered on the front door, and called 'Police!' in a stentorian voice. Somewhere inside a dog barked. The Inspector knocked again, and again.

Nothing happened. 'Nobody there?' asked one of the constables.

'Hush up,' said the Inspector. 'Quiet, everyone.' He beckoned Peter to stand beside him, and applied his ear to the door. Peter did the same. Someone was weeping, just audible through the heavy oak door panels.

'Mrs Cutwater?' Peter called. 'Can you hear me? Open up for us; we have come to help you.'

The flap of the letterbox was pushed open from inside, and a tearful voice said, 'I can't open up. They have taken all the keys.'

'Where are these people you speak of?' asked the Inspector.

'I don't know where,' she said. 'But when they get back they will kill me for this.'

'No, they won't,' Peter said. 'There are armed policemen out here ready to protect you. Stand well clear of the door, while we break it down.'

Three hefty constables charged the door without moving it an inch. One of them fetched a stout battering ram from the back of the van, and they tried that. The door splintered a little but did not give.

Losing patience, Peter took a revolver from his inner coat pocket, and asking everyone to stand clear, he put three bullets through the lock.

'I neither heard nor saw that,' said the Inspector. He looked horrified. But the shattered lock gave way at the next blow from the battering ram. The constables who were wielding it fell through on to the flattened door panel.

Peter stepped over them and put on the hall light. 'Where are you?' he called.

Mrs Cutwater emerged out of the shadows. She was wearing a red coat, and carrying a suitcase. She had the disorientated and fearful look of a refugee. She might have stepped straight off one of those pre-war trains from Germany bearing people in just-in-time flight.

'It's all right now,' Peter told her.

'They will come back soon,' she replied.

'Before they do, we will have taken you somewhere quite safe,' Peter told her.

'Just a few formalities,' said the Inspector. He was quite right, of course, Peter conceded, to take Mrs Cutwater's name; to make sure she consented to be taken into protective custody. But when it became apparent that his idea of a place of safety was a police cell, Peter intervened.

'That's a bit rough, Inspector,' he said. 'After all, this lady hasn't broken the law in any way. Let me look after her; I will produce her for interview any time you like.'

'Would that be acceptable to you, madam?' the Inspector asked.

She nodded.

'Off you go, then,' he said. 'But I rather think we will hang around here in the shrubberies and see who turns up.'

'Excellent,' said Peter, who had intended leaving the hapless Bunter in a shrubbery to do just that.

Once safely in the comfortable back seat of the Daimler, Mrs Cutwater revived a little.

'Where are you taking me?' she asked.

'For tonight, what's left of it, back to St Severin's,' Peter told her.

'Oh, please not, please not there!' she said.

Peter paused for thought.

Bunter cleared his throat. 'Mr Arbuthnot has a place in Henley, my lord,' he said.

'Brilliant, Bunter! And Rachel Arbuthnot is a kindly soul. Henley it is.'

Freddy was in London overnight, but Rachel took it in her stride being woken at four in the morning, and asked for her spare bedroom.

'Come in, my dear, at once,' she said to Mrs Cutwater. 'Do you need something to eat? I'm sure you do. Have a bite to eat and then you can go to bed, and sleep it off, whatever it is.'

She put bread and cheese and a bowl of strawberries on the table, and sat down in her dressing gown to look after her guest, and talk to Peter. Bunter went upstairs, and unpacked for Mrs Cutwater as he would have done for Peter or Harriet. As soon as they decently could, Peter and Bunter were in the car back to Oxford, in fresh early morning light.

'There was nothing of a personal nature in that suitcase,' Bunter told Peter, 'except a photograph in a silver frame. A rather good-looking young man, my lord. And signed David.'

They found Harriet, who had waited up for them, asleep in an armchair. Peter put a bedspread over her, and went to bed himself.

It was no surprise to Peter when Troutbeck presented himself while he was quietly breakfasting with Harriet. Troutbeck looked a strange combination of agitated and grim.

'Someone I care for has been abducted during the night,' he said. 'Do you know anything about it? If you do, you will tell me where she is.'

'I take it you refer to Mrs Cutwater?' said Peter, rather pointedly not asking Troutbeck to sit down.

'You do know about it!' Troutbeck exclaimed. 'Tell me where she is; I very urgently need to speak to her. And if you have kidnapped her, I should remind you that that is a criminal offence.'

'Nobody has kidnapped, nor yet abducted the lady,' said Peter. 'She asked to be rescued from a locked house, and she was duly rescued, by the Oxford police. I wish you luck in trying to establish that that worthy body of men has committed a criminal offence.'

'Where is she now?' asked Troutbeck.

'Safe,' said Peter.

'I urgently need to speak to her. Tell me where she is.'

'I could arrange to discover if *she* urgently wants to speak to *you*, Troutbeck, if that would help,' said Peter.

'May I sit down?' said Troutbeck. 'May I confide in you?'

'You may sit, certainly,' said Peter. 'As to confiding in me, that is as you wish.'

Troutbeck looked anxiously at Harriet, who made the slightest movement towards rising to leave. Peter almost imperceptibly shook his head, and she stayed put.

'You must be wondering why I am so concerned about Mrs Cutwater; Emily, that is,' said Troutbeck. 'The fact is that I am engaged to her. Naturally I feel protective of her.'

'A secret engagement?' asked Peter.

'For the moment, yes,' said Troutbeck.

'Your protective instincts did not extend, though, to securing her personal liberty; I take it you knew that she was confined to her house?'

'The servants I employed to look after her did so rather too enthusiastically, I'm afraid,' said Troutbeck. 'I did not intend that she should be locked in; merely that there should be someone in the house at all times.'

'Would you care to tell me why such a thing was required?' Peter asked. 'Against whom did she need protection?'

'Against herself,' said Troutbeck without hesitation.

'In what way was she not fit to have charge of her own coming and going?' asked Peter. He was using his quietest and steadiest tone. Harriet wondered why he was playing Troutbeck along instead of confronting him with what they knew about him.

'For one so young she has had a lot of trouble in her life,' said Troutbeck. 'She is – how shall I put it? – fragile. She sought my protection after her husband died; and I gladly offered it. I was a friend of that husband, as I think you know; during his lifetime I fell deeply in love with Emily, and I spoke of it only when his death left her without a friend and guardian.'

'Very touching,' said Peter. 'Do I take it that Mrs Cutwater inherits her husband's estate?'

'You can find that out at Somerset House,' said Troutbeck tartly. 'But yes, for what it is worth she inherits. The estate is encumbered by debts; inspecting the will in the Public Records Office will not tell you that.'

'So it is not from fortune-hunters that she needs protection,' said Peter dryly.

'Look, this is what I need to tell you about,' said Troutbeck. 'Emily has become delusional. There is mental illness in her family, and she is succumbing to a form of it. She suspects her friends of conspiring against her; she imagines that servants are spying on her, and old friends are cast off on the most absurd grounds. She wanders at night, sometimes clad only in her nightgown, and fights and curses the servants who find her and bring her back. She is suffering, in short, from some dreadful form of paranoia but she resists admission to the clinic in which she could receive treatment. That is why she has been locked in. As I say, for her own protection. She will no doubt, as we speak, be telling the police all sorts of wild stories about her situation, none of which should be believed unless confirmed by myself or one of the servants.'

'And yet you still want to marry her?' said Peter.

'There is no accounting for love,' said Troutbeck smugly. 'Now, will you tell me where she is, so that I can take her home and look after her as best I can until I can get her into a clinic for treatment?'

'What you say could account for Mrs Cutwater being frightened,' said Peter. 'But she also said she was angry. Do you know why she was angry?'

'She is beyond reason,' said Troutbeck. 'It is cruel to keep her from me. I ask you again to tell me where she is.'

'I cannot do that,' said Peter. 'I can ask her if she wishes to see you. If she does, of course, that can be arranged. I could also arrange for a letter from you to her to be delivered to her.'

Troutbeck sat frowning for a while. Then he said, 'I shall need an hour to write such a letter.'

'Take your time,' said Peter serenely. Then, as Troutbeck reached the door, he said, 'It is good news at least that the Warden has been found.'

'Oh, of course,' said Troutbeck stiffly, closing the door behind him.

'I thought you would confront him with the allegation that he has been blackmailing the Warden,' said Harriet, as soon as he was safely out of earshot.

'More fun to play him along a bit,' said Peter. 'Besides, the blackmail story isn't quite cooked yet. Better to keep it in our hands until we can fully account for it.'

'You mean that there is a missing link: how did Troutbeck get to know the Warden was the wicked reviewer?'

'Exactly, Harriet. I always thought it would be fun to be married to you.'

'May I make a suggestion? When a piece of paperwork is missing, it's always a possibility that it has been thrown away.'

'Accidentally?'

'You said Troutbeck needed it for evidence in order to blackmail the Warden. But it would also be evidence against him, wouldn't it? If the Warden ever accused him of blackmail, he wouldn't want to be found in possession – he would want to be able to deny all knowledge.'

'So he would bin it? Tearing it up first, presumably.'

'When I walked in the Fellows' Garden the other day,' said Harriet, 'the gardeners were having a bonfire. They were feeding it with waste paper from a row of bins.'

'Then it will be gone without trace? This is a very long shot, Harriet, but why don't we ask young Gimps to ask the gardeners?'

'If they've ever saved a brand from the burning, you mean? No harm in asking. Meanwhile I was thinking that I hadn't yet kept my promise to the formidable Miss Griffiths to show you the Alfred Jewel. I don't want to bump into her on the High and have to confess to slackness.'

'Righty-ho,' said Peter. 'Just give me a minute to set the Gimps hound on the trail.'

'You do that,' Harriet said, 'and I'll ring Rachel, and make sure she can cope with Mrs Cutwater for a few more hours.'

As they walked along the Broad, towards the Ashmolean Museum, Harriet reported that Rachel had sounded quite serene, and Mrs Cutwater seemed 'perfectly normal to her'.

'Good,' said Peter.

'She said she owed you, Peter, and was glad to help. Exactly what does she owe you?'

'Well, Freddy, I suppose,' said Peter. 'I don't think of it as a debt. Now, this jewel we are to see, how do we know it is Alfred's?'

'It says so,' said Harriet cryptically.

Soon they were looking at it, propped on a stand in its glass case. A figure holding two wands in bright enamel looked up at them through an oval slab of crystalline quartz, surrounded by a band of pierced work in gold. The band said: 'Alfred mec hect gewyrcan.'

The label deciphered that: 'Alfred had me made.' At the bottom of the quartz the gold band became a boar's head, decorated with filigree, and a round hole in the boar's mouth showed it had once held something. A pointer, Harriet told Peter, used when reading to direct the reader to one word after another.

'And we know about that,' Harriet told him, 'because Alfred wrote a preface to one of his translations – not the Boethius, the one about the duties of bishops – saying he was sending a pointer worth fifty gold coins to each bishopric in his land, and the pointer was to be kept with the book, and the book always in the cathedral.'

'How does it come to be here?' wondered Peter. The label told them that. 'Found in 1693 near Athelney, where Alfred founded a monastery ... Bequeathed to the University of Oxford.'

'It's at least as weird as it is beautiful,' said Peter. 'But it's numinous all right. Who is the figure looking out at us from all that gold? Is it Alfred, or a bishop, or Christ?'

'I don't know,' said Harriet, 'but whoever he is, I like his candid gaze.'

'Is there any bad news about Alfred,' wondered Peter, 'or was he our only good, as well as our only great, king?'

'He is widely thought to have been an inattentive cook,' Harriet reminded him. 'He burned some cakes.'

'So 'tis said,' said Peter. 'We should forgive him, Harriet, we are being inattentive ourselves. Back on the job. Let's awa to Carterhaugh as fast as we can hie.'

21

Waiting for them on their return, they found Inspector Gimps, with Sidney, the lithe young gardener who had wriggled under the racks of port what now seemed like an age ago.

'This fellow has a tale to tell,' the Inspector said.

Sidney was bursting with his news. 'You was asking about burning papers, sir,' he began. 'Well, sometimes fellows give us stuff to burn, because we often have a fire going for leaves and the like. Before you ever got here, sir, Mr Vearing give us a laundry basket full of papers to burn. Head gardener asked me to roll some of the stuff up as spills to start a new fire with, same as we used to do newspapers for my gran, sir. So I was rolling up pages and making a pile of spills when the head gardener come up to me, and he seed something on a bit of paper, and he said, "Hang on, my boy, not sure as how that ought to be there," and he took it outer my hand. Where'd that come from? he wanted to know, but I'd emptied all the papers from bins all together in a heap, and I couldn't say for sure to save my life.

'The head gardener said, "We better ask someone." And just then Mr Troutbeck was coming through the

326

garden on his way into college, and so we asked him. And he said no, we was quite right, it shouldn't have been sent for burning, and he would take care of it, but where was the first page? So we looked about for it a bit, but it was like a needle in a haystack. I think it must have been one of the spills I had already made, sir. Anyhow, we couldn't find it, and in a bit Mr Troutbeck said he would have to go, and off he went with the papers he'd already got.'

'And the papers in question, Sidney, they might have come from Mr Vearing?'

'Could of, sir. I can't say.'

'Sidney, thank you,' said Peter. 'You have been a great help.'

Sidney stood grinning till Peter remembered that last time he had been useful he had earned half-a-crown, and produced such another.

When the boy had departed, Peter thanked Inspector Gimps.

Harriet said, 'So that's the link.'

'Nearly there,' said Peter, 'not quite. It has to be foolproof to put a rope round a man's neck. Fill in Inspector Gimps, Harriet, could you, while I go and find the head gardener.'

That gentleman remembered perfectly the incident described by Sidney. He was taking cuttings in a greenhouse when Peter found him, and he went on working deftly as they spoke.

'What I'd like to know,' Peter told him, 'is what made you rescue that particular document? What caught your eye?'

'Mr Outlander's name, sir. That's all.'

'Why was that an alarm call?' Peter asked him.

The gardener stood up and faced Peter, with a cutting knife in one hand, and a sprig of Plumbago in the other. 'Mr Outlander was one of ours, sir,' he said. 'We were all cut up about him. Don't reckon the college has been the same place since he died.'

Peter said, 'Are all and any of the fellows one of yours?'

'We are all college men,' was the reply. 'We work for the college all our lives, most of us. We make a garden for the college now and the college in years to come. Some of the fellows like the garden, and talk to us, some of them don't. Makes no difference. What we make is ours as much as theirs.'

'And Outlander was one of those who noticed, and talked to you?'

'He was, yes. No swank about him. He was a scholarship boy when he come here. He did a bit of odd-job gardening for his pocket money in the vacations. And his sister worked at Kew.'

'Thank you,' said Peter.

'Your missus likes the garden,' the man added. 'She talks to us.'

'Yes,' said Peter, 'she would.'

'So we can track the carbon copy every inch of the way,' Peter said to Harriet. 'Vearing stole it from the Warden; then he sent it to the bonfire; then it was given to Troutbeck.'

'Does Troutbeck have it now?' Inspector Gimps asked.

'No, he's too clever for that,' Harriet said.

'I expect you're right,' said Peter.

Harriet glanced out of the window. 'Peter, look,' she said. 'Who is that?'

An old man was being helped across the quad in their direction, supported by the head porter and one of his deputies. Miss Manciple was running out to greet him. The Warden looked grey and worn, but he was basically walking back into his lodgings on his own feet. Peter sent Bunter down to ask about Mr Vearing; after all, he had been much less ill than the Warden.

Mr Vearing, Bunter reported, had been brought back to his rooms in college an hour ago.

Peter turned to Inspector Gimps.

'Would you get across the quad to Vearing's rooms,' Peter said, 'and read his rights to Mr Vearing, and charge him with the murder of Mr Enistead, and Mr Oundle, and the attempted murder of Thomas Ludgvan, Warden of this college.'

'Ready to go, are we, sir?' said Gimps. 'What about Mr Trevair?'

'What about him indeed,' said Peter. 'But I don't think he's Vearing's work. He'll only cloud the water.'

'Should I take an extra constable or two with me?' asked Gimps.

'I don't think you'll need to,' said Peter. 'The man is too ill to put up a fight or flight.'

'Peter, what will happen to Vearing?' asked Harriet anxiously. Her anxiety was not for the man who had always given her the creeps, but for Peter, who was known to have a hard time living with an execution that he had had a hand in bringing about.

'If his lawyer is worth anything, he'll plead insanity,' said Peter. 'He'll be in Broadmoor for the rest of his life.'

'He won't hang?'

'The uproar about the Bentley case has abated public support for hanging somewhat,' said Peter. 'I rather think the days of capital punishment may be drawing to a close.'

'So the only loose end is Trevair? He doesn't fit the pattern, does he? I suppose he couldn't have fallen over that balustrade?'

'What do you think?' said Peter. 'But I would like to know why. There's no fun in this,' he added plaintively. 'I used to think when you know how you know who; but that isn't working well at all. We can all see *how*; it's *why* that is the problem.'

'I thought we knew why: they had all thought an economist would vote for land, and he voted for the book.'

'But mad Vearing was killing people to keep the majority for the book; why would he go for Trevair? It suggests a second murderer. As unlikely as a second actor once was in a Greek tragedy.'

At that moment the Warden appeared, knocking lightly on the communicating door, and stepping into the guest room.

'I should have been here to welcome you when you first appeared in college,' he said. 'Better late than never. I hope you will get us all sorted out very soon.'

'Please sit down,' said Harriet anxiously. 'You don't look well enough to be on your feet.'

The Warden sat. 'Do you know why Vearing tried to poison me?' he asked Peter.

'Yes, I do,' Peter told him. 'I took the liberty of reading your blue exercise book.'

'Ah,' said the Warden. 'Well, it spares me the unwelcome task of telling you. Since I am told I shall recover in a while, I shall not press charges. We can forget about this.'

'It might perhaps be forgettable, Warden,' said Peter, 'if the attempt on you were the only one. Alas, Mr Vearing has made several attempts, and has succeeded in killing two others: Mr Enistead and Mr Oundle. He will certainly face charges of murder.'

'What will become of him?' asked the Warden. 'For a fellow of the college to hang . . .'

Peter explained what he thought would become of Mr Vearing.

'Well, he must indeed be mad,' the Warden said.

'Unfortunately, though madness rules out responsibility, it does not prevent malice,' said Peter. 'But you have had more to contend with than Vearing. I think if I am right, Troutbeck has been blackmailing you.'

'In a way,' said the Warden. 'He was threatening to let the whole college know that I had written the review that so upset poor Outlander. But that was the truth; I thought I ought to face the music rather than turn myself into Troutbeck's puppet. I took a degree in law, as well as one in history, Your Grace; and although you hear people say the greater the truth the greater the libel, the law takes no such view. In law a man is not entitled to enjoy a reputation that would not be his were the truth about him known. I could and did face down Troutbeck.'

The Warden got unsteadily to his feet. 'Stay here as long as you like,' he said. 'Stella Manciple is taking me to the seaside to stay with her sister, and recover in peace.'

'That's a good idea,' offered Harriet. 'She is an excellent woman.'

'Indeed,' said the Warden. 'That book will have to be sold, you know,' he added. 'But it will no longer be my concern. I am not well enough to continue; I shall resign and let younger men bear the burden.'

'Take life easy for a bit,' said Peter. Miss Manciple was lingering anxiously at the door. 'And thank you for your hospitality.'

When he had gone, Peter said, 'I think a little drive to Henley now, Harriet. I think Mrs Cutwater can tell us the rest of this story, and we should certainly make sure that Rachel Arbuthnot is not overburdened by her unexpected guest.'

'Is Gimps coming with us?' asked Harriet.

'No; she will talk more freely to just us. We shall take Bunter, and leave Gimps to keep an eye on Troutbeck, and tail him if he goes anywhere. Shouldn't be hard. A dodgy customer should not have such a conspicuous car.'

A ride across rural England on a sunny afternoon in late spring has pleasures all its own. At Shillingford Peter stopped the car, and Bunter got out and bought a bunch of flowers and a pot of honey from a roadside stall. A frothing white surf of cow parsley foamed at either side of the country roads, and the pastures were ablaze with buttercups. By and by a Sunbeam Talbot could be glimpsed in the rear mirror. Peter slowed down, but the Sunbeam slowed down also, keeping well back.

'I wonder when the pursuer will realise he is pursued?' said Peter.

Quite soon, perhaps, for when they reached the outskirts of Henley no pursuer, no flashy car was in sight.

The Arbuthnots had a large and pleasant house with a driveway screened from the road by trees. It was in the style affectionately known as stockbroker's Tudor, which was nearly right for Freddy, who was a commodities broker, with a splendid financial brain, and partly responsible for the wealth that Peter had accumulated before the war, and was now steadily sinking into the estate at Denver. Because the Sunbeam had not been in sight in the rear mirror when Peter turned into the drive, and because of the screening trees, Peter was pretty sure the pursuit had been shaken off.

But the crunch of their wheels on the gravel had announced their arrival, and Rachel came flying round the house from the garden with arms extended in affectionate greeting, and Mrs Cutwater coming behind her. 'Peter!' she cried. 'Harriet! We have been having such a good time.'

'I perceive these are coals to Newcastle,' Peter said, presenting Rachel with the flowers.

'Oh no, they're not,' she said, 'I adore Sweet Williams, and they're hard to grow. Most biennials are.'

'Oh, good,' said Peter. 'There's honey, too.'

'Come in, come in, everyone,' said Rachel. 'Freddy will be home soon. But I expect you've come to talk to Emily. Here she is.'

Emily Cutwater looked a different woman from the last time they had seen her. She was glowing from the fresh air, and had lost the wary look and the rings under the eyes she had had before. Her remarkable beauty was fully evident again – the chestnut hair, the grey-green eyes . . . No wonder, Peter thought, Troutbeck was after her.

Rachel led them through to her pretty, chintzy sitting room. Bunter melted away into the background as he often did, and Peter and Harriet sat down with Mrs Cutwater.

'This girl has quite a tale to tell,' Rachel said. 'I'll go and make some tea.'

'Mrs Cutwater,' said Peter.

'I think you are a friend,' she cut in, 'and I like my friends to call me Emily.'

'Emily,' Peter said, 'Mr Troutbeck has told us you are engaged to him. Is that true?'

'I was,' she said, 'but I'm not now! The cheating rat!'

'You have changed your mind about him,' Peter said. 'Was that because he had you locked in?'

'That came later,' she said.

'Could you bear to tell us from the beginning?' said Peter.

She folded her hands in her lap, and wrinkled her brow in thought. Then she looked steadily at Peter, glancing from time to time also at Harriet, and began.

'It starts with Andrew,' she said. 'Andrew Cutwater, my husband. I told you whoppers about him. He was nearly eighty when I met him, and a sad old chap. He needed a hand in the house and garden, and I was looking for work somewhere near Oxford. He employed me as a housekeeper. Michael Troutbeck was a friend of his, almost the only one who ever visited him. Otherwise all he had were mates he took a drink with at the pub. He didn't work his farm any more; he had bits of it let to other farmers. He bought it just before the war, not thinking then that it would get too much for him. Anyway, he was harmless, and kind. He did drink far too much, but he was a bit of a gentleman if you know what I mean. Of course you do.

'When I had been running things around there for a while he asked me to marry him. "You see me easy out of this world," he said, "and I'll see you all right after I'm gone."'

'You didn't mind that?' asked Peter gently.

'He didn't want to lay hands on me,' she said. 'He just wanted someone for company, and someone to leave things to, since he hadn't got family of his own. I don't mind being kind to someone who is kind to me. What's wrong with that?'

'Nothing at all,' said Harriet.

'I asked David, of course, and he thought it was okay. A bit unusual, he said, but then unusual suited me. And then it turned out that Andrew and David got on terribly well. Andrew was interested in things that interested David. Seems he had been picking up bits and pieces from the furrows when he was ploughing, and David thought there must be a Roman villa somewhere on the land, and maybe an Anglo-Saxon village too. They had a fine old time telling each other things, and going down to the local for a drink. We all had quite a good time together for a few months. Michael Troutbeck came calling nearly every week, and Andrew said, "It isn't me he comes to see, it's you, my dear," and I didn't know the truth of that till later.

'And then David died, and the bottom fell out of everything.'

'David – you mean David Outlander?' Peter asked. 'Emily, was he your lover?'

'What?' she said. 'What? What in God's name makes you think that?'

'You carry his picture round with you, even escaping from a locked house.'

'I did love him more than anyone in the world,' she said, her eyes filling with tears. 'He was my brother.'

'I'm so sorry,' said Peter, 'we didn't know that.'

He waited for her to recover a bit, but she paused only a little before going on.

'It knocked the stuffing out of Andrew. I wasn't surprised at what it did to me; David and I had always been close. But I hadn't realised how Andrew would feel. But then, you see, it was Andrew who found him. David used the beam above the trapdoor in the hayloft to do it. Everything went horrible for us. Andrew could hardly get out of bed most days. All we knew was it had something to do with a book in the college library that David had written about. Andrew knew that; David hadn't told me. I'd have told him what I thought about getting miserable about a book, any book.

'We were having a very hard time. Michael Troutbeck came very often, just to cheer us up, he said. I believed him, I didn't know any different. He and Andrew talked a lot. Then Andrew cut his finger on a bit of barbed wire out in the field somewhere, and it went septic, and he got a very high temperature, and the doctor tried something called M and B, but it didn't work. I think Andrew didn't want it to work. He said to me, "Everything's yours now, Em. If you don't want it all yourself, you do something with it David would have liked."'

She paused.

'Give yourself a break now,' Peter said. 'This is all very painful for you.'

'I want to tell you, though,' she said. 'It's good to tell somebody.'

'Have a cup of tea and a turn round the garden, and then we'll go on,' said Harriet.

Peter joined neither the cup of tea, nor the turn round the garden. He watched from the window as the three women in the house wandered across the lawn, and toured the borders, bursting with the glories of early summer. His gaze lingered on the graceful form of the unfortunate Mrs Cutwater. But surely some cavalier would come riding to her rescue. He wished whatever cavalier appeared good luck.

In half an hour Emily was back again. She seemed calmer. 'After the funeral, Michael Troutbeck came more often than before. He told me he loved me. He talked to me a lot about how we should marry and go abroad. I felt as if I hadn't a layer of skin left on my body, and it was nice to think somebody cared about me. You'll think me a fool. I think I was a fool, but I let him put a ring on my finger, and keep on talking. He told me all this stuff about the college getting into arguments, wanting to sell the book that David had thought so highly of, and I thought David would have hated the thing to be sold to America – not that I have anything against Americans, but it's so far away. So I said to Michael Troutbeck there was something he could help me with: he could give the farmland to the college so they wouldn't have to sell the book. The land would be worth a fair bit, and that would be doing what Andrew asked me to do.

'He said he would see to it, but then he got rather strange. He didn't want me to talk to anyone about it, and he got terribly angry when he found out I had written about it to a friend in Scotland. He got some servants in: a cook and a gardener, he said to give me a break from housework in a big house all by myself, and I thought that was kind of him, but then they kept watching me. They offered to take my letters to the post, and they began to lock the door. After you came to the house the door was locked on me all the time, and they did something to the phone, so it made funny noises and kept cutting out. For a while I thought he was just looking after me, but then I began to wonder why I wasn't to talk to anybody.

'I said to him I would have thought somebody in the college might have liked to say thank you for a present of all that land, and he went storming round the room shouting at me, telling me I would spoil everything for us if I tried talking about what I didn't understand. He said he would kill to keep the plans on course. I think he was just letting off steam, but for a moment I believed him.'

'How frightening for you,' said Harriet.

'It got worse,' said Emily. 'I wandered into the kitchen looking for a drink one evening when the cook had a day off, and there was a copy of the *Oxford Mail* on the table, so I sat down to read it. And it gave me a horrible shock. It said the college was thinking about selling their Alfred book to afford to buy some land. It was the whole thing turned on its head; I didn't want them to buy the land, I wanted to give it to them, so that they could keep the book. So somehow it was the exact opposite of what I meant to do.'

'What did you feel about that?' asked Peter.

'I felt betrayed. I didn't want him touching me any more, I wanted to get away from him. He kept saying he was doing what Andrew wanted, looking after me, and giving away my property was a silly little girl thing to do, and he was only after protecting me and acting in my best interests. And then he said we were going to need the money.'

'What did you say to that?' Peter asked.

'I asked him what for. And he told me that all that lovely talk about going abroad and seeing the world, and showing me the south of France, and Italy . . . it was going to be very costly. So I said, let's stay in England then. And he said he couldn't do that, he needed to be out of harm's way.

'So I said I wasn't in harm's way in England if he would just leave me alone. And he said I had a choice. I could sign the deed to sell the land, and go abroad with him and have a nice time, or he could have me sectioned and put in a mental home. He said he could easily do that; he had friends who would do it to me on a nod and a wink. And he said if I started telling anyone about the quarrel about the land it would make it easy to convince people I was mad. And he said once I was called mad he could take over Andrew's estate and do what he liked with it. And he said anyway there was madness in my family – hadn't my brother committed suicide? So then I remembered your card, stuck behind that plate, and I tried and tried to telephone you.'

Peter had become very flushed during this account. Harriet, almost shaking with rage herself, recognised this as anger.

At this point suddenly Freddy appeared. 'I might have known you would be here,' he said cheerfully to Peter. 'Where there's trouble . . . There is a gentleman, unknown to me, and a police officer having a ferocious argument at my front door. I just slipped round and let myself in at the back. Drinks, anyone?'

'Please, don't let him talk to me,' said Emily Cutwater.

'Certainly not,' said Peter. 'He will never talk to you again. He is about to be arrested for murder.'

22

Peter and Harriet spent the night in the second-best spare room in Freddy's ample house. 'That's just about the nastiest thing I have ever heard,' said Peter, 'and I have heard plenty of nasty things in my time.'

'Poor, poor woman,' said Harriet. 'She has been in hell.'

'Let's call it purgatory,' said Peter, 'since we will get her out of it.'

'I have been wondering what she could possibly do,' said Harriet. 'That farmhouse will be full of bad memories.'

'I didn't want to suggest this while Troutbeck was still at large,' said Peter, 'because he would have come looking for her. But shall we take her home to Denver for a while? Would you mind?'

'Not at all. Good idea.'

'I had a sort of idea you didn't take to her.'

'I didn't, at first. She seemed hostile and defensive. But I didn't then know what was happening to her.'

'You don't suspect my motives?'

'I have reason not to,' she said.

'Ah, moon of my desire, that has no wane . . .' said Peter.

'Stop quoting, Peter, and come to bed,' she said.

As they drove through Oxford on their way back to St Severin's they found the streets thronged with people in gowns. A light wind blew the black grosgrain out behind them, tugging at their shoulders like wings. The white rabbit fur of BA gowns weighed some of them down; they grabbed at their mortar-boards or trenchers to stop them flying off. They were pouring out of the Examination Schools, and thronging the High. A procession of laughing young men and women, so very oddly clad, were making for Christ Church Meadow, accompanied by friends with champagne bottles and picnic baskets.

'Exams over,' said Harriet. 'School's out.'

'Alas, regardless of their doom the little victims play,' said Peter.

'Not all of them are regardless,' Harriet said. 'Jackson wasn't.'

'He's doubtless somewhere in the throng,' said Peter. 'The best of luck to him.'

Somehow the quadrangles of St Severin's College on a sunlit morning, with the shadow of death no longer hanging in the air, struck them again as beautiful. Proportionate and calm.

'Well, now,' said Peter, 'let's roll up our sleeves and have at this Augean Stable.'

★   ★   ★

A meeting of the fellowship. Everyone present except three – no Vearing, no Troutbeck, no Warden. Ambleside presiding. Peter explaining. Carefully, step by step, he took them through events, and his investigation. There were shocks; not everyone had known the full tally of assaults, and at the news that the Warden had written that destructive review himself there were raised and agitated voices, and expressions of disbelief.

'This is terrible, terrible,' said Mr Cloudie. 'Three murders; one fellow sectioned, one to hang. How will we ever recover?'

'Colleges have long lives,' said Peter. 'This will be lived down. But at the present moment you have work to do. You have lost three fellows, and have appointments to make. I advise you to emend your statutes, so that a matter once settled by vote cannot be raised again for – shall we say five years? – and you should heal the breach that has opened up between you. A good place to start would be to acknowledge that people taking the other view from your own are not necessarily less devoted to the college than you are. It is true that there has been real malignity at work here, but that canker is now removed. I think also that in financial matters the days when the Bursar can manage the money as well as the domestic affairs of the college are now over. You should seek, and pay for, proper financial advice. I can recommend somebody to you. And I suggest that you restore to your statutes the clause forbidding the sale of college property above the value of fifty thousand pounds, or some such sum, without unanimity or the approval of the Visitor.'

'But have I understood you?' said Gervase. 'In the end you are telling us we can have both the book and the land?'

'It would seem so,' said Peter, 'if Outlander's sister can forgive you for the Warden's conduct.'

'We must make emends,' said Ambleside. 'We must bring Outlander home. I don't mean exhumation,' he added hastily, 'I mean a decent memorial.'

'I think I have done what I can for you now,' said Peter. 'I am leaving you to your own devices. You may summon me to install the new Warden when you have elected him.'

Ambleside proposed a vote of thanks to the Visitor. Peter extracted himself from the babble of excited voices, and rejoined Harriet.

'Your mother will be glad to see us,' said Harriet. 'And she will like Emily Outlander, I'm sure.'

It took a few days, however, to extract themselves from Oxford. Emily had things to sort out before leaving the farmhouse. She dismissed Troutbeck's choice of servants, and found a neighbour willing to keep an eye on the house.

Harriet dined in Shrewsbury College. The golden light of a late summer evening was still shining through the windows as they rose from the table.

'Can you play bowls?' asked Dr Baring of Harriet.

'I'm like the man who was asked if he could play the violin,' said Harriet. 'I don't know, I've never tried.'

The company strolled out towards the bowling green, which had not been there in Harriet's time; she rather thought that corner of the garden had been devoted to compost heaps and tool sheds. Helen de Vine eagerly instructed her; how to hold the bowl, and roll it towards the jack, or if evilly minded towards an opponent's bowl to knock it from an advantageous position. To her own amazement, Harriet proved adept at this, and won the first round.

'Give her a violin, someone,' said Dr Baring.

To gusts of laughter they left the game and went indoors.

The next day Harriet delivered her promised talk on detective fiction and literature.

There had been no such distinction, she pointed out, when Wilkie Collins wrote *The Moonstone*, or when Dickens wrote *Edwin Drood*.

A girl in the audience asked what was the oldest detective story she knew.

'It's in the Book of Daniel,' Harriet told her, 'the story of Susannah and the elders. Do you remember? Susannah is accused of adultery by two lustful elders whom she has refused her favours. And Daniel separates the two accusers, and asks each of them to say under which tree they saw her lying with a young man. And one of them says under a mastic tree, and the other says under an oak tree. Case dismissed. That's a good detective plot. Now, can anyone think of an earlier detective than Daniel?'

Her talk was received with gratifying applause.

Peter owed George Mason both dinner and an account of things; on the evening when Harriet was delivering her talk he dined in Balliol, and did his duty by George.

Not till old friends had been satisfied did the Wimseys feel free to go.

One morning early, when Peter was walking up from Magdalen Bridge, having taken a punt for an hour to reassure himself that falling in was an aberration he could put behind him, he met Jackson coming down the High. Jackson was looking extremely unhappy.

'Oh, Your Grace,' he said to Peter, 'you wouldn't do something for me, would you?'

'What is it?' asked Peter.

'They will be pinning up the lists of exam results this minute outside the Examination Schools,' said Jackson. 'And everybody will be there – and I can't bear to go and look.'

'And if you haven't got a first you want to skulk away and bury your head in shame?' said Peter. 'Skulk right there, and I'll go down and look for you.'

He turned back towards the bridge. The great curving street opened itself to view, with that crucially placed tree at the curve beside Queen's College; green leaf breaking the vista of grey stone. Peter trotted down to the Examination Schools. The crowd of youngsters reading their fate in the lists got in each others' and Peter's way. Groans and cheers filled the air. A girl was in prime position at the top of the steps, reading out names and classes to people.

'Jackson, from St Severin's?' Peter called to her.

'He's got a first,' she said, and Peter went back up the High with a light heart to relieve Jackson's anxiety.

'Moreover,' he said, when he had given the news, 'the Boethius will still be in St Severin's library next year; I can promise you.'

Emily Cutwater didn't stay long at Denver; old friends turned up, anxious to reconnect with her now Troutbeck was out of the way. She put the farmhouse up for sale and bought herself a pleasant house in Witney. When she left them, Peter and Harriet took the promised trip to Venice.

'When you actually get to a great and famous tourist sight, you always see why it's great and famous,' Harriet said.

They were riding back from Torcello in a gondola. 'Does it actually remind you of Oxford?' she added.

'I'd say I'm very glad we don't have to choose,' he said.

'You mean, we can come here again?'

'Any time you can stand the train ride,' he said. 'But this is the occasion on which I want to buy you some Murano glass. Would you like some of those gold-flecked beads to wear?'

'Thank you, Peter,' said Harriet, 'the golden glass is lovely. But I don't want to wear it. I'd rather have those ornate golden candlesticks.'

'Yours for the asking,' he said.

They were very fragile, and had to be packed in large crates full of wood shavings and crumpled paper.

But they arrived safely at Denver. Harriet put them on a mantelpiece, where they were doubled in a large mirror, and between them she put the only survivor of the set of ivory chessmen that Peter had bought her in Oxford once, long ago.

23

One of the more conventional duties of the Visitor was the installation of a new Warden. The college took time to deliberate; fully eighteen months. Of the two contenders – Gervase and Ambleside – the college chose Ambleside, to Peter's quiet satisfaction. So in October of the following year the Wimseys were again in Oxford, to do the honours for Ambleside.

A blazing and golden autumn had transformed the city. A soft and gauzy autumnal mist drifted from the twin rivers, and tissue-wrapped the streets and buildings until nearly mid-morning. The plane trees on St Giles were butter-yellow and adorned with little brown balls of seed-clusters. Carpets of gold were spread under the avenue of trees on Christ Church Meadow and the trees in the University Parks. Slightly overblown roses and clusters of rose-hips hung on in the Botanic Gardens, and the city was seized with the annual delectable contrast between the end of summer, and the start of a new university year. The autumn would be a time of beginning for ever after for each generation of students who arrived, recurring like the seasons, in that lovely phase of the year.

The majority of the undergraduates of course were blasé second and third years, but the mood was suffused with the excitement and bewilderment of the freshers, agog at what was now theirs for an inconceivably long prospect of three years. Even four years for the classicists. Every college notice-board was surrounded by anxious young people looking for instructions about what to do now they had unpacked their cases, when and where to meet their tutors. The anxiety dispersed like the morning mist, to be succeeded by excitement. They did not have to attend lectures in their own subjects, and soon they were flocking to hear lecturers in other subjects – J.L. Austin, or J.R.R. Tolkien, or C.M. Bowra, or C.S. Lewis, or whoever they had heard recommended. Professor Wind announced a whole term of lectures on one single painting – Raphael's *The School of Athens* – and the lecture had to be moved to the Oxford Playhouse because there was not room enough in the Examination Schools. To attend lectures or tutorials, one had to wear a gown, and the streets were full of the silly sleeveless undergraduate gowns, with tapes hanging from the shoulders. The scholarship winners had more dignified affairs, almost like those of graduates, which blew out behind them like black sails in the wind. In the morning lectures there were always some people falling asleep, exhausted by the marathons of talk that filled the first years' rooms till the small hours; in the afternoon the lectures competed with the punts on the river, for as long as the sunshine lasted.

And all day long from every quarter the clocks in college towers struck the time, taking, if you timed it, nearly twenty minutes from the first note to the last note, collectively approximate, however accurate one among them might be. Those bells insinuated themselves into memory, so that the sound of them would unwind generations of Oxford men and women back to their student days, and to their rash and joyful younger selves.

In those streets you might have seen, that year, an older couple, walking together not hand in hand, but perfectly in step with each other, moving from one fine sight to another, seeming to walk in a dream. In Duke Humfrey's Library the man said to the woman, softly, 'And Bredon says no to all this . . .'

Out in the courtyard again, the woman said to the man, 'Family tradition is a burden, Peter, which you should know better than most people.'

'Give me time, Harriet. I'll get used to it,' he said.

'Oxford feels itself again to me, Peter,' she said. 'Does it to you?'

'The sick rose healed, and all invisible worms exterminated?' he said. 'Yes; it feels like our Oxford again. And it's striking eleven. Can we make it to the Wind lecture, do you think?'

They did.

The installation of the new Warden – the most grave of Peter's duties as Visitor in normal times – was to take place that afternoon. It didn't turn out to be either onerous, or much fun for Peter. It consisted of his waiting with Ambleside in the drawing room of the Warden's Lodging, while all the action was going on in the college chapel. Harriet was allowed to sit quietly watching from a corner.

'So what exactly are they doing in the chapel?' Peter asked.

Ambleside said, 'They are casting votes.'

'But I thought you were already elected,' Peter said.

'I am,' said Ambleside. 'But once there is a clear majority for someone the tradition dictates that everyone votes again for the winner. A Warden is always elected unanimously.'

'That's a graceful way of doing it,' said Peter. 'It shouldn't take long then.'

'The votes are collected in a chalice,' Ambleside said, 'and then they have to be counted. The last Warden was in office so long it's pretty well only the Senior Tutor who can remember the last time it was done.'

'That would be Cloudie?'

'Yes. And I believe here he comes.'

Mr Cloudie entered the room, smiling, and shook hands with everyone.

'I have pleasure, Your Grace, in presenting to you John Ambleside as the duly elected Warden of this college,' he said.

'I have pleasure in accepting him as such,' said Peter.

The college butler entered, carrying a large tray with decanters and glasses.

'Oh, do we drink to that now?' said Peter. 'Hurrah.'

'We must sign the great book first,' said Cloudie, indicating a huge volume lying ready on a side-table. 'It records the election of every Warden back to the sixteenth century.'

Peter and Ambleside and Cloudie all signed below a beautifully handwritten declaration. Cloudie handed Ambleside a copy of the Bible, and holding it he read firmly an oath of office, of fidelity to the college at all times and in every way. And presto! Ambleside was the Warden.

The room began to fill with other fellows, who had walked across from the chapel to offer good wishes, and share the party. Peter and Harriet joined in, aiming, as they would have done at home, to talk to everyone in the room.

The atmosphere in St Severin's had changed. It felt hopeful and slightly precarious, like the mood of someone recovering from an illness. Ambleside had in effect been discharging the Warden's duties for some time, and hardly needed a novitiate. The new fellows had, of course, all heard about the perturbations and trials of the previous year, but they were over – history – of no more immediate interest than the reign of Alfred the Great. The exception to taking that view was, naturally, Jackson, one of three new research fellows.

In the college chapel the broken wing of a carved angel had been fixed back in place, and the height of the balustrade on the minstrels' gallery had been raised. A new slab of dark slate was mounted on the wall opposite the door, where it caught the eye. It bore the inscription:

DAVID OUTLANDER
1921–1948
LATE SCHOLAR OF THIS COLLEGE
DECUS REIPUBLICAE LITTERATORUM

'What does it mean?' Emily had asked Peter when he told her about it.

'An ornament of the republic of letters,' Peter had said. 'An ornament to learning.'

'Good,' she had said. 'I like that. I'll go and have a look at it some time.'

Looking at it now, Peter said, 'Quite right and proper.'

As they left the chapel they saw Jackson, crossing the quad, and hailed him.

'Congratulations on the fellowship,' Peter said.

'I think I owe you a lot,' Jackson replied. 'I think you saved Boethius for the college.'

'Nothing saved Boethius for himself,' Peter replied. 'Poor chap died a nasty death in the end, in spite of philosophy. That reminds me, Jackson, of something I wanted to ask you. You remember that odd phrase in the manuscript that we all got so excited about, that Bunter photographed?'

'Of course I remember,' said Jackson. 'It's a king-pin of my thesis.'

'I never asked you what it meant,' said Peter.

'It means: *I hope to do good deeds in my lifetime, and to be remembered for them after my death*,' said Jackson.

'Nothing about seeing God, or immortality?' asked Peter.

'Not a word,' said Jackson. 'And perhaps that's odd, now you mention it, because he certainly believed in God.'

'But his hope was just to do good and be remembered. At the same time not much to ask, and a lot to ask. I'd gladly settle for that myself,' said Peter Wimsey.

Jill Paton Walsh

The Attenbury Emeralds

In 1921, the Attenbury emeralds were stolen –
and Lord Peter Wimsey made headlines when he
recovered them.

Now it is 1951. There is a new Lord Attenbury and
a baffling new mystery about the emeralds.

It will be the most intricate and challenging case
Lord Peter Wimsey has ever faced.

'A pitch-perfect Golden Age mystery; not a pastiche
but a gem of a period puzzle that belongs on the
shelf beside the Wimsey originals.' Christopher
Fowler, *Financial Times*

'An absolute treat: civilised, intelligent and
spellbinding.' Barry Forshaw, *Daily Express*

'Sayers would not have recognised that it wasn't her
own work.' Marcel Berlins, *The Times*

HODDER

The best books live on in your head long after they are finished. As you read, you are turning the pages faster and faster to find out what happens next, only to feel bereft when you reach the end.

If that is how you feel now, you might like to join us at www.hodder.co.uk, or follow us on Twitter @hodderbooks, and be part of our community of people who love the very best of books and reading.

Whether you want to find out more about this book, or a particular author, watch trailers and interviews, have the chance to win early limited editions, or simply browse our expert readers' selection of the very best books, we think you'll find what you're looking for.

And if you don't, that's the place to tell us what's missing.

We love what we do, and we'd love you to be part of it.